FOR THIS CHILD

Based on a true story

EDIE LIVESAY

Copyright © 2015 by Edie Livesay

For This Child
Based on a true story
by Edie Livesay

Printed in the United States of America.

ISBN 9781498440233

All rights reserved solely by the author. The author guarantees all contents are original and do not infringe upon the legal rights of any other person or work. No part of this book may be reproduced in any form without the permission of the author. The views expressed in this book are not necessarily those of the publisher.

Unless otherwise indicated, Scripture quotations taken from the Holy Bible, New International Version (NIV). Copyright © 1973, 1978, 1984, 2011 by Biblica, Inc.™. Used by permission. All rights reserved.

www.xulonpress.com

This book is dedicated to:
Ryan Iverson my nephew and his family
Stephanie, Berea and Ezra

For this child I prayed.
I Samuel 1:27

Preface

In the mid 1980s Jillian Townsend continues to pursue her lifelong dream of teaching and ministering to the children of Ecuador, as evil conspirators Marta and Lucia do everything in their power to discredit and hurt the big hearted American missionary. Carlos and Elena anxiously await the birth of their child after two miscarriages as they enjoy the friendship and hospitality of Eric Perez, the wealthy owner of Hacienda Tulcachi. The lives of the precious children still imprisoned in the "orphanage" held in the tight clutches of Marta Brewer and Lucia, the jungle Indian, continue to hang in the balance as Jillian and local officials feverishly work to free them. Can Dr. Raquel Torres help Rolando escape his alcoholic father's fate and begin to move on with his life? Will Raquel provide the friendship Jillian so hungers for or is she in for more heartache? How will the residents of the Tumbaco Valley be affected by the intricate way these lives intertwine as the Jillian Townsend Trilogy concludes.

Chapter 1

After her devotions one morning, Jillian hurried through breakfast and preparations for her first class of the day in the one-room schoolhouse two miles up the mountain behind Pachuca. Driving the narrow, dirt mountain road would be difficult and time consuming and she didn't want to be late. She unlocked the door and stepped onto the sidewalk. From across the street a young boy rose from a bench and walked timidly toward her. "Buenos dias, señorita."

"Buenos dias," Jillian replied shifting her bag of school supplies to her other arm, squinting at him to see if he would be in one of her classes. "May I help you with something?"

He shook his head and thrust an envelope in her hand. Watching her for a moment, he then backed away. "Hasta mañana, señorita."

"Gracias, hasta mañana." She recognized Marta's handwriting on the envelope and it took everything in her not to tear it open. Instead, she walked calmly down the block, past the telephone office and three homes and stopped in front of a house with a driveway. For the equivalent of five dollars a month the resident family, the Ortegas, kept the vehicle safe from thievery. She called greetings through the open window and got into her car as the señora of the house came out to unlock the gate. Jillian waved her thanks and drove to the road above Pachuca and turned toward the mountains. Halfway to the school, she stopped the motor and opened the envelope. Marta's familiar handwriting brought an errant tear to Jillian's eyes and she brushed it away. How she wished things hadn't changed. In spite of everything, she still wanted to be with Marta and the children. Steadying herself, she inhaled deeply and began to read:

Dear Jill,

I have tried in so many ways to talk with you, but I finally decided the only way is to write you a letter. You are never home. I've driven by your house a number of times, but the padlock is always secure.

I can't understand what is going on. I thought you were going to move into that house in Quito. I waited for you the day after we went to see it, but you didn't show up. I know you told me in the letter you sent that you had to pick up your cargo, so I thought maybe we could go later on that day and sign the papers. I waited by the road in Tumbaco all afternoon, hoping you would go to Quito and I would see you pass. I can't believe that you would give up an opportunity to be with the children. Maybe I was wrong about you. You gave me the impression that they were the most important people in your life, but now I hear you are working in the Pachuca schools. Have you forgotten Andy and Ryan?

Perhaps you have the idea that I am no longer interested in visiting with you in Quito. You're wrong if you believe that. I hope you still want a friendship as much as I. Look at the next page. You can see that it's a lease for the house in Quito. It's still available. If you'll go ahead and sign it, I will take it back to the owner and then you can move out of that old dump you're living in and move into a nice new house. I know how much you must want that. Just sign the lease and I'll send a boy to your house tomorrow morning to pick it up at the same time.

I can't wait to see you again. I'd have delivered this letter myself, but you know how Lucia would react if she ever found out.

Love, Marta

The second page was indeed a lease written by Marta in Spanish. *Apparently,* Jillian thought, *Marta figured that a mere signature would secure the house. Her letter seemed so sincere as if Marta wanted to be her friend. What a liar she is!* She shook her head at the sickness welling inside her. *Thank goodness Flora came to see me at the risk of being noticed that night.* Jillian was shocked that after all this time Marta was still asking that she move. She would have to reply tonight. It was essential that her letter be worded very carefully to

Chapter 1

avoid closing permanently any door in the future that might allow her to have the children and at the same time not implicate Flora.

Deep in thought, her spirit ebbing with the despair that she so often suffered while living with Marta, she wound up the steep, almost impassable, cow path to the tiny one-room six grade schoolhouse. Built of mud, it clung to the side of the mountain, its face peering opposite at Quito across the wide Tumbaco Valley. The interior of the schoolhouse featured a board of slate hung from thick, blackened beams. The dirt floor was bumpy and hard packed and she saw a dead rat off to one side. A dozen small, worn tables and benches held two students each, half of whom faced opposite walls.

For Jillian's classes, English and crafts, the students turned the benches in one direction and sat facing her with shining brown faces. At the end of each class she told a story from the Bible usually, demonstrating each drama with flannel graph background and figures she was able to buy in the United States. She taught them songs, exulting in the straining young voices that wafted through the glassless windows and floated up the hillsides. To round out the class Jillian handed out two cookies to each child, a rare treat for these mountain children.

Several weeks into the school year Jillian began hearing favorable reports from parents scattered throughout the villages and she was invited to work in each of the seven schools in the zone. They were delighted with the results of her teaching, the crafts they carried home and the few English words they were learning. New songs were being sung, some with English words. There were comments from some villagers who doubted her commitment to the community fearing that once she won the hearts of the people she'd return home to America, leaving her work with the children unfinished, dashing their hopes of a better life. It was her hope that in time, those rumors would be dashed.

After the class, the children gathered around her to show off their accomplishments. She stood with them for a time and engaged in conversation with the teacher, a young man who for a pittance, walked the same steep mountain path each morning to teach six grade levels, drawn from a substandard education. Burdened and frustrated, dogged by poverty, his dreams of a bright future had long ago been thwarted. Caring deeply for his plight, she prepared to leave and waved good-bye to the teacher and children as they disappeared into the schoolhouse.

At midmorning she was scheduled to hold a class at the boys' school in Pachuca and then return to prepare materials for the next day. Late afternoon she drove to Quito for supplies unavailable in Pachuca. Driving to and from the capital city allowed her uninterrupted time to think of how she would word her reply to Marta. Finally, late in the evening, following much fretful deliberation she drafted a letter. Lifting the paper, she read it aloud.

Dear Marta,

Thank you for the letter of this morning. It was nice hearing from you. I'm sorry that we've had a hard time getting together again. I remember with fondness the last time we drove into Quito to see the new house. I do want to thank you for all the trouble you have gone to in order that I move into it.

Well, I've put a lot of thought into this. Between the time that you and I saw the house and the receipt of your letter yesterday, a number of things have happened in my life. You, of all people should know how I feel about working with Ecuadorians. Since our last time together, I have been blessed that many doors have opened for me to help children. You probably know this already, but I have several classes that I teach each week in the public schools. I'm able to visit in many homes also and I have made friends with influential people.

You expressed something about my not caring about the children. Nothing could be further from the truth. I still care very much for Andy and Ryan; however an occasional visit with them isn't what I need. The chances of you forgetting about me living so far away are too high. If that happened then I would be stuck with a one-year lease and no children. I think you can understand that my decision to stay in Pachuca is for the better.

I trust you are rejoicing in my new life here. It's been a long time since I've been this content.

I hope you and Lucia are doing well. You have to admit that this way you won't be running the risk of her finding out about our relationship. The burden would have been on you to be careful all the time if we had continued to see each other.

Chapter 1

Kiss my children for me. Tell all the children I love them very much. My hope is that someday soon we can all be together again.
Love, Jill

She leaned back and reread the letter. Her brow crinkled at the thought of her children and her friend, Flora still in the clutches of that woman. She felt a surge of weariness. "If only things could be different. If only we could sit together and discuss this face to face. I hope Marta isn't too upset. I can only pray she won't take it out on the children or Flora," she murmured.

Placing the letter in an envelope, she left it unsealed so she could look at it again.

Suddenly there was a rap at the door. A glance at her watch showed it was still early enough for visitors. Eric? Could it possibly be him? Gladys had told her about his visit weeks ago and said he might be returning soon. She looked down at the old grubby clothes she had thrown on after classes and patted back her wayward hair. With a thudding heart, she slipped open the latch and peeked out.

"Philip!" She exclaimed with surprise. "Philip Rios."

"Buenas noches, Jill." The young doctor stood hesitantly on the stoop. "Would you mind if I came in to talk with you?"

She paused. "I don't know. I don't think we have anything to talk about."

"Yes, we do. I must speak with you."

"I see that you are still driving the same American-made car." She stepped aside to allow him entrance as she recalled with bitterness the many times they had ridden together through the streets of Quito.

"Yes, you remember my pride in owning it." He tugged nervously on his well-trimmed beard. He was as immaculate as ever. His glasses hung low on his nose giving him the appearance of a wise old man. Wise he was, old he wasn't. A young dedicated and brilliant doctor, he worked not only in the government hospital teaching doctors much older than he, but traveled each day to work in the Yaruqui clinic, northeast of Pachuca. He was tireless and truly in love with his profession.

"I don't know that I want to speak with you, Philip. I still think of the terrible thing you did to me."

"That's why I'm here. That's what we must deal with."

"Never will I believe you if you tell me again that I mean something to you. You used me, embarrassed me and then walked away without a word of explanation."

"Please, let's sit for a moment and I will explain."

"It's been years since I've seen you." She led him into the kitchen and put Marta's envelope on a counter. She was far too upset to offer him refreshments.

Joining her, he removed his glasses and with his thumb and forefinger he rubbed his eyes. "When you and I were seeing each other I was in a very confused state."

"You were also married," she interjected, "and I didn't know it."

"Please, let me explain." He wet his lips and smoothed his mustache. "Do you know what it feels like to be a popular sought-after doctor while still in his late twenties? My colleagues, family and friends treated me as if I were a god. It seemed that everything I did was right. When a sick person faced me and gave me their symptoms, it was as if a puzzle was being put together before my very eyes. Of course, I had to spend hours reading medical journals and books. I was getting by with very little or no sleep. The money my family spent on reading materials and my continued schooling was an enormous amount and because of that I became successful, but you know all of this."

"Yes, if there is anything admirable I can say about you, Philip, it's that you are a wonderfully capable doctor."

"Try to imagine what effect it had on me, to be lauded from Quito to Yaruqui as one of the greatest doctors in Ecuador, whether that be true or not." He leaned on the table, an imploring look in his eyes.

"Do you think this is an excuse for what you did?" Jillian backed away from him.

"No, of course not. I'm trying to explain that I wasn't mature enough to handle the acclaim." His eyes fell. "No matter how much people made over me, I needed more. It became an obsession and then I needed more and more. I bought an imported car but that wasn't enough. I needed a companion that would draw attention to me, so I became involved with you."

"Weren't you afraid that you would draw the wrong attention? What if your family had seen us together?"

Chapter 1

"Didn't you notice where we ate lunch? In the old part of Quito, in little back street restaurants. Didn't you wonder why I never took you to beautiful, luxury restaurants, theaters and concert halls?"

"No," she gave him an incredulous look. "No, I didn't think a thing about it. You know I'm not comfortable in places like that. I thought you were catering to my whims."

He chuckled. "You are so naïve. I was trying to keep you away from people who ran in my social circle. To me, you were like a breath of fresh air and you also carried the impact of being an American; on top of everything else happening in my life, I had an American girl in love with me."

"Well, isn't that strange. I don't remember telling you that I was in love with you." Jillian's eyes turned cold.

He frowned, a little stunned. "You wanted to marry me."

"You know why I chose to marry you. It was a way out for my children. By marrying you I could take Andy away from Marta and I wanted to reclaim Anna, the little girl that was sent out of the country for adoption. I can't remember if I had Ryan then or not."

"I don't remember," his voice trailed off in a moment's silence. "I was in such a confused state. It seemed every day the situation became more involved and pretty soon I didn't know what to do about you."

She hit the table with an open palm. "What you should have done was tell me that you were married, but I know now that you had no intentions of telling me."

"That's not true. I tried to tell you several times, but I just couldn't. I started to care for you too much. My problem was deciding whether I was going to get a divorce so I could marry you."

"You are a fool if you believe I would have married you had I known you were already married. Never, never would I have married you."

"I know that now. I was too confused to see it then." He played with his glasses that were sitting on the table. "That's one reason I'm here tonight. I came to apologize. I want to tell you how sorry I am for deceiving you."

"Apologize?"

"Yes, about what happened that night when Marta found us…"

"That was one of the most embarrassing moments of my life," she interrupted. "I have gone over the length of our relationship, all of the conversations. Nothing you ever said or did made me think you were married."

His hands rested. "I'm trying to explain. That night was a turning point for me. I realized how close I had come to ruining my life, our lives. I was frightened by our encounter with Marta; frightened enough to go home and take a new look at my marriage, my wife and my family. It scared me and I made a new commitment to my wife. Since I saw you, we've had a baby, a little boy."

"I'm truly happy to hear that, Philip, however you don't understand at all what I went through. You betrayed me. You lied to me."

"What do you want me to do? All I can do right now is apologize."

"How can you live with this on your conscience? Have you told your wife about us? How about your conscience before God? I'd feel like dying with the pressure."

"I've done all that. I've talked with my wife. She knew something was wrong so I told her although I was never unfaithful to her sexually, I misled you and in that way I was dishonest to both you and my wife. I've gone to church and prayed as well as I know how. I confessed with tears and sincerity and to the best of my ability and dependence on God I will never betray my wife again. I've racked my brain trying to figure out what else I can do. Some people in this country purposely suffer physical pain to rid themselves of sin and I've even considered doing that."

Jillian softened. "No, don't do that. If you've turned to God for forgiveness and believe that you have settled things with Him, there is no reason to do penance. Penance isn't the answer anyway because if you have been forgiven by God and your wife, what right do I have to hold something against you? I'm happy that your marriage is doing well."

"Thank you. This has been very heavy on my heart for a long time. Now, as I have told my wife, I intend to be a better doctor and husband. At least I don't have all the problems I did with my inflated ego. I simply want to be a good husband, father and doctor and Jill, now that we've talked, I want to be a good friend to you. I do feel so much better, so much cleaner."

Chapter 1

"I guess, in an indirect way, we can thank Marta for that." She felt a sense of relief, some of the old hurt dissipating. "How did you find me here?"

His face brightened. "I heard that you were working in the schools. Never did I dream you would be living in the plaza. Here I thought you still lived with Marta and her helper. Did you bring Andy with you? Did you bring any of the children with you?"

'No," she said sadly. "Marta still has the children. I've thought of every way possible to take those children from her, but there is no solution."

"Why did you leave the orphanage without them?"

"Marta forced me to leave and I still don't know why. You have probably heard they shut down her outpatient clinic. She believes I had something to do with that, but the more I think about it, the more I believe she is hiding something so incriminating that if found out, she could be deported. Of course I don't know if that is true, right now it's just a suspicion. Perhaps everything she does is within the law, although I must say, one day years ago she mentioned to me that if the government saw her records on the children she would be in trouble, but since then, she must have taken care of the records. I wonder about her adoptions. If they aren't legal, how then is she able to get the babies out of the country?"

Philip leaned forward until he made direct eye contact with her. "Stay out of it. If you want to continue living here in peace, don't start trouble when you don't have to."

"What about the children?"

"You must leave them alone."

"I can't do that." She stood angrily. "Why doesn't anyone understand they are innocent children who need help?"

"Do you think Marta is still mistreating them?" He replaced his glasses and peered at her.

"I don't know. I need to talk with the maid who works there. I need to be alone with her for a couple hours."

"If you need help, please contact me. If you ever find out that she is harming the children, I will do what I can."

"Thank you. Now, tell me how you found me."

He grinned a white smile and adjusted his fine tie. "I met a young doctor who works here in Pachuca in the government clinic. She doesn't know you, but she has heard of you because she mentioned that a gringa was working in the public schools. The more she talked about you, the more I wondered if the gringa was you. By the way, you should meet her."

"The doctor is a female?" Jillian's eyebrows lifted in question.

"Yes, she's in her final year of medical school, working in the government clinic here in Pachuca. You will like her; in fact you have a lot in common. She is also evangelical. Yes, I'm sure you will like Raquel very much. During the week she lives in the Martinez house and on weekends she goes home to Quito."

"She lives with the Martinez family? Rolando Martinez?" Conversations about Rolando always piqued her interest. "What about Rolando? I had heard that his parents passed away."

"Yes, he was here for the funerals but right after the burials he just disappeared, but anyway, Raquel lives with Geoff and Opal Martinez. I wasn't available the Sunday Geoff's dad died so he called Raquel in Quito. She's a friend of the family so she came the distance. Geoff's father was found dead in the middle of the road, hit by a car, the driver had taken off. Poor Raquel had to travel from Quito to dress the body in a suit and prepare him for burial. Then of all things, Geoff's mom died a few days later. During this time, I met Raquel and found her to be a very nice person. I think you should go see her at the clinic someday."

"Perhaps I will." She sat down again. "Philip, I just thought of something. There is a family who has a little store next door. It's a family of women, except for Gladys' husband. The other day when I was there I noticed Gladys' grandmother sitting in the kitchen, her feet in a basin of water. She seemed to be in such great pain, I stopped to ask her what was wrong. When she lifted her feet out of the water, I was horrified. She has such blisters and corns on each foot. Is there anything you can suggest we do for her?"

"These poor people," he sighed, shaking his head. "They work so hard in bare feet or in shoes that aren't fitted to their size. There's not much we can do."

"Don't you have any medicines for corns?"

Chapter 1

He thought for a moment. "You know, I think I can get something from our pharmaceutical department in Quito. I can get some pads for the corns and perhaps some painkillers. I can bring something for athlete's foot just in case. If you will cut arch lifters to size, you can put some in her shoes."

"Will you do that for her? Oh, thank you."

"The trouble is I won't be able to obtain the medicine until next week. That means I can't get the supplies back to you until then. Can you wait?"

"Of course, just so you remember her."

He stood and held out a finely manicured hand. "Thank you for forgiving me. I feel now that I can lift my head with dignity."

"You are forgiven and I promise you, if for some reason I need you to help me get my children from Marta or if I hear they are being mistreated, I will call you."

"I'd be disappointed if you didn't."

Chapter 2

One week after Philip promised to bring Jillian the medical supplies for her neighbor, he knocked at her door.

"Oh, gracias," she said as she piled the items on the kitchen table and studied each one. "This is for the corns and possible bunions. Oh, look at the pads for her shoes. I can't wait to show them to her."

He picked them up one by one and explained how they should be used.

"You know," she exclaimed. "I'd like to take the medicine and show them to her now. Can we do that?"

Adjusting his lab coat, he thoughtfully replied. "Let's see. This is midweek so possibly Raquel will be home. Perhaps while you take these things to your neighbor, I will step next door to the Martinez' and discuss something with her. If you have a problem, maybe you can come and get me, but I must get home and will only take a few minutes with Raquel."

"Maybe you can stop by to see if I have applied the medicines correctly?" she asked hopefully.

Philip ran a hand over his hair, adjusted his tie and smoothed his mustache. "Jill, I'm sorry. I can help you put them back in the sack but I can't stay. I must return to Quito."

They stepped onto the sidewalk and Jillian pulled the door shut. We'll only be gone a few minutes. I'll leave it unlocked."

"Shall I drive you down there?"

Chapter 2

"Please take a few more minutes and let's walk. It's such a short distance." She started walking.

"Okay."

They passed Pachuca's resident nurse's home. Olivia Nieto stood in the doorway and greeted them. "Buenas noches, Doctor Rios. Buenas noches, señorita. Are you making a house call this evening?"

"Buenas noches, Señorita Olivia," replied Philip. "No, I'm going down to visit with Doctor Raquel."

"Buenas noches, Señorita Olivia," smiled Jillian. "And I'm on my way to visit my neighbor Gladys Baca's grandmother."

"Doctor Raquel should be at home. We left the clinic about an hour ago. She told me she was going to spend the evening reading." Olivia ignored Jillian to acknowledge Philip.

"We must be on our way," Philip said. "Buenas noches."

They walked beyond Olivia's house and passed by the church. "She acts as though she doesn't like me," remarked Jillian.

"Stay away from Olivia. I know her well because we've worked together a few times at the government clinic where she's a nurse. She likes men too much. She leads a questionable life and in fact, I've heard a lot of unpleasant things, for instance, sometimes she doesn't charge patients for inoculations, but she will take payment in things. Some of her patients have been hired to guard things such as crops, materials from construction sites or some such things. She'll take cement or wood or something else in payments. It's very bad practice."

Jillian was appalled. "I'll remember your warning."

They passed the school for Catholic monks, then two houses and stopped before Gladys' home. "Perhaps I'll see you when I'm finished." Jillian sent him on his way and knocked on the door.

Gladys opened the door a crack. "Buenas noches, señorita."

"Buenas noches, Gladys. May I come in?"

Gladys gave her a cold look and hesitated a long moment before opening the door. "Si Entre."

Puzzled by the chilly reception, Jillian stepped inside.

"What do you want, señorita?" Gladys withdrew to the dim hallway.

"I want to visit with your family," explained Jillian. First Olivia had treated her rudely and now Gladys.

She led Jillian down the hallway and into the main room, where her grandmother sat at a table drinking a cup of hot water, a look of perpetual pain on her face. Gladys' mother sat on a sofa, knitting. The room had the typical mud walls, but someone one had attempted to paper it with newspaper. The floors were laid with wide planks of wood, so worn and uneven that she wondered how the elderly women could walk across the floor without tripping.

Focusing her attention on the woman's feet, Jillian stepped carefully over to the table beside her. When the woman looked up, she saw the cold distrust in her watery eyes. "Buenas noches, señora."

"Buenas noches, señorita. What brings you to our house?"

"Señora, I have been very concerned over the pain in your feet. I have brought medicine for you."

The woman's eyes opened wide but her face remained set and hard.

"I would like to help you," explained Jillian.

"We don't have enough money for the medicine." The woman pushed her cup away and looked over at Gladys. "We did not ask for the medicine, did we?"

Jillian was confused. Just a few days before Gladys and her grandmother had been very warm toward her but now they were aloof and suspicious. What had happened? "I don't expect you to pay me money, señora. I only want your pain to go away." Jillian sat down next to her. "Will you let me do this for you?"

"You don't want money?" The woman looked confused.

"What kind of medicine?" Gladys asked.

"This." Jillian turned in her chair and opened the sack pouring out the contents on the table. "As you can see, some of them were made in the United States. I had Doctor Rios obtain them in Quito. He brought you the very best."

"Doctor Rios," the grandmother took one of the corn pads in her hand, stared at it and showed it to Gladys and her mother who had put down the knitting and joined them.

"Gladys, please bring me a basin of warm water, soap, scissors and a towel," said Jillian.

The young woman hesitated for a moment and then left the room.

"I need to wash your feet," Jillian explained.

"Señorita," the old woman intoned softly. "I can't let you do that."

Chapter 2

"But I must. Look, you can see the medicines that will help you feel so much better. May I see your shoes?"

Leaning over with a grunt, the woman picked up her shoes from beneath the table where she had slipped them off. They were the common, inexpensive plastic shoes worn by the nationals. Jillian picked one up and tried to judge the size. "You need to buy some sturdier shoes. No wonder your feet hurt."

"We don't have enough money to buy better shoes," the old woman answered gruffly, her eyes becoming hard again.

"Señora, you must talk to your family. You must somehow save some money to buy good shoes. You can't wear plastic shoes any longer. I will put pads in them right now, but for your own comfort you need leather shoes."

Gladys walked into the room, a basin, towel, soap and scissors in her hands and set them on the table. Jillian in turn placed them on the floor and knelt. She took the gnarled hardened and crusted feet and gently washed them. She opened the bottle of medicine, placed drops on the corns and covered them with pads, then placed pads on bunions, cut pads for the shoes and handed her a bottle of pills. "When the pain is very bad, take two of these with water. Gladys, if you notice any infections in between her toes, wash her feet and apply this medicine."

Tears filled the woman's eyes. "That already feels better." She looked at Gladys. "She washed my feet."

Gladys' eyes softened and her mother joined in. "Gracias, señorita."

"Gracias, señorita," the old woman echoed. She stood to test her feet. "You are not the bad person that Señorita Marta said you are."

Jillian's eyes bulged. "Señorita Marta said I was a bad person?"

"Si, she came to our home the other evening and told us to be very careful, that we should not trust you. She said the only reason you are here in Ecuador is to take our money. She said that you are teaching our children many evil things in the school."

"Yes." Gladys put the basin on the table. "She warned us that you would give us smiles but try to steal from us."

"I am sick in my heart," Jillian placed her hand on her chest. "Señorita Marta is supposed to be my friend. Never would I hurt you. Have you heard of me taking money from your people? Have you heard of any evil that I teach in the school? I don't ask for one centavo for the time I give to your children. Most of the parents are pleased with the English words, the stories and the crafts I teach."

"The American nurse said that the English words are evil, but I knew in my heart that she was lying. I know that you do not steal. I am beginning to be very angry that she is doing this against you, señorita."

"Do you know if she has gone to other people in the plaza?"

"Si, she went to everyone in the plaza one day while you were away. She went from door to door. She even went to the girls' school, but I understand that the teachers told her to go away."

Despite herself, Jillian smiled. "Now I understand why Olivia Nieto treated me very coldly tonight."

"Si, the American went there also," the grandmother voiced regretfully. "We are very sorry for the way we treated you, señorita. It is because the people of Pachuca don't know you well yet. Señorita Marta has lived here many years and although she is a difficult person to understand, she has come here to stay."

Biding them farewell, Jillian promised to return again the next day. Resisting the temptation to go next door to see if Philip was still there, she returned home. Her heart was in turmoil. Why was Marta spreading false stories about her? Was her old friend so desperate to have her leave Pachuca that she was attempting to force her out under pressure from the townspeople?

By the time she arrived home she was angry. She had hoped Philip would have waited, but his car was nowhere in sight. Slid under her door was a note from him, explaining his need to get home for dinner with his family. If only Eric would come back. She sensed that he had been right. One way or another, Marta was going to try to get her away from Pachuca. Now, filled with embarrassment and too afraid to face him and admit her mistake, she would do nothing to contact him.

Instead, Jillian vowed determinedly, Marta is not going to make me leave. I will continue to teach the children, taking time to explain each lesson to the teachers so I cannot be accused of any wrongdoing. With a sinking heart, she feared for the first time that the door for Andy and Ryan was indeed closed.

Chapter 3

Eric decided to visit Jillian in the late evening when she was most apt to be at home. Several weeks had passed before he was able to pull away from his work at the hacienda. Now that the potato planting was completed he decided he must see her. Since alluding to a broken relationship in his conversation with Elena the previous week, he now could not get Jillian off his mind. Perhaps he could talk her into a picnic beside the creek they had visited several months before, or a day of window shopping in Quito. He would ask her forgiveness for demanding that she live in Quito. Hindsight made him realize how self-centered he had been trying to control someone he had no claim to, someone he may never be able to call his own without proceeding carefully. It seemed he had fallen in love and he needed to find out if Jillian felt the same way.

His truck turned the corner, passing Ernestina's grocery store and rolled toward Jillian's house. He peered through the darkness, surprised to see a large, imported car parked in front of her house. He backed up to the corner and got out of the truck, locking it securely. It was quiet except for the mute sounds from the park. The car was familiar, American-made and sporty. With dread he recalled Doctor Philip Rios drove such a car. He saw lights on in the house but heard no voices. A stab of anger and jealousy wrenched his heart. How long had this been going on? Could this be why Jill rebelled when I made demands on her? Come to think of it, when had she given me any indication that she loved me or wanted a future with me? I just assumed that I was the only man in her life. She hadn't talked about Doctor Rios at all. He thought back to the first time he had seen her. She had been with the doctor that day too. He felt like a fool knocking on her door and disturbing them. No, he wouldn't knock on the door, but he was too curious about what was going on to return to Tulcachi. He stepped back on the sidewalk and looked up to her balcony. It was dark.

He didn't want to talk with Gladys again. He was embarrassed enough, but perhaps if he asked Gladys to not say anything to Jillian, he could at least discuss the situation with her. He started down toward Gladys' home and walked past the house next door where Olivia Nieto, the town nurse, shared living quarters with her father, Don Eduardo. The door was open and he saw the old man sitting at the dining room table eating dinner. He was spotted by Don Eduardo but before he could get to his feet, Olivia appeared around the corner. The nurse was a very large woman with short dark hair and a round face. Eric immediately disliked her and wished he had not been wandering around gaining attention.

"Buenas noches, señor," Olivia called after him.

"Buenas noches, señorita."

"May I help you with something? Perhaps you need medical help?" Her eyes gleamed with interest, her smile suggesting something more intimate.

"I'm Eric Perez from Tulcachi. I'm looking for information."

"Yes, I know who you are. I'm Olivia Nieto." She stepped out of the house as her father came up behind her.

"Señor Nieto." Eric gave a small nod in the man's direction. "Buenas noches."

Nearly toothless, the fat old man tried to reach out to shake his hand. Eric noticed and quickly stepped forward to the take the extended hand. "I must speak with the señorita who lives next door. I don't want to disturb her if she is busy. I'm hoping you can tell me who owns that car and whether I should knock on the door."

"Of course, I know the car well." Olivia cast him a coy look. "It belongs to Doctor Philip Rios. He visits her often. He's married but that doesn't seem to bother her at all. It's really quite disgusting, isn't it?"

Chapter 3

It was her small mouth that he didn't like and he ignored her flirtations, replying humorlessly. "Jill and I have been friends for several years. It's been a long time since I have seen her; I thought I would see how she is tonight."

"Would you like to come in for a cup of tea?" Don Eduardo pushed himself forward.

"Yes, yes, do come in." Olivia took his arm possessively.

"No, I must be on my way."

He left them staring after him. His confidence crushed, he got into his truck and started the drive back to Tulcachi. "Never again," he murmured, "will I allow myself to be drawn into a relationship with Jillian. If she prefers married men then I will no longer pursue her. I have too much pride to grovel any more. From now on Tulcachi, Carlos and Elena and their baby will be my whole life."

Chapter 4

Opening the front door to Aunt Mariana's house he walked in. Hearing noises in the kitchen, he padded through the living room and dining area and stepped into the bright, blue room. His aunt stood at the sink peeling potatoes and he stood watching her for a moment.

"Hola, Tia," he said softly.

"Oh, oh, Rolando!" she screamed with pleasure, potato and knife flying as she turned to him. He was in her arms in a flash. "Oh my darling." She exclaimed. "Where have you been? I've been so worried."

"Everywhere and nowhere, Tia, but it's good to be home."

"We didn't know where to look for you. Where have you been living for a whole year?"

Sitting at the table, he sighed. "After leaving here, I went south for a while, then to the jungle; after that, up north, then over to the northern coast. Like I say, everywhere and nowhere."

"How did you live?"

"I had jobs here and there, enough to eat and travel."

"Oh, Rolando, why did you leave?"

"I had to."

"Geoff blames himself for your disappearance."

"He shouldn't do that." A touch of guilt moved his conscience. "I don't blame him."

"Perhaps you should tell him that."

"I will, right now."

Chapter 4

She laughed. "I didn't mean right now. Have something to eat first. He won't be home now anyway."

It was dark when he arrived at his family home. To his surprise, a sedan was parked in front, indicating guests. He decided to find out first who was inside so he walked to the side of the house and peeked in the living room's small window. Geoff and Opal sat facing him, cheerfully entertaining the couple sitting on the sofa, their backs to Rolando. A pang of jealousy shot through his heart. That was what he wanted. Why was he always on the outside looking in? He wanted to belong to someone. He was tired of being alone and living only for himself. For several minutes he watched and finally Opal rose from her chair. The man seated beside the woman on the sofa raised his arm from her shoulder and she stood to join Opal. When Rolando recognized the visitor, he let out a small agonizing cry, not believing what he had just seen. Raquel. He had spent countless hours thinking about Raquel during his travels this past year. She had become the perfect woman in his imaginations, one who would help change his life with her love. In the short conversations they had during the week of his parents' funerals, he had found himself more and more attracted to her. It was incredible. Her strength and ability to speak her mind to him without fear was compelling. Over the year he dreamed of pursuing her. This was the reason he had come back, but now, it looked as though she had married or was about to be married. It was more than he could bear.

Walking to the back of the house, he sat on the stoop. He would have to wait until Raquel and her husband left before he could let Geoff know he had returned. Placing his head in his hands, he despaired of his life and his failures. Somewhere in the depths of the Ecuadorian jungle he had decided to return to Pachuca to win Raquel.

The morning he left Playas, he had taken a broken dream. Elena didn't want to be with him. It didn't take long to believe that. Actually he realized it the minute he saw her standing outside the restaurant waiting for Carlos. By the time he reached Guayaquil, he had surrendered knowing Elena's marriage was meant to be and that it had been he, Rolando, who pushed her out of his life, not Carlos. Because of this misguided hatred for Carlos he had hurt and destroyed all those he loved, almost taking someone's life. Wandering the country of

Ecuador, he saw himself as others saw him and it was then he thought of Raquel. Perhaps she could help him change. Because he feared he would also destroy her, he rejected the idea time and time again, until after a year of running, he decided to find her and see if she had any interest in him. Perhaps she would be pleased with the new resolutions he had made. But tonight he had seen her with another man. He felt more alone now than ever. A nagging desire to have a drink wormed its way into his belly. Rising, he turned back to the street, but when he heard voices, laughter and a car's motor, he waited until it had driven off. He debated several minutes whether he should see Geoff tonight or the next day. Walking halfway to the street he hesitated and then turned again in an agony of indecision. Realizing he could no longer put off seeing his brother, he walked to the back door and came face to face with Raquel.

"Oh!" she jumped with fright. "Oh, Rolando, what are you doing back here? You scared me."

Rolando stood, looking down at her, his mouth hanging open stupidly.

"When did you arrive in town?" she asked lifting a lit candle closer to his face.

"Raquel, I thought you just left for Quito."

"No, I stay in Pachuca during the week and in Quito on my days off." She frowned again. "You haven't answered my question. Geoff doesn't know you're here, does he?"

"No," he replied, delight and dread spreading through his heart. He was afraid to ask about the man he'd seen with her. "Did your husband go back to Quito alone?"

"My husband?"

"Yes, the man who was with you on the sofa."

She put one hand on a hip and gave him a questioning look. "Were you watching through the window?"

"I came earlier to visit with Geoff and saw the car. I didn't want to barge in and disturb you, so I waited out here."

She stood back and looked into his eyes, studying his face. "You've changed, haven't you? Where have you been this past year?"

"No place special and yes, I guess I have changed a little. Perhaps you had a lot to do with that."

Chapter 4

"Why do you say that?"

"Remember how you talked to me the night of my papa's death?"

"Vaguely, but I hardly believe you heard anything I said."

"Oh, but I did." He looked at her carefully, the flickering candle in her hand changing the color of her eyes as he remembered them. He had traveled many miles trying to remember what she looked like. Taking a step forward, he gave her a small pleading look. "Raquel, who was that man? Is he your husband?"

She giggled. "No, he's my brother. He came to Pachuca today to help me look for a building to set up a practice. I'm living here during the week and completing my studies while working in the government clinic across the street. I like Pachuca enough that I would like to live here."

But Rolando had not heard a word she said beyond the fact that he had no rival for her affection. "Would you please sit with me a minute? I must talk to you."

She hesitated a moment and then sat beside him. "Opal will wonder where I am."

"That's all right. I will tell you quickly what I have on my mind." He rubbed his hand against his knee nervously and turned to look at her. "I have changed. I've done nothing but travel for a year and most of that time I thought about you."

"About me? You hardly know me."

"I not only know you, but I love you."

Raquel started to stand. "That's impossible."

He put his hand on her arm. "It's the truth. I love you and would like to see if we can develop a relationship."

Fighting off his hand, she stood. "That's impossible," she repeated. "We live worlds apart. I appreciate the fact that you seem to have changed, but Rolando, our lifestyles are so different. Why start something that we can never continue?"

"Why are our lives different?" A cloud started to settle over his spirit.

"Our goals, priorities and desires are different. We think differently, our philosophies, theories and understanding conflict. I believe that before you can ever find yourself, you must make a lot of things right you have done wrong. There has to be a real change of heart.

It's not something that you do to please someone else but because you know it is the only way. There are a lot of people you must ask forgiveness and money you have taken that must be returned. It's called restitution."

She had hit the mark and he felt miserable. Again, she had seen past all of his pride, right into his heart. He felt as though all his evil acts and thoughts were exposed before her. The walls he had so carefully built fell at his feet. He stood and walked from her into the night.

The next morning he was gone again, leaving behind a grieving Raquel who believed she had mishandled their conversation and had driven him further from his family.

From now on, thought Rolando, I don't care who I hurt or what I do. He caught an early bus to Quito and disembarked at the bank, withdrawing all of the money he had stolen from Geoff. From this day forward he would steal to live and drink all the liquor he had been denying himself for months. His face burned with embarrassment remembering the way he had exposed his feelings for Raquel. Now he detested her.

Chapter 5

Oyambarillo, a hamlet two miles northeast of Pachuca had once been an immense hacienda encompassing several thousand acres, but over the years the land had been sold parcel by parcel to farmers having roots in the hacienda's history, leaving a remnant of the family's original holdings in the hands of two elderly descendants. At one time, before the completion of the new highway, the primary road leading north passed through Oyambarillo. The narrow, cobblestone road barely wide enough to accommodate two trucks had been used extensively, giving rise to a few huts, a store and a school for the growing community. The advent of the new highway had changed all that as now few trucks and cars made their way through town.

Jillian had decided to walk to her school class in Oyambarillo. The morning sun promised a beautiful day and on impulse she set out on foot. After class, with a heavy heart, she made her way toward home chastising herself for her lack of gratitude at how well things were going. The children always greeted her enthusiastically and the teachers expressed their thanks for her endeavors. Still, her spirits sagged.

A year had elapsed since Marta had tried to turn the people of Pachuca against her, but the tainted plot proved futile for rather the opposite had occurred. Among the town populace Jillian seemed more popular than ever. She suspected Gladys Baca had something to do with that.

Her depression had grown steadily, yet subtly over the months. Finally she had to face the facts. Never again would she see Marta and the children. All this time had passed and not a flicker of interest had she seen on Marta's part. Then there was Eric, who had faded from her life without so much as a backward glance. She would not allow herself to admit how much she missed him, for she might break down and drive to Tulcachi. The fear of rejection bridled her.

Before the road intersected with the highway, there lay a path wide enough for a small vehicle which led up the mountain to the Oyambarillo Hacienda. Jillian followed it halfway, where she climbed a small rise upon which sat an old deserted church. Ancient custom led owners of large haciendas to build their own churches for hacienda residents, but over time lethargy toward seeking God seemed to have crept in. The church had been gutted inside and was being used for storage purposes. The long and narrow edifice, built of stone with high open windows still maintained a loveliness of simplicity. With its tall steeple, it perched on the hill like a sentinel keeping watch over Pachuca in the distance.

While living with Marta, Jillian had oftentimes gazed out her bedroom window facing north and studied the church. The sight of it brought her hope and comfort when her heart felt, at times ravaged by hopelessness and pain. From afar, the little church looked new and well cared for, but now up close it was evident it was in a state of neglect. In her mind she imagined this house of God once teeming with families in search of a deeper spiritual walk but now it stood sadly quiet and empty. The windows and door had been removed allowing the cold night breezes and driving winds to penetrate its crushed heart.

"I'm all alone," she whispered as she scrambled up the steep knoll and found a grassy spot on which to rest. She brushed the back of her hand across her eyes, smearing two hot tears. "I feel so empty, just like this church." She turned away and faced Pachuca, searching for her former post at the bedroom window on Marta's property. Her watch indicated it was midmorning so the older children would be at school; the younger ones, Andy and Ryan would be at play either outside or in their rooms.

Chapter 5

She saw Flora for short visits once a month. She reported that Marta was gone so much that the children had some reprieve from her harsh discipline. Flora merely shrugged and shook her head at Jillian's inquiries to the woman's whereabouts. Again the shroud of mystery cloaked Marta's movements.

Despite her popularity with the students, Jillian was not happy. Nothing, it seemed was turning out the way she had expected upon her return to Ecuador. Deep within the recesses of her mind laid the hope that Marta would have repented of her scheme to rid herself of Jillian and welcome her return to the orphanage, but from all appearances, it seemed as though Marta had no desire to see her again. "How I miss the children," she wept aloud as tears flowed. "I miss them. I miss Marta, Lucia and the friendship we had. I want to have the security of a home surrounded by people." A fresh wave of weeping shook her as she turned her thoughts to Eric. It had been over a year since she had seen him and she had no doubt that he was out of her life for good. After all, she sobbed, who wants a friend who can't control her temper? She almost resented Philip's happiness. His visits had been few and far between since the night she had tended her neighbor's ailing feet. No, she thought, not even he is sensitive enough to know how much I long for companionship. He is too preoccupied with his career and family to consider my needs.

She knew she could count on the people of Pachuca to be friendly, but they had their own families, their own cultures. It was difficult to find the companionship she needed to satisfy her lonely heart. Perhaps it's time to leave Ecuador, she thought. This was not the first time she had considered the possibility. She spoke in prayer to God. Face to face with Him, her inner desires revealed, she questioned her original intent in coming to Ecuador. "Lord, why am I here?" She asked. "Am I supposed to remain? What am I accomplishing? Is it worth leaving my family in the United States?"

It was like reading a dragging novel with no apparent plot. What if the plot starts on the next page? If she closed the book now, she might be just a few pages away from an exciting intrigue. What if I'm nearing the end of my dilemma? The answer could be around the next turn! What if I left Ecuador, only to find out later that I could have had the children back? The thought was tormenting. No, it was too big of a chance to take. No, she concluded, I'll endure loneliness if I have to as long as there is even a remote possibility that I might be reunited with Andy and Ryan and, hopefully, Marta.

Her shoulders slumped forward and she placed her chin in her hand. It was a shame that from this vantage point she could only see the second floor of the house she once lived in. She longed to see the playground, but there were too many obstacles and the distance was too great. If a woman had birthed a baby last night, there would be dirty sheets this morning, she mused and Lucia would be hanging out her sparkling white wash. If Marta was away again today, then Lucia and the children would be alone.

For months she had resisted the temptation to visit the property, the drastic urge tempered by her fear of Lucia's and Marta's wrath, but now, she reasoned, perhaps with the passage of time Lucia's hatred had abated. Should I take a chance to see her? She weighed the idea. Perhaps my old friend would be happy to see me. While Marta's out I can meet with Lucia alone in the clinic. If I'm able to win her understanding and don't get killed in the process, she mused sarcastically, then perhaps she'll permit me to see the children and if Lucia can be persuaded, then she might persuade Marta to allow me to move back to the property. What if Marta allowed Andy and Ryan to come live with me in the plaza? Oh, could it possibly work?

With a surge of new hope and knee-knocking resolve, Jillian rose, grabbed her backpack and hurried down the hill. On the new highway, she searched in the distance for a bus from Yaruqui. There was none so she set out for Marta's property, full of fearful determination. "I must hurry before the children are called in for lunch. Marta may come home for the meal and the older children will be out of school. There will be too many distractions," she muttered. "I hope there are no new patients ready for baby delivery." Her pace picked up. She searched behind her for a bus, but still none appeared. The day was warm and she was without protection from the sun. A bead of perspiration rolled down her back. She regretted how wilted she would look by the time she arrived. A glance to the west showed no signs of a cooling cloud cover. Though she rushed, it took her thirty minutes to cover the distance.

Chapter 5

At one end of the compound, close by the road was a high, narrow wooden gate built into the mud wall. It had been several years since the gate had been used, but with extra effort she was able to push it open. Her nervousness left her feeling weak so walking cautiously toward the closed outpatient clinic she peeked across the picket fence at the small group of children playing. Straining to see her two boys, she spotted Andy playing with Sarah in the sandbox. Ryan was not in sight. A longing stronger than the will to live swept over her. If she had been physically able to climb the high fence, she would have bounded over in a rush to embrace her boy, but she held onto the fence in an effort to remain calm. Her only hope was to convince Lucia she had a right to see the children.

After checking to make sure Marta's truck was not in the carport, she walked timidly to the patient door of the maternity clinic convinced she was being watched from inside. Any moment she expected the door to fly open with Lucia lunging after her. Closing her eyes, she breathed deeply and knocked. A minute passed and Jillian knocked again. She pressed her ear to the door and heard distant pounding noises. Lucia was at her tool bench in the attic. It was a moment of decision; perhaps she should leave.

"No, I must have the boys with me." She pounded as hard as she could on the door. "I must take the chance that Lucia will be happy to see me."

Being light on her feet, Lucia flung open the door without a warning sound. Shock registered on both of their faces but it took only a moment for Lucia to recover. Surprised and angered, the Indian attempted to slam the door shut. "What are you doing here? Get off my property."

On reflex, Jillian flung herself at the door and blocked its closure. "Wait a minute, Lucia. I must talk with you."

"Get out! Get out! I would rather die than see your face." Lucia screamed, leaning on the door.

Jillian put her whole weight on the other side, pushing inward. "Lucia, please, I must talk with you. Please, I beg you." She felt the door give a little as if Lucia had hesitated. "Please Lucia, just a minute. I'll stay just a minute."

The struggle stopped and slowly the door opened. Lucia peeked around the edge and then stepped into full view. The two women stood face to face. Jillian felt a strong stir of emotion. They had once been best friends, sharing warm fellowship. Two cultures had once been united, hurling aside the barriers of different backgrounds, education, countries and customs. As close friends, they had embraced the contrasts as stepping stones to understanding each other. Where and when the abundant waters of companionship had drifted off into separate tributaries Jillian couldn't remember or comprehend. All she knew was that at one time they had loved each other dearly and now there was hatred and animosity as deep as the Andes ranges were high.

"Please let me come in for a moment." Jillian opened both hands displaying them to the Indian as if to show she was holding no ill will.

Lucia's black eyes narrowed and seemed to go blank. She didn't speak but stepped back to let the girl past. With shaking legs, Jillian made her way into the hall and waited for Lucia to face her.

"Well?" Lucia waited.

"I'd like to go somewhere other than the hall to talk. Can we go into the clinic or the kitchen?"

"No."

"Lucia, please give me a chance to talk with you. I won't bother you again. I just need a little of your time," she begged.

The Indian frowned. "I don't want you in the patient area or the kitchen. Someone may come in and see you. If Marta returned early from her errands and found you here, she would be very angry with both of us. Let's go into my sewing room." Lucia led her into what used to be her bedroom before moving to the defunct outpatient clinic. "Here, come in and sit."

Jillian followed her into the room where they had spent many hours waiting for patients to dilate enough to deliver their babies. During those hours they would play board games and chatter, planning their future in the orphanage. Almost everything remained the same; Lucia's old bed was in its usual place against the wall, a place no doubt to rest during the long nights before infant deliveries. Her clothes bureau had been replaced with a table piled high with cloth

Chapter 5

and patterns. "I see you are still making clothes for the children." She inspected the hem of a tan dress.

"Of course. Who do you think would sew if I didn't?" Lucia's face remained noncommittal. "Okay, what do you want?"

"I want to know if there's any way that you can tell me where our relationship went wrong."

Fiery, angry emotion stirred in Lucia's eyes. "Relationship? Señorita, there was never a relationship."

"Lucia, how can you say that? I can remember the evenings we sat on this bed playing games, reading or just talking while waiting for deliveries. Remember all the good food we would bring in here to eat? I recall what close friends we were then."

Lucia smiled. "You are a romantic fool to think of those days. They are gone."

Jillian started to return the smile when she realized the Indian's mouth was set in a sneer. A cold finger of fear flicked her heart. "How could you forget? Those evenings were so special to me."

"If you came here to talk about the past, I must ask you to leave. I don't have the time or the desire for this."

"No, that isn't the real reason. I'm really here because I need to talk with you about Andy and Ryan."

Lucia stood motionless. "What about them?"

The girl moved forward in a pleading manner. "Lucia, if there was anything about our friendship that meant something to you, please listen to me. I love Andy and Ryan. You remember how Marta gave Andy to me and you know how I delivered Ryan. You heard the mother say she wanted me to have him. Oh, please talk to Marta. Tell her that I should have the boys. They are really mine." Tears sprang to her eyes.

Lucia moved backward to the bed and sat by the pillow, never taking her eyes from Jillian. All of a sudden her face broke into a sardonic smile. "Of course you are here because of the boys. Oh, Jill, I can imagine how you must feel, having Andy and Ryan so close and yet not be able to see them."

Smiling hesitantly, she agreed. "It's been terrible. I think of them all the time. That's really the reason I came back to Ecuador. I want them with me."

Resting on her hands, Lucia chuckled. "So that's why you came back. I wondered. You left your home in the United States, your family and friends and came back to Ecuador to live in an old mud house without plumbing and electricity just to claim the boys."

"Yes, although the house does have electricity." Jillian was more hopeful with each passing moment."

"What would you do if Marta gave you the children?"

"I'd start looking for a way to adopt them."

Lucia laughed. "In Ecuador a single woman can't adopt a child. They can't even care for them without governmental permission. That is, unless you plan to marry."

"Marry? Me?" Jillian's hand went to her heart, realizing Lucia was remembering Eric's presence on her balcony. "I have no intention of marrying. Are you sure about the Ecuadorian law?"

One side of Lucia's mouth curved upward. "Yes, I am sure. Well, I guess adoption won't be possible if we give the boys to you."

Jillian's mind was whirling. "Do you think if I worked something out, you know, like governmental permission, that Marta would give the boys to me?"

"What do you mean, 'work out'?" Lucia frowned.

"I don't know." The girl turned to face the window. "Maybe I can think of something."

She turned back toward Lucia and gasped as fear exploded like an electric shock in the pit of her stomach. The Indian had moved so close to her that Jillian felt her breath on her face. She backed against the window. "What are you doing?"

Her eyes emotionless, Lucia leaned toward her. Jillian's glance slid to Lucia's hand. It cradled a gun, the same gun that she had used to scare Jillian with suicide many years before. She lifted her eyes. "I thought Marta had taken that gun from you. Where did you get it?"

"You are such a fool. Sometimes your innocence and stupidity astounds me. Do you think that I couldn't get this again from Marta?"

Jillian licked her lips. "Why do you have it now?"

Lucia pressed closer and lifted the gun. "I would love to hurt you. I have dreamed of doing it day and night."

A cry escaped Jillian's mouth. "I thought you were being friendly with me a minute ago. You really do hate me. Well, all right, shoot

Chapter 5

me. I don't care anymore. You have hurt me so many times and I have continued to love you. Go ahead, shoot me. If I can't have the boys I want to die anyway."

For a long time the women, breathing heavily stared at each other. Then Lucia frowned and looked down at the gun in her hand. She stepped back and glared at her. "Get out of here, Jill and never come back here again. I will tell you with all certainly that you will never again see Andy and Ryan. They were not yours when you lived here and they are not yours now."

Carefully moving past Lucia, she grabbed her backpack and hurried out the door. She just wanted out of this room, away from the terrible oppression and danger.

Chapter 6

Everything had happened so quickly. Before Jillian realized where she was, she was standing on the grass outside the clinic, staring at the closed door. She laid her hand on her chest and felt the rapid palpitations of her heart. All she could think of now was to get away from this dreadful place. Scampering toward the old gate, she turned her head to see if Andy was still at play in the yard but it was empty of children.

Safe on the road, her breathing steadied; she leaned weakly against the mud wall. Lucia could have easily harmed her and who would have been the wiser? She had stopped at Marta's property on a whim so no one would have considered she had gone there. Remembering the garbage pit behind the main house, she shuddered. It was as deep as a house was high. She knew because once she had tied two tall ladders together to rescue a cat that had fallen in. After this latest experience, she knew Lucia wouldn't hesitate a moment to kill her and throw her into the pit. Even Marta wouldn't have to know.

Carefully watching her step on the rough cobblestone road, she adjusted the pack on her back. What a fool she had been to visit Lucia. Her chances of securing the children were now more remote than ever. Imagine how angry Marta will be when she hears that I was at the clinic, she thought. I just hope the children won't be the target of her displeasure.

A glance at her watch showed it was siesta time. Lifting her eyes from the road, she was shocked to see black clouds rushing toward

Chapter 6

her from the west. The bright and shining day of a few moments ago was quickly becoming as dim as dusk. The turbulent clouds billowed across the valley toward Pachuca. Lightning bolts darted earthward and claps of thunder rumbled simultaneously overhead. She had, on a few occasions seen terrible storms in Pachuca but as yet had not been caught in one. Lightning bolts struck the road several yards in front of her. Frightened, she wondered if she would be able to make it safely home. The gray curtain of rain appeared suspended from heaven, ready to engulf her.

She ran past the volleyball stadium and stopped in front of the market. The streets were empty, probably because others had seen the storm coming while she was with Lucia. The strain of exertion in the high altitude was taking its toll on her body and she rested a moment waiting for the dizziness to subside. At that moment the torrential rain reached Pachuca, the bolts of lightning performing a maniacal dance above the town. The terrifying booming thunder shook the very road on which she stood. She felt faint from fear but dared not run into the street as the water was already gathering, forming into streams. In no time it would become a muddy river. She looked around for a place of shelter and realized she was a few feet from the government clinic. Hurrying across the walkway, she tried the door and found it open; entering she stood inside the waiting room, soaked and cold in the dim, empty waiting room. At least I can rest on a bench until the rain passes, she thought. She pulled off her pack and laid it on the bench beside her.

An anxious voice called out from a room on her left. Curious, she padded to the door and tapped on it.

"Come in, come in," the voice called out, evidently relieved.

Jillian opened the door and paused in shock. A young woman knelt next to a man propped against a desk. A great deal of blood was smeared on the floor and on his clothes.

"Come here and help me. There's a lantern in the next room. Get it out of the cabinet and find some matches. I can't see what I'm doing," commanded the woman.

Jillian returned to the waiting room and entered a room next door. She tried the light switch but it failed to respond. The storm had probably knocked out the power. The shadowy room contained

For This Child

an examining table, three wooden chairs, a small desk and a cabinet. Flinging open the top doors of the cabinet, she peered in but saw nothing but medicine bottles, syringes and boxes of cotton. Behind the next door was a box of matches. She grabbed it. Down on her knees, she opened the bottom door and found the lantern. Taking it, she set it on the desk and lifted the glass. Striking a match, she pushed the flame onto the wick until it caught. Closing the glass, she turned up the fuel, lighting her passage back.

"Good," said the woman. "Now I need you to hold this compress on his hand until I can get my suturing needles. Here, come closer and put down the lantern."

Placing it on the floor, Jillian skirted the large pool of blood, quelling a wave of nausea against the heavy horrid smell that filled the room.

"Here." The woman relaxed her hold on the man's hand and made way for Jillian. When she saw that the compress was being held correctly, she left the room. Thunder clapped around the clinic shaking its foundations. The pounding rain on the windows and roof was deafening. The room flashed white repeatedly, intensifying the macabre scene. Minutes passed agonizingly slow and it seemed the woman had been gone a long time. She scrutinized the man's face; it had taken on an ugly gray color, then suddenly his mouth sagged. "He just died!" screamed Jillian. "He's not breathing! Please hurry!"

The woman came crashing in and fell to her knees, oblivious to all the blood. "Keep holding that hand tight!" she commanded falling forward and starting to breath into the man's mouth. She then leaned on his chest in an attempt to restore his breathing. Over and over she repeated the process until there was an abrupt intake of air. The man was breathing again. "I brought an IV. That's what was taking so much time." She reached up to take a metal tray, holding suturing needles, thread, cotton and a cleansing solution. "I will need you to help me with this."

Jillian tried to find a more comfortable position and noticed how her skirt was sopping up the blood. She placed the metal tray at her side as the woman took a plastic bag filled with solution and hung it on the back of a chair. Scooting it near the patient, she pulled a long tube with a needle attached from the side of the bag where it had

Chapter 6

been taped. Quickly she rubbed the back of his uninjured hand with treated cotton. "Now, hold up the lantern. I must see what I'm doing while I push this needle into a vein."

Jillian held the lantern over the man and watched her search for a good place to put the IV. He had lost plenty of blood, so she was forced to prod and probe until she found a good vein. She expertly inserted the needle and then she sutured the man's injured hand.

For the first time, the young woman looked at Jillian. "You came at the right time. I was desperate for help. Gracias, señorita."

"De nada." Jillian rose and looked at her skirt. It was blotchy with blood.

Regulating the IV, the woman tried to make the unconscious man more comfortable. She stood to her feet and opened her desk's top drawer to remove a stethoscope. Kneeling, she listened to his heartbeat for several seconds. "On the wall you'll find a blood pressure device. If you will bring that I will see how he is doing. Also, in the room across from the waiting room, you'll find a cot. Bring the pillow and blanket. When he awakes and is stronger I will need your help to put him on the cot, but for now we'll have to make him as comfortable as possible." She took the blood pressure apparatus from Jillian's hand and knelt beside the patient again, deep in concentration.

Jillian hurried into the waiting room and looked around. There was a doorway to her far left, but a glance through the window showed that it led to a courtyard and a room with a dental chair. Directly ahead was a door standing ajar. She pushed it open and peered through the semi-darkness until she saw the outline of a cot. Grabbing a pillow and blanket, she returned to find the woman leaning against the desk, studying her patient. They carefully stretched him out on the floor, covered him with the blanket and tucked the pillow under his head.

"Is his heartbeat strong?" asked Jillian.

"It's steady but I need to find a truck that will take him to Quito. I'm very concerned." She stood and held out her hand. "By the way, my name is Raquel Torres, Pachuca's resident doctor. I believe yours is Jill."

"I guess I shouldn't be surprised that you know who I am," Jillian replied, taking Raquel's hand. "There aren't many gringas in Pachuca."

Raquel laughed. "Not many gringas walking the streets of Pachuca on a rainy afternoon." She turned serious. "Would you mind looking out the window to see if it's still raining?"

"Sure and I'll look for a truck." She hurried into the waiting room and opened the front door. Scampering around a dozen mud puddles to the street, she scanned the plaza for a truck. The water still flowed like a stream in the streets but the sun struggled to peek from behind the skirts of the clouds. She ran back to Raquel. "The sun is starting to shine again but the streets are full of water. I couldn't see a truck."

The doctor checked the man's vital signs again. "Do you think between us we can carry him into the back room and put him on the cot?"

"Is he strong enough to move?"

"I hope so. We can't leave him on the floor like this and my office isn't quiet with patients coming in."

"How are we going to carry the IV and him?" Jillian frowned, her mind conjuring up the awful consequences should they drop him or pull out the IV. "Maybe we should just bring the cot in here and you can see your patients in the examination room."

"Of course. That's a better idea. I'll bring it. Please stay with him."

When she returned, together they lifted him, Jillian at his legs, Raquel with hands under his shoulders, her eyes focused on the IV inserted in his vein. After making him as comfortable as possible, they pushed the cot against the wall.

Raquel looked at the puddle of blood beside her desk. "I guess I'll have to clean this."

"Please, let me help." Jillian joined her.

They found a mop in the back room, the streaming sun now flooding the clinic. Armed with a bucket, rags and the mop, they returned to the room and prepared to clean. After Raquel checked the man's vital signs again, she was encouraged that he had a stronger pulse and set about helping Jillian with the cleaning. In no time, the old worn floor was clean and the mop and bucket put away.

Chapter 6

Although she and the doctor had been through an intense ordeal, Jillian was awkward with the fact that they were strangers. She wasn't quite sure if she should stay a while longer or take her leave. Raquel must have sensed her nervousness for she waved Jillian to a chair. "Thank you for your help."

"What happened to him?"

"It was one of the biggest shocks I've had as a doctor. Olivia had gone home for her midday meal and a siesta. I was writing out a list of medicines for Olivia to buy in Tumbaco this afternoon, when I heard a noise in the hall. We had finished treating all of our patients for the morning, so I went out to tell whoever was there that I couldn't see him until this afternoon. I couldn't believe what I saw. The man was slumped on a bench, leaning against the wall almost unconscious, but his hand was what caught my eye. Jill, he had, I don't know what else to call it, but he had a bag of blood attached to his hand. It looked bigger than a baseball."

Jillian screwed up her face. "How can that be? What kind of bag?"

"You've worked in señorita Marta's maternity clinic. You know that after the babies are born, the placenta is then expelled."

"Yes, I'm aware of that."

"Well, the outside of the bag of blood looked like the skin covering the placenta. I can't explain it any other way." Raquel turned her palms upward.

"How did he do that and how did he injure his hand?"

"He came from the east, from a banana plantation many miles away. He told me he had cut his hand with a machete while chopping bananas. Apparently he knew he would bleed to death if he didn't get to Quito in a hurry. What he applied to his hand to form the bag is something I don't know. He said it is some kind of jungle cure. He had also applied a tourniquet. He passed out before I could question him further.

"But he still lost a lot of blood."

"Not as much as he would have had he not curtailed the flow. These jungle Indians are very wise in the ways of self preservation. He was able to travel many miles and many hours without losing enough blood to die, even though we almost lost him a few minutes ago. I think the bus driver must have made a special trip down here because he knew the man wouldn't make it to Quito."

"Wait a minute. Do you know that I read somewhere that jungle Indians can use huge spider webs as bandages? I bet that's what he wrapped his hand in."

"How very interesting."

"It's unusual to see an injured national traveling without his family."

"He probably didn't have time to return home. He could have lived several hours away from his work. If he sent a co-worker to his home, perhaps they will come looking for him. Hopefully they will catch the same bus as left him here."

"Unless the rain brings landslides onto the eastern passages, then they'll never make it. You know how difficult it is to travel on those dirt roads."

"You're right," groaned Raquel, glancing toward the unconscious man. "I'll see what I can do about getting a truck to carry him to Quito this afternoon. I'm just thankful he didn't die. If you hadn't come when you did, he could have died and I wouldn't have wanted to be alone if that happened."

"Death still bothers you and you're a doctor?"

Raquel pushed her chair back, crossing her legs. "I may be a doctor, but I never forget that first I am a human being. I will never get used to someone dying. It is something that is intolerable in my family. You see, I come from a family of doctors."

"When I worked at the maternity clinic, I once had a man almost die right before my eyes. Marta was driving him to Quito and I had to sit in the back of the pickup watching to keep him still. When he started making funny breathing noises, I didn't know what to do. I'll never forget that sound." Jillian shuddered at the memory.

Raquel's voice took on a note of understanding. "He must have been quite ill."

"He had just been hit by a car and we were taking him to the hospital in Quito."

"Then you shouldn't feel guilty, uncomfortable perhaps, but not guilty."

Jillian grinned at the pretty doctor, a petite woman in her twenties. Strong sunlight streamed through the window highlighting the

Chapter 6

brown glints in her dark hair. Her eyes were large, brown tinged with green. She surmised that Raquel had a few drops of European blood in her family history. The contrast of dark lashes and brows made her hair and eyes seem lighter than they were. She had an engaging full smile, good teeth and a short yet shapely nose. Attired in a doctor's smock, she was an alluring sight. "I have to deal with death and poverty quite a bit now. It was very difficult at first but now I have come to expect it."

"Perhaps you need to look at life, Jill, instead of death."

"Life is beginning to appear twisted to me. I once had feelings much like yours when everything looked so positive, but since then there have been situations in my life that has made me less optimistic."

The doctor looked purposefully into Jillian's eyes. "You have been hurt, haven't you? Someone has hurt you very much."

Averting her eyes, Jillian felt suddenly vulnerable from Raquel's probing. Walls that she had so carefully built up around her the past year seemed in danger of being undermined. The doctor was knocking on walls of protection strong enough to withstand the pain from rejection and loneliness. Further heightening Jillian's discomfort was the realization that Raquel sensed all of this. "I think I'd better go home. I can hear your patient breathing evenly. He must be doing better and I'm sure you will soon have your afternoon patients knocking at your door."

Breaking her gaze, Raquel stood and walked to the patient. She felt his pulse and laid her hand on his chest. "Yes, I think he is doing better." Replacing his arm on the blanket, she turned back to Jillian. "I've heard a lot about you."

A feeling of alarm swept through her, negative thoughts coursed through her mind. Could Marta have talked with Raquel? "What things?" she replied harshly.

Raquel returned to her chair and leaned back in it. A warm smile lit her face. "Wonderful things, things about the stories you tell, about your classes, reports of how you give of your time, your special supplies and the fact you teach without charging any money. I hear how you are available to listen to children and high school students who need help. I understand that sometimes you take patients to the hospital in Quito when they have no transportation. I have wanted to meet you for a long time."

Jillian relaxed. "Gracias."

"Why do you think I would hear a negative report?"

"I'm sorry," she shrugged. "I have had a very difficult year here in Pachuca. I thought when I moved here that it would be different."

Raquel leaned forward and placed her arms on the desk. "Do you want to tell me what has happened?"

"Maybe I will someday, but now I must prepare for my classes tomorrow." She rose.

"Perhaps you can teach me English. I would love to speak your language."

"Yes, I can do that."

Raquel rose, following her to the door. "The government has asked me to spend a day tracking down children who have not been inoculated against whooping cough. I have been doing this about once a month. Next week I will be walking to the north. Would you like to go with me? We could take a picnic lunch." She looked at her hopefully.

"I have classes almost every day." Jillian replied with a touch of reluctance, wondering if she was being pulled into a relationship.

"Almost every day?" smiled Raquel.

"Every day but Thursday."

"Please go with me. Just once. I'll plan on next Thursday morning."

"All right."

"Good, come very early. I think it will be a wonderful experience for you."

Chapter 7

Lying on her stomach, Jillian spit dirt from her lips. She reached as far under the bed as she could, clasped a small ankle in her hand and gave a grand tug. Uttering a torturous scream, a struggling four-year-old boy appeared, grappling for something to hang onto. His mother took the child's flailing arm and pulled him out the door to where Raquel was waiting to gently admonish him that the shot would not hurt.

Rising to a kneeling position, Jillian dusted the filth off her clothes. A scraggly dog nervously crept forward to sniff at her, his curiosity having won out over his fear. She glared at him and he yelped, trotting backwards. A pig grunted from some dark corner and a hen wandered through the front door, searching the dirt floor for anything palatable.

An elderly woman lay in the bed cradling an infant. The thin straw mattress could hardly have been comfortable, but the woman rested in a thick padding of clothes, her entire wardrobe, no doubt. Jillian respectfully nodded her greeting. "Hasta mañana, señora." She backed out the door.

"Hasta mañana, señorita. Gracias."

Jillian joined Raquel who was explaining to the mother that she would be back in a month for the booster shot. This was not easy for as the mother tried to console the child, he stood, mouth wide open howling with all his might. As the doctor turned to replace the syringe in the metal tray, she gave Jillian a meaningful glance and nodded toward the road. They left the family and started the two-mile trek back to Pachuca.

"Your clothes are dirty." Raquel grinned.

Jillian pulled back Raquel's cardigan and inspected the doctor's white dress. "There's hardly a spot on you. It's probably because you did all the easy work. I crawled on more dirt floors today than I care to think about."

"Pardon me please." She shifted the metal tray to the other hand and stepped in front of Jillian. Putting her hand up to the girl's face, she frowned and flicked something off her cheek. "Did you wash your face today? Oh, and by the way, when we get back to the clinic, you're going to get your own shot. All the dirt you ate today is probably filled with unsightly little bugs."

A flicker of irritation flared at Raquel's familiarity and then Jillian saw the humor of it. How silly she must have looked, crawling under beds with only her legs showing! She laughed then and Raquel followed suit. In a moment they were weak with laughter leaning against a mud wall to remain on their feet. Their howls of humor floated though the quiet countryside, inviting a few wide-eyed stares from occupants of the huts they had visited earlier that day. That made them laugh even harder and in those moments a friendship forged a bond between Raquel and Jillian that would last a lifetime.

Jillian left Raquel at the clinic after getting a shot against any bacteria she may have picked up in the huts and went directly home. The euphoria of their hysterics remained with her during a shower and lunch, bringing intermittent chuckles. For the first time in years, Jillian was happy. She could almost forget what Lucia had done to her the other day. Duller now was the pain of her separation from Ryan and Andy. She picked up her dirty dishes and piled them in a plastic dishpan, ready to carry them outside for washing when a knock came at the front door. She peeked through the opening between the double doors and saw a light-haired man standing on the doorstep. Jillian thought he looked American. Opening the door, she took a better look. He was tall, thin, balding and wore glasses. "Buenas tardes."

"Hello, please speak English with me," he greeted her. "My name is Larry Parker. You are Jill Townsend I believe?"

"Yes," she said hesitantly. "May I help you?"

Chapter 7

"Maybe I can help you. My wife Heather and I live a few miles from here. When we heard that there was an American living in Pachuca, we decided we'd like to invite you to our house one afternoon for coffee. I'm here to extend that invitation."

"How did you hear about me?"

He shifted the weight of his feet and thrust his hands in his jacket pockets. "Your name was brought up in a conversation I was having with another American in this area."

"An American?" A warning sounded in her mind. "Who?"

"Well, actually it was Marta Brewer."

"Are you a friend of Marta's?"

"Not really." One of his hands came out of his pocket and he adjusted his glasses. "She's merely an acquaintance of ours."

"Why would you want me to come to your house for coffee?" she asked suspiciously.

"Why not?" He looked genuinely perplexed. "We're both Americans in a foreign country and this can act as strong bonds. I sense you are wary of me."

"You are a stranger to me. That alone would make me a little suspicious, but more so because Marta Brewer isn't one of my greatest admirers."

"Really? I can tell you there was nothing in my conversation with Marta that would make me think she held anything but the highest regard for you."

"Are you serious?" Her eyes opened wider.

"I'm serious," he smiled. "I am here to invite you for coffee. We'd like to hear some of your adventures in Ecuador. We'd like to know what you are doing in Pachuca. Are you busy these days?"

"Yes," she exclaimed. "Just recently I was given permission to teach summer classes during school break and also I will start classes here in my home for young people."

"You see? This is interesting to us. Please come to our house," he said beaming a smile.

They discussed the day and time and after he left she sat in the kitchen feeling foolishly lighthearted. What a wonderful day! First her experiences with Raquel this morning and the promise of a new, close friendship and now the revived hope that Marta did care for her after all. A softening on Marta's part of course could mean a reunion with Andy and Ryan in the future. Maybe something good had come from her visit with Lucia. Could Marta have seen how desperate she was to have her children back because of her encounter with Lucia? Oh, if only she could believe that. She picked up the dishpan and headed for the backyard when again, someone knocked on the front door. She placed the dishpan on the bench in the foyer and opened the door. A young boy stepped backward off the cement steps. "Buenas tardes, señorita."

"Buenas tardes."

"Señorita, come. You must hurry. The doctor needs you right now."

"The doctor?"

"Si, Doctor Raquel. She asked me to bring you very fast."

"Where is she?"

"In the clinic. She said you must bring a heavy sweater and good walking shoes. You may be gone several hours." The boy backed off the curb onto the road and waved her forward.

"Gracias," called Jillian, turning to run up the stairs to her room. She grabbed a sweatshirt out of her bureau and checked the jeans and cotton top she had on. That would have to do. As she slipped on a pair of heavy socks and tennis shoes, she wondered why Raquel needed her so soon after they had returned from their medical trek of the morning. At the last minute she put a comb, toothpaste, toothbrush and washcloth in a paper sack. Returning to the kitchen, she snatched a handful of rolls and some cheese, stuffing them in another sack. She threw handfuls of corn to the chickens, checked the back door to see if it was firmly locked, covered the dirty dishes and dashed out the front door, locking it behind her. She ran across the street, past the park, the school and toward the clinic. It was afternoon and Pachuca's townspeople were gathering in the park and storefronts to spend a lazy evening visiting and eating a light meal bought from street vendors.

"Buenas tardes, señorita." Greetings followed her.

"Buenas tardes," she replied, giving a slight bow with her head as she passed her neighbors. With concern she hurried. What emergency was Raquel facing that required her help? The waiting room

Chapter 7

was empty, but she heard voices coming from her office. She knocked lightly.

Raquel quickly opened the door. "Jill, come in."

She gave the doctor a questioning frown and stepped inside. A woman holding a ragged poncho sat nervously on a corner chair. Raquel pointed to another chair indicating Jillian should take a seat. She then returned to a wooden table where a man lay, clutching his hat close to his abdomen. He looked at Jillian and despite his apparent pain lifted himself up to greet her.

Returning his salutation, she looked at Raquel questioningly. The doctor ignored her, lecturing on what seemed to be a dissertation on sanitation. Raquel allowed the man to rise to a sitting position and continued talking as she took a bottle of medicine from a cabinet behind her desk. Counting out a few capsules, she put them in a small plastic sack and explained to the patient what they were and when to ingest them. The man slid painfully from the table to a standing position, pulled a few sucres from his pocket and placed them in Raquel's hand. She guided the couple to the front door and turned toward Jillian, eyes rolling upward.

"When will these people ever learn that you can't drink the water from an *acequia?*"

"I know. It makes me sick to think of drinking the same water that they use to wash their clothes, bathe and one can only guess what else."

Raquel held her head. "That man is so full of worms they choke him in their search for food."

"You must be kidding me." Jillian felt ill.

"No, I'm not. Worms will work themselves up into a person's mouth looking for food if they get hungry enough."

"Oh, that is the most sickening thing I've heard in a long time. I don't want to talk about it." With a wave of her hand, she changed the subject. "Why did you call me?"

"I need you to go with me. I sent Olivia to Quito for medicine, so I'm alone."

"Where? Go where?"

"Up the mountains behind Pachuca. There's a woman having a hard time delivering her baby. They need a doctor."

"Up the mountain? You can't be serious. Look at what time it is." Jillian followed close behind Raquel, extending her arm to show her watch. "It will be dark soon."

"I know." She glanced at her own watch and then at Jillian. "I don't know why they couldn't have brought the woman down here, but they didn't. They claim she is so weak that she would have died on the way. Why do these people wait so long to call on a doctor? And unfortunately the baby doesn't know what time it is."

"Do you know anything else about the patient?"

"Not much more. About a half hour ago, two men came rushing in here and begged me to go up to their mountain hut. The younger man's wife is having her first baby. She was planning to deliver with the help of a midwife, but she's been in labor for four days now and they're afraid she might die. She is very weak." She peeked out the window. "I asked them how I was going to get up there and they said they would provide a horse. They brought three horses with them. I said there was no way that I could travel by horseback up a mountain, especially that far." She giggled at Jillian's look of horror and then returned to her post at the window. "So I sent them to find a truck."

"I'd be glad to go with you, Raqui, but we may have to spend the night or at least we may return very late tonight."

"I know and I wouldn't have asked you to go with me if I wasn't afraid to go alone with those men. I thought about asking my friend Opal Martinez, whom I live with, but she's married and I hate to take her away from her husband." She gave Jillian a pleading look. "You don't have an early class, do you?"

"My first class is ten o'clock tomorrow morning."

"I know we'll be back before....oh, here they are."

"Do you have a coat?"

"I sent someone to the Martinez house to get it and to tell them you would go with me." She hurriedly grabbed her medical bag and coat from her office, giving Jillian a smug smile. "I knew you'd go with me."

Chapter 8

They hurried out the door and Raquel locked it after her. A young man met them on the sidewalk and after introductions all around he apologetically explained. "I found a truck whose driver will go past my home on the mountain." He waved a pointed finger behind him. "But you and the señorita will have to ride in the back. The driver's family is with him in the cab."

Loud salutations greeted them coming from what appeared to Jillian to be a crushed multitude of people in the forward compartment. The truck was a long flatbed with wooden slats built up on each side. Large double doors were erected into the end; a huge canvas tarp was secured tightly to the sides of the truck covering the top of the back end.

"It's better that I sit in the front so I can guide them to my house," continued the man. "My brother-in-law will take the horses home tomorrow morning."

Raquel nodded in wide-eyed agreement to this explanation and looked at Jillian in disbelief, who gulped back a giggle.

"We must hurry." The man ushered the two to the back of the truck and opened the doors. Jillian placed their belongings inside and took an uncoordinated giant step onto a metal rung, falling forward onto a pile of alfalfa. Raquel followed, tumbling after her.

"We will be at my home in just a few minutes." The man grinned hugely as he closed the big doors.

"Oh, yes," exclaimed Jillian. "I've been in Ecuador long enough to know that a few minutes to them is a few hours to us." She crumbled in a heap as the truck lurched forward. "I'd like to see where that man is going to find a place to sit. Years ago, on my first trip to Pachuca, I had to find a place in a crowded truck cab. I hope I never have to go through that again. The experience remains a terrible memory. I'd rather be back here."

"At least we have a bed." Raquel leaned back and then sat up again, yelping with laughter. "It was enjoyable watching you climb into this truck. You were very dignified."

"And so were you. It was my leg you grabbed onto trying to find your balance."

They giggled in the darkened interior.

"This is fun, isn't it? Aren't you glad you came with me?"

"Fun? It seems I've been getting into difficult situations ever since I met you." Jillian laughed. "Fun? Fun is when I can see where I'm going."

"It's probably a good thing you can't see the terrible roads that we'll be traveling."

"What if we arrive too late to help the mother or what if the midwife is able to deliver the baby?"

"Actually they aren't really midwives. They're really witchdoctors." Raquel snuggled back in the sweet alfalfa. "There's a good probability we're too late one way or another but I could never take a chance by staying home."

I can tell you're a very committed doctor and I'm proud that the people have so much confidence in you."

"Pachuca has had a few women doctors working in the government medical clinic. I think when it comes to a delivery women prefer to have a woman doctor. Maybe I'm wrong but it seems that way to me." She rolled toward Jillian as the truck leaned to one side. "I wonder why they didn't go down to Marta Brewer's clinic and ask for help. She has a jeep, doesn't she?"

"I don't know if she has a jeep any longer but I do know she doesn't like to go out on house calls."

There was a long silence of several minutes. "Are you asleep, Raqui?"

Chapter 8

"No," she mumbled. "What's the matter?"

"If that man had worms crawling up his throat, why did he wait so long to come and see you?"

"I thought you didn't want to talk about worms."

"It's your fault because now I can't forget it."

"I could tell you a lot of horrible stories."

"No thanks," she replied forcefully, then continued happily. "However I remember one time when I first moved to Ecuador and Lucia, the aide who works with Marta pulled a bunch of flies out of an old man's nose."

"I've heard of that. It's because there are so many flies looking for a warm place to lay their eggs. The old man probably slept through the whole thing."

"He wasn't sleeping when Lucia was digging them out." She yawned. "When do you think we'll get there? I'm getting cold. I bet it's dark outside."

"Put on your sweatshirt."

"Are you hungry?"

"Why? Did you bring something to eat?"

"Si, rolls and cheese. Here, I'll get them." She rose to her knees and crawled toward the door in the darkness, falling as the truck swung around a corner. "I understand what you mean. I'm glad we can't see the roads we're traveling over."

"Or the edges of the road we are barely missing."

"Don't even think about that."

"Where are you, Jill? Can't you find the food?"

"No, I don't know where it went." There was more pawing across the truck floor until she gave her location away with a dull thump followed by a low groan.

"Are you all right?"

"I can't keep my balance," Jillian screamed with laughter. "What are we doing here? If my friends back home could see me now they wouldn't believe it. Why aren't there any windows in this thing, or at least a light?"

"Can't you find your way back here?" Raquel joined in the laughter.

"I'm not returning without the food." Grunts of exertion and pawing brought more laughter. "Here it is," she cried triumphantly as she fell onto the alfalfa.

They ate, gabbing companionably about their families, religion and cultural backgrounds. They were amazed by the basic philosophies and theological beliefs they had in common. Much time passed when finally the truck slowed to a halt and their conversation hung suspended as they waited to find out if they had indeed arrived at their destination. Loud conversations surrounded the truck and the doors opened.

"Buenas noches, Doctor. Please hurry," beckoned a middle-aged woman holding a lighted candle.

"Buenas noches, señora. I will find my medical bag and follow you."

"Here it is," Jillian found the bag in the truck corner.

The woman helped them down with her free hand and turned toward the house. The bright half moon and star crusted sky revealed they had traveled nearly to the summit of the mountains behind Pachuca. Outlined in black against the glowing sky the familiar humps and crags seen normally from afar now seemed at arm's length. Jillian gasped at the night's beauty.

Raquel and the woman disappeared through an open door. Jillian folded her arms across her body to protect herself against the night chill and looked around at the sky-lit landscape. Unfamiliar ghostly shadows surrounded her, but despite that, she walked to the road and looked down across the Tumbaco Valley. The lights of Quito so far away lay like a slim necklace upon the thick neck of Mt. Pichincha. Automobile headlights snaked up and down the ascent sparkling like diamonds on her portly bodice. Reluctantly Jillian backed away from the mesmerizing scene, the night chill robbing her romanticism. Stepping inside the hut, she hesitated in a narrow hallway. Two flickering candles placed on a bench lit her way to an open door at the end. Several people milled about inside the room, so she decided to remain in the doorway.

Raquel knelt beside the patient who appeared to be a child still in her early teens. She called out for a basin of water and jumping into action the woman who had met them at the truck pushed her way past the people standing about, in search for a container.

Chapter 8

Jillian wondered if the baby had already been born and tried to look beyond the dozen people in attendance for a bassinet. In the murky light the room appeared very cluttered and dirty with litter scattered about. In one corner a fire had been built over a shallow rock well; the smoke from its smoldering embers cast a light haze over them before its escape through the tiled roof. Three candles glowed on the bedside table providing the only other light.

A dog meandered in and out between the legs of family members until a casual kick to the animal's backside sent him scurrying with a yelp. This seemed to discourage him little for soon he returned in a search for food. Jillian shuddered as the dog discovered the patient's partially eaten dinner bowl left on the floor by the bed and eagerly lapped at it. A pail of slop sat beside the doorway and in spite of herself she looked in it, the content of which would be later thrown to the pigs.

The patient cried out as Raquel began stitching up the birth canal. The baby must have been born already, Jillian thought as she turned to leave. The smell of smoke, childbirth, rotting garbage and the press of dirty bodies was overpowering. All she wanted was a breath of fresh air.

"Jill, come here," Raquel called.

All eyes turned toward her and a pathway opened as she turned and approached the patient and Raquel.

"I need you to find the baby."

"The baby?' she asked stupidly.

"Yes, it was born before we arrived." Raquel looked at Jillian with a jerk of her head. "The mother says it's wrapped in a blanket."

"Si, señorita," the young mother pointed with her chin. "He is close to the fire in order to keep warm. Please find him."

Jillian noted the blood lost during birth and the greenish complexion of the mother. Her eyes settled on the bedside table. Caked with a mixture of food, hair and still wet with blood a filthy penknife lay open. This must have been what they used to cut the umbilical cord, she thought. A sudden premonition struck her. Why was the baby so quiet? Why wasn't someone holding him? Surely a newborn infant should be in someone's arms, not casually placed in a corner. She searched around the smoky fire but all she found was a pile of rags, garbage and gunny sacks filled with potatoes and corn. Through the blue fog she noticed a bench a few feet from the fire. On top lay bowls, pots, a pan and various eating utensils. More rags lay beneath. Carefully picking her way to the bench, she patted the pile to see if someone had placed the baby under them.

"Ah, success," she muttered to herself pulling the layers of cloth aside. "Oh, God, why isn't the baby moving?"

Chapter 9

Her fingers felt flesh and she gently rubbed the clammy skin. There was no doubt that the baby was dead. Dreading to expose the entire body, she rewrapped the infant and pulled the bundle toward her. Rising to her feet, she held the unresponsive baby in her arms and found a corner of the bench to sit on. Someone would have to unwrap it.

"Raqui," she called gently through the whispering conversation surrounding the bed. "Raqui, I found the baby."

All eyes turned in her direction as Raquel stood and walked to her. "How is he?" She knelt on the dirt floor by the bench."

"He's dead," Jillian moaned. "I feel so terrible that we didn't get here any sooner?"

"Are you sure he's dead?"

"Yes."

"I need to look at him." Raquel rose and leaned over to take the bundle from her and as she did she let out a horrified cry.

"What's the matter?' Jillian pulled away.

"What's the matter with this baby?" Raquel gawked at the child.

"Why?" gasped Jillian, moving backward on the bench. "What do you mean?"

"It doesn't feel right." The whites of Raquel's eyes seemed to glow in the dim light. "Here, let me sit down."

Jillian noticed the crowd of people moving closer around the patient's bed as if to protect her from the adverse news. A murmuring and whispering among themselves rose in volume. She traded places with Raquel as the doctor peeled away the layers of rags. "What is wrong with this baby?" She drew in a sharp breath.

"What? What!" Jillian bent closer and saw the head of the child. It was misshapen, with globs of bloody substance covering the hair and face. She turned, gagging.

Raquel hastily covered the baby and placed it on the bench, unconcerned that the utensils and plates landed on the floor. Marching to the center of the room, she faced the patient's family. "I need to talk with the person who delivered the infant."

"Where is my baby?" The weak young mother lifted herself up on her elbow.

Ignoring her, Raquel motioned for the woman who had met them at the truck to follow her to the hallway. Jillian followed close behind, not wanting to be near the baby.

Her hands on her hips, Raquel faced the woman. "Señora, are you the patient's mother?"

"Si, it is such a shame."

"What happened to the baby? His head is broken."

"It wouldn't come out. My daughter couldn't push out the baby. His head was too big." Tears ran down the grandmother's face. She tried and tried and we pulled and pulled. I thought my daughter was going to die. Even the midwife said there was no hope and returned to her house."

"Why didn't you bring your daughter down to the clinic the first day you saw she was having trouble?"

"Because we thought she would be able to eventually have the baby up here. She was in such pain. We hated to have her go all that way by truck. What if the baby was born on the way? This was the fourth day that my daughter was in labor and the baby didn't come. The head was there, but it was too big for my little daughter, so we cut the spot on his head, the part that is soft and then cut open his head. That way we were able to drag him out."

While the grandmother wiped her tears and nose on her poncho, Raquel with slumping shoulders returned to the birth room. As she passed, Jillian who had remained in the doorway asked, "Can they get in trouble for what they did, Raqui?"

Chapter 9

"Maybe. I'll have to talk to the magistrate and they will want the baby blessed by the priest, so maybe they will. This is a new one on me. I'm trying to think like the mountain peasant would think. What else could they have done? They were desperate. The mother was dying so they had to make their choice between her and the baby. Actually the mother and the baby would have died otherwise. She still may not live. I've told them they must get her to a hospital in Quito. She's lost too much blood during the difficult delivery. If only she had gone to Quito the first day."

"Do you think they'll take her?"

"Maybe." She put her hand on Jillian's back. "You're angry, aren't you?"

"I'm angry at their ignorance, their filth and their poverty," she cried.

"I, too, become very angry." Lowering her head, Raquel shook it sadly. "The baby probably would have died anyway. Did you see the knife they used to cut the umbilical cord and probably the soft spot? It was so dirty that the baby's navel would have become infected. That would have been a much worse death."

"This whole evening has depressed me terribly. Have you thought of how we're going to get home?"

"I don't think we'll return to Pachuca tonight. That's why I had you bring something warm to wear."

"Are you saying that we have to sleep here, in this house with all the filth and a murdered baby?" Horror filled Jillian's eyes. "No, gracias, I'd rather walk home."

"You would find more trouble walking home than staying here, Jill. These roads are narrow and can wind around very deep canyons. Also we have no idea what kind of nocturnal animals roam the mountains at night. I'd rather face the discomforts here and get a ride back tomorrow morning."

Disgruntled, Jillian left Raquel and walked to the edge of the corn field.

"I appreciate that you came with me," the young doctor said, following behind her. "I know this is the last place you want to be."

"I don't mind being with you. I enjoy that part, but where will we sleep and where is the outhouse? Where is there water to wash with?"

"I don't know where we'll sleep. I'll speak with the señora." Raquel responded with a hint of humor in her voice. "Jill, they probably don't have an outhouse. I suppose they use the corn field, just as we'll have to. In fact you'd better watch where you're walking."

Jillian stepped back gingerly. "I'm sorry I'm acting so spoiled, but I've not gotten used to this part of Ecuadorian life as yet."

"I haven't either. I've never had to live like these people. The only way I know about their lack of material goods is by stories they tell me in the clinic. I'm also too spoiled to live this way."

"How do we find a way home tomorrow? Remember that I teach a class midmorning."

"I'll go ask."

Swiftly moving clouds swept across the half moon, creating eerie shadows against the wall of the mud house. Creeping closer to the doorway, Jillian waited for Raquel's return. She longed to go home. The doctor re-appeared minutes later with the señora and another woman. Raquel told Jillian. "We're not going to sleep here." She gestured toward the second woman. "The señora has invited us to stay with her family for the night. Tomorrow her husband will drive us to Pachuca."

Jillian gazed at the poncho-wrapped woman and dipped her head in salutation. "Buenas noches, gracias for the invitation."

"Buenas noches, señorita. You and the doctor are invited to our home. If you will come with me I will show you where you will sleep."

Raquel took her medicine bag and coat in one hand and shook hands with the patient's mother. "If you have any problems during the night, please come for me; however you must get your daughter to a clinic or hospital for care as soon as possible. Perhaps she can travel with us."

"Si, gracias, vaya con Dios." The sad mother wiped at her eyes before shaking hands with Jillian. Following their hostess, the two girls hung onto their belongings and strained their eyes for holes and obstacles in the narrow road. They climbed a few meters until the woman led them through an opening in a corn patch. Raquel followed while Jillian stepped through hesitantly, not forgetting the multi-purposes of a corn field. The brilliant moon and stars drenched

Chapter 9

the opening in the tall swaying stalks, revealing a small hut sitting snugly beside a ditch flowing with rushing water.

"Entres, Doctor Torres and señorita. You are welcome here."

The girls stepped inside the small mud house and waited for the woman to direct them to their beds for the night. The room was lit only by the dying embers from a fire in the corner.

"Come with me." The woman led them to a doorway and allowed them to enter first. Inside, she found a candle on a protruding shelf and lit it with matches lying alongside. Two single beds filled with sleeping children left little space for anything else except for an old broken bureau. Puzzled glances were exchanged between Jillian and Raquel as the mother started shaking the children awake.

"No, no señora. Don't wake the children." Raquel moved forward to stop her. "We'll be happy to sleep on the floor."

"We will?" Jillian silently mouthed the words as she stared at Raquel.

"Our guests must never sleep on the floor." The woman gave Raquel a horrified look and loosened her poncho. "You will sleep in this bed." She pushed two small children from a bed and shoved them toward the door. The sleepy-eyed, tousle-haired youngsters gave them dreamy, somewhat confused looks and ambled toward the main room of the house. "They have a straw mat and they enjoy being close to the fire," explained the señora, pulling up the thin mattress the children had been sleeping on.

But Jillian, so fascinated with the bed she and Raquel were about to sleep on took little notice of the exodus. As the children departed, the woman opened a bureau drawer and pulled out two thin ragged blankets. Placing them on the vacated wooden bed planks, she turned and gave a sharp order to three remaining children peeking at Jillian and Raquel from the foot of another bed across the room.

"You three, go to sleep. You must get up early to go to work in the fields." The heads disappeared amid giggles. Ignoring them further, she directed Raquel to the bed. "Doctor, this is where you and your friend will sleep." Looking pleased, she failed to see the glances of dismay flash between the two girls. "Hasta mañana," she said with a nod of her head. She withdrew, the mattress tucked under her arm.

"Hasta mañana," echoed the girls.

Jillian's heart sank as the realization struck her that they were to sleep on wooden planks without a mattress.

With the departure of their mother, three pairs of dark brown eyes peeked out at the two guests from over the top of their blanket. They giggled behind hands clamped over their mouths.

"Are we going to have to sleep on these wooden planks, Raqui?" Jillian whispered in her friend's ear.

"It looks like it." She looked around the room. "All we have are these thin blankets. I don't see anything else and I don't feel comfortable looking in the bureau with those children watching us. I hope we don't get too cold."

"It's already chilly."

"Well, I'm tired. We only have a few hours until dawn." Raquel set her medicine bag close to the bed and proceeded to climb onto the planks, pulling her coat up over her. "Blow out the candle."

After snuffing out the flame, Jillian tiptoed back to the bed and sat on the planks shivering. "I must say, you sure know to entertain your friends and what a fine hotel you've found. It's equipped with feather beds, a luxurious bath and room service. I'd like to thank you for thinking to invite me."

"Shut up, Jill or you'll make me feel guilty. Lie down and snuggle in your sweatshirt."

"Good idea. There's so much to snuggle into," she groaned, her hip bone digging into the wood. Turning over, she tried to find a more comfortable position.

"I wish those children would stop whispering and giggling," muttered Raquel.

"What's the difference? I couldn't sleep anyway."

There was a long pause and eventually the children quieted.

"Are you sleeping Jill?"

"Are you talking to me? Of course, I fell asleep the minute my head hit the pillow. I feel like I'm floating on a cloud."

"I'm really worried."

"About what? That someone will have to carry you on a stretcher to the truck tomorrow because your body won't unfold on its own?"

"I'm worried about the new mother." Her whisper lowered even more.

Chapter 9

"Why?" Jillian was suddenly serious.

"She's in poor physical condition. I don't think she's going to live."

"Oh, no." She turned her numb head on the wood. "Did you tell her mother?"

"I didn't because there's not a thing we can do until she gets to a hospital. Tomorrow morning, if she lives through the night I'll insist she goes down with us. Then they can take her on to Quito."

"Was it because of the long delivery?"

"Partly. She has no strength left and because she lost so much blood. They used such primitive procedures to get the baby out."

"How terrible. I guess I shouldn't complain about this horrible bed."

"Why don't you use the blanket for a pillow?" She paused a moment. "I'm glad we could sleep together. At least that will keep us warm."

"You'll never sleep. I have to turn over every three minutes because my entire body is numb." Jillian folded the blanket and laid her head on it. "Oh Lord, just get me through this long night."

Raquel giggled. "You are such a coddled American."

"Coddled? How can you say that? I live in a two hundred year old mud house that has no indoor plumbing and inadequate lighting." Jillian felt a wave of anger sweep over her. "I have to heat water for a shower. Ha! A shower! If you can call pouring water from a cup over my body a shower."

"Hey, I'm sorry. I was just kidding." Raquel lifted herself a bit and tried to see her companion through the darkness. "I was trying to make a silly joke."

"That's okay," she replied sheepishly. "I'm in a horrid humor."

They settled back with their thoughts.

Chapter 10

"What's that noise?" Jillian sat up.

"What noise?"

"Listen to the terrible wailing."

"Oh dear, that's exactly what it is, wailing. She must have died."

"Who? The patient? Oh, Lord, please no. Oh, Raqui, it can't be. We didn't do all we could, did we?"

"I knew the minute I saw her that there was little we could do," she sighed. "I'm going to have to walk down there and see what's going on."

"You're going to leave me here alone?"

"You're not alone. The children are here." Grunting, she hoisted herself off the hard bed and stood over Jillian. "You can go with me if you want, but why do that? It isn't going to be pleasant."

"Maybe I'll stay. I don't want to go back to that awful house."

"I talked to her about God and prayed with her when we first arrived."

"What did she say?"

"Nothing much. She only nodded her head. I hope she understood how important it is to have a secure relationship with God before she died."

Raquel was gone and Jillian turned her body to the wall, trying to ignore the distant wailing. It seemed an eternity had passed when, through a crack in the boarded up window and openings in the tile roof she saw a dim gray light. A rooster announced the new dawn. Sitting

Chapter 10

up slowly, she groaned at the stiffness in her limbs and looked across the room expecting to see the same row of big brown eyes staring at her. She gawked at the empty bed. Had she slept? Shivering in the chilly air, she stood and tried to stretch. Hesitantly opening the door to the main room, she peered around. One small child lay sleeping on a mat next to the fire. She envied his peaceful slumber. It would have been more comfortable to have slept on the floor. Two covered plates sat on a table in the middle of the room and she clenched her fists in order to resist looking under their covers. She and Raquel hadn't eaten since the previous day in the truck. Hindsight was teaching her that she should plan for all emergencies. Next time she would pack more food and maybe bring her sleeping bag.

Pushing open the front door, she walked into a brilliant morning. The clean, fresh air welcomed her after a night in the stuffy room. Corn and potato fields climbed up the mountainside just shy of the summit. The fertile land situated so close to the equator yielded plant growth at great altitudes.

She found the path through the corn field that led to the narrow road and followed it until she came to the edge of the property. Poised on the rutted dirt lane, she looked down upon the stretch of valley below her. Lying at the base of the mountain Pachuca was hidden from her view, but the Tumbaco Valley dipped and rose in deference to the height of distance Mount Pichincha. Quito nestled in its bosom as contentedly as a cat basking in the early morning sun. She descended the road, drawing nearer to the mournful cries, and then passed through still another corn field before arriving at the house.

A few weeping mourners stood around a large truck that resembled one that had first brought her to Pachuca several years before. It was a large flatbed with high wooden sidings, big double doors at the back topped by a giant tarp attached to the cab much like the back end of the truck that had brought them here, but on this vehicle the cab had been lengthened, added three hard narrow benches with a door opening to each one.

Jillian greeted the small group with a quiet salutation and entered the hallway uninvited. The door at the end of the narrow hallway was closed but the first door on the left stood open. Peeking in, she saw Raquel sitting alone at a table sipping from a cup. "Hi Raqui."

The doctor's head swung around. "Oh, Jill, come in and have a cup of corn colada and some rolls."

"I'm starved." She sat beside Raquel and picked up a roll taking a big bite. She drank deeply from the cup that Raquel pushed toward her. The thick sweet corn flavored liquid tasted good to her ravenous appetite. "Did she die?" she asked, already knowing the answer.

"Yes and I feel terrible. She was so young."

"When you didn't return to the other house last night, I worried."

"I wasn't sure I could find my way back and I hated to ask someone to take me, so I just sat in here most of the night."

"What will they do with the bodies?"

"We're going home in that truck parked out in front. The bodies will stay here. Several people will go with us to Pachuca and then on to Quito to buy coffins for the mother and baby."

"How terrible. It seems like we came up here for nothing."

"I know. I feel that I'm not a very good doctor. I just didn't know what else I could have done for her. I did stop the bleeding and gave her a shot to try and stop the infection that was sure to come, but I'm so limited without proper equipment." Her head drooped with depression and weariness.

"Raqui, you're a very good doctor. I know you did everything possible to save her. We got here too late to save her and that's not your fault. They should have taken her to Quito days ago."

"Thank you." She stood and glanced at her watch. "Did you get enough to eat? We must return to Pachuca. They've been waiting for daylight to gather all the family. It's six-thirty."

"I want to leave very much."

They walked into the front yard as the small group broke up and faced the girls. Raquel directed her attention to a man standing by the cab. "If you are ready to leave, señor, we are also ready."

"Si, we are ready."

The group bustled into action. One of the women called into the house and waited until the patient's mother appeared, red-eyed and huddled in her poncho. She shuffled to the cab leaning on her companion.

"Señor, what do you have in the back of the truck?" Raquel asked the driver.

Chapter 10

"Sacks of potatoes."

"Is there room for us back there? If there is a place for us to rest, we would appreciate that. We have a very busy day ahead of us."

"Certainly, please come with me." He opened the big doors and raised his eyebrows at the girls, as if asking their approval.

"This is very nice." Said Raquel.

Along the back of the flatbed bulging gunny sacks were stacked and secured behind a wooden fence. The front area contained layers of empty bags. They climbed onto the floor of the vehicle and waited for the man to close the doors.

"We'll be home in a couple hours." Raquel placed her medical bag beside her and lay back. "Oh, this feels good, so much better than that terrible bed."

"Are you still very depressed about the deaths?"

"I'm doing better, thanks but now I'm a little worried about Geoff and Opal and your neighbors. They must be wondering what happened to us."

"Do you think Geoff might try coming after us?"

"No, he wouldn't know where we were because I didn't know until we got here."

Though the weaving, bumpy ride precluded their sleep; the chance to lie stretched out helped drive the kinks from their sore limbs. Jillian closed her eyes, planning her upcoming class at the girls' school in Pachuca. Remembering the stack of paperwork waiting for her at home, she groaned to herself, but inwardly she was thankful for it kept her from thinking about last night.

Chapter 11

On the day Jillian was to visit Larry Parker, Raquel decided she would accompany her as far as Tumbaco to purchase medicines and visit one of her patients. Jillian gave her explicit directions to the Parker's home on the outskirts of Tumbaco and left her off at the plaza. They planned to meet there in two hours for the return trip. Jillian returned to the highway and drove a few hundred meters west to a rutted dirt road that led to a locked wide metal gate. A small middle-aged peon came running at the sound of her automobile horn and greeted her cheerfully and pointed to the top of a long driveway when she mentioned she had an appointment at the first home on the right. Following his direction she crested a gentle slope and came upon a row of six brick houses.

 At the first house, Larry and a young woman waited beckoning her to enter. She was glad she had decided against casual clothes and had dressed in a brown wool skirt, white blouse and a tan blazer. With a pat to her curly head she took a deep breath and parked the car. The woman walked down the steps to greet her. She was of medium height and weight, her brown hair curled too tightly, indicating a recent permanent. She was dressed in a white skirt and sweater, accentuating her already pale complexion, free of makeup. Her brown eyes matched her hair, giving her pallid face a mousy look. A straight nose and thin mouth made her appear rather harsh, but when she smiled she looked friendly and eager to meet Jillian. "You must be Jill. I'm Heather, Larry's wife. Please come in."

Chapter 11

Larry remained in the doorway and stepped aside when the women entered. "Have a seat here on the davenport," he said as Heather and he took their places in two armchairs facing her.

The house interior was built of white painted brick and polished oak. The furniture was of no particular period but comfortable and expensive. An oriental rug partially covered a highly polished parquet floor and several pieces of native art hung on the walls.

"This is a lovely home." Jillian looked around, smiling. "What community is this that you live in?"

"We are one of several American and European families living here," said Heather. "We work for a large European company in Quito. It's worth the commute each day to live in the country. Our children attend school in Quito, so since the men have to travel each day, they take the children with them. We were able to bring a nice van through customs when we moved here, so that helps. It's just nice living among the country people. You get more of the flavor of Ecuadorian living."

"Where do you do your grocery shopping? Do you buy from Tumbaco's open market?"

Heather's eyes betrayed the horror she felt. "Oh, no. There's a wonderful shopping center in Quito. It's much cleaner and safer there. The problem with buying in the marketplace is that you have no idea where the food has been or who has been handling it, but you should know that, Jill. After all you do live in Pachuca. You don't buy your food in the market, do you?"

"I buy meat and a few vegetables in the market Sunday morning and during the week my neighbors sell cheeses, bread and milk."

"Goodness." The hostess wiped her hands on her white skirt, like she was trying to wipe off amoebas. "I once saw milk that had just come from an hacienda. There were flies and specks floating in it."

Despite herself, Jillian giggled. "The answer to that is running the milk through a dishtowel to catch the flies and specks and then you must boil the milk for twenty minutes."

"You don't tire of doing that?" Larry leaned forward.

"No, because that is real life in Ecuador. I don't think twice about it. I have to boil the water anyway."

"We have our own well here on the property so we don't have to do even that," said Heather, frowning slightly. "Larry said the house you live in is nothing more than mud bricks. Do you have running water and electricity?"

"Sure. Someone recently installed electricity. The electrical wires are on the outside of the walls, but it's very economical. I only pay a couple American dollars a month and I have running water. Of course it's outside in the back area, but it meets my needs. The mud bricks are just fine. The walls are so thick that the house stays warm at night and cool during the day. The house has been standing for over two hundred years and that's longer than some houses built in the United States."

Heather attempted a smile. "You almost seem to enjoy what you're doing, living in this country. Don't you ever miss your home in the United States, wherever that is?"

"My family's home is in Oregon. Of course I miss them, especially when I receive letters and read of their activities. Holidays are also difficult, but I'm really very happy here. I love the people and my work."

Coughing gently, Larry interrupted. "Do you mix with the people very much? What is it that you do? You mention working with the schools and having young people come to your house."

"I've received permission to have classes during the summer in the schools throughout our district. I plan to take crafts, stories and songs all over the mountains. I'll probably do that in the mornings because in the afternoons I'd like to open my home to the youth of Pachuca. They also need to learn English. Already I've had so many parents approach me with their approval. This can all begin in about two weeks. I've already spent several afternoons passing out flyers inviting the children to come."

Jillian was becoming more animated with each word, but slowed down when she realized Larry and Heather were not joining in her enthusiasm. The man leaned back and brushed his hand across his balding head. "Aren't you afraid of the many dangers of living alone?"

Beginning to realize she was being questioned too intently, she replied, "Not at all. If anything, the people of Pachuca would protect me. I have had some of the pueblo's men tell me that if I ever

Chapter 11

needed help to just call and they would come running. No, the longer I live in Pachuca, the better the people are in accepting me. I think it's because I have chosen to live like them, you know, eat their food and count my best friends among them."

A corner of Heather's mouth lifted. "Perhaps you'll marry one of them."

Cautiously grinning, Jillian shook her head. "Marriage is the last thing on my mind right now. Larry, you told me you know Marta Brewer. Where did you meet her?"

He shrugged. "Somewhere, I can't remember. We've been out to her orphanage."

Heather piped up. "Yes, we were so impressed with her children. What a wonderful work Marta is doing."

"Yes, the children are wonderful," replied Jillian, feeling a little sad.

"Why did you leave her work?" asked Larry. "Weren't you happy there?"

Jillian judged the situation. Were these people just curious about her reason for living in Ecuador and merely being friendly? How much could she tell them about Marta? Dare she mention the children appeared so well behaved because they were afraid? Why hadn't they recognized the child abuse? Dare she tell the Parkers that Marta was a master at hiding her sins?

"Yes, I was happy, however Marta asked me to leave."

"Oh?" Larry's eyebrows lifted. "Why would she ask you to leave?"

"She felt I was responsible for the government closing the outpatient clinic and inspecting the maternity clinic."

"Were you?" Heather asked.

"Of course not. I would never do anything to lose my position there. I loved the children too much."

"Hmm." Larry's head lowered in thought. "I wonder why she would feel you were responsible if you had nothing to do with it. Do you have any idea, Jill?"

She stiffened a little but tried to relax. Although these people seemed concerned and interested, yet they were a little too inquisitive. "I don't know. One day Marta suggested I get away from the house. I had just been through a traumatic experience and she felt

I needed a change of scenery, so I went into the plaza. While there I decided to get something to eat and at the little eatery I met a friend who asked me to join him for lunch. It so happened that in his company was the town's policeman. Even though I didn't bring up Marta at all, by coincidence the policeman and the health department showed up a week later to close down the outpatient clinic. It probably seems like I had something to do with it, but there was nothing I said or did to instigate the closure.

The couple looked at each other and nodded their heads in agreement.

"What was so traumatic that you had to go to the plaza that day?" asked Larry gently.

Jillian was beginning to feel uncomfortable with all the questions so she hesitated, torn between a desire to tell of the tragic relationship she had with Lucia toward the end of her stay at the orphanage and a surprising loyalty she still felt for her. "Lucia was angry with me because I was spending too much time with Marta in her room. She attacked me with a hammer."

Again, the Parkers seemed to show concern so Jillian continued, warming up. "One time Lucia placed a gun to her temple to frighten me. I thought she was going to kill herself because I had spent the day at the hospital housing quarters in Quito. I had a good friend there, we often lunched together. Lucia slapped me because she was so jealous."

"So Lucia was jealous of your friendship with Marta and this other girl?" Larry nodded, encouraging her.

"And you think these are the reasons Marta sent you away?" asked Heather.

"There were other things," said Jillian, her voice lowering. "Lots of unexplained things."

"Like what, dear?" prompted Heather.

"Marta punishes the children too severely. That's why they are so well-behaved. She beats them with a hose or a belt, usually for minor things. She will not allow them to cry, to be held or to be treated with love. I've seen her force a gallon of warm water down the boys because they wet the bed. They throw up the water and she forces more down. It's just terrible. She locks them in their rooms. I think

Chapter 11

she's taking babies illegally and selling them, at least there were so many incidences that point to it."

"My goodness, do you have proof of all you are saying?" Larry stood to wander around the room and then he stopped before her.

"No, not really. I just saw a lot, but I was never able to get any proof."

"You say you didn't tell the policeman this when you had a chance? Have you told anyone about all these terrible accusations? Heather leaned forward in her chair.

"I did not say a word about this to the policeman or my friend during lunch that day. You two are the first I've mentioned this to at all. The reason I'm telling you now is that recently something happened that makes me realize there's little chance I'll ever get my children back."

"Reason? What happened?" Larry sat beside her on the davenport turning toward her.

"Yes, and what children are you talking about?" asked Heather.

"There are two boys living with Marta who are mine. She gave them to me. In fact I delivered one of them. I feel that I still have claim on them. That's why I went to see Lucia."

Larry pulled back a little. "You went to see Lucia after what she has done to you?"

"Yes, it was foolishness, but it's been over a year since I'd seen her last and I just had to see if her feelings had changed for me. I needed to know if I could have the boys for my own."

"What did she say?" asked Heather on the edge of the chair.

"She detests me and pulled a gun."

"A gun?" Larry voice was incredulous. "She pulled a gun on you?"

"Yes." Jillian frowned, wondering suddenly if he was mocking her or was genuinely concerned.

"So now you are working in Pachuca, living in a mud house and making plans to work in the schools this summer?"

"I've been holding craft, English and Bible classes for several months but now I have permission to work in all the schools. The government has given me full rein in whatever I want to do."

Heather's pale face blotched with emotion. "Permission? Where did you get permission?"

"From the Board of Education, of course. The president of the educational department visited the school in Pachuca on Cinco de Mayo and during a ceremony he gave me a letter of permission and thanks for the work I'd already done."

"The president of the Department of Education visited Pachuca and gave you permission?"

"Yes, I have it at home, signed and sealed with the President of Ecuador's seal."

Larry stood and returned to the armchair, leaning forward to look her levelly in the eyes and spoke softly. "How long do you think you can get by telling all these lies?"

Jillian's heart stopped. "Lies? I'm not telling lies."

"From the moment you walked into this house you have blathered lies."

Her breath coming in short gasps, she rose. "I'm not lying. Everything I've told you is the truth."

"Listen to me. We know Marta Brewer well, obviously better than you do. In no way would she steal babies and sell them illegally. Lucia seems a little distant, but she's not a violent person. The children seem healthy and normal to us. I can see why she wouldn't want you with the children any longer," exclaimed Heather. "We know that it was not a small eatery you ate in that afternoon. You went into a saloon to eat. You met two men and spent the afternoon with them. No telling what you were doing and while there, you spilled all this venom on them, as you have on us right now. If you could tell us as strangers all this stuff, think of what you told those two as you sat in a saloon. What was your purpose? What were you after, the orphanage? Did you covet Marta's possessions?"

Jillian's face burned. "I want to go now. This was all a trick to make me talk. You're doing this for Marta, aren't you?"

"Wait a minute!" Larry rushed to grab her arm. He swung her toward him, his face ablaze with anger. "You leave Marta alone. If you ever go near her property again, I will wring your neck." He put his hands up in a wringing motion.

She backed away from him until she reached the door.

Chapter 11

"Forget the school classes, Jill. You're through in Ecuador. If you don't leave on your own in two weeks, we'll see that you are put out with force. Get out of Ecuador, do you hear?"

She opened the door and stood on the stoop. "I'll never leave Ecuador. This is my home and what I have told you are not lies. You have no idea what you're doing."

Larry stepped forward and grabbed her arm, forcing her down the three cement steps. "You think that I'm joking? I want you out of Ecuador in two weeks. This is your last warning."

Wrenching her arm away, in shock she turned and walked to the blue pickup and drove back to the highway.

Chapter 12

She was waiting in the pickup when Raquel walked past the Tumbaco plaza. "What are you doing here? I was going to walk to the Parkers to meet you. I thought you'd be there all afternoon." She opened the passenger door and got in.

"It was a short visit." A sick depression made her effort to smile futile.

"What's wrong?" frowned Raquel. "You don't seem well."

She managed a feeble smirk. "They didn't even offer me coffee."

"I thought you were invited for refreshments. What happened?"

"Their purpose for the invitation was not out of friendliness, but to warn me."

Raquel was alert. "Warn you about what?"

"Raqui, there are a lot of things I've never told you starting with the day I first met you. Remember the bad rainstorm and the man who almost died in your office?"

"Yes, of course I remember. Why?"

Leaning her head back on the car seat she began, "I had just come from classes in Oyambarillo. At the time I was feeling very lonely. Nothing seemed to be working out the way I wanted it to. For a year I'd lived in the plaza and still there was no sign that Marta was going to give my boys to me. Back home, it was one of my nephew's birthdays and I realized how stupid I was to be here and not there with my family. I almost decided to go back to the United States that day, but every time I considered leaving I thought of Andy and Ryan and the

Chapter 12

chance they will be returned to me. I have a lot of patience, but a year is a long time to wait. That day, I decided to stop by the orphanage and talk to Lucia."

"The nurse aide?"

Jillian closed her eyes and nodded. "Yes, I thought I could persuade her to convince Marta the boys should be with me."

"And?"

She straightened up and looked at Raquel. "I shouldn't have gone there. Lucia would have harmed me if I hadn't backed away and now Marta has friends helping her to remove me from the country."

A little sound of amusement burst from Raquel's mouth. "Send you from Ecuador? Do you mean the Parkers are going to send you away? How and why would they do that?"

"I don't know how they would do it, but I think I know why they would try."

Raquel was silent, waiting.

"I've never told anyone this until I told the Parkers today," Jillian continued. "I'm telling you now because I have finally lost all hope of getting the boys back and because I feel I can trust you. Raqui, I think Marta is selling babies for adoption."

The doctor's mouth fell open. "Selling babies? What babies and to whom?"

"I think they are going to America. She takes babies from mothers in the maternity clinic."

"Why haven't you told anyone?"

"Like I said, one day I think there's a chance I'll get my boys back, the next day something like this happens and I lose all hope. I wanted the boys and I believed if she thought I was no danger to her, she would eventually give them to me. Now I see that was foolish thinking."

"We need to go to the authorities, Jill. Let's go to Quito right now."

"No. I have no proof at all. I've never met her lawyer. I'm not sure that I've ever heard his last name. I think I heard Marta call him señor Fernando on the telephone once, but I'm sure that's not his true name. She used that for the sake of the telephone operators who she is certain are listening in. Anyway, Raqui, how could we find out? I'm almost positive she takes the newborns somewhere where they stay until their papers are completed. Once I knew where she took them, but the police raided it and deported the person in charge."

Raquel looked stunned. "I'm having a hard time understanding what you're saying. This is a terrible crime and to think you've not told anyone. What about the poor mothers? Did they give the babies to Marta knowing they would be sent to the United States?"

"Probably not." Jillian's head hung low. "I have felt so burdened over this. I hoped you would understand however."

"If you had told this to me before I had a chance to develop some feelings for you, I'd be so upset I'd never have wanted a friendship, but now I believe I understand you a little." She gave Jillian a crooked smile. "So you think it's not a good idea to take this to the authorities."

"Not now. Let's wait. I have an idea. One day Marta and I went to Quito to speak with a couple who had adopted a baby from an orphanage north of the city. Marta was leaving babies there until the government closed down the operation and took the children. The Livingstons were able to flee with their baby. That day the couple told us they used the same attorney as Marta's. If I can visit them, maybe they'll tell me the name of their attorney and in that way we can start to get proof.

Raquel looked hopeful. "That would be a start. What if he used an alias for them? Would he sign papers with a fake name?"

"Who knows? The more I think about this, I realize I was very stupid not to have told Rigo Estrada the day he came to Marta's house or the day I met him in the plaza. Oh, I didn't tell you that he happened to be in the plaza one day when I was eating lunch. He asked me several questions about Marta's operation and I said nothing. How foolish of me."

"But you don't think it's a good idea to go to the authorities now."

"Not now. Let's wait. I'll visit the Livingstons and once a month Marta's maid has a day off. We usually meet after dark so Marta or Lucia don't see us. This way I know what's going on at the orphanage. Perhaps next time you can be there to question her."

"Yes, she might tell us something that we can relate to the police."

Jillian started the motor and headed toward Pachuca. "You need to get back to the clinic. You probably have patients waiting."

Chapter 12

"Olivia is there. What are you going to do about the Parker's warning you to leave Ecuador?"

"Nothing." Jillian's eyes left the road to glance at her. "Nothing. With summer coming, I want to go into the mountains and hold classes and what about the English classes in my house? No, they can't make me leave."

"Good, because I will help you any way I can."

Chapter 13

Raquel relaxed against the pickup seat. "You might like to know what I was doing in Tumbaco today."

"Weren't you buying medicines and visiting a patient?"

"Yes, but I had another purpose. My year in Pachuca is almost over and in the next two months I must decide what I want to do with my life. Now that my schooling is over, I can work either in the government hospital in Quito or in a clinic."

"Have you made a decision?" Jillian's heart suddenly felt heavy. She was just beginning to find her loneliness lifting because of her new-found friend.

"Last evening my brother came from Quito to visit Opal, Geoff and me. We spent several hours talking over how we would build an outpatient clinic here in Pachuca."

"You mean you are thinking of starting a medical practice here?" Jillian's spirits suddenly lifted.

"Yes, my brother said he would support me in any way he could. We've already spent time looking for property. My parents have some money and I know they will help me. Now that Marta Brewer's outpatient clinic is closed, that leaves only the government clinic. Pachuca needs a clinic run by a doctor, not a student." Raquel was becoming animated. "Last week, after the young mother lost her life up in the mountains, I made the decision that I would do what I could to help these people and build a fully equipped clinic."

Chapter 13

"I'm so happy you've decided to do this. I would hate to just find you and then have you leave Pachuca."

"I feel the same way," she smiled. "Anyway, I spoke with the drugstore proprietor. He will be happy to supply the more common medicines. The hardware store will supply the materials for construction. This way, I won't have to go all the way to Quito every time I need something."

"What about the property?"

"Geoff and Opal have a lot one block beyond the plaza, two blocks from the new highway. They will ask for a small payment on it. Everything seems to be working out well." She suddenly sat up straight. "Oh, you might be interested in this. Rolando Martinez has come back from his wanderings. After my brother left last evening I wandered behind the house. I was surprised to find Rolando sitting back there."

"What was he doing? Why didn't he go into the house?"

She shook her head. "He is the strangest man I've ever known. Did I tell you that I first met him the night of his father's death? I was amazed then how angry and bitter he was. When I met him last evening, he frightened me at first. I think there's something wrong with him."

Jillian made a left hand turn onto the road leading to Pachuca. "You're right. Something is wrong with Rolando. He's an alcoholic."

"I know, but there's more. I've seen him so angry that I think he might be dangerous."

"Did you feel he was dangerous last night?"

"It's strange you asked that. A year ago, before the funeral he acted so hateful I was frightened of him, but last night I sensed he had mellowed some. There was something different about him."

"What did he say? Where has he been?" She pulled the pickup into the Ortega's driveway.

Raquel got out and walked to the road. "Well…"

"Wait a minute." Jillian walked to an open window in the house and yelled a greeting. "I had to let the señora know I was back. Now, what were you saying?"

85

They walked past the telephone office and onto the main street. Waving to Ernestina at the corner store and several passing pedestrians, they held off in their conversation until they reached Jillian's house.

"What did Rolando say?" repeated Jillian. "And where has he been?"

"He's been traveling all over Ecuador. He claims he's done a lot of thinking about his life and that he has decided he's in love with me."

"What?" chortled Jillian. "You say he's in love with you? A year ago he frightened you and the next time you see him, a year later, he loves you? You're right, he's the strangest man I've ever heard of."

"There's something sad about him."

"Raqui, he's an alcoholic, that's why." She opened the door. "Do you want to come in?"

"No, I must get back to the clinic. Olivia is there alone, but I do want to see you again. We must talk about summer classes and what we can do about this threat from the Americans. Also we must meet with Marta's maid."

"Yes, please come when you have a chance. I think I'm going to drive to Quito and visit with the Livingstons."

Raquel started toward the clinic.

"Raqui." Jillian caught up with her. "What did you say to Rolando when he said he loved you?"

The doctor pushed out a lower lip. "That it wouldn't work because he and I don't agree on much of anything. The most important difference is that I'm a Christian and he has no roots in any religious belief. Never could we build a relationship on such a shaky foundation."

"Is he staying with Geoff and Opal?"

"No, I told Geoff I had seen him, but after he searched all evening and this morning, no one has seen him. I have to admit my heart has been very heavy. No one knows where he went."

"Don't worry, as long as his family is here, he'll be back."

"I'm not worried about that. I'm concerned that he'll get so drunk he'll hurt himself." Raquel gave her a sad smile. "Well, I'd better go to work. Why don't we have coffee later and we can talk about what you learn at the Livingstons."

Chapter 14

One evening two months later she and Raquel sat around the table in Jillian's kitchen. She had prepared a quick dinner of fried llapingachos, a mashed potato pancake with a slice of cheese enclosed and a finely ground peanut soup, flavored with onion, chicken stock, cream and a few diced potatoes. Much had happened in the past weeks. Jillian had begun opening her home to the young people of Pachuca, offering English classes. The first session had garnered twenty students; however difficulties with scheduling and comprehending English had narrowed the attendance to eight. Raquel came as often as possible, exhibiting a flair for remembering basic English grammar. Even more successful were the classes in Pachuca's suburban schools scattered throughout the mountains. The district's seven principals had encouraged Jillian to summon the children to their local schools during the summer break for the purpose of learning crafts and English. Bible stories told with flannel-backed pictures were met with wild enthusiasm and the cookies she offered were accepted with wide-eyed gratefulness. At the end of two months, she had become a topic of conversation among the nationals.

As thrilled as she was with her reception among the people, she had failed to realize how much work the summer project would require. Here, Raquel was able to volunteer a few hours each evening to the preparations. Many evenings they separated kits of colored paper, scissors, paste and pencils and placed them in plastic bags purchased in Quito. A local carpenter had built a ping-pong sized table with two long benches which Jillian placed upstairs in the room adjoining her bedroom. Along two walls he had built wooden shelves, large enough to contain several hundred pounds of colored paper and craft books.

After Jillian mentioned the need for more paper, Raquel found a paper factory in the south end of Quito. An afternoon trip to the large factory warehouse proved fruitful where for a small amount of money she was allowed to fill her pickup with as many paper scraps as it could carry. Once a month she made the trip, returning to Pachuca with scraps enough to provide the children with more opportunities to work on crafts. A commercial bakery allowed her to buy bags of animal cookies at a discount. She found the paper and cookies to be of substandard quality but to the children of the mountains they were sparks of brightness in a dark and dreary world. Because Jillian knew the children would probably never know any existence beyond Ecuadorian life, she offered the materials without embarrassment.

Earlier that day, Flora's brother had appeared at her door to report his sister had the day off and would pay her a visit that evening. Immediately Jillian contacted Raquel to come for dinner; she wanted the doctor to be there to hear Flora's monthly report on the well-being of Marta's children.

"Do you want another llapingacho, Raqui?" Jillian asked from the stove.

"One more, please."

Jillian took a portion of mashed potatoes and pressed it into a patty. Next she placed a thick slice of white cheese across the potato and added another patty on top to create a sandwich which she place in a thin layer of hot butter in the skillet. After making another for herself, she left the stove to sit beside her friend while the food cooked.

"Perhaps you should have invited Flora for dinner."

"No, Flora never visits here in daylight. She must wait until after dark. Marta has no idea that we are friends. We must wait to see each other on her day off. Anyway it's her only chance to eat with her family."

"What would Marta do if she found out?" Raquel absently moved her fork back and forth over a small piece of fried potato.

Chapter 14

"I can't imagine how angry she would be. She'd fire her and that would be a final blow for those children. Flora is the only consistently stable person in that house." She stood to turn the llapingachos. "That's why this past year we have been so careful to meet only after dark."

They ate, turning to the subject of the Livingstons again. Jillian's trip to Quito had been in vain. She found the Livingston's apartment empty and after questioning a neighbor on their whereabouts, they reported not knowing where the family had gone. That put a damper on ever finding out Marta's attorney's name. When the conversation drifted to the latest developments in the construction of Raquel's clinic, there was a knock at the door.

"I'll get it." Raquel pushed back the chair and went to the door. Jillian followed close behind and held out her arms to greet Flora as the girl hurried into the house.

"Buenas noches, señorita Jill," cried Flora, hugging her tightly.

"Buenas noches, Flora." She released her and turned her toward Raquel. "Do you know Doctor Raquel from the government clinic?"

Flora's eyes opened wide in an expression of admiration. "No, I haven't been to the clinic since I started work at the orphanage. Señorita Marta has always given me the medicines I need. Buenas noches, Doctor."

"Why don't you come into the kitchen?" Raquel led the girl to the table and sat opposite her.

"Do you want something to eat Flora?" Jillian walked to the stove.

"Gracias, I ate with my family, but I'll eat something."

"I made colada just for you and we have some soup left. Remember when you taught me how to make colada?" She found a cup. "I bought corn meal, boiled it in water and flavored it with cinnamon and brown sugar and a pinch of salt."

Flora's eyes twinkled with the memory. "Yes, that is right and it sounds good. I'm too full for soup but I'll drink some colada."

They drank the hearty drink and munched on fruit and cookies, talking largely of Flora's family. Then Jillian sighed deeply and asked the question she had been dreading for fear of the answers. "How are the children? How are Ryan and Andy?"

Deep sadness cast shadows beneath Flora's eyes. "It is very bad. In all the time I have worked for señorita Marta, I have never seen the children so sad."

"What is she doing?" Raquel drew her chair closer to the table as if to pull the answers out of her. "What's happening?"

"I don't know what happened. One day Marta and Lucia started behaving strangely. They talked a lot in whispers away from the children. When they are with the children, they yell and punish them a lot."

"Oh, Lord, help those poor children." Jillian's head swung in Raquel's direction. "That's what I mean. That's why I want to take them away from Marta."

"She will never give them up. In fact, just yesterday a construction crew began building a high brick wall around the property," said Flora.

"A wall?" repeated Jillian, astonished. "Why would she build a high wall around the property? She already has a mud wall and fence blocking people from getting inside."

Flora shrugged her shoulders. "I'm not sure, but I did hear señorita Marta crying. She said to Lucia one day last week that she has come to the conclusion you will never leave Pachuca."

"It's my fault, Raqui. She's taking it out on the children. Sometimes I think it's better that I leave and go back to the United States. I should have left when those Americans, the Parkers told me to leave."

Raquel jumped in her chair catching Jillian and Flora by surprise. "The Americans," she cried, making a quick gesture with her hand. "I forgot to tell you, Jill."

"What?"

"The Americans you visited. This afternoon I went to Tumbaco, to the hardware store to see about some things for the new clinic. I put the articles on order and was waiting on the highway for a bus to return to Pachuca when I had a sudden inspiration. You know how often we've spoken about the Americans and why we've never seen them again? I decided to speak with them and ask them why they treated you so harshly the day you visited with them. I was sure that Marta had filled them with many lies about you, but I wanted to face them myself. Anyway, I went back to the plaza and found a taxi. I

Chapter 14

talked the driver into taking me to their house. I remembered the directions you had given me. We arrived at the big complex. I was surprised to see the gates, but after the taxi driver honked a few times, an old peon, he must have been seventy years old, came hobbling up. I asked him where Larry and Heather Parker lived. To my surprise he said he didn't know. I told him that my friend said they live in the first house on the block, but he just shook his head and pointed up the hill. Did you have trouble finding them the day you visited?"

"No," frowned Jillian, puzzled. "I just told him I had an appointment, I think that's what I said, at the first house. He acted like he knew about it. I didn't mention the Parker's name. They were waiting at the front door for me."

Raquel continued. "The old man said no one was living in that house and that the residents hadn't lived there for six months because they were on a furlough in the United States. I asked about the house across the road but he said that house had been unoccupied for a year. Finally, after questioning him at length, he remembered a couple that had stayed there a few days two months ago but he thought they were probably friends of the owners and had come from the United States to do something in the house for them. He couldn't remember their name but said Parker was not familiar."

Jillian sat in stunned silence up to that point. "You mean they aren't residents of Ecuador?"

"Apparently not. Oh, and there was another thing he said that I think is very strange. When the couple arrived they had no children that he saw, yet on the day they left, they had a very small baby."

"Raqui, maybe they were here for the short stay so they could get one of Marta's babies."

"That's what I think."

"Do you know about this, Flora?" Jillian asked. "Is Marta giving babies away?"

"I don't know but of course she tells me nothing." The girl frowned, pondering a moment. "But it seems like I remember the name Larry and Heather but Parker wasn't the last name. One afternoon they came to look at the orphanage and maternity clinic. I remember how Marta made them feel at home. She had me serve them coffee and cake and after that day I didn't see them again."

"Did you hear anything they talked about?" Jillian asked in a hopeful tone.

"No because every time I came near them they stopped talking and then they went to the clinic and I didn't see them again."

"Raqui, that's it!" Striking the table with her fist, she exclaimed. "That's what Marta does with the babies. She has the adoptive parents come for them."

"That may be the case sometimes, but she probably has many different ways of getting children to new parents. That's why she wants you out of Ecuador. You are a real threat to her. She was afraid that someday you would start putting incidents together until you were able to figure out what she's been doing all this time."

"If I could have the children in my care I would leave her alone. I'd never say anything about what she's doing." Jillian turned tear-filled eyes in Flora's direction. "You say she is mistreating the children? What is she doing?"

The girl sighed. "Like I say, she yells at them and punishes them. Last week she did something very bad."

"To whom?" asked Jillian.

"To Peter."

"He's one of the boys living in Marta's house," explained Jillian to Raquel. "What did she do?"

"It was Sarah's birthday so Marta was going to make sugar cookies. I feel so sorry for the children because all they eat for breakfast is that terrible cereal."

"Yes," explained Jillian. "She buys bulgur and oatmeal in bulk. It takes so long to cook in the morning, Lucia told Flora to start cooking it the night before. I tried to talk Marta out of that idea, but she said she doesn't want Flora wandering all over the house so early. So the evening before, she has to cook the cereal and then heat it up in the morning. It tastes terrible."

Despite herself, Flora had to giggle at the grimace that crossed Raquel's face, but then she became serious. "The children eat early in the morning and then go to school. They are not allowed any more food until lunch which doesn't come until noon. That's five hours. The other day when Marta was making cookies, Peter did something he's not supposed to do. He went into the kitchen where Marta says

Chapter 14

no children are allowed. She had just taken cookies from the oven and put the pan on the counter when she was called into the next room for something. Apparently Peter took a cookie. When señorita Marta returned, she saw an empty space on the pan. It was very bad. She made all the children come into the kitchen and then demanded the person who stole the cookie confess. Over and over she asked. She was very angry. Everyone kept saying that they didn't do it. They were frightened she would beat them. Then Marta took each of them by the arm to the window where she looked at their faces, shirts and into their mouths to see if she could find any traces. Of course Peter had remains of the cookie in his mouth. She demanded he tell the truth but he kept crying, saying he didn't do it. Finally she screamed to the other children that they had to go to their rooms and then she took Peter into the bathroom. She made me go in there too. She put him on the cabinet where she changes the baby's diapers and made him climb on top and lie down. She called for Elizabeth to find Lucia and when Lucia came, she sent Elizabeth away. Then she made me hold down Peter's arms while Lucia held his legs. Marta took a rubber tube, hooked it to a big syringe and put the tube into Peter's mouth and then she forced it into his stomach and syringed out the cookie."

Tears were coursing down Jillian's face and Raquel turned pale.

Flora continued. "She found the eaten cookie and then she decided maybe he had stolen something else and kept syringing until I saw blood. Then she made Peter go upstairs where she whipped him with a belt and made him go without food until the next day. He missed the party."

Jillian had never yet seen Raquel angry, but through her tears she saw the doctor's mouth set in a thin line and her eyes flashed with hatred.

"Is Peter all right?" Jillian pumped. "How is he now?"

"He is so sad but of course his wounds are better. I've been so worried about all the children. This morning Sarah couldn't eat that terrible oatmeal. When it was reheated it burned on the bottom of the pan. The taste was awful and Sarah couldn't swallow it. Marta made her sit there for a long time and when she couldn't force anymore down, Marta spanked her. Sarah vomited onto the table, but Marta forced her to continue eating and she vomited again. Jill, you are right. I can't leave my job. I hate it there. I hate what Marta does to the children, but I can't leave them. They need me. Tommy begged me to take him to my house one day." With a desperate gulp, she choked back tears.

After Flora left for her parent's home, Jillian and Raquel sat deep in thought. Finally Jillian spoke, "We have to do something. I told you I want to get Ryan and Andy out of there. Can you help me?"

"I've got to be honest with you. I don't think there's anything we can do."

"Why?"

"Because Marta is a powerful woman and because she has a lot of money."

"What does that have to do with it? She's hurting those children."

Raquel reached out and patted Jillian's arm. "Someone as determined as Marta uses her means to get what she wants. If she is really building a brick wall around her property that can mean only one thing: she doesn't want you or anyone else in there. Those children are trapped."

"We can go to the authorities and tell them what Flora told us."

"We have no proof. We have only what Flora has said. If we take her with us to the authorities, Marta will remove her from the children's care and if Marta uses her influence to keep them then we've lost all the way around."

"But what if the authorities believe us and close down the orphanage? We can tell them about the dozens of babies being taken from mothers and sent to the United States."

"Jill, listen to me. If Marta is getting children out of the country, she has help from someone in the government. How do you think she gets the proper papers? If as many children have been sent from this country as you say, then someone is helping her. You could lose your residential visa."

"I think that's why I'm so angry at Eric Perez. I told him about some of these problems a long time ago. If he had paid attention and used some of his influence, perhaps he could have done something."

"He probably saw the same problems I see. He probably didn't want to hurt you."

Chapter 14

"No, he was interested in what Marta was doing for the sake of Rigo Estrada's interest as the town policeman and in investigating the possibility of illegal activities." Jillian sat up with a start. "Raqui, we can go to Rigo. He asked me to tell him about Marta a couple years ago. Oh, how I wish I had told him then. It's really my fault that those children are suffering. I was trying to protect myself by not telling him about Marta."

"Stop upsetting yourself about something you can't change now. Yes, I suppose we can go see him, but before we do, promise me something."

"What?"

"I want to take you somewhere. On your next day off I'll not work on the new clinic. I'd like to spend the day in Conocoto."

"Conocoto? Isn't that the valley south of Quito? What's there?"

"Just wait and see."

Chapter 15

Jillian was wrapping sandwiches when a child's voice yelled her name from outside her front door. She hastily opened it to find a boy of six or seven motioning to her. "Come, come, señorita Jill. The Doctor Raquel wants you at the clinic. She says to come quickly."

"At the clinic? Which clinic?"

He pointed toward the government clinic and motioned again for her to come.

Jillian ran to the kitchen and made sure the lunch was sealed and in the refrigerator and then she rushed out the front door toward the clinic. Why was Raquel at the government clinic? Her year had been completed and all her time was now devoted completely to the building of her new clinic. She barged into the waiting room and stopped short at the sight of a man lying unconscious in the middle of the floor. Raquel crouched at his side, checking his vital signs. A terrified woman standing over them threw her a quick frightened glance. A fresh, white strip of gauze wound around the man's head.

"What happened, Raqui?"

"He fell off his horse and was kicked in the head. His wife carried him here with the help of some neighbors." She pointed in the direction of several onlookers gathered at the end of the room. "Jill, we need your pickup."

"My pickup? Why? I thought we were going to Conocoto today."

Chapter 15

"We will, but on the way I need to take this man to Quito. I'm the only one who can go. The resident doctor is with a seriously ill patient in his office and Olivia is needed here with him."

"My truck is so small. The patient will have to lie in the back."

"Then he'll lie in the back. We don't have time to find another truck. Please go get it."

She ran from the clinic, past the plaza and the telephone office. Her little Austin Mini was smaller than most compact cars; barely able to carry more than two passengers in front as the back end was about three feet long. She pulled back the unlocked gates of the Ortega's home and yelled a greeting through an open window. There was no answer, so she backed the pickup into the street and re-closed the gate. Stopping by her house, she ran inside to put the lunch in a basket, grab a sweater, her driver's license and a few sucres. Driving to the clinic, she parked in front leaving the motor running.

The onlookers remained, standing in a close circle. Raquel met her at the door. "We must hurry to get him to the nearest hospital. He is still unconscious." She looked past Jillian and hollered to the group. "Come quickly and carry him to the pickup."

"Ask Olivia for some blankets and a piece of plastic just in case it rains."

Jillian coolly requested the blankets and plastic from Olivia, who responding in kind found them in one of the back rooms. Under different circumstances Jillian would have questioned Olivia about her unscrupulous practice of accepting stolen goods in return for medicines, but this was not the time. She ran to the back of the pickup and unfolded the blanket. Turning, she watched two men bring the patient on a wooden stretcher, lift him gently and lay him on the blankets turning him to the side and bending his knees so he would fit, while his wife and two men climbed aboard to sit beside him.

"Raqui, hurry." Jillian yelled into the clinic.

"I'm coming." She re-appeared, a worried look on her face. "I called the government hospital to tell them we're on our way. They can't afford the American hospital."

"It worries me the way they are sitting on the edge of the back end. They could fall." Jillian glanced back at the passengers.

"Don't worry. They're experts at holding on to moving vehicles."

They climbed into the pickup and Raquel turned around to look at the patient through the window. "I hope he makes it. I'm worried that he hasn't regained consciousness."

"This reminds me of the time that man died in the back of Marta's pickup. I still haven't gotten over it."

"You never really get over something like that. I still think of the young woman's death in the mountains. I'm sure we'd feel the same about this man if he dies."

They reached the main highway and then sped down the long hill to the bridge spanning the deep canyon, crossing at top speed. Because of the weight in the back end, the little pickup crawled slowly up the steep hill. Turning away from the canyon, they cruised toward Tumbaco and beyond to Cumbaya. Stopping at the train track that crossed the highway, a slight frown creased Jillian's brow. The brakes felt low and spongy. Had they reacted that way earlier on the trip? She pushed away a nagging thought of looming trouble and continued listening to Raquel's concern for the patient. Beyond Cumbaya, the highway started climbing toward Quito. The pickup with its heavy load crept steadily up the steep incline. Not until they reached Quito's city limits did Jillian have another occasion to use the brake. When she did, a current of alarm left her shaken. The pedal almost reached the floor. She decided not to say anything to Raquel; the doctor had enough worries on her mind. Quickly, she planned her strategy. What would be the safest route to the hospital? Stay away from the center of town and keep to the quieter streets.

"Why are we going this way? We must hurry."

"Just trust me and I'll tell you later. Right now, keep your eye on the patient and I'll get you there, I promise." She saw a policeman at the next street corner directing traffic. He had his hand in position to stop the line of cars she was leading. Starting to slow down a half block before reaching him, she ignored the angry honking of other drivers and rolled to a stop. Disregarding Raquel's puzzled look, she put her foot on the brake. It hit metal. Her brakes were gone. Sweat rolled down her back and she decided to tell Raquel. With a death grip on the steering wheel, she watched the policeman give her direction to pass him. "Raqui, I have something to tell you. We have no brakes."

Chapter 15

"No brakes? Why are you joking with a dying man in the back of our pickup?"

"We have no brakes. We're going to have to pull over."

"You're not joking." The awful truth was sinking in. "Jill, we can't stop because the man is dying."

"We have no brakes. That's why I'm crawling. That's why there are people honking at us."

"If you turn up this street, we can get to the hospital with little trouble. There will only be one intersection to get through and we'll be there."

Slippery with sweat, her hands turned the wheel to the left and she climbed the hill, hoping there was no reason to stop at the top. If they had to roll backwards there would be no recourse but to crash into something.

While Raquel prayed in a frantic pitch, Jillian maneuvered the pickup to the final intersection. "Oh, God, help that policeman to let us through. Oh, God! Oh, God!"

Just as they approached, he turned and swept his arm to let them pass. With a loud expulsion of relief, Jillian knew she had only one block to go. Speeding up, she put on the turn signal and started to turn left. Dismayed, she saw an ambulance racing toward them. In a split second, she decided to ignore the blaring sirens and flashing lights and barely avoiding a direct hit, she squeezed past the ambulance and rushed up the hill to the old hospital.

"Hold on, Raqui, we're going to have to crash into that pile of sand."

Turning toward an area under construction, Jillian put the pickup into low gear and rolled downward into the mound. Lurching forward, the patient's wife grabbed her husband before his head crashed into the end of the pickup bed.

"I've got to find someone to help us, Jill. Are you coming with me?"

"I'm too weak to walk. You'll have to go ahead. If I try to stand, I'll fall."

Raquel gave her a worried look and exited the cab. She leaned over the back of the pickup to study the patient who had by now opened his eyes and was looking around. "Wait here, señores. I'll be back with some help." She ran up a small hill and into the hospital. In a few minutes, two nurses and a doctor returned with a stretcher. Everyone climbed out of the pickup while the patient was carefully removed. They gave Jillian a signal of thanks, leaving her still shaking from the terrible ordeal.

"How could this have happened?" she said to herself. "Last night the brakes seemed fine."

Opening the door, she stepped out and leaned against the fender. Her vehicle was in the midst of a deserted construction site. Sand, cement and other building equipment were in evidence. She assumed the workers were on their siesta. Carefully she stepped around a mound of sand and walked toward the hospital entrance. Entering the ancient building, she found herself in a shadowy hallway with high ceilings, thick yellowed marble pillars, wooden floors and dark woodwork. Across the room, opposite the tall, heavy, double doors, an elderly woman sat at an antiquated typewriter behind a three foot high partition.

"Buenos dias, señora." Jillian approached her cautiously, not wanting to disturb the woman's work.

"Buenos dias." Tired eyes peered up at her.

"Do you have a telephone book I can use?"

"We don't loan telephone books," the lady squinted a frown.

"I need it just for a moment. I'll use it right here." She scrounged in her pocket and laid down ten sucres.

The woman eyed the money and picked it up, slipping it inside her blouse. "Just a moment, señorita." Disappearing behind the counter, she returned with a tattered outdated book.

"Gracias." Jillian leafed through the torn pages until she found the telephone number of her mechanic. Memorizing the number, she returned the book and offered her another ten sucres to dial the number for her. Then she walked back to the pickup with a promise from the mechanic that he would be there as soon as possible. By the time he arrived, Raquel returned with the news that the patient would live but the doctors didn't know if he had sustained brain damage.

"He'll have to stay here for a few days but I think he'll be all right."

The previous owner of the pickup as well as Jillian had periodically left the vehicle in the hands of this mechanic so he knew the pickup well. Now he placed rocks behind the back wheels and raised the front end of the vehicle with a jack. Feeling behind the left wheel,

Chapter 15

he twisted a cylinder and brought out the object in his hand. Puzzled, he studied it then placed it aside. Reaching underneath again, he looked at his finger.

"You're out of brake fluid, señorita." He looked perplexed.

"How can that be? You checked it just a month ago, didn't you?"

"Yes, I'm certain that I did." Shaking his head, he lay on the ground and slid his body underneath the pickup. Jillian and Raquel stared at each other.

He reappeared with another cylinder from the passenger side wheel and bent to pick up the cylinder from the driver's side, studying it again. "You will have to wait here for a few minutes until I have a chance to buy some brake fluid and replace it. You can't drive the car this way."

"Yes, I understand," Jillian replied, mystified. "How do you suppose I ran out of brake fluid so quickly? And on both wheels? The brakes were fine yesterday."

"Did someone else work on your vehicle last night or this morning?" He put the cylinders in his pocket and tried to rub his dirty hands clean.

"No, of course not. Only you have worked on it." Jillian shook her head, baffled.

"I think someone turned the cylinders just enough so every time you put your foot on the brake some fluid squirted out. By the time you reached Quito there was no more fluid."

Jillian handed him several sucres to buy what he needed to make the pickup operable and while he was away, the girls discussed the situation and decided that somehow the cylinders had worked themselves loose. Perhaps the mechanic hadn't tightened them enough during the last maintenance service. Jillian made up her mind that he was responsible and decided to discuss the possibility with him when he arrived. She met him as he pulled up beside the sand pile. "Señor, is there a chance you failed to tighten the cylinders?"

"Señoritas, I have no way of knowing all that has happened to your vehicle; however I do know that someone took a wrench and loosened the brake fluid container. If I had left it loose a month ago, you would have lost the use of your brakes long before this."

"Who? Who would do that?" Jillian's amazement clearly showed in her eyes.

"Of course, I don't know that," he smiled. "If no one else works on your truck, then I don't know the answer. With Austin Mini pickups made this year it is very easy to reach behind the wheel and turn the cylinder. Someone would have to understand this type of vehicle. There is no container of brake fluid under the truck hood, there are cylinders connected to the front wheels. They are both empty. Do you have someone caring for your truck at night?"

"Yes," replied Raquel. "Jill parks her pickup two blocks from her house under the care of a reputable family."

"Do they keep the gates locked at night?"

"I would think so, at least after everyone is at home," said Jillian, her voice trailing off. "Although this morning no one seemed to be at home and the gate was unlocked."

He cocked an eyebrow upward. "All I know is that someone did this to your car. It could have killed you. Traveling through mountains such as we have in this country you must have very good brakes."

"Jill, you should talk to the Ortega's. Perhaps they forgot to lock the gate last night," exclaimed Raquel.

"Señorita, if it was a prank, then it is not a funny one. Only an enemy would do this to you."

Jillian ran her hand through her curly hair, lightly pulling on it and looked at Raquel, a light dawning in her eyes and then she turned to the mechanic to hand him a hundred sucre bill. "Gracias, señor."

"De nada, señoritas." He replaced the brake fluid, tightened the cylinders and departed.

"Come, Jill. Let's go to Conocoto," said Raquel quietly.

With Raquel's directions, Jillian found her way to the valley south of Quito. Driving upward toward the summit, they rode in silence. Finally Jillian could no longer hold her tongue. "Why are you so quiet? Are you thinking about your patient?"

"No," she murmured and sighed deeply. "No, the patient will be all right. I'm more concerned about you."

"Me? Because of the brakes?"

"Yes, the brakes. We could have been killed. You know that."

"I must admit I was very frightened."

Chapter 15

Raquel turned to look at her friend. "At first I had planned to take you to Conocoto to visit friends of mine. I intended it to be a pleasant outing but now I feel it is imperative that you go with me."

"Can't you tell me what this is about?"

"No, because I want it to be a surprise." Raquel leaned back in the seat and seemed to study the landscape. They topped the summit and began winding back and forth across the mountain on the descent to the valley floor. The countryside looked much like the Tumbaco Valley, but the unfamiliarity of it brought an inexplicable desire for Jillian to turn back toward home. For her, Pachuca was without equal.

"How are the brakes now?"

"Fine, they are fine. Maybe somehow the cylinders came loose on their own."

The young doctor shook her head. "No, I believe someone turned the cylinders."

"Why would someone do that?"

"I believe things changed for the worst since you went to see Lucia. Marta realizes she can't watch you all the time, so over the months and little by little she has tried to wear you down. She's tried to turn the people of Pachuca against you and she's criticized you to the school officials. When that didn't work, then things worsened. She tried to scare you into leaving Ecuador by planting two Americans in Tumbaco. Now something happens to your brakes. No, I don't believe the cylinders turned by themselves."

A frown gathered on Jillian's brow. "I can't believe that Marta would do this. She really truly loved me at one time. What can we do?"

"You must be very careful."

They turned off the highway and drove toward Conocoto. After passing the plaza, they crossed a small river by way of a wooden bridge and followed the narrow road past several huts. A mile from the village center, they saw a building sitting alone on a long stretch of grassland. As they drew nearer, Jillian noticed the structure was built of stone and from its worn condition appeared to be very old. The driveway led beneath a large archway and wound around the back of the building. Raquel told Jillian to stop the pickup in front of a wide entrance.

The edifice reminded Jillian of the main building at Tulcachi, built in a rectangle that encircled a long patio, but this is where the similarity ended. Unlike Tulcachi, neither this building nor landscape had been maintained for a long period of time. The yard was austere and bare, without so much as a blade of grass. The yellow, hard-packed earth blended with the color of the building's walls. Life within was evidenced by a putrid stench and quiet childish voices. They walked through the tunnel entrance and entered the patio. There were no arches holding up the second floor as there were in Tulcachi but thick stone pillars placed every three yards. Much to Jillian's distress Raquel headed toward the source of the horrid odor, through a passageway and into a long shadowy kitchen. Several huge pots simmered on a wide hot stove. Two women stood at a long wooden table, dividing portions of wet greasy animal fat. One of the women turned and put a handful of it into a boiling kettle of water. Jillian realized that's what they smelled, the boiling fat.

Raquel greeted the women. "Buenas tardes, señores. We're looking for Cynthia Gato.

One of the women, with pieces of yellow suet stuck to her hand pointed down the passageway. The girls thanked her and followed the sounds of children's voices. Jillian walked behind Raquel through a double door into a room that stretched the length of the building. What she saw dismayed her. Small cots were positioned end to end down the middle of the room. Baby cribs lined the walls, interspersed with sets of drawers. Dozens of children of all ages sat on the cots or lay in the cribs. Most wore shirts, but were bare from the waist down. A stench rose from dirty clothes and messes left by the children wherever they chose to squat. Jillian shuddered at the chill in the room created by the mountain breeze blowing through the broken windows. Her initial shock receded and she wandered to a crib where a sallow toddler lay, rocking her head back and forth, her eyes blank.

"Hola!" Raquel's voice called out in an attempt to gain their attention. Dull indifferent eyes turned in her direction. A young girl appeared from behind a partition, a shirt in one hand and a naked child in the other. She walked toward them.

"Hola," repeated Raquel. "We're looking for Cynthia Gato."

Chapter 15

The girl pointed behind her before proceeding to lead the child to a cot to dress him. Jillian and Raquel walked to the end of the room where a woman sat at a desk behind the partition. She lifted her eyes and gave Raquel a broad smile.

"Buenas tardes, señora Gato. Do you remember me? I am Doctor Raquel Torres."

"Buenas tardes. Yes, I remember you, Doctor. You visited here a few months ago as a student."

"Yes, I was here during the whooping cough epidemic. May I present my good friend to you? This is Jill Townsend."

Cynthia grabbed Jillian's hand and pumped it congenially. "You are from America?"

"I am an American but I live in Pachuca."

"Are you also a doctor?"

"I'm not a doctor or nurse, but it seems since coming to Ecuador I have been involved with medicines and clinics."

Cynthia nodded. She was a short, young woman of about thirty. Her wavy black hair curled around her neck and ears giving her a girlish look, but fashionable glasses lent her a sophisticated professional style. Dressed in a well-tailored tan suit that did little to complement her olive complexion, she seemed out of place in this setting. "I'm very happy that the two of you came to visit us."

Jillian gave her a slight nod of thanks. "What is this place?"

Cynthia looked startled. "Why, it's a government orphanage. I assumed Raquel had told you about our work here."

Raquel explained. "I didn't know about the orphanage, Jill, until I was sent to the Conocoto clinic during my medical studies. I spent a month in this area with two other students. One day I was brought to the orphanage because several of the children had contracted whooping cough. We had to rush three infants to the hospital in Quito. That was when I met Cynthia and we had lunch together."

"Yes," smiled Cynthia remembering. "Well, Jill, what is it you want to know?"

"Where did these children come from? Who are they?"

The woman's arm swept the long room. "Some were left here by parents who couldn't care for them. Most of them were born to single mothers who couldn't cope with a new baby. Some of them are actual orphans. Last week we found a four-year-old wandering on the highway. Her parents have not come to claim her."

"Why aren't they dress adequately?"

"We don't have money for clothes, good food or care. The girl taking care of the children now is alone. When school classes are out, two other girls will come to help serve dinner to the children."

"I don't want to offend you, but I'm concerned about the food they eat. There is a terrible smell coming from the kitchen. What do the cooks serve the children? Oh, I'm sorry." A delayed look of horror crossed Jillian's face at the social blunder she had uttered.

"Don't apologize. It is an awful smell. Because we have so little money, we must feed the children soup made mostly of animal fat. The two days after market day a little meat is added. It's the fat you smell."

"Why doesn't the government give you more money?"

"They say they don't have enough for all the orphanages in this country. You should see just how poor the orphanage in Conocoto is. When you arrived, I was figuring the budget for the next month. Oh, Jill, you should see how the children must bathe. There is no water inside the building. They must stand under a spigot of cold running water in the chilly mountain wind. No wonder there are always sick children living here."

Jillian was horrified. "I see you have no glass in the window openings. This room must be very cold at night."

"They tell me it is. I don't live here. My home is in Quito. Each morning I go to work in the government office of the children's division in Quito. Every afternoon after lunch I travel here to oversee the orphanage for an hour or more and then I return to the city."

"Why is that baby moving her head back and forth? She looks so ill."

"The truth is we have so little help that those babies are never out of their cribs. Some of them are more than a year old and have never been outdoors. In fact many of the children never get out of this room except to bathe. There's no one to watch them and if they do go out, there's nothing to do but sit on the hard earth."

"Do you have proper bathrooms?"

Chapter 15

"No, because there is no indoor plumbing although we do have facilities, but sometimes the children aren't able to get to them. When the girls from school arrive, they will clean up the messes."

It was all too much for Jillian; she began to feel a wave of nausea and signaled her distress to Raquel.

"Well, Cynthia, I think Jill and I should be leaving. I have much to do this afternoon in Pachuca," she said, extending her hand.

They exchanged farewells and Jillian almost ran to the pickup. Leaning against the vehicle, she drank in the fresh air. Climbing into the driver's seat, she waited until Raquel sat beside her. "Why did you bring me here, Raqui? This is the most terrible place."

"My first desire was to let you see how these children are forced to live. I wanted you to see how well off Marta's children are in comparison to these orphans. I realize conditions aren't ideal in Marta's orphanage, but Jill, at least they have hot, indoor running water. They have good, nutritious food and warm clothing and from what you've told me only two children sleep to a room. That sounds a lot better than the way these children live. I was hoping that if you saw what these children go through you would be able to focus your attention on them and perhaps in that way, put Marta's children in the past." Raquel laid her hand on Jillian's arm. "No, don't look at me that way."

"And how do you think I can help these children? You know I don't have much money." She felt a spark of anger toward her friend. "And how do you think I can possibly stop thinking about my children?"

"You mean Marta's children," Raquel replied gently. "I don't expect you to forget them completely, but perhaps it would help if you found a new project."

"You don't think teaching classes in all of Pachuca's schools is enough?"

Raquel took a deep breath. "I've been thinking about what happened to the brakes. Frankly, I'm worried. What if someone did tamper with them? I would feel a lot better if you lived away from Pachuca and not so close to potential danger."

Jillian pulled away from Raquel as if to protect herself from the stab of pain in her heart. "Away? What do you mean?"

"I would miss you so much. I enjoy you as my dear close friend, but I think Pachuca is too dangerous for you. Perhaps you could move to this valley and start working in this orphanage. Then Marta won't bother you any more."

Tears sprang to Jillian's eyes. "How can you ask me to move? You know how much I love Pachuca. Never could I bear to live in any other village. It makes me angry that you don't understand."

"I'm sorry and I do understand. It was just a suggestion."

"So that's why you brought me here."

"I wanted you to see that Marta's children aren't suffering as much as you think. Come on, let's go. We can stop down by the river we passed and eat our lunch. After we eat we'll feel better."

During lunch, Jillian was quiet, thinking about what Raquel had said and what she had seen that day. After she relaxed and re-examined her friend's suggestion, she was able to see she had only concern for her safety. She thought about the conditions in the government orphanage. It was true that Marta's children certainly lived under much better physical conditions even though they suffered at times terrible emotional traumas, they were still better off than the listless neglected children she had just seen. If Marta had not taken in the children unwanted by parents, they would have ended up in an orphanage just like this, or as Marta many times reminded her, dead. She wondered if perhaps some of the babies she had just seen were ones included in the Marshall's raid and her heart sank at the terrible tragedy Marta had brought down on the heads of innocent children.

On the way back to Quito, Jillian finally spoke. "What do you suggest we do for the children in Conocoto? I don't see how we can help them. We're both busy; you with the building of your clinic and me with my classes, and neither one of us have a lot of money."

"You and I might not be able to help them but I know others who don't have much to do with their time. They might be able to do the work."

Jillian's eyes lit up with interest. "Who?"

"Think. Think of people we know with money and a lot of time."

For several minutes they rode in silence, Jillian's mind whirling. Finally it dawned on her. "There's someone I know with money and time. Eric's mother, Helen, but I don't know if she's well enough to

Chapter 15

be able to do anything for the children. Perhaps Philip Rios or his parents might help."

"That's right. My mother could do something and so could other women who live in the same neighborhood. We can find women from the more prosperous families in Quito who can contribute time and energy to those children in Conocoto. They need to discover ways to help people instead of wasting time at teas and card parties."

"What about the wives of government leaders?"

"What a brilliant idea! If someone who represented the government could go to the orphanage...."

"Raqui, we could call the president's wife." Jillian interrupted her friend.

"I suppose she is very busy with her own projects, but think about this, who, in your opinion would be in the best position to send his wife? Think of all the different offices in the government."

She sat thinking, a smile slowly forming on her lips. "Why, the treasurer's wife, of course."

"Yes, yes, that's it!" screamed Raquel, laughing.

"Wait a minute. Don't you think the government already knows about their own orphanages?"

"No, they all wear horse's blinders. In my opinion they ignore suffering, hoping someone else will do the work." Raquel jumped a little in her seat. "Maybe we should contact Helen Perez first."

"I really feel funny about bothering her."

"Why, because of Eric?"

"Yes, maybe she will think I'm running after him."

"You're not at all. When we go to see her, we'll not say a word about Eric. She'll know you don't have a special feeling for her son." Raquel gave her a secretive smile. "Won't she?"

"I don't," replied Jillian, a little too emphatically. "How can we set up an appointment with her?"

"Next time I'm at my family's home in Quito I'll phone her from there."

When they arrived in Pachuca, Jillian left Raquel off at the Martinez home and drove to the Ortega's driveway to leave the pickup. She pulled the gate closed, thinking she would come back later and check to see if the gates were locked.

With heavy thoughts, she ate dinner, gathered materials for classes the next day and as dusk settled, she stood against the banister overlooking the plaza. Several Indians scurried home, anxious to arrive before dark and the chill of night. The evening hour meant it was time for a light meal and fellowship with their families. The setting sun brought a blanket of cold mountain air that settled over the village. The lack of heat in their homes drove the villagers, fully dressed to bed early. All beds were shared for added warmth.

In the thickening darkness the plaza soon cleared of villagers and Jillian automatically turned her attention toward Marta's orphanage, hungry for any sign of life or light shining from the few windows exposed to her view. As always, the sight struck a poignant chord in her heart. She sighed deeply and leaned against a wooden post, her eyes sweeping the plaza. The few stores and residents surrounding the park had their doors opened to the night, the dim interior lights casting pale yellow pools on the sidewalk. Suddenly she was alert. Across the park, a dark swift shadow passed the open door of a house, moving furtively in an obvious effort to hide. There was something familiar about the way the shadow maneuvered. A red flag went up in her mind. Even from this distance, she sensed the sly stealth, the wily movements of Lucia. Hidden in the shadows of her balcony, Jillian was glad that she had closed her bedroom door behind her. She watched the dark figure move across the street to the store entrance. It was Lucia.

Jillian cautiously walked downstairs, closed the kitchen door against any light that might drift onto the street and carefully opened her front door. She was sure she knew where Lucia was headed and she wanted to join her. Jillian hurried to the end of the block and crossed to the dark side of the street. Past the telephone office she slowed almost to a halt. Now she was in pitch darkness and had to wait a moment for her vision to adjust.

The Ortega's house was dark, the family already having retired for the night. She sensed rather than saw Lucia and she leaned against a mud wall to wait, her heart thumping in anticipation. Lucia passed the store entrance.

"Lucia," she called. "Did you find what you were looking for?"

The woman gasped in shock, stopped abruptly and turned.

Chapter 15

"Buenas noches, Lucia. I was surprised to see you in the plaza after dark."

"Where did you come from?"

"Where have you been?"

The question gave Lucia time to recover her composure. "I've been to Quito and just returned if it's any of your business."

"Quito? Are you driving now? The last bus arrived an hour ago."

"I don't know why I should tell you what bus I came on, however if you must know, I caught a truck going to the jungle. I just walked down from the road south of here."

"You came from Quito without your purse or packages?" Jillian's voice peaked in a mocking, incredulous tone.

"I don't know why I'm standing here talking to you. I've got to get home." She started to walk away.

"Lucia," Jillian shouted after her. "Stay away from my pickup. If anything happens to me because of its malfunctioning, everyone in Pachuca will know it was you who messed with it. More than one person knows what you did to the brakes last night."

Lucia stumbled slightly and yelled over her shoulder. "I don't know what you're talking about."

"Oh, yes you do," she called back as the woman slipped into the shadows of the park. Returning home, she ignored the inquisitive looks on the faces of her neighbors, several of whom had gathered in the doorways of their homes.

Chapter 16

On occasion and for various reasons daily classes were canceled in Pachuca's public schools. One of Marta's strongest arguments to keep her private school open was her vow that for no reason would its doors close during the week. She ranted that the substandard intellectual level of the average villager was attributed to the many days classes were dismissed for everything from fiestas to dances to clean-up day and other sundry excuses that could be conjured up in the little luncheon room behind the school buildings. Jillian could see Marta's point. Poor wages and dilapidated buildings fostered a lethargic attitude among the teachers who in turn passed it on to the children, most of whom lived in squalid conditions and suffered from poor nutrition.

It was on one such vacation day from school that Jillian decided to drive beyond the boundaries of the school district and visit two small neighborhoods call Moya and Santa Fe, named after the haciendas which employed the inhabitants. She remembered clearly on her first visit to Pachuca years before when she peered from Marta's guesthouse window on a bright and sunny morning at the high mountains behind Pachuca. The tiny huts scattered up the heights had captured her imagination. Who lived up there? How did the people manage to survive? Each day when the sun began its descent to the west, the soft golden rays enhanced the view of small hovels and the patchwork of corn and potato fields. Part of the answers to those questions had been answered with the trip she and Raquel had made

Chapter 16

to help deliver the young mother's baby. Both mother and baby had died from lack of speedy medical help and the reluctance to move the patient from home.

Now she had cornered a patron at Gladys Baca's establishment and asked directions to the haciendas. The lad, panting under the burden of a sack of potatoes, dropped the bag to the floor and pointed eastward with his chin in a head jerking motion. Gladys finished helping a customer and assisted in giving directions until Jillian felt confident she would not get lost.

The morning smelled clean and fresh, a slight breeze stirring up delicious tangy odors of grass, fruit trees, kindling fires and baking bread. With a light heart, she packed a lunch and a large bag of prepared crafts, then drove past the northern end of the Hacienda Hermosa and found the small road which led up the steep incline.

Many times she had voiced a desire to Marta that the two of them should visit the mountainous back country of this area, but Marta had discouraged it, informing her that with so few people in the region it would hardly be worth the time and trouble to find them. No one was able to read or write and any type of teaching would be frowned on. It would be fruitless to try and teach them a standard of cleanliness for the sake of their health if they lived in mud huts with no indoor plumbing and were forced to use the ditch water for every bodily function and then use the same water for laundering, cooking and bathing. Who knew how many harmful bacteria were rushing downstream from communities upstream only to be picked up by those living below. Marta proclaimed that since every available hand was needed to work the land, no matter how young, there was no time for these youngsters to enjoy the folly of education. Despite the lack of encouragement, Jillian wanted to see for herself. She had considered taking a small quantity of aspirin, knowing that medicine always drew a crowd, but instead she decided this would be more of a scouting expedition. Her prime goal was to determine if it would be worthwhile to have classes during the three-month summer break.

Within a half hour she arrived at the first hut. Parking the truck, she called out a greeting. Minutes later, she had made her first friend in Moya and was surprised at the reception. Word of her work with the children throughout the school districts had preceded her. When she explained to the parents that she wanted to give classes during the summer, their enthusiasm was overwhelming. They led her to areas where dozens of children lived. None of the negative stories she had been told were true. These people had an eagerness to learn. Santa Fe proved to be the same. If she returned in the summer, the villagers promised there would be no lack of children to teach and no less enthusiasm.

Overjoyed, she descended the mountain and stopped under the shade of a eucalyptus tree to eat her lunch. She contemplated her good fortune, nearly missed had she listened to her peers. Her thoughts turned to the afternoon. She was expecting several high school students to attend an English class in her home and now would be her last chance for relaxation that day. Taking time to reflect upon how circumstances seemingly beyond her control had given her the opportunity to live out her life in Pachuca. Outside of the fact she still did not have Andy and Ryan with her, life was progressing quite well. The community of Pachuca had accepted her. She felt she was making a difference among the children of each district. Perhaps what she was teaching would never amount to much, but it was with some hope that a few of them would catch a vision of life beyond the limited boundaries in which their circumstances had confined them. She had greater hope for the high school students, the fortunate few who would not have to go to work until they graduated, for their families understood the need for education. Now they would have an opportunity to learn English.

Raquel's entrance into her life had made such a definite difference. In her heart she knew that Raquel would not deceive her as Marta and Lucia had. All in all, everything was going very well. Several weeks had passed since Larry and Heather Parker had made threats against her, threats that if she didn't leave Ecuador, they would see to it she did. Nothing had occurred that would make her feel in jeopardy except her car brakes incident and she suspected that was solely Lucia's idea.

Well, she thought, turning the ignition key, back to Pachuca, she could hardly wait to tell Raquel of the morning. She parked the car in Ortega's driveway and gathered the surplus crafts and lunch. As

Chapter 16

she stepped onto the road, she heard someone in a loud whisper call her name.

"Señorita, over here," hissed the voice.

Jillian eyes searched the dark interior of the small store that occupied the first floor of a mud house. Gladys stepped into view, beckoning her.

Perplexed, she hastened to her. "Hola, Gladys, what's wrong?"

"Buenas tardes, señorita. I've been waiting for you. I wanted to tell you that policemen from Quito are in front of your house. They are looking for you."

"Why? What do they want?"

"I'm not sure, but they seem to be unfriendly. They asked my grandmother many questions about you being here in Ecuador illegally."

The comforting memories of the morning fled as she listened.

Gladys continued, "My mother returned while the police were here and she and my grandmother assured them that you were here legally."

"Gracias, Gladys." Jillian's heart beat faster, anticipating a confrontation. "I have my papers at home. All I need to do is show them my visa."

"Oh, señorita, don't hand them your visa. Keep it in your hands. If they take it, you may never get it back and if you do, they may charge you much money for it."

"I'll do what you say. Now, I will go ahead. You shouldn't let them see that you have warned me." She patted Gladys' arm in thanks and nodded a greeting to the proprietor of the tiny store who had by this time crept up to hear the conversation. Spotting the unmarked gray van, she stepped from the street into the plaza. It was parked directly across the street from her house and as she drew near the van door opened. Two men descended and approached her. Jillian immediately recognized one as Rigo Estrada, Pachuca's policeman.

"Buenas tardes, señorita." The other man, dressed in plain clothes took out his wallet to display his identification. "May we speak with you a moment?"

"Buenas tardes, señor. Buenas tardes, Rigo. Certainly, please come into my house. She unlocked the front door and led the way into the hallway's cool interior. Motioning them to a mud bench, an extension of the wall, she sat on the end of another bench built on the wall opposite them. "What may I do for you?"

"Señorita, my name is Paulo Robayo. I am here to search your house."

"What? Search my house? Why?"

"I was given orders by my superiors to search your house." He rose and ascended the stairs.

Jillian stared at Rigo. "Can this be true?"

"Si, señorita, he has orders."

"What is he looking for?" Jillian rose.

"Sit down, señorita," said Rigo gently.

She sat and looked at the man sitting across the room from her. He hadn't changed much from the day she had shared a lunch with him and Eric on the saloon's porch. He was a short, chunky, dark skinned man with closely cropped black hair and alert black eyes. His bushy mustache covered his mouth. With his hand, he preened and smoothed it as if by habit.

"What is señor Robayo looking for?" she repeated.

Rigo twisted the hairs on his upper lip. "He will explain when he returns."

Frowning darkly upon hearing her closet and dresser drawers being opened, she thought about her visa and was thankful she had locked her purse away in the kitchen cabinet.

A bus braked at the end of the block and in a few minutes, sounds of low murmuring gathered outside her door. "My English class," she explained. "I forgot I have a class in just a few minutes." She looked at her watch and rose quickly to open the door before Rigo could object. Several young people, some townspeople, Gladys and her mother and grandmother were crowded around the entrance. Rigo rose too late to bar their entry and the crowd spilled inside, surrounding him. Gladys' grandmother faced him squarely.

"What are you doing in here, Rigo?"

At that moment, señor Robayo descended and stopped to face the crowd announcing, "I have orders to search the señorita's house."

"What are you looking for?" The old woman faced him angrily.

Chapter 16

"A complaint was filed with our immigration office that señorita Jill is a troublemaker. We were told the señorita had several men living in her house and I was sent to see if their clothes were in her bedroom. With this proof we could take her visa."

"Men living in this house?" exclaimed one of the students. "We are here several times a week and we've never seen a man here."

Gladys stomped over to Rigo. "You know that the señorita leads a very clean life. When have you known of a man living here in her house?"

"Señora, I was asked to accompany señor Robayo. I have done this."

Interrupting, Paulo Robayo said, "The complaint also said that you are taking money from the people, that you charge for your classes and for all the favors you perform. According to our records, señorita, you do not have a visa that allows you to work in our country for payment."

"I have never taken one sucre from these people. You can ask any of them."

The officer observed them nodding in agreement.

"Who filed this complaint?" Jillian was certain it was Marta or the Parkers.

He reached in a pocket and unfolded a long, legal paper. "It says an Alicia Abuelo entered the complaint."

"Abuelo?" chorused Gladys and Jillian. "Who is Alicia Abuelo?"

"What is this?" With a thrust, Raquel pushed her way into the hall. "Someone told me to come in a hurry. What's happening, Jill?"

"Oh, Raqui, I'm so glad to see you. A policeman, señor Robayo is here because someone complained that I have men living in my house and someone name Alicia Abuelo complained that I'm taking money from the people for the classes I give."

Raquel turned to the people standing in the hallway. "Everything is going to be all right. Go home and I will speak with the policeman." She motioned to the high school students. "Go upstairs to the workroom and Jill will be with you in a few minutes."

Three boys and four girls quietly climbed the steps and Jillian could hear them settle in the workroom. She then turned back to coldly face señor Robayo. "Now you must permit me to go to my class."

"Señorita, I can't do that until I see your papers."

She looked at Raquel and then at Rigo. When they offered no counsel, the four went into the kitchen and Jillian unlocked the kitchen cabinet's bottom drawer and withdrew a folder. When the policeman reached out to take the folder, Raquel stepped in. "You may look at the passport, but you can't take it. Jill has done nothing wrong. I can tell you right now who filed that false report. It is a small group of people who are jealous of the success Jill has had in this community. They want her to return to the United States, but as you can already see, the people of Pachuca want her to stay. The complaint is completely false."

Jillian saw señor Robayo relax and he glanced at the passport held in her hand. "Gracias, señorita, I'll return to Quito and tell them what I have seen. I think you should be careful, however because someone in Ecuador doesn't want you living here." He turned to Rigo. "I'll leave you now. Thank you for your help." He shook hands with Raquel, Jillian and Rigo and left.

"Raqui, who is Alicia Abuelo?"

"Think about it. Abuelo. Nieto. Alicia. Olivia."

Her eyes opened wide as she pondered out loud in shock. "Abuelo is grandmother is English. Nieto is grandson. Alicia is a first name. Olivia sounds a lot like Alicia. Raqui, do you think Olivia Nieto filed that report?"

"No. Olivia isn't intelligent enough to think of a plan like this, but she may have been questioned by the Parkers and Marta about your actions. I'm sure Olivia didn't file the complaint. Marta and the Parkers filed it with a false name."

Rigo's eyes took on an intense interest when Raquel mentioned Marta's name. "Señorita Jill, is it possible that I speak with you before I leave."

"The young people are waiting for me."

"I can get them started on a project." Raquel took one step toward the stairs. "What were you going to do today?"

"I was going to have them write a letter in English."

Raquel was up the stairs before Jillian could say anything else. She shrugged and turned to Rigo.

Chapter 16

"Please sit down." He returned to the bench and waited for her to sit. His hand smoothed his mustache.

"Rigo, I can't take time to speak with you now. I must attend the class upstairs."

He frowned a little and then nodded. "All right. I'll come back to see you after the class. In about an hour?"

With a hesitation, she nodded. "Yes, in about an hour."

Hiding a heavy spirit, she proceeded with the English class, assuring the young students the whole incident was a misunderstanding. When the students bent over their papers in deep concentration, Raquel motioned Jillian to meet her in the adjacent bedroom.

"I want to ask you a question. How well do you know Olivia?"

"Not at all. I've greeted her a few times but I don't think she likes me very much."

Raquel rested a finger on her cheek. "Of course I know her better than you do because I worked with her for a year, but she was not an easy person to like. After trying to build a good relationship with her, I finally had to give up because she seems to prefer the company of men and easily discarded any offer of friendship. She was very upset because the government sent a female doctor to Pachuca."

"Why would she say that I'm living with a man? Her house is next door. Can't she see who comes and goes from here?

"I did remember something when I was sitting in class."

"What?"

"Remember when Philip came to visit me one evening? He had just accompanied you to Gladys Baca's home next door. I think you were taking her some foot medicine."

"Yes."

"Philip told me the two of you stopped to talk with Olivia and her papa that night."

"Yes," replied Jillian thoughtfully.

"Don't you see? She saw you with Philip. Before that she has seen Eric visiting you. She probably reported that to Marta."

"And Lucia saw Eric on my balcony."

"I think Olivia is jealous you have male friends."

"I haven't seen Eric in months and Philip only comes once in a while. That certainly doesn't mean I live with them. No, there's more to this, but you're right. Olivia didn't file that report, but I'm sure she told Marta about Philip and Eric. This happened too soon after Larry and Heather Parker threatened me. I think Olivia is close to Marta, reporting everything that's going on in my house. They decided to use that silly name, Alicia Abuelo."

"Señorita Jill, did I spell this word right?" Adriana poked her head into the bedroom.

"I'll be right there." To Raquel, she lowered her voice. "We've got to get back to the class. Rigo is coming in a few minutes to speak with me. Can you stay?"

"Even if you hadn't asked, I would have stayed."

Chapter 17

Rigo refused a cup of tea, seating himself on the mud bench in the hall. "Please leave the door open, señorita, in case someone needs me for police business. I would like them to know I'm here."

Pulling the door open wide, she wondered whether Rigo, in light of the rumor about her really desired the protection of public view. She seated herself beside Raquel on a bench along the opposite wall. "What was it you wanted to talk to me about, Rigo?"

He scratched at his mustache. "I've known about the filed report for several days so I asked the government to wait until I could investigate on my own. The clerk who took the report remembers the applicant as a foreigner, a gringa."

Jillian swung her head around to Raquel and then back to Rigo. "A gringa?"

"Yes, she was a foreigner and the clerk remembers she spoke fluent Spanish."

"Raquel and I believe Marta Brewer filed the report using a fictitious name."

"I also believe it was the señorita or one of her friends," said Rigo. "Señorita Jill, for many years I have been trying to find out what Marta Brewer is doing other than delivering babies in her clinic. You must remember the afternoon you and I had lunch across the street in the saloon."

"I remember the afternoon you, Eric Perez and I had lunch on the porch of the saloon."

He nodded at the correction and continued. "If you recall, I asked if you knew whether the nurse had taken babies born to mothers in her maternity clinic. I ask you now, is Marta Brewer sending children to the United States for adoption?"

"I'm not sure," replied Jillian.

A spark of anger flickered in his eyes. "You lived with the American for several years and you don't know what is going on in her house?"

"I'm not sure, señor."

Rigo leaned forward, placing the palms of his hands on his knees. "Señorita, why are you living in Pachuca?"

"Why?" She replied, perplexed. "I work in the public schools."

He chuckled contemptuously. "Why should you, an American, come to a backward, poverty-stricken village to live when you could be in the United States? No, there must be more to it."

"Rigo," Raquel interjected. "If you must know, I doubted Jill's motives when I first met her. Sometimes I still wonder why she stays, but I believe her motives are pure."

He looked skeptical.

"This may be very hard to for you to understand, but I love Ecuador. I love Pachuca. I consider it a privilege to live here."

"Just what do you do everyday?"

"Every morning except Thursday I have classes in schools throughout the district. On Monday and Wednesday afternoons I drive to Palugo and Tababela for classes. Tuesday, Friday and Saturday afternoons I have classes in my house and classes in Oyambarrillo on Tuesday and Sunday mornings."

"Now, Rigo," said Raquel. "If you believe these false reports, I must tell you that I have joined her in some of these classes, have spent time with her in the evenings and know her quite well. She has begun to plan classes for children in the Moya and Santa Fe suburbs during the summer months. Don't you remember when the district superintendent of schools gave Jill a letter of thanks during a ceremony last month?"

"All right. If your motives are pure, then why don't you tell me the truth about what was going on in Marta Brewer's clinic when you lived there?"

Chapter 17

"Because I really don't know everything."

"Everything?"

"I'll tell you what I know," she relented.

His countenance softened as he stroked his mustache in anticipation.

"Marta is very secretive. I know very little about her work." Her mind drifted back to the years she lived at the orphanage. "I remember only a few cases that were suspicious. I happened to be in the clinic one day when a mother delivered a baby and I overheard Marta asking the mother to leave the baby with her. The mother refused but two hours later, at dinner Marta told a different story. She claimed the mother had offered her the baby."

Rigo's eyes lit with interest. "The baby is with Marta right now?"

Shaking her head, she said, "No, the baby disappeared."

"What do you mean, disappeared?"

Raquel frowned. "The baby disappeared from the clinic? What happened to it?"

"I don't know, Raqui. I guess Marta took it to Quito. She was gone all the next day."

"Where in Quito did she take it?" asked Rigo.

"I don't know. As I said, Marta was very secretive and became upset when I asked questions."

"Do you recall the time the parents of a newborn baby came to me and said Marta had stolen their baby?" asked Rigo. "I went with them to the clinic and asked the Indian Lucia, where she was keeping the baby. She said the infant had died. Do you remember the incident?"

"Yes," admitted Jillian softly. "The baby is alive and well and living with Marta."

Raquel stared at Jillian. "You knew this?"

"Raqui, what could I do?"

"Señorita, I would have listened to you. I nearly begged you to tell me what was going on the day we had lunch in the plaza."

"I was afraid." Jillian began to cry.

"Afraid of what?" asked Raquel.

"I was afraid if the police came to Marta's house to investigate that she would make me leave my children," sniffed Jillian, searching for a tissue and then looked accusingly at Rigo. "But you came anyway and because of that I lost my children."

"I did not go to Marta Brewer's house because of my suspicions. I accompanied the man from the health department who was ordered to shut down the outpatient clinic. It had nothing to do with the disappearing babies."

She continued to glower at him. "Well, I was unable to convince Marta of that. She thought it was because I had talked with you and exposed her."

Rigo, unruffled by Jillian's glare, continued. "Is there anything else you want to tell me about the nurse?"

"Rigo, you have to believe me when I say, she never talked to me about anything regarding her administration."

"What about mistreatment to the children living with her now?" He probed.

"Marta is very strict, but you must admit that the children live in better conditions than some of the children in this village. I don't know what else I can tell you." Suddenly she straightened, sitting upright. "Do you think if the government closes down the orphanage that I could have my two boys, Ryan and Andy, come here to live with me?"

"Not with the evidence you have given me here today, señorita." Rigo stood and walked to the open door. "I was hoping you could give me something that I could present to the government police. Hast mañana, señoritas." He turned with a wave and disappeared from view.

"Didn't you mention one time that Marta's papers might not be in order?" Raquel shut the door.

"That's not evidence and I'm not going to tell him something like that until I know, if the orphanage is closed down, the children won't be sent to a place like Conocoto."

Chapter 18

On the next visit to see her family in Quito, Raquel placed a telephone call to Helen Perez as she had promised. Señora Perez, delighted to hear from her, extended an invitation for Raquel and Jillian to have tea at her home in Quito. On the prearranged day, the girls set off from Pachuca late in the afternoon, following one of Jillian's classes.

"How has your truck been running lately? Anymore troubles?"

So far Jillian had refrained from mentioning to Raquel her late evening encounter with Lucia because she didn't want her friend to bring up the subject of a move away from Pachuca. Sensing the only reason Lucia had dared to appear in the plaza was for the purpose of seeing if the car had been involved in an accident, she believed she had given Lucia enough of a surprise to stave off any future attempts to bring her harm. What Lucia had done to the pickup could never be proven; right now it was all speculation. On the morning following the brake failure she had spoken with señora Ortega about making sure the gates were secured each evening. The woman declared the gates were always locked at night, so Jillian let the matter drop, though now she carefully checked the pickup's brakes before driving.

"Not at all. Everything is fine," she replied with a note of finality.

She felt Raquel studying her, but the doctor remained silent. Today Lucia and car problems were far from her mind. She was concerned that the meeting with Helen would not be as friendly as their visit in Tulcachi. Every time she thought back to that day and the lovely lunch they had, she remembered how she and Eric had permanently parted that same evening after a heated argument. Recalling Helen extending an invitation to her that day for a future luncheon date was an ache she could not dismiss. The very fact that she had not heard one word from Helen since then indicated there might be strained feelings on the part of the older woman. Now that she had an opportunity to see her again, she dreaded this meeting. Of course she had to put all these thoughts aside. Her feelings were small issues compared to the main purpose of visiting Helen and asking if she would become a liaison between the governmental departments and the Conocoto orphanage. That Eric might also be home produced mixed feelings in Jillian. Thoughts tumbled through her mind. Should I speak with him and ask his forgiveness for my behavior our last evening together? What if he rejects me?

They arrived at the beautiful home build into one of the slopes in the Batan district. Jillian tried to place Eric, in his high topped boots, ranch clothes and hat climbing the front flight of steps and walking through the fine oak door. Somehow she couldn't picture him in this setting. They rang and a young maid opened the door, ushering them inside. She took their wraps and led them into the living room.

Raquel walked directly across the grand room toward Helen, who had risen slowly from the sofa. Jillian smiling shyly, followed.

"Jill, I'm so glad to see you again," said Helen, stepping forward to take her hand in hers. Leaning forward, she kissed the girl's cheek.

At once Jillian relaxed. Helen was as lovely now as she had been at the hacienda. She wore a simple white linen dress with a pale blue belt at the waist, accented with ice blue topaz earrings and a delicate companion broach that reflected the loveliness of her clear blue eyes. She suddenly felt ill-clad in her white cotton blouse, blue skirt and matching cotton vest. Raquel had thought to wear pink, her best color that seemed to bring out the flush in her cheeks, giving her a healthy, wholesome look.

"Please be seated. Jill, if you'll agree for Raquel's sake, we'll speak in Spanish." Helen sank back onto the white sofa, slipping a mint green pillow behind her back for support.

Jillian and Raquel sat together under the huge windows on a matching white loveseat that gave Jillian a chance to look at the upper

Chapter 18

levels. Her mouth fell open a little as she looked up at three floors above her, to the broad beamed ceiling. On each level, a gleaming wood banister faced the living room. Opposite the balconies and behind her, tall windows filled the side of the house, divided horizontally by two feet of expensive, perfectly laid brick painted white. Mint green brocade drapes and sheer white curtains hung from numerous feet above. Behind Helen, covering most of the living room wall was a marble fireplace, where a fire burned, crackling gently on the grate. The second floor banister stood in front of what appeared to be a dining room. A woman, preparing a tray, bustled around a table and back and forth between cabinets and a door in the corner. Above that and out of view was perhaps a floor of bedrooms.

Helen saw her look and promised a tour before they left. She explained that the foundation and first floor of the house was actually built into the hill behind the house. On the second floor, behind the kitchen a section of the mountain of earth had been excavated far enough back that they were able to plant a garden, have a medium sized lawn and build an apartment for Isabel.

The woman Jillian had seen in the dining room descended a staircase carrying the tray in her hands. She greeted the guests politely and placed it on a glass coffee table before the hostess. Helen looked carefully at the prepared food and then dismissed the maid.

"Jill, how would you like your tea, with sugar or lemon?" She poured the brew and stirred in the sugar at her request. "Raquel?"

As Raquel served Jillian and herself, Helen lifted a dainty towel from a basket full of cut cakes, placing two each on their plates. She handed them to a waiting Raquel. "Jill, beside the end of the sofa you will find two lap trays. You may use them if you would like."

They settled down to eat and sip the tea. Jillian bit into a light yellow cake with fluffy white frosting and sighed deeply. "I have lived in Ecuador so long I had forgotten how good cake can be."

Helen's gentle laughter warmed Jillian's heart. "It is made from a recipe book published in a town high in the Rockies. Raquel, in case you don't remember, the Rocky Mountains are in the United States. The reason it is very difficult to make a tasty cake in the sierras is because no one has a recipe for high altitudes. I hope you like the tea. The last time I was in the States, I brought back several pounds of English breakfast tea. It brews dark and strong. I hope you like it that way."

"It's delicious." Raquel wiped frosting from her chin and took a sip of tea.

They discussed the weather, Jillian's classes and Raquel's progress with her new clinic. Finally the conversation turned to some of Helen's projects, which led to the reason why the girls had come to visit.

"Helen, I couldn't believe how those children must live in Conocoto," said Jillian.

"I feel ashamed to tell you that I was unaware there was an orphanage in Conocoto. Are you sure it's financed by the government?"

"Yes, I'm sure of it," replied Raquel. "I examined several children sick with whooping cough during my doctorate training."

"What is it you think I can do? If it's money you need, I can give some, but it sounds as though it will take more than a few sucres." The woman set her tea cup on the coffee table and leaned back.

"Yes, you're right. It will take a lot of money. We were hoping that you could discuss this with some of your friends," said Raquel, placing her elbow on the tray. "By chance, are some of your acquaintances involved in the government?"

"I met the president's wife at a social function many years ago. I doubt if she would remember me, but I do know someone who has friends in the government. What are you thinking?"

Jillian spoke up. "We thought if people in the government knew about the terrible conditions that these children are living in, maybe they could do something to change it."

"Let me see what I can do," smiled Helen. "My health isn't as good as it used to be. Don't be alarmed. "I'm not ill, I'm just slowing down."

"Are you under the care of a doctor?"

"As I say, I'm not ill, but yes my son Eric sees to it that I have a physical twice a year. When we fly to the United States to visit my son, Jorge, I always have a physical there also. So I'm well cared for. Now, let me see. Do you want more tea?"

This time Jillian served. They talked at length about the orphanage. Because of the difficulty of reaching Raquel or Jillian in Pachuca,

Chapter 18

Helen promised to leave messages at Raquel's family home where she could find them when she visited.

After the maid cleared the dishes, Helen leaned back and looked directly at Jillian. "Have you seen my son, Eric lately?"

Caught off guard, Jillian flushed brightly. "No."

"Sometimes I don't understand him very well," sighed Helen.

"Please don't blame Eric. It's my fault that he's not been back to see me. I acted foolishly the last time I saw him, which was also the last day I saw you."

"Do you mean he hasn't been to see you since then? I thought he had told me he was going to visit you more often."

"I believe he did try, but I wasn't home. That was over a year ago."

"Don't feel you are at fault. It seems I hardly see my son these days. More and more he is involved with his work on the hacienda. Actually, I'm thankful he has so much to do. I don't know what he would have done without the hacienda. He may have mentioned this to you, Jill, but several years ago his fiancée died from a cancerous tumor. He loved her very much and since then he has shown no inclination toward marriage or much interest in another woman. I've told him he cannot live in the past, but no matter, he can't seem to forget her. That's why when I heard Eric had invited you to lunch at the hacienda, I had to meet you. I pretended I was on a leisure excursion and ended up at Tulcachi, but of course he saw right through me. I don't complain that he doesn't come home as often as I wish he would." Helen leaned her elegant head to one side and closed her eyes momentarily. "It's strange but even as I say that, I realize that he's been changing. I noticed several weeks ago that he seemed more relaxed, more content. I think it has something to do with a young couple he hired recently to share in the hacienda work. They had been living on the coast of Ecuador but they seem to have adjusted quite well to the sierras. Why, the other day he mentioned that it's almost as if he had found a son and daughter. I was quite surprised as he finds it difficult to commit himself to anyone."

"I think I know the couple you are speaking of," Raquel nodded. "They aren't from the coast originally but were raised in Pachuca."

"Who do you mean? Do I know them?" Jillian looked at her friend, puzzled.

'You know who they are, Jill," Raquel replied and looked at Helen. "I think you are speaking of Elena and Carlos. If so, Elena is the sister of the family I'm living with in Pachuca. Carlos has been seen several times at Hacienda Tulcachi as Elena's family passes by to reach their property further up the mountain."

"Elena and Carlos? Elena Martinez?" Jillian asked.

"Yes, but her name isn't Martinez now."

"It's Tapia," said Helen. "Raquel, I don't understand. I thought they had moved from the coast. Now you say they lived in Pachuca instead."

"I don't know the whole story because Elena had already married and moved away when I started practicing medicine in Pachuca. As you know, Helen, I'm a Christian as you are. I had met Opal, Elena's sister-in-law several years ago at an evangelical high school we both attended for a short time in Colombia. When I discovered she was from Ecuador, we soon became good friends. She met her husband, Geoff a few years later at a church function in Quito. After they were married, I was invited to their home a few times. Geoff's parents died and I moved in. Carlos and Elena had no choice but to run away to be married because Geoff's older brother, Rolando was opposed to their marriage. Geoff is so loyal to Rolando that he's been rather quiet on the subject. The first time I met Rolando, however, I found him to be one of the rudest, most egotistical men on earth. I can understand why Elena and Carlos ran away." She blushed. "Please forgive the way I'm speaking. I have to be fair and say that when I last saw Rolando, he seemed to be a little different."

"Different?" asked Jillian, fully absorbed.

"Yes, he wasn't as rude. I don't know." Suddenly she looked at Helen. I'm sorry. I feel I'm talking too much. You were speaking about Eric."

Helen laughed. "I'm enjoying this very much. It's been a long time since I had young women in my home and I find it refreshing."

"It's been very nice for us also," said Jillian looking at her watch. "Now I'm afraid that we will have to be on our way. It will be dark in an hour and it's best if we're back in Pachuca before the sun sets."

Chapter 18

"Do you mind if I use your telephone?" Raquel asked Helen. "I want to ask my father if he's been able to purchase the lumber we need to continue construction on my clinic."

"Of course. You will find the telephone past the stairway in the hall."

When Raquel left, Jillian, her heart beating painfully, sat back to face Helen. "I have to admit I was hoping Eric would be here today. I owe him an apology."

"I don't know what happened between you two, but whatever it was, it hurt him very much."

"We argued the night he took my cargo to Pachuca."

"He didn't mention that to me and of course I haven't asked. It's not my business but I'm sure that's not what hurt him. Something happened since then. The night he went to visit with you a few months after our lunch at Tulcachi, something happened that hurt him."

Jillian screwed up her face thoughtfully. "What could have happened?"

Helen stood as she saw Raquel approaching. "I don't know, dear. Maybe I can talk to him. Since it's so late, why don't we postpone the tour of my house? It will be a good excuse for the two of you to return." With feeling, she hugged Jillian and then turned to Raquel, hugging her also. They parted with a promise that Helen would follow up on their concerns for the government orphanage.

Chatting away as Jillian drove toward the exit to Pachuca, she noticed Raquel's listlessness and lack of interest in the conversation. "Why are you so quiet? Are you not feeling well?"

"No, I'm feeling all right. It's the conversation I had with my mother. I had a message waiting for me to give to Geoff when I return home to Pachuca."

"What message?"

"Geoff's cousin Ricardo called Pachuca last night but couldn't get through, so he called my parent's home knowing that I would take it to Geoff."

"What was the message?"

"Ricardo said he tried for two days to contact Rolando in the hotel room where he has been staying and when there was no answer he started searching for him. He found him in a bar they both frequent.

Rolando was too drunk to find his own way back to the hotel, so Ricardo helped him and put him to bed. Ricardo left the address so Geoff could find him and bring him back to Pachuca. I blame myself for the worry Geoff has suffered." Tears glistened in her eyes.

"Why would you feel responsible? Everyone in Pachuca knows about Rolando's drinking problem."

"The night he returned from the jungle after being away for a year, he seemed different somehow, less bitter and more gentle. Remember when I told you that he proclaimed his love for me." She wiped a wet eye with her little finger. "He caught me so by surprise I nearly laughed in his face because my last image of him was the bitter, angry man I had seen the night of his father's death."

"My friend, you can't be at fault for that. He should have expected you to react that way. I would have done the same thing, I'm sure. You can't possibly be sorry you didn't accept his offer of love."

"Of course not," she replied a little too loudly. "But I should have been able to offer him some spiritual help."

"I'm sure there will be other chances."

"Yes, perhaps there will. Jill! Stop the truck!"

"What?" Jillian jerked her head around, alert for danger.

"I said, stop the truck! I want to get out."

The vehicle slowed. "Raqui, we're at the turnoff to Pachuca. What are you going to do here?"

"I'm going to catch a taxi and spend the night at my home in Quito. Tomorrow I'm going to visit Rolando."

Jillian's mouth hung slack from surprise and she automatically pulled over to the curb, allowing a honking truck to pass them. "You're going to visit Rolando in his hotel room?"

"Don't make it sound so unwholesome. I want to make amends."

"What about Geoff? Don't you think you should discuss this with him first?"

"Not until I apologize to Rolando for my unfriendliness the last time I saw him."

Studying her friend for a moment, she asked, "Are you sure that's the reason or might you be too fond of him? Don't get mixed up with Rolando because he will only bring you heartache."

"Tomorrow night I'll return to Pachuca with him, I hope."

Chapter 18

"I'll go with you. I can bring the two of you back in the pickup. In fact, I'll go with you to see Rolando."

"No, Jill. I need to do this myself. I'll return to Pachuca tomorrow." She lifted her eyebrows and smiled in an attempt to dispel Jillian's doubts. "Perhaps I'll be able to do some telephoning from my home about the materials needed for the clinic."

"You're in love with Rolando, aren't you?"

"Love?" Raquel laughed heartily. "Love? Jill, that's foolish. How can I love someone I've only seen a few times? The first few times he was an annoyance and the last time he was apologetic and gentle. Of course that makes me wonder about him, but love? How can I love him?"

"Because you're a doctor and you are compassionate. Raqui, by now you ought to be able to tell the difference between love and sympathy."

Anger flashed and died quickly in Raquel's eyes. "Don't worry," she said breaking into a winsome smile. "I can keep the two emotions separated. I'll be careful."

Reluctantly, Jillian said good-bye and waited while her friend flagged down a taxi. With a final grin and wave, Raquel departed for town.

Chapter 19

For Rolando, months passed in a blur of stolen purses and wallets to pay for his ever increasing need for liquor. During the day he slept off his drunkenness in a small hotel room on the south side of Quito. Late one afternoon he struggled awake, feeling the need for another drink. It was then that he realized someone was in his room. A blurry form sat on the end of his bed, and passing his hand over his eyes, he recognized Raquel. Certain he was dreaming, he closed his eyes and opened them again, expecting the illusion to be gone, but she was still there. "Raquel, is that you?"

"Yes."

Grabbing the blanket to his waist, he looked around at the cluttered, filthy room and was embarrassed. "What are you doing here?"

"I had to see you. You can't imagine what I've gone through since the last time we talked."

"How did you find me?"

"Your cousin Ricardo found you in a saloon and escorted you to this hotel room. Don't you remember?"

"No," he mumbled. "Why would you want to come here? The room is a mess. I'm a mess."

"I came because I can't forget you. I feel I did you an injustice that night in Pachuca."

"You had every right. Look at what you would have been getting into if we had begun a relationship."

"I feel responsible."

Chapter 19

"Everything that has happened to me, I have asked for."

"How can I help you now?" she pleaded.

"There's no help for me. If you weren't here, I'd already be on my way to the saloon. In fact, I need a drink so badly I can hardly think of anything else."

She sat at a loss for words.

"Raqui, I've always had a weakness for liquor. I'm following in the footsteps of half the population of Pachuca. Please don't blame yourself. My real problems started when I allowed hatred and bitterness toward a good friend to ruin my life. I thought I was destroying him, but to my surprise, my hatred had not affected him at all. I ruined myself. While my sister and her husband enjoy their life in Playas, I am an alcoholic living a life in hell. There's no hope for me."

"I will never believe that. There is always hope, but I don't understand what you mean by your sister being in Playas. Don't you know that they live here in the sierras, in Tulcachi? Your aunt and uncle have seen Carlos several times as they travel to their property in the mountains."

"Tulcachi? How can that be?" His mind whirled with the news. "I saw them in Playas."

"When were you in Playas?"

He sighed deeply and shook his head. "There's so much you don't know about me, Raqui. You were right to say it would be a terrible mistake to become involved with me."

She stood and glowered down at him. "Never will I believe there is no way for you to change. It's just as I told you before. You are going to have to want change and I believe God can help you."

"God?" He laughed cynically. "God wants nothing to do with me."

"I'll never believe that either. Will you come home with me?"

"Home? I can't return home."

"Yes you can. We all want you there."

"There's so much you don't know," he mumbled and looking up at her, he smiled. "You go on to Pachuca. Let me spend some time thinking."

"Are you going out to drink? Because if you are, I'll stay with you."

"No, don't stay. I don't know right now what I'll do, but I do need to think about something."

She left reluctantly and he sat on the bed late into the night.

Chapter 20

They sat close, leaning against the base of a eucalyptus tree, relaxing in the breeze of the late afternoon. She adjusted her bulk and tried to sit comfortably as Carlos tore a long strand of grass into strips. Out of the clear sky Eric had ordered Carlos to take the afternoon off and after some feeble protests, Carlos had agreed to spend time with his wife. During their first week at Tulcachi they had discovered this special place and claimed it as their own with the toasting of warm colas. So today, without debate, they decided to picnic at their favorite spot, a hearty hike away, behind the main house on a short plateau jutting from the side of a hill. Two trees stood at a slight forward angle as if to peer down on the activities of a productive hacienda. Romantically, Elena imagined the trees were protecting them from intruders, allowing them to pretend for a short time they were the only occupants of the world.

"If only I could make myself a little more comfortable," she groaned, struggling to straighten a thin blanket under her.

"Just two more months and you can get rid of that load," he grinned, patting her thigh. "How about something to eat. I'm starved."

"Starved? You ate a big dinner two hours ago." She stopped to look at him in surprise.

"That was two hours ago and now I'm hungry." Grabbing a small straw basket, he removed a ragged cloth and peered inside, examining the contents. "Mmm. Buttered rolls, cheese, bananas and

Chapter 20

look! A chocolate bar. Eric must have brought candy from Quito. Wonderful. Do you want some now?"

"Maybe a little chocolate, but I'm fat enough."

"I don't want to eat alone."

Quietness settled between them as they munched on the rolls baked that morning by Isabel. Puzzled, Carlos had told Elena it was strange that Eric mentioned an afternoon off the day after she had begged him to spend time with her. Elena insisted she had said nothing to Eric but smiled inwardly remembering her conversation with Isabel. She would thank her later.

High white clouds rolled lazily above them, drifting slowly toward Quito. From their vantage point the city appeared asleep and quiet under the rays of the hot afternoon sun, as if patiently waiting to be cooled by the approaching clouds.

"Look at the airplane circling the valley," Elena pointed.

"It's waiting its turn to land. It seems so long ago we flew into Quito." Brushing the crumbs from his lap, he lay back and put his arms under his head, looking deep into the breaks in the clouds. "It's still hard for me to believe we found a home so quickly. Do you miss Playas at all?"

Her answer was slow in coming. "A little."

"I'm not sure I want to go back to Playas. I've found so much pleasure right here in Tulcachi. I've thought many times we should have come here in the first place instead of running south."

"Oh, I wouldn't trade what we had there. Remember our honeymoon? I'm so glad we had that experience."

"Of course I remember. You're right, we have nice memories but I regret buying land there. We should have saved our money and bought land here. I'm thinking of writing my superiors in the Grand Hotel and have them send all the important papers I have in the box they're keeping for us. This is where our roots are."

"We could sell the land there and buy here, but I have a feeling Eric plans to give our son the hacienda. He didn't really say that, but he hinted. Has he ever said anything to you?"

"There have been little comments. I think he's waiting to see if the baby is a girl or a boy."

"Would you mind if he did give it to him, Carlos?"

"Eric has no heirs and he knows we would take care of the place, but Elena, he's still a rather young man; he'll be living here for years yet, so it's nothing we have to consider today. I'm thinking of taking a few days off and going to Playas. We need to put our piece of land up for sale." He positioned his head to sleep and their talking ceased as they listened to the distant lowing of cattle, the songs of birds and the buzzing of insects. Elena reached over and tousled his hair, content with her life, knowing they were in the right place. As much as she loved Playas and the sea, her place was with her husband here in the mountains of her youth.

His voice broke into her thoughts. "I saw your family today; your aunt and uncle."

Alert, her hand lay motionless on his head. "You did? Where?"

"Going to their property above Tulcachi. I've seen them many times but I didn't want to upset you by mentioning it."

"I haven't seen them once."

"That's because you usually stay inside or at the back of the house."

Her moment of peace having vanished, she shrugged clasping her hands in her lap. "Maybe because I haven't wanted to see them. Do they know we've returned to this area?"

"They've known for several months."

Sadness gripped her. "They don't want to see me because they think I've disgraced the family by marrying you."

"I'm sorry, amor." Before he could control it, a hurt look crossed his face. "Oh, Carlos, I don't mean that I feel disgraced. To me you are the most wonderful, gentle, kind man I have ever known. You are my life, the only reason I want to live."

Reassured, he teased. "What about the baby?"

"To me the baby is you," she said gravely. "I love him because of you."

"Don't you wish sometimes you had stayed in Pachuca instead of running all over the country this way?"

"Never. I would do it again many times. I've never regretted marrying you. Not for a moment. That is the truth, mi esposo."

"I'm glad to hear that because sometimes I worry a little."

Chapter 20

"Well, don't." Despite her bulk, she moved to his side and dropped a kiss on his cheek. "The only thing I really wish is I'd have this baby tomorrow. I feel so huge."

"You look beautiful to me." He gathered her to him, placing his face in her hair. "I love you so much, Elena."

"I love you too."

They slept in each other's arms until the coolness of dusk woke them. Startled, they sat upright, blinking in astonishment. "We must go." He helped her up. "I don't want you to become ill."

"I'm all right."

"We must hurry down the hill while we can still see our way."

Grabbing the blanket and basket, they laughed at her awkwardness as they trotted down the hill, through a large pasture and into the warmth of their home.

Chapter 21

Eric paced the uneven, worn brick floor of the old kitchen, sipping on a cup of hot, ground corn colada.

"Señor Eric, perhaps you should walk up toward the ledge to see if they are still there." Isabel turned from the stove and folded a damp cloth nervously.

Looking at her absently, he pondered the situation. "No, I think we should wait until dark. Perhaps they wanted to watch the dusk approach. I can't believe Carlos would take any chances with Elena." Walking to the table, he put the cup down forcefully. Truthfully he wasn't as much concerned as he was lonely for the two young people. The supper hour had been quiet and uneventful, driving home the reality that he had become extremely attached to his two friends. As he walked past the worried cook to peer out the door, voices in the distance made him freeze. Springing into action, he returned to the table and Isabel turned to her chores as the kitchen door burst open. Elena and Carlos rushed through, stopping in the center of the room, their hair mussed, their clothes dusty and their eyes sparkling. Eric looked up in anger but his heart softened at the sight.

"I'm sorry we're late, Eric. We fell asleep on the ledge and didn't waken until a few minutes ago." Carlos gave him an apologetic look.

Elena hurried to Isabel's side. "We missed supper, didn't we? Oh, I hope you didn't worry about us."

Eric gave Isabel a warning look and smiled at Elena. "We did wonder where you were, but certainly it wasn't a worry."

Chapter 21

"Would you care for your supper, children?" Isabel bustled past Eric to take the basket and blanket from Carlos.

"Not too much for me, thank you. We ate the rest of the rolls on the way home." Carlos smiled at Elena.

"Perhaps we'll have some hot colada and cheese, thank you," replied Elena, as she peered into Eric's cup. "But please go to bed, Isabel." She put her hand on the cook's arm. "I'll serve Carlos and myself."

"All right," Isabel nodded, putting two cups on the table. "Now that you're home, I might as well. Please excuse me and have a good night."

"Good night," they chorused as Elena dipped colada into the cups from a pan. She found the plate of cheese under a cloth in the cupboard. They washed in a basin and then joined Eric at the table. For an hour the three discussed the past events of the day and plans for tomorrow.

Carlos finished his second cup of colada and put his hands on the table. He was concerned with a neglected ridge east of the main buildings that had been ignored due to the steep slope. "I know we can use the new tractor in that area and eventually harvest many hundred kilos of corn, Eric."

"I won't do it, Carlos because it's too dangerous. What would happen if the tractor lost its balance?"

"It won't. I rode my horse up there two days ago and walked the length and width of it. We're losing money by not planting there. There's plenty of room. We can let Raul drive the tractor. He's always careful and if we measure off his boundaries, I'm sure nothing will happen. I also ran my horse down the slope and found it's really not that steep."

Thinking a few moments, Eric scratched his head lazily. "I agree we have been wasting valuable land but I won't let Raul use the tractor. We'll use men with picks to loosen the earth."

"It's time to plant corn now, but if we take men from the potato fields or from tending cattle, the crops and cattle will suffer. The tractor can do in one hour what five men can do in three days. Please. Let me be responsible for Raul."

Throwing up in hands in resignation, Eric said. "All right, Carlos. I want you to know that I don't like the idea, but you're right about wasting time and land. There's a strong market for corn in Quito this year, so we can use the extra yield. I'll go out with you tomorrow and talk things over with Raul myself. If we all agree about his safety, we'll go ahead."

They sat for another hour discussing cows, cheese and Elena's upcoming prenatal checkup until weariness drove them to their beds.

Chapter 22

Carlos was gone by the time the sun appeared over the mountains the next morning. This was the time of day she hated. When he left her, it was as if he took a part of her with him. She comforted herself with the thought that it was only a few hours until they would spend the siesta and evening hours together. Without him, she felt alone and cold until she grew accustomed to the empty place by her side and then she would stretch and sleep for another hour.

Each day she grew more tired and required more rest. After a nice breakfast she sat on the bench behind the house knitting and talking with Isabel. Feeling out of place with the women who worked on the front porch, she loved the cook and spent hours with her while the men were away.

A week later, Elena was disappointed when news was sent that Eric and Carlos could not return for lunch due to a breakdown on one of the farm trucks. The day seemed unusually long and she was not feeling well. After complaining of being overly warm, Isabel suggested Elena lie down after lunch for a nap. She guided the girl to her room, helped her into bed and bent to feel her flushed face.

"I think you may have a fever. Try to sleep and see if it will pass. We have only about eight weeks to wait until the little one arrives." Isabel smiled tenderly at her.

"I'm fine, really. Perhaps I sat in the sunshine too long this morning. I just feel so tired." Closing her eyes, she took a deep breath. "I will sleep, but if Carlos comes before I wake, please tell him to come in and see me. I don't want to sleep if he is home. Please."

"I will, ninita. You rest now." Isabel closed the wooden shutters and shut the double doors behind her, leaving Elena alone.

She hadn't been feeling well. During the night she had awakened with what she decided was a touch of indigestion, but after a few minutes it had passed. All morning she had been ailing caused by a heavy pressure in her heart region due to carrying the baby high and it was beginning to bring a great deal of discomfort. Difficult to pinpoint the pressure, she felt queasy and dizzy. Finally she drifted into a deep sleep. Terrible and realistic dreams plagued her but she could not wake herself. She heard voices in her room, but she could not speak out; no sounds escaped her open, dry mouth. Sweat poured off her body and her heart beat so loudly she could hear it in her sleep. Faces appeared and dissolved and then suddenly she was in Playas, frolicking in the ocean until she realized the water was too hot and rough. Panicking, she began flailing her arms in the surf and cried out for Carlos. He appeared on the shore, laughing and waving to her. She noticed Eric struggling to swim out to her, but he was unable to reach her and she didn't have the strength to move toward him. She heard herself screaming and there was a horrible roaring in her ears. Then she was suddenly awake. Sitting up in bed, everything was quiet and she threw of the covers in the unbearable heat. Immediately she was asleep again, peacefully this time.

The door opened slowly and she awakened feeling refreshed. He was there and she turned to smile at him.

"I heard you were sick."

"I'm feeling much better."

He knelt by her bed and took her hand and with a handkerchief wiped her face. A strange feeling suddenly possessed her and it seemed every fiber in her body tingled.

"Look at me," she ordered.

He turned and the light from the doorway shone on his face and then she noticed his reddened eyes.

"Open the window. Open the window." She cried in a panic. "What's wrong?"

Chapter 22

Standing, he went to the shuttered window and opened it, pausing for a moment.

"What's wrong," she repeated, feverishly adjusting her body as he turned back to her and knelt again. She saw his swollen eyes were full of tears.

A roar started in her ears and she grabbed at the bedding, fighting the feeling she was falling into a dark, black hole.

"Carlos, where is Carlos?" She screamed.

"He's dead, my carina," sobbed Eric.

Chapter 23

Late the next morning following the visit from Raquel, Rolando was on the bus to Tulcachi. At the turn off to the hacienda he descended the bus and began to walk a seven kilometer trek to the large ranch. The siesta hour having just ended as he drew near, he met a peon on the road returning to the fields. Stopping him, he smiled tiredly.

"Buenos tardes, señor. Could you tell me where Carlos Tapia is?"

"Buenos tardes. Carlos?" The broad-cheeked, weather-worn face squinted up at him. "I think he's working on a ridge beyond the main buildings and up the road that heads east. If you continue on that road a kilometer you will reach a side road beside a grove of bushes. Take that road for another kilometer and you'll see an odd-looking ridge. It looks like a very long, very wide-backed animal lying there. Anyway they're going to start planting corn today, I think."

Rolando thanked the man and moved on. As he approached the large house which stood beneath a grove of eucalyptus trees, he saw a long porch covered with stuffed burlap bags, piles of potatoes and a group of women working. He searched their faces for Elena but she wasn't there. Walking to the bottom of the hill, he then began climbing upward until he reached the side road and turned to the left passing several hundred yards of thick brush. He traveled at a slight incline until in the distance he saw a ridge about seventy-five meters high that spread several hundred meters to the east. Sitting on the summit he saw a tractor, a lone man and a horse grazing nearby. Recognizing Carlos even from this distance, he walked

Chapter 23

rapidly toward him. Carlos sat on the tractor, leaning forward on the steering wheel, deep in meditation. Rolando stepped up the side of the ridge and came out behind him. His heart quickened as he gently called Carlos' name.

Carlos' head snapped around, the fear and surprise evident in his eyes. "Rolando. What are you doing here?"

The big man shuffled his feet for a moment and put his hands in his pockets. "I'm not sure. I guess I need to talk with you." He held his breath as Carlos studied him in bewilderment.

"What do we have to talk about?" He looked behind him as if to search for help in case Rolando had mischief on his mind.

"I'm not here to make trouble. I'm not the blustering, raging proud man you have seen in the past. I'm troubled and defeated and I need you to help me."

From the look on his face, nothing could have surprised Carlos more. "What is it you need of me?"

"I need your forgiveness."

Carlos blinked his eyes and sat dumbfounded for several moments. "My forgiveness?"

"Yes, both your forgiveness and Elena's. I thought it best to talk with you first, since I did such a stupid thing in Playas." He lifted pleading eyes to the man on the tractor. "You don't know what I've been through. Years ago I was so blinded that I thought I had everything under control. I thought that because of who I was, I could hold people within my power. I manipulated Elena's life and tried to destroy yours." He smiled without humor. "I thought you could never make anything of your life, a poor downtrodden Indian, I told myself. You would never get anywhere in this world and then you went out and proved me wrong. Here I stand, a poor downtrodden man who made nothing of my life and I started with everything in my favor."

"I have nothing to forgive. Actually you did us a favor. By forcing us to run away, we had only each other and because of this, our marriage has become cemented in a way that would not have happened if we had been surrounded by loving families and friends. We wouldn't be in Tulcachi right now. I have work that I love. Elena is healthy and happy." He smiled. "By the way, did you know your sister is pregnant and will be delivering a baby in a few weeks?"

"A baby?" Rolando's eyes widened and misted. "A baby. It's hard to believe my little sister is old enough to care for a child."

"She's not a little girl any longer. She's a fine woman and will make a good mother. Please, come visit with us. If I didn't have to stay here and finish this project, I'd take you with me right now but we're behind time and short of men. I'm waiting for the hacienda owner to return from his trek further up the mountain. I'm just resting until he returns." His eyes brightened. "Would you be able to come back tomorrow or the next day?"

"I'd love to."

"Come for the noon hour. I'd like you to meet Eric Perez, the hacienda owner."

"Thank you, Carlos. I can't believe you have accepted me so readily.

"I had no hatred against you. I just wanted to protect my wife, your sister."

A great burden lifted from Rolando's heart and he felt a childish desire to yell with delight and run the length of the ridge. Instead he grinned, embarrassed by his feelings. "You have a nice tractor. It looks new."

"Actually it's an older model but new to us. It came through customs just two weeks ago. Would you like to see how it operates?"

"Sure."

"Come and sit behind me and I'll show you."

As Carlos studied the controls, Rolando looked at him. "You act as though you don't know how to run this machine."

"To be truthful I don't know anything about it. I thought that all I had to do was turn the key and press the gas pedal. We have a man who usually operates the tractors. As I said, I was just sitting here resting for a minute. Eric went on a quick ride and the peon went to Tumbaco for truck parts. I've been waiting."

Rolando leaned forward and touched the starter. "Here, I can teach you."

"Please do."

"Put your left foot on the clutch and push the gearshift forward. Yes, that's right. Now, as you lift your left foot up, press your right foot on the gas pedal."

Chapter 23

The tractor lurched forward and stalled.

"That's the idea, but you have to lift your left foot and press your right foot a little slower and at the same time." With patience, Rolando taught him all the gears and then jumped down from the tractor. "I don't think you should try driving this yet. I can give you another lesson when I come back in a couple days. How's that?" He looked at his watch. "I guess I'd better leave. I have to get back to Quito."

"You're living in Quito?" He switched off the tractor's motor.

"Not after today. I'm going home. I have some other wrong deeds to make right."

They shook hands and Rolando leaned forward to hug his brother-in-law. As he walked away, Carlos started up the motor again. Alarmed, he turned, raised his arm and started running back. "Carlos, wait! I don't think you're ready to drive."

The tractor lurched backwards at a rapid speed and lost traction. He watched in horror as the machine fell, turning over and over until Carlos was thrown free. A large wheel glanced off him until it finally came to rest against a large bush. The man lay in a broken, crumpled heap. Racing down the hill, Rolando reached Carlos and put his arm under his neck. He patted his cheek and put his ear next to Carlos' lips to see if he was still breathing. He was.

"Carlos. Carlos. Please wake up. Please don't die," he cried. "Please, not now." Putting the man's head down carefully, he jumped up. He must get help. Where was Eric? Where had he gone? Rolando ran with all his might toward the road hoping to find someone. It seemed forever before he covered the kilometer, but soon he saw the intersection. There was no one in sight. Suddenly, he realized he should have carried Carlos with him. Turning back, he ran the distance in a few minutes. To his surprise, he saw a tall man bending over Carlos and a stallion on the ridge. He started to move toward them but then he realized he couldn't present himself. There were too many people who knew how much he had hated Carlos. No one would believe it was an accident. He must leave before anyone saw him.

Anxiety and grief accompanied him to Quito. The day had started out with promise but by the time he reached Quito, his mind was in a whirl of conflict. He'd been forgiven. There was no bitterness or hatred left in him against his brother-in-law. Only this recent turn of events saved him because another drinking binge might have killed him. He knew that. He would have to take what had happened this afternoon and build on it. Anyway, there was every chance that Carlos would live. He was thrown clear of the tractor; just the tire glanced off him. Perhaps there would be a few broken bones, but Rolando wouldn't believe he was dead. When he regained consciousness he would tell señor Perez and Elena that he and Rolando had reconciled.

He packed his belongings, paid the landlady with some of the stolen money and took what remained of Geoff's savings and resolved from that moment on the only money he would spend would be the money he earned.

Chapter 24

The news of Carlos' death sent shock waves through the town of Pachuca. Rolando learned of it at the breakfast table in his Aunt Mariana's house, where he had been welcomed back with open arms.

"I heard about it when I went down to the corner store to buy bread this morning," said Mariana. "Ernestina was crying. You know how she feels about all you young people who have grown up around here."

He sat stunned, surges of disbelief rippling through him. Dead. He couldn't believe it. Just yesterday they had parted with a firm shake of hands and a hug. It was his fault for showing off and trying to teach him to drive that tractor. Oh God, he should have carried him in his arms down to the hacienda.

"Rolando, what's the matter?"

"I don't feel well. I think I'm going to be sick." He ran from the room with Mariana in pursuit. Finding a bucket of water on the back stoop, he leaned over and splashed water on his face and then sat against the house wall until the nausea passed.

"Dear, I can't believe Carlos' death would affect you this way. I always thought this is what you wanted."

"I don't want anyone to die, Tia. Please leave me alone. I need to rest a minute." He leaned his head back taking deep draughts of air as she reluctantly stepped inside. Tears ran freely and a lump in his throat hampered his breathing. Life is so miserable, he thought. Is there happiness anywhere?

Guilt prevented him from attending Carlos' funeral. He told Geoff he had to go to Quito but actually he left early in the morning to wander in the mountains above Pachuca. He walked beside deep canyons, climbed small hills and sat beside tiny streams that flowed through the farmlands. If only he could have told Elena about his new friendship with Carlos, but if he had, Eric would want to know why he left the scene and why he hadn't returned. The foolish mistakes he had made that afternoon in a state of panic would always haunt him.

The sound of tolling church bells echoed off the mountains behind him, filling the valley with their mournful strains and he grieved. All day he wandered and meditated, trying to organize what was left of his life. At nightfall he returned to town and walked to his family home, hoping to find Geoff. He found him sitting at the kitchen table frowning over the business records. Looking up, Geoff saw his brother.

"Rolando, come in. Would you like something hot to drink?"

"No, gracias." He waved Geoff back to his chair while he pulled one up for himself.

Geoff pushed back the book and smiled at his sibling. "I needed an excuse to stop this torture. I have such a hard time with mathematics."

"Did you see Elena today?" He turned weary, questioning eyes to Geoff.

"She looked terrible. I was surprised to see that she is pregnant, several months along. That will make Carlos' death even harder to bear. My heart went out to her and I approached her for a few moments to give my love and to offer an explanation why you weren't able to be there."

A long silence ensued until Rolando could no longer bear it. He thumped his fingers on the table nervously. "Geoff, I took the money. I stole it from your room."

"I know."

"It wasn't that I needed it for myself. I thought I had to have it because somewhere in my crazy, mixed-up mind, I thought I had to go after Elena and bring her home. I wanted to destroy Carlos."

Geoff stared at his brother and slowly an uncontrolled look of horror crossed his face.

Chapter 24

"No, I didn't harm Carlos, but I did go to Playas. I found out from Laura that Carlos and Elena were living there. I went to bring Elena home and found, much to my dismay and surprise that Carlos was a wonderful, kind and gentle husband to our Elena and that she didn't want to come home after all. My hatred against Carlos all these years has been for nothing. I only brought damage to myself and my family. I made a terrible mistake. The money I took from you has been spent on things you won't want to know about. It fell like water through a net. I am so ashamed. Will you forgive me? Will you let me work for you again and pay back what I owe?"

"My dear brother, you never did work for me. You worked with me. This is a family operation and I have needed you very much these past months. We could do twice the work I do if I had proper help." Geoff sat back and thoughtfully played with his ear lobe. "Yes, you can work and pay me back and when you have earned the amount you took, we'll talk. Until then, it is a subject we'll not speak of again and Rolando, you have always been forgiven."

"Why is everyone being so nice to me? I don't deserve it, you know."

"Perhaps not, but your family loves you. You just haven't allowed us to get past the walls you've been putting up around you for years. I've always loved and respected you. The truth of the matter is I've never despised you, as you have accused me in the past. I've never thought any less of you, nor have I stood in judgment against your lifestyle. After I married Opal, my love and appreciation grew for you. Much of what I am today is due to your sacrifices while I was a child and now that I'm responsible for a wife and a growing business, I have nothing but love and respect for you."

The front door opened and shut and the voices of Opal and Raquel filled the house. Rolando stood and prepared to leave.

"Where are you going?" questioned Geoff. "Please stay."

"No, I must get home. Thanks."

"You're not leaving because of us, are you, Rolando?" inquired Opal, walking into the kitchen.

Rolando shook his head no and greeted Raquel who was standing behind Opal. "I've got a lot of things to do." Turning back to Geoff, he held out his hand. "I'll see you in the morning."

Geoff agreed and stood to hug his brother. He returned the hug affectionately and excused himself, passing by Opal. As he opened the front door to leave, Raquel reached him.

"Why are you leaving? Can't we talk?"

"There's really nothing for us to talk about, Raquel. Thank you for all your interest and concern, but I think I can handle things now."

Her face fell and she frowned. "For someone who told me he loved me a few weeks ago, you have certainly changed."

"You were right. There's no way we can work things out. Despite the changes that have occurred in my life, we still live in two different worlds. I don't need what you have. I have been able to turn my life around on my own these past few days and I feel so much better. Everything is looking up." He saw her crestfallen face and gently touched her cheek and then reached for her hand. "Oh, Raqui, please don't take this wrong. You're a fine girl and I like you very much. In fact, it was your help that turned me around. Ever since we met on the night of my papa's death, you have influenced me. You helped me back then and in Quito too. I really do appreciate you." Giving her a kiss on the cheek, he walked out the door, leaving her with tear-filled eyes.

Chapter 25

As quickly as the sun rose behind the mountains of Pachuca, the news of Carlos Tapia's death swept through the town. The son of Maria Laura Tapia, the brother of Joel, Jerman and Yolanda had lost his life while driving a tractor on the Hacienda Tulcachi. Some villagers believed it was God's judgment. After all, they reasoned, hadn't Carlos and Elena fled from the bosom of their loved ones, leaving behind two grieving families? Residents of the plaza clashed with those in the upper suburb where Carlos had lived over who was at fault. Plaza residents staunchly believed that Carlos coerced Elena into running away. No, retorted those in the suburbs; Elena had turned his head, seducing Carlos away from his family until he fled unwittingly from his roots. Now God surely had brought punishment. Others grieved. Ernestina, the corner store owner, received the news with disbelief and then wept in sorrow. And then, there was Fausto, the poverty-stricken child who had pinned all his hopes on Carlos, his hero. He had waited for years hoping to see him again but now, his future uncertain, he hid in a corner of the church cemetery, huddled in despair. Surprisingly, of the Martinez family, only Geoff and Opal seemed to care about Elena's loss wondering what she would do now that she had no husband.

From behind Jillian's house, the church bells pealed mournfully. Raquel swirled her fork in the yolk of a fried egg, bereft of appetite.

"Aren't you hungry?" asked Jillian, breaking the corner off of a piece of toast and dipping it in her egg.

"Not really." Raquel leaned back in the kitchen chair and studied the thick white painted logs spanning the ceiling length. "You know, Jill, this is an ugly room. Why do you live here?"

"I know it's ugly but why should I care? It's a place to stay." She paused. "Why are we talking about the ugliness of this house when I know you're just depressed over Carlos? I'm depressed too. Even though I never met him, I've followed his life through gossip. You probably feel more depressed than I, living with Geoff and Opal."

Raquel straightened up in her chair and began picking once again at her food. "I don't think the family is very sad over his death. I don't think Geoff has ever forgiven Elena and Carlos for eloping. He feels it destroyed the family, but he's very concerned about her future right now and thinks there's a chance she might return home to Pachuca. I think they are sad and hopeful at the same time."

"That doesn't explain your feelings," Jillian remarked between chews.

Raquel scooped up a fork of egg and placed it in her mouth, deep in thought.

"What's wrong, Raqui?"

"Rolando has come home to Pachuca."

"I've been wondering what happened in Quito. Did you go to see him?"

"Yes. After the siesta hour I took a taxi downtown and found his hotel room. I thought he would be destitute, living in a slum, but actually the hotel wasn't that bad. It's a middle-class tourist lodging. I knocked several times at his door but there was no answer. Finally I paid the clerk several sucres to let me in so I could wait for him. Imagine my disgust when we entered and I found him sprawled on the bed sound asleep. He was in such a drunken state that I could not wake him. The room was a mess; his clothes were laying everywhere. I asked the clerk why the room hadn't been cleaned and he said Rolando had rented the room for several days and had requested no maid service. He asked that his towels and sheets be placed outside the door. Jill, I sat in that room for an hour or more before he began to stir. Finally, when he opened his eyes and saw me sitting there, he thought I was a dream. At that moment, the lecture and scolding I had planned to give him left me. All I could think about

Chapter 25

was the foolishness of his life, wasting it by hating the man who had married his sister."

"What did you do?"

"Not much. He was very apologetic and humbled, so different from the first time I met him. I told him the way I saw it, help from God was his only chance." She put the last pieces of egg and toast in her mouth and stood. Placing her dirty dish and utensils in a tub of water for rinsing, she stood dejected.

They fell into a lengthy silence, their thoughts accompanied by the tolling bell.

"I think the procession is closer." Jillian inclined her ear toward the door.

"Let's go to the balcony. At least I can tell Geoff that we saw it pass."

Raquel crossed the hallway and started up the stairs with Jillian following, having her own reasons for being in sight. She wanted to support Raquel and to show the townspeople she was a part of the populous. Remembering the Sunday afternoon so many years before, she had sat in the pickup with Marta in a crowded plaza and watched Elena and Rolando pass by them. From their looks centered on Marta, they had shown their hatred toward her. So much had happened since that day; what terrible tragedies had occurred in their young lives. If only Jillian had understood then how Marta inflicted grief in the lives of those who put their trust in her. Now she was eager to see if Elena had changed. She must have. But her deepest desire was to see Eric. Surely he would be there in the procession somewhere as Carlos' employer. Maybe he would be a pall bearer.

The girls walked to the banister and looked down just as the procession rounded the corner in front of Ernestina's store. The bells rang loudly, monotonously. They leaned out to see who was standing along the curbs. "There's Geoff and Opal on the steps of the church walk."

"Do you see Rolando?" Jillian followed the direction of Raquel's point.

After a moment of searching, the doctor shook her head. "I have a feeling he won't be here. Perhaps he's never forgiven Elena."

"I wonder if her Aunt Mariana and Uncle Hector will be in the procession."

"I doubt it. She will never forgive Elena for hurting her family and her beloved Rolando. They blame her for what has happened to him."

"That's foolish. Rolando is an adult. He has hurt himself."

"Rolando's aunt adores him." She gently slapped her hands against the railing. "Sometimes I think she has harmed him more than helped him."

"Here they come." Jillian's attention was drawn back to the corner where the procession had stopped momentarily before proceeding to the church sanctuary. She saw Eric first; his commanding presence stationed behind the six pallbearers, all strangers to Jillian. He leaned toward the woman at his side, protectively holding her close. A sharp pain of jealousy caught her by surprise as he focused all his attention on Elena, who seemed to will her legs forward. No tears were visible on her face, though Jillian recognized signs of shock and grief. This might be a fatal blow to her reputation, as most of the townspeople would not sense this and seek to use Elena's seeming lack of grief and her connection to Eric against her.

On Elena's other side and two steps behind walked Laura, Carlos' mother. She and her two sons, Jerman and Joel carried candles. Behind them a weeping Yolanda struggled to stay on her feet. A short stout man rushed to catch her and his companion, a woman took Yolanda protectively to her side. Probably family members, Jillian assumed. Isabel and Ramon walked directly behind Elena, Isabel weeping and Ramon keeping an eye on her in case she stumbled. Scores of people walked behind, many from the suburb above Pachuca where Carlos was born and raised. Bringing up the rear were several men on horses and a few driving trucks and tractors.

The priest, garbed in a long robe, with his monks passed directly below them now, swinging smoking bowls of incense and casting holy water from a scepter. The repetition of their prayers rose and dipped in intonation. Strangers to Jillian lined the curb and surrounded the casket, no doubt friends of Carlos from Tulcachi. They murmured and wailed as they cupped their hands about the flames of candles keeping them from blowing out in the gentle breeze.

The pallbearers moved on and Eric and Elena started to pass below them. Suddenly Eric lifted his head and stared directly at her. Jillian's heart contracted and she started to smile, but his face

Chapter 25

registered no friendliness toward her; instead there was a hint of hostility. Any hope she had that he had forgiven her for their argument died in that moment.

"Oh Lord, help her," groaned Raquel at Jillian's side.

Fighting back her urge to cry over Eric's rebuff, Jillian responded. "Who?"

"Elena. Look at Elena. She's pregnant. She must be eight months along."

Studying the girl, closer now, she saw that she was large with child and a great sorrow wrung her heart. Where was the young, sweet carefree child she had seen that Sunday afternoon? Grief etched her face, aging her beyond her years. She had borne more sorrow in the past few days than most women twice her age. All at once, compassion for Elena flooded her, supplanting the momentary jealousy she had experienced just minutes before.

The line of mourners reached the walkway to the church. There it stopped allowing Geoff and Opal to step forward to offer their condolences. Eric stood close by in a posture of protectiveness. He had not given Jillian another glance.

"I wonder if Rolando knows she's pregnant." muttered Raquel."

The thought of Eric's snub brought renewed pain. "Did you see the way Eric looked at me?"

"Yes. Now I'm glad you haven't tried to make contact with him. I can see what you mean."

"I had considered driving to Tulcachi to visit him. I wanted to see if we could remain friends despite the way I acted that night. Now I can see that I would never be welcomed."

"I cannot believe that a man his age would hold something as silly as a little argument against you." Raquel touched Jillian's arm. "There has to be something else that caused his actions today."

Turning to seat herself on one of a pair of rocking chairs she had recently purchased from a local carpenter, she absently watched Raquel sit down in the other. "You know, Raqui. I can't forget what Eric's mother said to me the other day when we were visiting her. She said that something other than our argument had hurt him. Frankly, I let it pass because I don't know what it would have been. I thought maybe she was speculating."

"Let's think a minute. You said he came to visit you when you weren't home several months ago?"

"Yes."

"How do you know that he came to visit you?"

"Don Eduardo told me he had stopped by to see me."

Raquel leaned forward. "Don Eduardo? Olivia's father?"

"Yes." She frowned, puzzled at Raquel's question.

"Why weren't you home that evening?"

"That was the evening I took medicine to my neighbor who has the shop next door and lives next door to you."

"You mean the night Philip Rios came to visit me?"

"Yes. Why?"

"Because Philip told me something that may help us understand why Eric is acting the way he is."

"What?"

"You and I had not yet met, but Philip suggested I pursue a friendship with you."

"Yes, I remember he wanted me to meet you, but what does that have to do with Eric?"

"Nothing really, but as we talked he mentioned that the two of you had stopped to speak with Don Eduardo and Olivia."

Jillian didn't reply as she tried to recall the happenings of that night, but alarm was beginning to spread through her. That was the night Gladys had been so suspicious and aloof blaming Marta for spreading so many tales against her character.

"I know Olivia, Jill. She was my nurse the year I worked in the government clinic. I disliked her the minute I met her. When Philip talked to me that night, he was concerned that Olivia might take advantage of you in some way."

"What do you think happened?"

"I think she intercepted Eric and told him something."

"What? What could she have told him?"

"Of course I'm not sure, but I do know that she's in her late thirties and not married. This is a terrible tragedy for someone living in a small village like this. You can count on one hand the single women living in Pachuca and all the surrounding suburbs right now."

Chapter 25

Jillian seated herself on the edge of her chair. "Do you think she told Eric I was with a man?"

"Weren't you?"

"Yes," she yelled. "With Philip, a married man who loves his wife and has no romantic thoughts toward me and Olivia knows that."

"If I know Olivia well enough she made it sound much worse. Remember what she told Marta? Remember the story she told the authorities?"

Jillian's heart sank. "And Eric would believe it because the first time I saw him, years ago, I was with Philip. He's always known we were close." She was silent for a long moment. "Yes, Olivia could have told him that I have many male friends. No wonder he looked at me that way."

"Maybe you should go see him after all."

"Not now. Not while Elena is grieving and ready to deliver a baby."

"Listen, the bells have stopped. The procession must be in place and the priest ready for the funeral.

"I don't want to see Eric pass by again. I'm going into the house." Distraught, she began preparing for her next class.

Chapter 26

Nothing in Elena's young life prepared her for what she faced now. The agony was unmerciful even though the doctor had sedated her. She would awaken in the night screaming, tearing at her clothing and at her heart in an attempt to rid herself of the pain, the overwhelming pain. At night she longed for the day but when the day arrived she wept for the night. Above all, she hated her bed, so cold, damp and empty now. They moved her to the living room, but in the dark hours she mourned for the evenings they had spent together in the room. Finally Eric stayed with her during the nights until exhausted they both slept as the sun came over the mountains.

In the depths of despair, he was riddled with unnecessary guilt, grieving for a lost son. None of those in his social circle had earned his respect as had the degraded, downtrodden Indian from the back mountains of Ecuador. Eric had been led to believe nothing productive could come from an uneducated mountain Indian and he simply tolerated their drunkenness and lack of initiative. Nothing beyond satisfying their sex drive and another drink seemed to interest most of them, but now he wondered if this was true? Could the fault have been in his distorted thinking? Perhaps there were more like Carlos in these mountains. The realization that he was a prejudiced man came to light when unprepared, he fell under the spell of Carlos' directness and friendliness and thankfully, Eric had taken time to listen and learn despite his preconceived ideas. Now as he reflected on the past few months, he realized that if he had stubbornly clung to his

Chapter 26

unyielding bias, perhaps he would never have known his beloved Carlos. He had loved him as a son and Eric's last will and testament included the young man's offspring. If the baby was a boy, the hacienda would eventually become his. If Elena bore a girl, the child would be provided for the rest of her life, her education secured. If he had lived, Carlos would have had a home with Eric to the end of his life. The couple would have been able to live there, if they chose, until they died of old age. The loss was tremendous. Having grown accustomed to sharing his burdens and ideas with Carlos, Eric felt now there was no one to whom he could turn. Elena, as much as he loved her was suffering so deeply she couldn't see his pain. Having suffered the premature death of his own fiancée many years ago, he could relate to Elena's heartache. He was helplessly inadequate with words and found by simply holding Elena he helped soothe her heart. He considered the thought of marriage to the girl to give the child a father, but he pushed the idea aside. She was a mere child herself and he middle-aged. No, marriage wasn't the answer, but he was determined to be there for her as long as she needed him.

Chapter 27

The funeral passed like a dream for Elena. The doctor had sedated her to keep her calm and she heard onlookers gossip in murmurs that she appeared to be without emotion as she passed on her way to Pachuca's central plaza. It was the first she had been there since the day she ran away with her husband.

Traveling slowly, a truck carried the pallbearers and coffin to the edge of town while the people of Tulcachi formed a procession, following in farm trucks, tractors and on horses. Elena, Eric, Isabel and Ramon, the driver, rode in Eric's private car until the caravan reached the outskirts of the village proper. The pallbearers pulled the coffin to the ground while the assemblage stood waiting for the Catholic priest and the monks to arrive. Heavy silence was broken by the mournful tolling of distant church bells punctuated by an occasional moan or cough, or the sound of a mother hushing her child. As the small group of church men approached, the priest, attired in white vestments stepped out to sprinkle holy water over the coffin while softly intoning a prayer. He turned and the entire funeral party followed, with Carlos' fellow workers serving as pallbearers. As they walked into town, members of the procession began to chant in sporadic fashion; candles were lit and moans and wails mingled in sync with the rising volume and intensity of the prayers.

Eric guided her as they began the near mile walk to the church and she lay against him, finding some comfort in his nearness. They had passed Carlos' house where Laura, his mother and his brothers

Chapter 27

joined the cortege. Yolanda followed them alongside Aunt Carlota and Uncle Jose. Laura walked to Elena's side and with a sad, tearful smile took her hand. Elena smiled back and gave her a hug. "Thank you for giving me your son."

Eric reached out to shake her hand. "You raised a wonderful young man. I can't give you enough thanks for bringing him into the world."

The road led past the home of Mariana and Hector and as the procession passed by, she saw the couple with Elena's cousins grouped in the doorway, but there was no movement toward her. She felt Eric hold her tighter as if to protect her from this unkindness. Strangely, she felt no pain or tie to them any longer. She had married a man they believed to be socially beneath them and they had been wrong. Eventually their bitterness and loss would eat away at their spirits and destroy them but she knew she had made the right choice and that made her a victor.

Everything passed in a haze. She recalled various people coming forward to offer their condolences. She hugged Carlos' sister, Yolanda who was overcome with grief. Fausto stood tearfully in the background and her heart went out to him. Because of Fausto's faithfulness, she and Carlos had been able to run away. She promised herself to speak with Eric about offering him work. In that way, she could thank him.

Uncle Jose, Aunt Carlota, Alfredo and a girl she presumed to be his fiancée, in turn hugged Elena. They extracted a promise from her that she visit soon, but Elena knew she would never return to their home in Quito so full of poignant memories. The only person she longed to see was Rolando and he wasn't there. That hurt her more than Aunt Mariana's snobbery. Surely after all this time he had forgiven her.

Geoff, with a young woman stepped forward and Elena recalled her brother was now married. He took Elena from Eric and held her closely for a long while, tears brimming in his eyes as he told her he loved her and was sorry he had delayed visiting her in Tulcachi. She responded with understanding and asked about Rolando. To her sorrow, Rolando was in Quito and had not been able to attend the funeral. Geoff promised he and his wife would travel to Tulcachi in two months, after the baby was born.

Contrary to common practice, arrangements were made with the priest to bury the body outside the church plot. Elena was adamant that Carlos be buried behind the hacienda under the two trees at their special spot. He had loved the mountains more than anyone she knew and was convinced he would be happier there than lying in a neglected churchyard. As the final benediction was offered, the pallbearers returned the coffin to a truck now parked in front of the church. Carlos was buried on the plateau that same day without Elena in attendance as she lay in a drug-induced stupor on the living room sofa.

Chapter 28

And now Eric was responsible for Elena. When Carlos lay dying, Eric had promised that he would care for her. It took several days before Elena was able to question the circumstances of her husband's death, but she finally found the courage and Eric carefully explained, trying to spare her needless pain.

That fateful day, he had been having trouble with one of the farm trucks and had borrowed Raul from Carlos. Raul had spent much of the morning trying to get the truck started and was finally forced to drive a jeep into Tumbaco to find a mechanic. Eric rode his horse up to call Carlos back for dinner, since the plowing of the ridge could not continue without Raul. He found him frustrated and impatient that his project had suffered setbacks. On the spur of the moment, Eric had decided to ride the length of the ridge in order to estimate the amount of time they needed for plowing. On the way, he stopped to survey other possibilities for plowing as the ridge dipped and rounded the base of the hill. For several minutes he studied the potential for using this area not only for potatoes and corn but possibly wheat. He spent time figuring how they could build boundaries for safety keeping his workers from plowing too close to the drop offs back where Carlos was waiting. On this end, the rise was gentle. He had to admire the young man for seeing promise where he had failed to look. Smiling, he made his way back and as he reached the summit, his eyes searched for Carlos and then he noticed the tractor was gone but Carlos' horse remained. A small fear gathered in his stomach but he pushed it away with a dry chuckle. Was he imagining things? Where was the tractor? Perhaps Raul had returned and driven away, but no, Raul couldn't have gotten back from Tumbaco this soon and Carlos wouldn't leave his horse unattended.

He could only guess at what happened while he was away. For some unknown reason Carlos, while sitting on the new tractor with as little knowledge, if any, for operating motorized vehicles, had started the motor. Instead of pushing the stick into forward gear, apparently he had pulled it into reverse and as he let out the clutch the tractor had lurched backwards down the slope. The tractor lay on its side a distance from his friend. The scene that met him as he neared the accident would live with him forever. It froze him to his horse for a several seconds before he could manipulate his legs into action. There was no logic to this. Carlos was usually a careful, alert young man and it took those seconds for him to convince himself he was not dreaming. Having been thrown clear of the tractor, Carlos lay halfway down the slope, a large gash on his head and his limbs turned in awkward positions obviously broken in many places. He was still alive when Eric reached his side, but he could only whisper, suggesting his lungs had been punctured. In labored speech he told Eric to care for Elena and the baby. His last words were, "I love you, Eric. Thank you for giving us a home. Tell Elena I have never loved anyone as I love her and the baby."

And then he died.

Nothing Eric did for Elena seemed to help. Her agony and grief were frightening. They talked by the hour, but there were times when she would become abnormally still. At other times she babbled, describing her pain like waves of the ocean. Eric tried to understand. She complained that her body felt numb and described herself as having no feelings, yet at the next moment, her emotions hit a high, roaring peak from which there seemed to be no release. Then her head would roll from side to side as desperate moans escaped from her mouth. It was unbearable. She loathed the bulkiness of her pregnancy and despised herself for not being with Carlos when he was in danger. She cursed bittersweet memories that produced blinding headaches and spasms of vomiting.

Chapter 28

On one occasion as they talked, she suddenly burst into tears and ran to the door, screaming and begging Carlos to come to her. On another day, Eric and Isabel found her in her room packing her suitcase. When they asked where she was going, she replied she had to hurry to Playas for someone had been playing a terrible trick on her. Carlos was waiting in Playas searching for her. Eric could only take her in his arms as they wept together. The days passed slowly, but soon she approached her ninth month. Eric wondered if the only reason she continued to live was for the child.

But their difficulties weren't over as Eric became caught in a terrible web of circumstances. One evening they took a small dinner in the living room and remained at the coffee table to talk. Much to his relief, he noted Elena was beginning to rationalize a little, her thoughts turning more to the imminent birth of her child. He felt a spark of hope that this could temper her grief over Carlos. Her sudden fits of weeping and lamenting seemed to be fewer and further apart. He let her talk as much as she desired, knowing it was a healing outlet.

"Would you like to play a game of checkers?" he asked, his blue eyes hopeful.

"Yes, I'd like that," she attempted a smile.

He squeezed her hand and then fetched the checkers from a bureau. Moving their plates aside, he laid out the game and gave her the choice of colors just as the telephone rang. The central office in Pachuca had a call for him from his Quito home. Elena watched him as she listened, her eyes growing large and fearful. Returning the phone to its base, he sat on the sofa, putting his arm around her shoulders.

"That was my mother's maid. My mama is very ill and they aren't sure what's wrong. You know she's been all alone since my papá is dead. She needs my help. They've taken her to the American hospital in Quito." He lifted her trembling chin. "Querida, my beloved, you understand that I must go see what's wrong."

She let loose with a loud wail.

"Do you want to go with me? Of course. I don't want to leave you alone."

It wasn't until the next day that they returned to Tulcachi. Eric was beside himself with concern as there was a possibility that his mother needed open heart surgery and with little faith in Quito's medical services, he had already started proceedings on a special visa for himself and his mother. They were to leave the next day for New York where his brother worked as a surgeon, but he was equally concerned about Elena. Because she had never obtained a cedula or identification papers, he was unsuccessful in securing a passport for her. It became obvious she would have to remain in Ecuador. He encouraged her to stay at his home in Quito, but she refused to leave Carlos in Tulcachi. More frightened now by her calm demeanor as she had shown no emotion after her initial outburst; it was as though something had died in her.

"Elena, I'll be gone for a week at the most. Tomorrow I'll take my mother on the plane and we'll arrive in New York tomorrow evening. My brother is handling everything; she will be given tests and if she needs surgery, she will be operated on. If there are no complications, I'll leave and come back for you."

She averted her eyes and replied in a dull voice. "I'll probably have my baby while you're gone."

"You still have a little over two weeks to go." He took her hand gently. "Anyway, niña, I've already talked to Isabel and my mama's chauffeur, Ramon. I'll close up the house in Quito so they'll both be here for you. I've given them instructions to care for your every need. Together, they will see to it that you need nothing."

Her resolve seemed to fall apart. "I can't live without you, Eric."

"I think I know how you feel. I don't want to go, but she's my mother."

"What if I do have the baby while you're away?"

"Then Ramon and Isabel will take you directly to Quito. The minute you start to have pains, call Isabel." He pressed her hand. "However, I see little chance of that happening and I promise you I'll call the central telephone office in Pachuca every night. If they are able to put the call through, we can talk together. If, for some reason I can't contact Pachuca, I'll call a friend in Quito and he will get hold of you. One way or another we will keep in contact." Shaking his head, he told her, "I would give anything if this hadn't happened right now.

Chapter 29

When Eric left Elena, she wept bitterly. Holding onto him at the airport, she begged him to return quickly. He turned from her reluctantly, promising to see her in a week's time as Helen gave her word that she would send him back the minute she was in the recovery room. As the airplane melted into a speck in the sky, Ramon led Elena to the car and drove back to Tulcachi. Meeting them at the door, Isabel comforted her, tried to entice her to eat a good lunch and then gave her a mild tranquilizer. Elena fell into an exhausted sleep on the sofa. She slept through supper and into the night, awaking at midnight when a dull, intense pain shot through her middle section. Stumbling to the door, she walked the hallway length to Isabel's door and knocked. Hearing noises, immediately Isabel appeared, concerned and ready to help. By midmorning, Elena was in labor and as it was Sunday, they could not locate a doctor by telephone, so Isabel and Ramon decided to call Marta Brewer in Pachuca. Marta told her to bring Elena as soon as possible.

"I don't know what to do. Shall we take a chance that her doctor will be at the hospital in Quito?" Preparing the suitcase, the stout woman nervously folded and refolded Elena's clothes, looking over at Ramon anxiously waiting for instructions.

"I think that we should take a chance since señor Perez left instructions that Quito was first choice."

"What if no doctors are available?"

"There are always doctors in the hospital."

"What if she has the baby before we arrive?"

"Haven't you ever delivered a baby?"

Isabel gave him an incredulous look. "I've had my own babies delivered at the hospital in Quito, but I'm not able to help Elena have one in the car." She shook her head with impatience. "We can't stand here talking. We must get her to the hospital. Let's try to make it to Quito. It will only take an hour."

Within minutes they were settled in the car driving quickly toward the Pan American highway. Elena tried to rest in the back seat. At the entrance to the main highway, Ramon slowed the car. Blocking the way were several policemen amongst a crowd of people. Rolling down the window, he called to one of the officers. "What's the matter, señor?"

"We have a car race today. No one can go to Quito."

"But we have a lady with us who is in labor. She's going to deliver a baby at any moment."

The officer shrugged his shoulders. "Sorry, I can't help you. The race has already started in Quito and should be here in an hour. In a few minutes we will be closing this highway completely and you'll not go anywhere. If you can wait until all the racers pass by, then the road to Quito will be opened again."

Elena sat forward and asked nervously, anxiety closing her throat. "What shall we do? I feel another pain coming on."

The policeman waited until her cries died down and leaned toward the window fearfully watching her. "You'll have to go toward Pachuca or Yaruqui. Each town has a clinic, but you had better hurry. You have about thirty minutes and no cars will be allowed at all on this highway, even if you have the baby right here."

Ramon turned to the women. "What shall I do? We can't go to Quito."

"We'll have to go to the American clinic in Pachuca," Elena said calmly, resigned.

"Are you sure?" he asked.

"I don't think we have any other choice. I just need to hurry. My pains are closer together then they were when we left home."

Quickly Ramon turned away from Quito and drove rapidly toward Pachuca. As her pains were about fifteen minutes apart, she wished

Chapter 29

desperately Eric was with her to hold her hand when the cramps overcame her. Maybe she should have stayed in his house in Quito. What a fool she had been. Now she was about to deliver her baby in the clinic of her enemy. She hoped desperately that Marta would have forgotten the animosity she and Rolando had shown her in the past. In a matter of a few minutes they arrived at the clinic and Lucia opened the door. She invited Elena and Isabel inside, instructing Ramon to remain in the car.

Leading Elena into the prenatal room, Lucia found that Elena was dilated and would deliver sometime during the night. Informing Isabel she was no longer needed, she led her to the door.

"No, you can't stay with her. We never allow family members or friends to spend time with the patients. Who knows what we would be missing in the morning. Come back on Tuesday to take Elena and the baby home and be sure to bring six hundred sucres, so please be prepared."

Isabel stood nervously at the door, but held her ground swallowing her anger at the barb about thievery. "I need to spend the night with Elena. She doesn't like to be alone."

Lucia gave her a hard cold stare. "No one spends the night here but patients. I told you to come on Tuesday morning with the money and you can see her and the baby then." Pushing her out the door, she shut it and left Isabel standing on the doorstep, tears in her eyes."

Elena was taken to the showers and bathed, handed a white hospital gown and led to a high bed with the whitest sheets she had ever seen. Lucia worked around her without saying a word. Feeling an overwhelming sense of loneliness, she thought the woman cold and ugly. Finally Lucia left her alone and for two hours Elena cried into her pillow along with intermittent labor pains. After being fed a light dinner, Lucia checked her vitals and how dilated she was and then she was left alone again. Early in the evening the pains became more intense and she forgot everything but her need to deliver the burden she had been carrying. She longed to hold Carlos' baby in her arms thankful she had this much left of him. Confident that she and Eric would raise the baby and love it as much as she and Carlos could have, she was content that at least the future of their child was secure.

The painful hours that passed were almost welcomed by her. They blotted out the agony and loneliness of her soul. As the contractions came closer together, Lucia appeared more frequently until finally she was led to the labor room and helped onto a table with two metal stirrups attached. Her legs were placed in these and she was strapped down. An injection was prepared and given and she was prepped. Then they waited for the next thrust of pain.

Looking up, she saw Marta Brewer in the doorway. Several times Elena had met with the nurse during prenatal checkups, but had never noticed before the kindness showing on the woman's face today. She was radiating love and tenderness. This confused Elena as Marta took Elena's hand in hers and comforted her.

"Please relax, my dear. This will all be over soon," she soothed. "I'm so sorry Carlos can't be with you."

Tears flowed from Elena's eyes as she absorbed the attention and love. How could she believe this was the same woman who had rejected her mother so many years ago on the day of her own delivery? Had she and Rolando misunderstood this kind nurse all these years? Her pain created a longing to have Marta sweep away all the hurt and sorrow she had borne these past weeks.

With love and gentle hands, the baby was delivered after a few minutes of hard labor. The last pushes were unbearable, but when Elena heard the lusty cry of her firstborn, she was able to relax. Twisting her head to see the baby, she watched Marta suctioning the infant's mouth.

"Oh, how beautiful she is. It's a girl, Elena. Gracias a Dios, how we've been waiting for a girl."

"I have a girl? It's not a boy?" Elena asked, disappointed.

"No, it's a beautiful little girl, somewhat premature, but not too much." Marta laid the baby in a waiting bassinet and re-examined the child. "Perhaps we miscalculated the due date a little, but that's all right. She's a beauty."

Elena's first disappointment was being replaced with a spark of excitement. Carlos had wanted a girl. Through the night she cradled her baby next to her breast, hardly able to sleep. Excitement and unspeakable love toward the infant filled her thoughts. As dawn arrived, Isabel and Ramon appeared at the window, knocking softly.

Chapter 29

Elena sat up in bed, opened a small door in the glass window and spoke quietly through the screen.

"Buenos dias, Elena. We could not sleep for thinking of you."

Elena beamed, gathering up the small bundle and presenting her daughter to the peering guests. "I have a little girl."

"A girl. How wonderful and isn't she beautiful, Ramon?" Isabel exclaimed, turning to the man.

Ramon pressed forward, smiling broadly. "Señor Eric will be happy to hear about the child. His friend in Quito called last night telling us there was no way for the señor to get a line through to Tulcachi. He was very concerned about you, señora Elena. Wait until the señor hears of the child. He will be delighted."

"Will we be able to come in and visit with you later, Elena?" Isabel struggled to see through the screen.

"I'm sorry, but apparently señorita Marta has rules that visitors aren't allowed inside. I don't understand because I would love to have you hold the baby. There are no other patients. I'm all alone."

"Perhaps we can ask, if we see the señorita. Right now, you should rest. If we hear from señor Eric, we will send the wonderful message of your daughter."

"Thank you and please send my love." Elena fought a growing desire to leave the clinic. "I can go home tomorrow. Please pick me up as soon as possible."

"We will. We'll be here early tomorrow morning. Give our niñita a kiss."

"I will."

Isabel and Ramon backed away from the window and walked to the end of the clinic to watch for movement in the distant house. They waited a moment and then returned to the car. Elena started in fright when suddenly she noticed Marta in the doorway. She hadn't heard the nurse enter the clinic and wondered how long she had been watching. Without a word, Marta walked to the patient's door and called to Isabel.

"Señora, may I have a word with you?"

"Oh, Buenos dias, señorita," exclaimed Isabel. "We were looking for you. We would love to visit with Elena and the baby for a moment. Would that be possible?"

Marta glanced toward Elena, whose face was framed in the window. "Visitors are not allowed inside the building until they come to pick up the patient. I'm sure you have seen the baby through the window." Leaning closer, Marta dropped her voice and Elena strained to hear her words, but she was out of range.

When Marta turned into the clinic, Elena frantically motioned for Isabel to come to the window. "What did she say to you?"

"That you had a difficult delivery and needed your rest. She said she wants us to leave you alone until we pick you up on Wednesday."

"Wednesday? Do you mean I must stay here until Wednesday? Oh, Isabel I feel fine and ready to go home now. Please come sooner," pleaded Elena.

"Querida, that is the day after tomorrow and we will come very early."

Elena heard a noise and turned to see Marta at the end of her bed.

"Tell your guests to leave as you must rest. The baby needs the care that only you can give her."

"I must rest, Isabel. I will miss you so." Elena spoke through the window, holding up her baby for one last peek.

Ramon started the car motor and the two bid her goodbye with sad waves. She turned and snuggled with her baby before turning her attention to Marta. "I don't see why Isabel couldn't come in to see the baby," she remarked angrily.

"It's bad enough that we have unclean patients in here but at least they can shower. Visitors don't bathe and therefore we are exposed to all kinds of disease. That's why."

Elena bristled. "Isabel and Ramon are not dirty. I admit I don't know much about giving birth, but it didn't seem to me that my delivery was so difficult that I must stay here until Wednesday."

Marta's mouth opened in puzzlement. "Wednesday? No, that's not right. I told the señora to come on Tuesday. Tomorrow morning."

"Tuesday?" Elena struggled up, pressing her baby close to her bosom. "No, señorita. Isabel said you told her Wednesday morning."

"Then she made an error."

"We must send her a message." Panic filled Elena's eyes.

"Don't worry," the nurse spoke soothingly. "I'll give them a telephone call and tell them to come tomorrow."

Chapter 29

When Marta departed, Elena buried her homesickness after gathering the baby to her again. "Your popi wanted me to name you Little Elena, but I have been thinking and I have decided I want to call you Angelita because you are a little angel sent from your popi wherever he is today." She caressed the infant's soft, downy cheek, ran her fingers over the thin eyebrows and touched the tiny nose. She was astonished that she and her beloved husband had been responsible for the beautiful infant. Reluctantly, she relinquished Angelita only during the time it took for Lucia to give the baby a bath and change the bedding and for her to take a quick shower. Other than that, they remained together the bond growing stronger each moment. She prodded the baby to suck until her milk came in a heavy stream. As the tiny mouth sought the source of nourishment, Elena felt a prolonged depth of joy, the first since Carlos' death. She knew that she would survive if for no other reason than for this child.

Her desire now was to leave for Tulcachi with the baby. She would return and make a home for her daughter. Eric's arrival would complete her contentment. Remaining at the clinic was beginning to wear on her. Her first impression of Marta was being replaced by a sense of wariness. It seemed the nurse no longer felt concern for Elena, but rather a mild hostility. Marta and Lucia had been involved in a violent argument before lunch in the kitchen, which caused the nurse to leave the clinic slamming the door. Lucia stomped upstairs to the attic where Elena heard loud banging for the next hour. She felt the clinic was cold and impersonal and she longed for the next morning.

After supper, Marta came to her side and glanced at the sleeping baby. "Buenas tardes, Elena. I wonder if I may speak with you."

"Of course," Elena replied, holding the baby close to her side.

Marta pulled up a chair from under the window, sat beside the bed and patted Elena's hand. "When you first started coming to the clinic for prenatal care, I wasn't sure who you were since you used your husband's name, however when I heard of his death I was able to connect you with the little Elena Martinez from the plaza."

Elena's throat closed with the threat of tears and she looked down at Angelita's curly black locks.

"What are your plans now?"

"I will return to the hacienda in Tulcachi and raise my daughter there."

"Without a father?"

"No, the hacienda owner plans to help me."

The nurse's face turned scarlet. "Do you mean you will live with Eric Perez alone?"

"We're not exactly alone, but why not? My husband and I lived there with him before….."

"But now you're not married and neither is señor Perez."

Elena stared at the red-faced woman, sickened at her implications. "He's like my father. You will never understand what he has meant to me and my husband this past year." Clearly Marta was horrified and Elena became confused. "What are you saying to me, señorita Marta?"

The woman pressed her lips together and shook her head in wonderment. "Leave it to you people to raise your children in conditions like that."

"Conditions like what?" Elena stared at her with disbelief. "My baby will receive nothing but love and attention."

"Yes, she'll grow up with two people who aren't married. That will certainly confuse her. Have you thought perhaps I could take her and raise her?"

"No!" Terrified, Elena clutched the baby to her breast. "I wouldn't think of giving this child to you. She is all I have left of my marriage to Carlos. Never!"

"I can give her everything you can't," continued Marta, undaunted.

"No! Don't talk to me about it. I will never, never give you my baby."

"All right." The nurse stood with a look of disgust on her face. "You don't have to act like I've done something wrong. I was just trying to save her from a questionable future."

That night Elena slept little, waking every few minutes to see if the baby was by her side. The relief was tremendous when morning came and the threat lessened. Reproaching herself for her needless fear, she began preparing for her trip home. After breakfast Lucia told her to get up, take a shower and change into her street clothes.

"Did señorita Marta telephone Isabel at Tulcachi?"

"Your ride home will be here shortly."

Chapter 29

"Is it all right if I wait awhile? I don't have any money with me to pay you so I would rather wait until my ride comes to start getting ready," she protested timidly, fearful of leaving the baby alone. "Are you sure my friends were telephoned in Tulcachi?"

"Yes, they are supposed to be here early this morning as I told you already. You must take a shower before you leave, so please do that quickly."

Elena did not want to displease Lucia so she disrobed, merely stepping into the shower to wet her body and then dressed quickly in her street clothes. Hoping to find Ramon and Isabel waiting, she left the bathroom and walked to one of the windows. The car was not in sight. She saw Lucia in the labor room and walked to her. Catching her breath sharply, she noticed Marta also standing inside the room. Turning toward the bassinet, Marta stopped her. "Lucia said you don't have money to pay for the delivery."

"No I don't, but my driver will be here any minute and he'll pay the bill. You were supposed to call them at the hacienda and tell him to come today. Lucia said that you did."

"I'm sorry, but we need your bed for other patients, so we have to ask you to leave." Marta ignored the question.

A terrible thought struck Elena and she turned again to the big room where she had left the baby. The crib sat in the same spot with the small bundle inside. Reassured, she returned to Marta and Lucia. "I don't understand. No one else is here. I must wait or I can try to call the hacienda."

"No, you'll have to leave. You can come back later for the baby, but I won't give her to you unless I have the money in full."

"My baby? I'm not leaving without my baby."

"And I'm not going to give her to you unless I have the money."

"Oh Dios mio. Where is my baby?" Panic engulfed her. She ran into the patient's ward and took up the bundle. Blankets fell through her hands to the floor. Angelita wasn't there. Elena ran from room to room shouting for her baby. Everything went blank as she fought for breath. Then the realization that Marta had taken her baby dawned on her and she rushed at the nurse with a murderous fury. "Where's my baby? Where's my Angelita?" She shrieked, clawing and scratching.

"Lucia, will you take her outside before someone gets hurt?"

The woman pulled the screaming girl into the hall, opened the patient's door and put her outside. Elena stood in shock, not believing what had happened. "All we need is the money, Elena, and we'll give you the baby. Try to find some money quickly," said Lucia.

In a nightmarish panic, she ran as if in a dream to the plaza, pounding on the doors of her own home. No one was there and the doors were locked. She stumbled, wailing hysterically, pleading for money from door to door. People ran to their windows and entrances to see who was making the commotion. They turned away embarrassed, remembering her state of mind at her husband's funeral. She appeared intoxicated and incoherent. Disgusted, the townspeople retreated behind closed doors.

Elena wandered the streets weeping. An hour later, she had finally found Ernestine who was able to give her the needed money, but stood helplessly trying to understand the ravings of the young girl standing before her, tearing at her hair and clothes. Gladys tried to stop Elena to ask what the matter was, but as the girl was rushing toward the Martinez home and she decided Elena was probably going home. But instead she was running back to the clinic and as she rushed to the door, she pounded with all her might.

Marta had been waiting and she opened the door quickly. "Do you have the money?"

Elena showed her the sucres, but the nurse started to shut the door. The girl pushed against it, until Marta lost patience. "You bring me only six hundred sucres?"

"That's what you told me I needed."

"It's double that amount now that you have caused such a problem for us." Marta pushed the girl down the steps.

Elena fell backwards and lay helplessly on the ground.

"Where are your friends? They've forgotten you, I see."

Noting Elena was dazed and unable to speak coherently, Marta relaxed a little. "Did you call the hacienda or tell a town official of your need?"

She shook her head dumbly.

"Elena, my dear, my mission in life is to rescue children's lives from ungodliness and place them in respectable homes. You'll be able to have other children in the future." She ignored the wild eyes

Chapter 29

and pathetic form lying on the dirt walkway. "I don't know if you can understand this, Elena, but the truth about your baby is that she is dead. She died while you were in the shower."

The words hit a nerve in the girl's confused mind. "Died? She didn't die. She's in your house. I want my baby." With a cry, Elena struggled to her feet. "I want my baby."

"No, it is the truth. She really did die." Marta reached into her pocket and unfolded a paper and thrust it into Elena's face. It was a death certificate. The words blurred, but Elena made out her own name and the words, 'Baby Angelita Tapia'.

She fainted. When she aroused, she was lying near the road and the door to the clinic was closed. Rising, she walked down to the Pan American highway and wandered slowly home.

Chapter 30

Now Rolando had a goal. Working in the truck was pleasurable because he knew each day's work would bring him closer to restoring Geoff's money. He had gone several weeks without an alcoholic drink; work was steady and Geoff was his friend. Even though he still kept his brother at a distance because of his leanings toward the church, he knew they could talk together and that was a far cry from their relationship the previous years.

The loss of Carlos hadn't affected him as much as he thought it would. That they had parted friends was sufficient, but Elena's condition worried him. Geoff's report of her state of appearance at Carlos' funeral surprised him. He understood that she loved Carlos, but he hadn't suspected the extent of her love. Geoff had seen through the drug induced sobriety and saw the wild grief in her eyes, but Rolando could comfort himself that Eric Perez was there to help her.

If he would have let his true fears be made known, he would have admitted he was afraid to visit Elena in Tulcachi just in case someone remembered him walking past the buildings that day. Maybe the peon already recalled he had given directions to a stranger; maybe the man would recollect what he looked like. He would have no good excuse for not coming forward and decided it would be better to call on Elena after the baby was born, thereby absolving himself of any feelings of neglect and guilt. By then everyone would have forgotten he had been in the region.

Chapter 30

All day he had been driving the truck on the road beyond the pueblo's swimming pool and up into the mountains where there was a large rock quarry. Hauling rocks for the construction workers who were laying a foundation a kilometer west of Pachuca had kept him busy the entire morning. He had taken a short nap after lunch in his father's bedroom and was now anxious to complete the job.

Turning a bend, he was surprised to see a little blue pickup sitting alongside the road. Since no one was inside the vehicle, he slowed down and looked around for Jillian, the American girl who was now living in the plaza area. Despite the fact he had seen her several times in the pickup carrying children back and forth to school or to some other function; he had never met her personally. He thought back to the conversation he had with Laura's children about her handing out postal cards with pictures of her homeland. Perhaps this was his chance. Braking the truck, he pulled up behind her pickup and softly closing the truck's door, he padded across a patch of green grass and around a small rise. Stopping short, he looked down on the girl napping on a large towel. Smirking with good humor, he sat several feet away from her.

As if she detected someone's presence, she opened her eyes, squinting against the brightness of the day and peered into his smiling face. Sitting upright, she adjusted her clothes, patted her light hair and looked at him sternly. Clearly she was fearful and probably wanted to be alone, but then she smiled and he saw she had a face that wasn't beautiful, but one that would be hard to forget. Her green eyes mellowed and he sensed a compassion and love that made him want to sit with her all afternoon, just to talk. There was no need for introductions.

"You're Rolando Martinez, aren't you?"

"Yes and I'm sorry if I woke you. I only came over to see if you were all right. I saw your pickup and wondered why you would be here." Looking around he saw a brown paper sack. "What is this, a picnic?"

She laughed. "No, I just wanted to get away for a while. Sometimes my house can get rather crowded. Do you know me?"

"Of course I do. You're señorita Jill. I've waited a long time to meet you."

"Please just call me Jill." She looked at him steadily. "I guess we had the same desire. I wanted to meet you too." Turning around, she dragged a thermos from the sack. "Would you like some cookies or coffee?"

"No thank you. I just ate my lunch."

There was a lengthy but comfortable silence between them. He rubbed the toe of his shoe into the grass aware she was studying him. He lifted his head and their eyes met. "How is it that we have lived in the same town for so long and haven't met each other?" He asked with a smile.

"I don't know. I guess because I'm seldom home."

"Yes, I've heard about your classes and have seen you driving into the mountains with your pickup full of children."

She laughed again. "You're right. I'm always going somewhere."

He didn't want to leave but when she moved to a more comfortable position, he realized maybe she wanted privacy. "I'm sorry. Am I bothering you?"

"Not at all. It's just that I'll have to return home soon. This was a special time for me. It's not often I can get away."

Making himself more comfortable, he grinned. "Maybe I will take a cookie. They look good."

She handed him a clear plastic bag and he took it, pulling out half a dozen. "Tell me about yourself. I hear you used to work with señorita Marta."

"Yes, for a few years."

"How was it living with Lucia and Marta?"

"It depended. Some days were wonderful, others difficult. The children made it worthwhile."

"I've heard about the children she took in. Did any of them live with you?"

"Yes, before I left I had several in my care."

"The nurse is a strange woman. I've had a rather sad experience because of her."

"Oh? How was that?"

"My mother was never the same after my sister, Elena was born. I blame her illness and death on señorita Marta. I begged her to help my mama when she was lying by the side of the road in heavy rain

Chapter 30

in full labor. She treated my mama like she was not worthwhile. I believe her words were not about her but why I didn't have a jacket on. What did that matter? Jill, because the señorita didn't help my mama, nothing was ever the same again."

"I've heard part of the story from friends. It's hard for the townspeople to forget rumors like that." Jillian leaned forward. "I'm aware of the suffering you endured when you were young and I'm so sorry. I would like to be your friend, Rolando."

His eyes brightened and he wiped his mouth with the back of his hand. "I'd like that. It's nice to be able to sit and talk with you."

"Did you know Elena is at Marta's clinic with her baby right now?"

Rolando's face fell in astonishment. "No, why would she be at that woman's clinic?"

"Apparently she couldn't make it to Quito yesterday. Marta's maid stopped by to see me and gave me the news. Elena's sister-in-law Yolanda stopped by also. She said she was going to wait to visit Elena in Tulcachi later because Yolanda claims she wants nothing to do with Marta. We've become rather good friends."

His heart missed a beat. Imagine what Yolanda would have told Jillian about his extended stay in her home. Praying that he looked unperturbed, he merely shook his head.

"Have you seen Elena since the funeral?" Jillian must have noticed his discomfort because she changed the subject.

"No." Regaining his composure, he replied curtly, covering his uneasiness.

"Why don't you go down to the clinic and visit her?"

"I haven't seen her in such a long time, I don't know if she wants to visit with me."

"Oh, Rolando, that's silly. Of course she wants to see you."

"There are a lot of things you don't know."

"Perhaps, but I can assure you there are a lot of things I do know." She leveled her eyes at him. "Don't miss this opportunity."

Feeling uncomfortable, he stood. "I must leave. I'd like to finish my other haul job today."

"If you ever need to talk or just need a friend, please come to see me."

"Thank you." He grabbed her hand gratefully. "I will do that."

Sitting inside the truck, his heart beat with excitement. Elena. She was only a few hundred meters from where he was sitting. He could run the truck down to the clinic in just a minute and visit with her. No, not yet. He would wait until tomorrow. As it was he had sat for two hours this morning waiting until the peons at the quarry showed up for work. He would finish the job today or tomorrow morning and then visit Elena. Maybe he could ask Geoff to go with him, but no, the desire to see his sister and ask for her forgiveness was something he needed to do alone.

Early Tuesday morning he rose, eager to see Elena. Grooming himself carefully, he ate a hurried breakfast, laughingly ignoring his aunt's inquiries. She had not yet forgiven Elena.

By the time he arrived at the clinic it was eight o'clock. Pausing at the bottom of the driveway, it struck him what he was doing. How did he know Elena would be glad to see him? He remembered her temper and the silent treatments he received when she was angry with him. Perhaps Carlos had regained consciousness long enough to tell Eric that Rolando had been there. Maybe they were waiting until after the baby was born to speak with him concerning Carlos' death. Maybe with a baby Elena would have no room for him in her life. He could not bear another rejection from her. After all, Elena had left him in the first place. In agony, he stood on the road and with a final shrug of his shoulders he turned and walked back to the truck he had parked at Geoff's house. Geoff and Opal had gone by bus into Quito on an errand and Raquel was enjoying four days off with her family and wouldn't return to Pachuca until late morning. He would wait until after work this evening and talk Geoff into going with him after all.

Sadly he drove to his next job, his mind heavy with thoughts of Elena. He would ask for her forgiveness later when he visited with her in Tulcachi. Perhaps if Geoff went with him, she would be happier to see him.

Chapter 31

Teaching classes in the boys' school was more pleasurable than at the girls' school because the building was spacious and well lit. Each room had several windows either broken or opened allowing the gentle morning's breeze to freshen the well-populated interior. Jillian looked forward to the mornings she spent with the boys because many of the rooms in the girls' school had no windows resulting in poor lighting. Children, desks, supplies and teachers were stuffed into rooms slightly larger than Jillian's balcony. The smell of smoke that clung to the children's clothes, unwashed bodies and lack of fresh air made her long for the out of doors.

She mentally checked off the supplies in her shopping bag as she made her way to the boys' school: scissors, paste, stacks of colored paper. As she approached the white two-story building north of the market and soccer field, she met a nine-year-old girl trudging home with a baby strapped to her back and a basket of meager provisions on her arm. She knew the child had attended school for a year, but would never be able to return because her mother was pregnant again and working in the fields leaving the baby's care to the young girl. It was an oft-repeated story. Jillian acknowledged the girl's murmured greeting, grimacing only when she was well past her at the sight of the child's face, prematurely worn and lined.

Today, Jillian planned to instruct the second grade boys on how to make a freight truck. They would cut out the parts: wheels, cab, windows and back end in various bright colors and paste them on the outline of a truck which Jillian had traced the night before. The remaining few class minutes would be spent in teaching the boys the English words relating to the truck.

While the children lowered their heads to concentrate on cutting out the colored papers, Jillian wandered behind the teacher's desk. A row of windows provided a good view of Marta's property. The yard was empty of children but, as always, a strong sense of loss squeezed her heart. The feeling lingered when a shy boy half way to the back of the room softly asked her for help.

She was bent over his desk, guiding his hand around a black tire when one of the teachers rushed into the room, calling her name. Alarmed, she lifted her head and then followed the teacher into the corridor.

"Señorita, you must take your vehicle to the mountains. There has been a terrible accident."

The rapid-fire Spanish was lost on Jillian. She tried to calm the agitated teacher. "Señor, please speak a little slower. I need to understand."

He gave her a bewildered look as if to question why she couldn't understand simple Spanish. "There has been an accident in the mountains close to Papallacta," he sputtered.

"You say there was an accident in the mountains?" She asked to make sure she understood the second time, as the agitated teacher was again running his words together.

"Si, señorita Jill," he repeated patiently. "Doctor Raquel sent a messenger to tell you to go to the mountains on the road to Papallacta."

"Papallacta. The road to the jungle?" She asked, further alarmed. "Was a vehicle involved? What kind of accident? The roads are very dangerous."

"I'm not sure, but I believe a pickup truck filled with many people fell over the side of a cliff into one of the deep ravines. They will need every available vehicle to help carry out the dead and injured."

"Am I to meet Doctor Raquel somewhere?"

"Señorita, the doctor arrived from Quito and has already left Pachuca." The man wrung his hands. "She said you are to drive toward Papallacta until you get to the accident."

Chapter 31

"Will you please gather my materials when the children have finished their project? Gracias."

With a sense of doom she ran home, passing several Pachuca residents standing quietly on the road, their faces rigid from shock and their hands covering their mouths in horror. News of the accident had reached them and now they must wait to hear if the victims were members of their families. She grabbed two pieces of bread, some fruit and peanuts. No telling how long she would be gone. Gladys' family gathered around their front door and watched her with large, fearful eyes as she drove her truck out of sight.

The Sierra region lies between two chains of the Andes, the Cordillera Occidental and the Cordillera Oriental. The giant mountains divide like two twin backbones. Pachuca sits at the base of the eastern ridge at about nine thousand feet altitude. To reach Papallacta, she would have to crest the eastern heights several thousand feet higher before descending the treacherous road leading to the jungle. Well traveled by buses, trucks and other means of transportation, it was not uncommon for accidents to occur on the narrow, unpaved road. Jillian suspected, however, this accident was more severe than some. She drove past Carlos' family home and thought about his recent burial. A dark heaviness bore down on her as she drove up the steady incline before taking the turn off toward Papallacta. She twisted around hairpin turns and drove between huge boulders before emerging on a vast hilly highland that stretched as far as the eye could see, carpeted with tough yellow-green grass, punctuated by scrub brush. The road continued to climb beside a ravine carved so deeply in the earth that one could perhaps see bottom only by stopping the car, getting out and leaning out perilously over the edge. She shuddered at the thought and focused on navigating her way around the gullies and deep potholes. The road was without benefit of guardrails and noted for heavy landslides. She rolled down the window and could almost feel the silence beyond the pickup's small puttering motor. She hated this area for its isolation. For miles there were no homes, no people and no cattle. Now and then, almost by magic, a hacienda rose from behind a hill and round about it would be a scattering of small huts like children surrounding their parents. Beyond would lay fields of corn, wheat and herds of animals. Then shortly, the bustle of peons, tractors and horses would be replaced with desolation and unearthly silence.

I wonder how far I have to go, she thought, skirting a huge pothole and keeping an eye on the deep drop to her right.

Off and on during the past few days Eric had crept into her mind. She thought about him now. Will he come to Pachuca to visit Elena at Marta's clinic? Sunday evening, Flora had dropped by Jillian's house to inform her Elena had been admitted into the clinic to have her baby. She was surprised to hear Eric hadn't been with her when she arrived. Instead a man and woman from the hacienda had transported her in their car, according to the report Flora had heard from Lucia around the dinner table that evening. Jillian surmised the man and woman were Ramon and Isabel. Now, today, Elena would be going home. Maybe Eric would come to pick her up. She was puzzled why he hadn't been at Elena's side when she had arrived as he had been during Carlos' funeral.

Her mind drifted to Rolando and then to a small landslide which covered half the road. She slowed the pickup down to a crawl in order to pass it. Safely past the obstacle, she released a deep breath and returned her thoughts to Rolando Martinez and their visit. For years she had wanted to meet him. It seemed from the first day she had lived in Pachuca she had heard about him in one way or another. Yesterday following an English class in her home, she left her students putting together a colorful jigsaw puzzle while she went for a drive. Seeking peace and quiet she drove to a tiny steam behind the town swimming pool. Parking by the road, she scouted out a spot further upstream beneath a tall tree. After drinking a cup of coffee from her thermos and eating two cookies she had baked last week, she leaned back on a large beach towel and fell asleep. To her astonishment, when she opened her eyes, Rolando was there, sitting on the grass, watching her. With great control she hid her surprise and stared back. She had to admit the reports she'd heard about him were true. He was a very handsome man. His brown hair and eyes, which lent him a foreign look, contrasted with the black eyes and hair common to most Ecuadorian Indians. Though his face was friendly as they conversed, she sensed hardness beneath the veneer of cordiality. Was that a result of the hatred and bitterness he harbored of

Chapter 31

which Raquel had spoken? Jillian had told him his sister, Elena was at the clinic. From the surprise on his face she realized no one had taken the trouble to tell the family.

Almost two hours into her trip, her thoughts returned to the present at the sight of a throng of people and several buses and trucks halted beside the road. She nosed the mini-pickup as close to the crowd as she dared and searched for Raquel. The doctor was kneeling over a woman at the edge of the cliff, examining her. Beyond Raquel she saw Philip Rios squatting on his haunches holding open a man's eyelids, peering into them.

Jillian slowly got out of the pickup, aware again despite the crowd, of the eerie pervasive silence of this vast countryside. Audible only were the distant sounds of words and groans rising from the chasm below. Earthly concepts of time and space felt foreign now, almost as if she were on another planet. Slowly approaching Raquel, she watched as her friend looked up at her without recognition so overwhelmed was she with the extensive casualties and lack of proper medical supplies. Philip too, was burdened; he saw Jillian and nodded only a greeting. Walking to the chasm's edge, she looked down upon a red pickup lying in a mangled heap. Some of the bodies lay around the vehicle and some hung out the windows and the back end. She realized the groans were not coming from the victims but from the men who, on makeshift stretchers were carrying bodies up the side of the cliff. Their grunts of exhaustion bounced off the ravine walls and echoed faintly in her ears.

Raquel ordered the half dozen men to place three bodies in Jillian's pickup bed. "Turn your truck around," she solemnly instructed Jillian. "Take them to the clinic in Pachuca. We'll find a big truck or bus to haul them from there."

Horrified, Jillian followed Raquel who had turned her attention to another stretcher being hauled from below. "But Raqui, why can't we put them in one of these big trucks right now?"

"Because they are full of supplies and there is no more room in the trucks. You have to take the bodies to Pachuca. I'd piled more in your pickup, but I'm afraid the weight will put your truck out of balance on these terrible roads. Please go slow, as I'm sure you did on your trip here. We have other pickups coming from the hacienda you passed so you won't have to return up here. I know it won't be pleasant, but you have to do it." She flung her arm toward Philip. "Doctor Rios, the doctor from the Pachuca clinic and I have our hands full. We can't go back with you."

"Who will be at the clinic when I arrive?"

"Go to the government clinic and Olivia should be there. She'll have someone to help her, I hope."

It was her worst nightmare and as the helpers squeezed three mangled bodies, a deceased woman and two men in the back of her truck, she asked that they cover their faces with jackets. Gunning the motor, she slowly ascended the dirt road to the summit and down the other side, carefully skirting the drop-offs and pot holes, praying all the way she could soon rid herself of this hideous burden.

Ages later, or so it seemed, she finally drove up in front of the clinic and Olivia ran from the building, followed by several young men. Some women huddled at the curb, straining to see if one of the dead was a loved one. It was apparent the faces of the victims were unfamiliar to them for they stepped back and heaved sighs of relief and said grateful prayers of thanksgiving.

Parking the truck in front of her house, she went inside and returned with a bucket of soapy water and a broom to scrub the pickup bed. Leaving her truck at the Ortega's, she numbly ambled home. A cluster of women waited for her, eager for news. Did she recognize any of their loved ones? Did she see the vehicle that crashed? Did its owner live in Pachuca?

Not knowing the vehicle's make, she was reluctant to name its color, so she claimed to know very little. The women would hear soon enough.

After the group dispersed, Gladys found Jillian sitting in her kitchen. "Buenas tardes, señorita. I brought you some soup. I thought you would need something to eat after what you have been through today."

"Gracias, Gladys," she said sniffing deeply of the aromatic vegetable soup. "I took some food along but I had no appetite." She took a spoon from the cabinet and seated herself again. "It was terrible."

The woman took a chair opposite Jillian and leaned forward on her elbow, concern wrinkling her face. "Were there many dead?"

Chapter 31

"I don't know how many. There are some. I really don't think anyone lived. Oh, Gladys, why do they have to put so many people in those pickups? I heard people talking about it while I was waiting for them to load the three bodies in my truck. There must have been seventeen people in that little pickup. They said the driver was speeding. I think he was just a young man, too young for such a responsibility."

"The fares he charges will help make payments on his truck. That's why they put so many inside. Did you recognize the truck?"

"No, I couldn't even tell what model it was. I'm sure we will find out soon. Hopefully it wasn't from Pachuca." Her voice drifted to a whisper.

"Something else happened today."

Her head came up. "What?"

"Just after you left I heard a terrible noise. It sounded like yelling. Someone was pounding on doors in the plaza and trying to interrupt people waiting for news from the accident."

"Who was it?" She stopped chewing.

"I thought it was someone who heard his relative had been killed in the accident so I ran to the door of our store to see who it was. I was so surprised to see Elena Martinez—er, Elena Tapia running from door to door and group to group.

Jillian put down her spoon. "Elena? What was wrong?"

"I don't know. I thought I heard her begging for money, but it was hard to understand her. Jill, she was crazy, like a lunatic. I think she has lost her mind since her husband's death. Maybe news of the accident near Papallacta reminded her of Carlos."

"Money? She was begging for money? Did anyone give her some?"

"I don't know for sure that's what she wanted but I saw Ernestina give her some. I don't know. I think everyone thought she was crazy and because the townspeople had their minds on the accident, I think they thought she was upset because of it."

"But, Gladys, she just delivered a baby. She's been in Marta Brewer's clinic for the past two days."

"A baby?"

Jillian stood hastily. "Yes, she was supposed to deliver a baby yesterday or the night before."

"Why was she asking for money? Surely she has enough living with Eric Perez."

"I don't know why, but I do know that Marta Brewer cannot be trusted. Do you know where Elena went?"

"No, I thought of following her, but she was going to her family home, I think. She went in that direction, so I returned to the store."

More distressed than she had been all morning, Jillian escorted Gladys to the store and then walked up and down the street, asking the residents where Elena had gone. Geoff, Opal or Rolando weren't home. Raquel had spent a four day weekend in Quito and had hurriedly returned to attend the accident. Anyone she met in the street didn't seem to know or care. The accident in Papallacta and the bodies that were slowly being trucked in had everyone preoccupied.

Chapter 32

Early Wednesday morning Ramon and Isabel arrived at the clinic. They peeked through the window and saw that Elena's bed had been made up. Running to the door, they knocked briskly. Lucia opened it and seeing who stood there, reached to ring a bell. While Lucia was busy with the bell, Isabel ducked past her and started toward the patient's room, but Lucia hurried after her and blocked the woman's way.

"Señorita Marta will be here in a moment. Will you please wait?" she requested coldly.

Isabel gave Lucia a dark stare but turned back to where Ramon stood. In a matter of moments a kitchen door opened and Marta approached.

"Buenos dias," she said roughly. "I'm very busy."

"Buenos dias," they chorused.

"We have come for Elena Martinez Tapia," said Isabel. "She delivered a girl child on Sunday."

"I told you to come for her on Tuesday. She's not here."

The couple was shocked speechless. Shaking her head, Isabel finally found her voice. "What do you mean? You told us to return on Wednesday, not Tuesday. Here we are and now you say Elena is not in the clinic?"

"That's what I said. She left yesterday."

Ramon stepped forward. "I don't understand. How did she leave? Where did she go?"

Disdainfully, Marta put her hand on her hip. "I don't know what happened to the girl. How she got home is not my concern."

Isabel and Ramon shook their heads and turned to each other and then Marta ushered them out and shut the door.

"I feel funny about this." Ramon shook his head. "The American told us Wednesday not Tuesday. She made a point of telling us. I'm confused."

"Shall we call the United States and tell señor Eric?"

"No, let's wait. We can check around the plaza. I'm not sure where her family lives, but I think she would have gone there until she could find a ride this morning. She's probably at the hacienda right now. Maybe we just missed each other."

Isabel wrung her hands. "Yes, no doubt. Our poor little girl. To think she had to go through all this by herself."

Ramon chewed on his lower lip and grabbed the wheel tightly, avoiding potholes as they drove up and down the streets, searching. "I know señor Perez is going to be upset that we were not with her."

"Yes."

They stopped and asked a few people about Elena, but no one knew where she was.

"We're strangers to them," Isabel complained after their fourth stop. "But I feel strongly that Elena isn't here."

"Let's go on to the hacienda," agreed Ramon. "We're wasting time here."

The trip seemed to take forever but upon their arrival they found Elena hadn't been there nor had anyone seen her. They immediately drove to Quito and telephoned the United States. Eric said he would leave for South America very early the next morning and would arrive in Quito just after noon.

Frustrated and frightened, Ramon and Isabel neglected their duties and sat sadly the rest of the day in Tulcachi waiting for Elena. After they had left Quito they returned to Pachuca and had driven through the plaza asking more questions, but no clear answer was received. Everyone seemed to be more pre-occupied with a terrible accident that had happened the previous day which left many dead and injured in a neighboring town.

Chapter 33

Eric arrived in Quito the next day. He was beyond reasoning when they related the story. Ramon drove quickly back to the hacienda under Eric's instructions, but Elena was nowhere to be found. He decided to visit Marta and Ramon drove him to Pachuca. Jumping from the car, Eric ran to the door and began banging loudly. Lucia opened it, smiling as Marta appeared behind her. The nurse asked him into the kitchen, after he introduced himself and invited him to take a chair.

"What may I do for you señor Perez? I have heard a great deal about your productive hacienda."

His blue eyes blazed with impatience. "I'll stand, thank you. I'm here about Elena Tapia. I understand she left here with her baby on Tuesday, but I've not been able to locate her."

"Yes, she did leave here, but not with the baby."

He leaned forward in dismay. "Not with the baby. What do you mean?"

"I mean she didn't have the baby with her."

Sagging backwards, his head began to pound. "Why? What happened that she would leave without the baby?"

"Because the baby died."

"Died?"

"She was hopelessly premature and didn't survive more than thirty-six hours." Shaking her head sadly, she reached into her pocket. "Here's the death certificate."

Eric studied it. There was Elena's name and Baby Angelita Tapia spelled out on the line designated for the child's name. There was also the scribbling of some other name at the bottom that he assumed at the time was a medical official. He lost hope. "Oh, dios mio, help her. Where is the baby?" he choked on the words.

"We rushed her to the government hospital, but the baby died on the way."

"Where is her body?"

"We left it in the care of one of the doctors. I'm sorry. I didn't get his name and I can't read his name at the bottom of this paper. No telling where the body would be now. She's probably already buried."

He stumbled from the clinic and into the car. Through tears of grief, he explained the situation to Ramon and Isabel.

"Why didn't the señorita tell us when we were here yesterday?" sobbed Isabel.

They all shook their heads, unable to comprehend the news.

"Where could she be?" Eric mumbled.

"Perhaps she went to Carlos' uncle's house in Quito," offered Ramon.

"Of course." Eric sat upright. "We must go to Quito. That's where she is."

They drove off. Days later he would think to follow up on where the child had been taken but by the time he tried to find the trail, the baby's body was hopelessly lost in governmental red tape and Marta claimed she no longer had the death certificate but had released it to a governmental official. It would haunt him the rest of his life.

He and his companions raced to Quito. After an extensive search they located Jose's home, but were stunned to hear Elena had not turned to them for refuge. In an effort to calm Jose and Carlota, Eric promised to call them the minute he learned where Elena was.

They returned to the hacienda. No one had seen her. Eric called his workers together and told them to be ready at dawn to form a search party. They were to walk every route from Tulcachi to Pachuca, searching inch by inch for the girl. He, in turn, was going to visit Elena's family again. He had stopped by the family home, but, though they were deeply concerned, her brother Geoff confessed they hadn't seen his sister since the funeral. They promised to join the search team the next day. Rolando would also be there. Eric was very interested

Chapter 33

in knowing where Rolando had been all this time, but Geoff said he had been faithfully driving the family truck and had not mentioned Elena at all.

Eric spent the night in the living room, wringing his hands and pacing the floor. He blamed himself for leaving her. He was angry with Isabel for not insisting on staying with Elena. Why hadn't they returned to visit her on Tuesday? No housekeeping duties could be that important. It was both Isabel's and Ramon's faults for not returning on Tuesday. Couldn't Ramon make a decision on his own? What was wrong with the man? His mind refused to function any longer; in sheer exhaustion he sat on the sofa. Finally, just before dawn, as he started to fall into a stuporous sleep, he knew where she was. Wrapping his poncho about him, he walked slowly out the back door. Dragging his feet, his heart pounding in his ears, he stumbled through the pasture behind the house and up the steep hillside to the unusual ledge jutting from the edge of the ridge. Under the two eucalyptus trees the earth still appeared fresh where they had buried Carlos. Eric knew he would find her nearby and as he searched in the predawn light, he saw her lying beside one of the trees. Time stood still. He heard the birds singing, announcing the morning's arrival. Roosters crowed in the distant barnyard and the soft lowing of cattle reached his ears. Looking down across the valley, it struck him why Carlos had so loved this spot. He watched the tip of Mt. Cotapoxi light up with a blazing orange glow and in the distance Mt. Pichincha turned from grey to green. He didn't want to look at Elena. Not yet. A thousand memories flooded his mind and each one reflected her laughter and joy. There would be no remembrance of her sorrow. He resolved to keep it that way.

Turning his back on the sunlight that had begun to engulf Quito, he forced himself to walk to her. Exposure in the harsh cold mountain night had sapped her life; he was stunned at her condition. In her grief she had torn her clothes; and her long black hair framed her face wildly, but it was her face that captured his attention. In death, it was finally at peace; more so than he had seen it since Carlos' death. He took off his poncho and laid it across her body and from somewhere in the depths of his being, a low moan escaped as he lay beside her and wept.

Chapter 34

Marta dropped the curtain into place and sighed deeply. She couldn't remember when she had been so badly frightened. Who would have dreamed Eric would have returned so quickly from his mother's bedside in the United States?

"You're lucky he didn't question you further about the baby's body," Lucia spoke in perfect English behind her.

With a startled jump the nurse stomped her right foot and turned. "Will you stop sneaking up behind me?" She glared at the Indian for a moment. "Why would he have questioned me further? I think I handled things very well."

"I don't like it." Lucia's small dark eyes closed for a moment. "You should never have taken this baby. There are too many important people involved: Rolando, Eric, Geoff…"

"I need this baby. Did you check on her in my bedroom like I asked you to?"

"Of course."

"Look." The nurse rummaged through a large pocket in her uniform. Transferring a wadded handkerchief to the opposite pocket, she retrieved a piece of notebook paper along with another paper. Unfolding them, she pushed one toward Lucia.

"A family in New York needs a baby girl and look what they're willing to pay for her. We can have her in their home in six weeks. I have the death certificate here. Our attorney will produce papers that will appear as though the baby is an orphan and up for adoption.

Chapter 34

No where in the papers will Ecuador be shown as the birthplace. That's it."

"I just want to get her out of here. She makes me nervous."

"Why? Both Elena and Eric believe she's dead. Rolando is too drunk to care. Elena's parents are dead and Geoff is certainly no threat. His character is so weak, he'd never try to follow up or do anything about it. Her uncle and aunt, Mariana and Hector don't seem to have anything to do with Elena now that she ran away to marry so they'll never ask about the baby."

"I don't know. I've had a funny feeling about this since Elena started her prenatal care here. She's been like a splinter in my hand."

"Yes and a thorn in my side, but the family has been that since Elena was born. Well, she'll never find out. I have even made sure the little girl will never know where she's from. My lawyer will extract a promise from the couple in New York that they will never tell the child where she was born. They'll just say her family lived in Mexico or some other Latin American country and somehow she ended up in the United States. I'll give the attorney her death certificate and he can put it in his files along with all her papers, just in case there are questions. In that way, even when she is old enough to show interest in her birthplace, she will never know it was Pachuca, Ecuador. You see?"

Lucia shook her head in resignation as Marta returned the request for a baby and the death certificate to her pocket.

"Now, I should call the lawyer. He'll just have to take care of the baby at his house. I agree with you. I want her out of here as soon as possible."

Chapter 35

When two days passed with no news of Elena, Jillian decided she must drive to Tulcachi. Geoff had heard early Wednesday morning that his sister was still in the clinic but when Rolando and Geoff tried to visit her, they were told Elena had already left for home. They tried questioning everyone who worked on señorita Marta's compound but had come away with very little information. Marta and Lucia had not been home and Flora, the maid, offered all she knew about Elena just prior to her exit from the clinic. Yes, Flora confirmed, Elena had delivered her baby at the clinic but she had left for home the previous day. No, Flora hadn't personally seen her leave, but because new mothers normally remained in the clinic only two days, she had thought nothing of it. Baby? Of course the baby was with Elena. Where else would the baby be?

They had driven to Tulcachi, but the peons they spoke with knew nothing of Elena's whereabouts and they were told that Eric Perez was still in the United States. Every time they tried to connect with señor Perez's chauffeur and cook, the couple was away.

When Geoff stopped by Jillian's house later that afternoon, he was greatly agitated. The urgency to find Elena prompted Jillian to drive to Tulcachi herself. She could not rest until she knew Elena was safely at home. She was also curious why Eric would travel out of the country when Elena remained at home to deliver her baby alone. Why had he not seen to it that the girl be attended by doctors in Quito? Why would Elena have delivered her baby in Marta's

Chapter 35

clinic, of all places? "It's as if I had never spoken to him about the nurse's shady dealings with patients. Why can't he hear what I say?" muttered Jillian angrily. She vowed she would speak with every peon on the hacienda until she found the answer. Isabel would know. Thank goodness Elena and the baby would be in the capable hands of Isabel. The thought that kept nagging her was the report that Elena had been running through the streets asking for help. She had to admit she didn't believe it was Elena at all. It didn't make sense. It was probably a frightened girl resembling Elena who believed one of her loved ones had been injured or killed in the dreadful accident in Papallacta. If Isabel and Elena weren't at the hacienda, then she would drive to Quito and speak with Helen. Elena and the baby were probably resting comfortably in the beautiful house with all the comforts a new mother could hope for.

She was unable to get away from the house because of two important errands she had saved for her day off. By the time she was free of her obligations, the sun was nearly overhead. Perhaps it is better, she thought, to arrive at Tulcachi at the onset of siesta for by then the peons will have gathered for lunch, saving me the trouble of tracking them down.

When she drove into the front yard of Tulcachi Hacienda, she was surprised to find the yard deserted. There were no workers on the porch, no children and no saddled horses. She looked at her watch. The siesta hour had not yet begun so the yard should have been a beehive of activity in preparation for the noon hour.

She parked the pickup and walked to the back of the central house. The kitchen was cold and dark supporting her theory that Isabel and Elena had gone to Quito. Passing through it to the patio she stopped, puzzled. The entire hacienda seemed to be deserted. On impulse, she retraced her footsteps through the kitchen and went around the corner of the house. She was shocked to see Eric's truck parked under a eucalyptus tree. Could he have returned or was he driving the sedan? A dark ominous thought struck her. Something was terribly wrong.

Hurrying through the kitchen again and along the outside corridor of the house beside the patio, she entered the living room. There she found Eric, slumped in a sofa corner, asleep. Her heart lurched. She hadn't seen him at close range for over two years. He looked aged. Perhaps it was the way his head hung on his chest that deepened the lines on his face, the features of which, in sleep, wore a look of pain. He was huddled under a blanket, his muddy boots pushed out before him. Two days' growth of gray beard lent him an unkempt look. Had he been drinking? Why hadn't he gone to Quito with Elena? With this thought came a feeling of guilt. She was intruding on his privacy. In sleep he was unable to protect his dignity. Turning to leave, she stopped as she heard footsteps sounding overhead. She lifted her head and by doing so, failed to see the wastebasket by a chair in the narrow room. There was a clatter and Eric bolted to an upright position.

"What's the matter?" he uttered wildly, disoriented.

She whirled around, a smile of apology on her face, but her smile froze as she looked at him. His face was haggard and gaunt, his eyes deep-set and hollow.

"Jill?"

"Yes, I came to see you."

To her dismay, he buried his head in his hands and groaned. Then as the blanket moved, she saw the pile of tissues on his lap. "Eric, what's the matter?" She sat beside him. "I came about Elena."

"What do you know about Elena?" His head swung toward her. "What about Elena?"

"I'm so confused. I came because I heard she delivered a baby. I came to see if she is here." She stopped talking, waiting for him to say something. When he didn't she sat beside him and continued lamely. "Someone told me they thought they saw her in the plaza asking for money and help. I wanted to know if it was really Elena. That's why I'm here."

His blue eyes darkened with anger and his voice lashed out at her. "When she asked, did you give her money?"

Taken back by his outburst, she replied. "So it was Elena. Eric, I wasn't home. My neighbor told me about her. Her brothers and I have been trying to find her. They went to the clinic but the maid said she left two days ago. From your response, I guess you haven't found her either."

Chapter 35

He leaned his elbows on his knees and his head sank into his hands. "I found her."

"You did?" Her face showed a mixture of delight and puzzlement. "When did you find her? Where was she? Eric, what's the matter?"

"I found her this morning on my property. She was lying beside her husband's grave."

Her heart plummeted. "Is she here? May I see her?"

His voice dropped to a whisper. "Jill, she's dead. She was dead when I found her. If I had just thought of where she was the evening before, I could have saved her."

"Dead?" Jillian sprang to her feet. "How could she be dead? Two days ago she was in Pachuca. Four days ago she delivered a baby. It was on Sunday wasn't it? How can she be dead?"

He remained motionless, his eyes fixed on the floor at his feet. "It's my fault. Why didn't I think of where she'd be yesterday? Jill, I was in the United States. I left her here alone." He gave her a pleading look. "I couldn't help it. Everything seemed to happen at the same time."

Sitting at his side, she leaned toward him. "Why were you in the United States? You must have had an important reason for leaving."

A sob caught in his throat. "My mother was having difficulty breathing and her chest was painful. The doctors here said she could have a heart attack at any moment, so they stabilized her heart until I could get her to New York. She's to have surgery tomorrow morning and I won't be there." He gave her a dry chuckle. "I don't even know how she is."

"How awful for your mother. Oh, Eric I'm so sorry."

"Elena wasn't supposed to have her baby for several days. I thought I would be home before it happened."

"Wait. The baby—where is the baby?" A dark suspicion gathered in Jillian's mind. "Is the baby here?"

"Nothing that has happened makes sense to me. First Carlos dies, then Elena and now the baby is dead."

A silence fell on the room and Jillian took a deep breath. "Dead? The baby is dead? How can that be?"

"I don't know what I did to deserve this. Just a few months ago I was more content than I've ever been in my life." He turned his gaze on her. "Jill, I had never been happier. Carlos was like a son to me and I loved Elena as a daughter. Everyone looked forward to the birth of their baby. I was to be the baby's godfather. I had made the child heir in my will. I had everything, now I have nothing."

She suppressed a desire to brush back a lock of hair fallen in his eyes. "Who told you the baby is dead?"

"Marta Brewer told me when I went to look for Elena." His eyes closed in memory.

"Marta Brewer." Jillian's voice fell to a low growl. "Marta Brewer told you the baby is dead and you believed her? Don't tell me you believed her."

His head came up, an angry look clouding his face. "Of course I believed her. She showed me the death certificate."

Jillian laughed without mirth. "Death certificate. Oh, Eric, Marta Brewer can whip out death certificates as easily as you can saddle a horse." At once his eyes looked sharp and alert. "You have been deceived. I will guarantee the baby is now on its way out of Ecuador. Some nice family will adopt it, believing the infant has been abandoned by its parents. They will innocently tell their friends and family that Marta Brewer saved yet another baby from death's door. Why didn't you ask to see the baby, even though it was dead?"

"I wasn't thinking straight. All I could think about was Elena. Marta said Elena had left the clinic, distressed because of the baby's death. Marta said the baby was premature and dying, so they rushed it to the government hospital. And there she died."

"That's a lie. She? The baby is a girl? She was probably alive and well at the time Marta was talking to you. There was no hospital trip. You can believe me. Elena left to find money. We both know that now. Marta wouldn't give her the baby unless she had money. When Elena couldn't find any, she sent her away. Even if she had found the money, Marta would have had another excuse. She would have said the baby had died."

"Dios mio." He stood shakily. "What Elena must have gone through."

"Yes, because Marta can be cruel without realizing it. She always thinks she is being helpful, but actually she is shortsighted. She thinks only of herself and her friends in the United States, the ones on the

Chapter 35

receiving end. She has no understanding of the nationals. In all the years she's lived here, she's never learned that they are human beings too, with deep emotions."

"You tried to warn me." He walked unsteadily back and forth, running his hands through his hair. "Why didn't I listen? I thought you were obsessed with your boys." He stopped in front of her, his eyes fixed on hers. "If I hadn't been so stubborn and proud, you would have remained my companion and become Elena's friend. You could have warned her about Marta. Oh God, what have I done?"

She placed a hand on his arm. "Stop it! It's too late to think about that."

"What you must think of me," he said in a self-loathing tone.

"I won't listen to you degrade yourself. If anyone knew about Marta, Elena did. It's no secret that the Martinez family believes their mother's sickness and death was a result of Marta's neglect. Why would she have gone to that clinic? Marta doesn't usually take in a woman who hasn't had her prenatal care there. Why was Marta treating Elena?"

"Marta's clinic was a place to go only if Elena couldn't get to Quito. The day she went into labor, there was an automobile race on the highway to Quito. Ramon, my mother's driver could only drive toward Pachuca. It was all a set of terrible circumstances."

Memories of living with Marta flashed through her mind. During her five years with the nurse, she had seen and heard enough to know that if Marta wanted a baby badly enough, she could find a way of taking it from its mother. She could only imagine the trauma Elena had experienced that day as the baby was ripped from her arms. This was evident from the anguish she had demonstrated as she ran through the streets of Pachuca begging for money. What a disastrous coincidence that she would lose her baby the same day the residents of Pachuca had suffered the loss of several friends in a neighboring town in the fateful accident on the road to Papallacta. The townspeople had been unable to handle both tragedies and as a result many lives had been lost from the valley in one day. In that moment Jillian surrendered any feeling of friendship she had nursed for Marta over the years as she imagined the torment young Elena Martinez Tapia had suffered at the hands of the over-zealous nurse.

That sick woman, Jillian thought. She really believes she is acting in accordance with God's will.

"Where is Elena now?"

"She's upstairs. I'm keeping her there until the funeral tomorrow. Would you like to see her?"

"Yes."

He smiled for the first time and reached out to take her elbow. "Come then."

They walked to the end of the corridor and climbed a flight of stairs to the second floor. He hesitated before an open door and gently guided her into a large room. At the far end a set of shuttered windows stood open allowing a soft, cool breeze to stir throughout the room. Along the walls sat several empty straight-backed chairs. Elena lay on a long table in the center. The room contained no other furniture and the walls were bare. She surmised that the space was being utilized for the first time in years. Because the Perez family was not Catholic, there were no candles, no pictures of the Madonna and no religious trinkets in evidence.

As she entered the room, Jillian noticed a young boy seated close to the body. In one hand he waved a large fan, his other hand held a fly swat. Eric saw her looking at him. "He's here to wave away any flies that might land on her. The more persistent pests will be dealt a flow from the swat. I have seen to it that someone will be here to keep vigil until she is buried."

Moving forward, she stood by the girl who had weaved in and out of her life for years though she had seen Elena only on two occasions, many years before on Jillian's first weekend in Pachuca and at Carlos' funeral. Now she looked down at the girl. Elena was dressed in a dark blue dress with a white collar. Her eyes were closed and her black hair was in a thick braid over her shoulder. She was glad she couldn't see the girl's eyes, afraid that one glimpse of them might have revealed Elena's suffering which would have haunted her for the rest of her life. Poor Elena. Jillian knew firsthand what it was like to lose her dearest possession to Marta's cunning. She studied the fine, delicate formation of Elena's face and understood why Carlos was willing to leave everything behind to be with her. She had seen Elena laughing that day in the plaza so many years ago. It had been

Chapter 35

a lilting, charming laugh, a reflection of the freshness of her young womanhood. How unfair life was that through their own craftiness, Marta and Lucia should survive and the innocent should suffer premature death. It was also obvious that Elena hadn't been dead for many hours and wondered if things would have been different if Eric had found her even an hour sooner. But she would not add to his burden and firmly shut the door on the thought. She looked up and saw tears well up in his eyes as he bent over the lifeless body.

"I loved Carlos and Elena as I would my own children." His voice broke and he bowed his head, the tears falling on Elena's dress.

As Jillian moved around the body to touch him, she caught sight of Isabel shuffling to a chair in the corner. The cook walked like an old woman, hunched over in grief, appearing to lack sufficient strength to stand erect. Jillian left Eric and went to her and, throwing aside the custom of restraint, pulled the woman into her arms, the effect of which triggered in Isabel the release of deep, pent-up sobs. She leaned on Jillian aching with grief.

Jillian looked over Isabel's shoulder at Eric, whose face revealed a mixture of compassion and embarrassment and she turned back to Isabel. "Why don't you go to your room and rest?"

"Yes, Isabel," Eric agreed. "I don't expect anyone to work today. I sent everyone to their homes. There will be no labor in Tulcachi today." He pulled the cook gently from Jillian's embrace, led her out the door and on her way.

Noticing the boy sitting in a frozen position, staring toward the ceiling, Jillian followed his gaze toward a fat fly resting on a thick beam. Eric stood behind her.

"You said you found her?" She asked.

"I did. One of the things that troubles me most now is that by the time I thought of Carlos' grave it was too late. I kept thinking she must have gotten lost on one of the roads between here and Pachuca and it wasn't until sunrise this morning before I realized where she was. If I had thought about it last evening she would be alive right now. Her body was still warm when I found her." He threw out his hand in a pleading manner. "But Jill, I was so confused. I searched everywhere I could think of."

"I know you did." She reached for his hand. "Come on. Let's go from here."

He turned to glance at Elena. "It's hard to believe there will be only a few times that I'll be able to see her before she is taken from me forever." He patted the lad's shoulder. "Chico, you keep those flies away from her."

Chapter 36

They stood on the balcony overlooking the patio. She still held his hand. Suddenly she felt him stiffen and then he looked down at their clasped hands and as though he had just awakened from a deep sleep, his free hand flew to his face and rubbed the stubble on his chin. "How terrible I must look. I haven't shaved since I left the United States early yesterday morning."

"I understand. Why don't you shower and shave and I'll make us a lunch?"

His eyes watered and his mouth trembled with emotion; he nodded yes.

When he left the balcony, she went to the kitchen and searched through the cupboard coolers. By the time he returned, she had set out cold meat, bread, cheese and bananas. Lighting a match to start a fire on the propane stove, she set a pan of water on top for instant coffee.

He sat and reached for a piece of bread. The sight of food must have made him realize his hunger because he ate as one long deprived of food. When the water boiled she poured them each a cup of coffee and sat across from him.

"Eric," she said hesitantly. "Eric, I want to ask your forgiveness for the way I yelled at you the last time we saw each other."

Two spots of red appeared on his freshly shaven face. "Oh, Jill, we must talk about that night. How I wish that hadn't happened. So many times I've regretted the things I said to you."

"Why didn't you come back to see me? I was over my anger almost immediately."

"I stopped the truck that evening and considered returning, but I am a very proud man. I kept thinking I would return someday and make amends but time passed so quickly." He leaned forward across the table, his eyes level with hers. "I did go to see you one day but you were not at home. I waited in Rigo's office for an hour and then another time I came for the evening, but I left because there was a car sitting in front of your house and I thought you had a guest."

"By chance did you come the night Philip Rios was there?"

Anger flickered in his face but only for an instant. "Yes, I recognized his car."

"Eric, Philip is my friend and that is all. Just my friend. He is very much in love with his wife. That evening he came by to give me some medicines for my neighbor. In fact we weren't even inside the house. He just left his car there. I was at Gladys' house and Philip stopped by to see Raquel."

His voice registered a note of contempt. "Someone told me there are men at your house all the time."

Her jaw clamped in anger. "Who? Olivia Nieto? What a lie. Marta started a lot of those rumors. Marta and Olivia. Men do not come to my house just to visit. The only men I see are the young people in my English classes. I don't have time for such visits. My evenings are spent preparing for the next day's classes."

"I believe you. Please forgive me for ever thinking any differently. Will you forgive me?" His face dissolved into a smile. "Let's forget all of that."

"Of course. I'd rather not talk about it any more. Have you had enough to eat?" She rose without waiting for a reply to cut two more pieces of bread at the counter behind him. Purposely, she turned to scrutinize the back of his head. The wet gray hair he had slicked back after his shower was drying and curling around the base of his neck and ears. Her heart raced with pleasure. She had dreamed of this moment for over two years. Taking a deep breath, she placed the bread in front of him, her arm brushing his.

Chapter 36

He flashed her a warm smile as she sat opposite him. "I believe that despite everything going on in my life right now, a heavy burden has been lifted from my heart. I'm so glad you came today."

"So am I."

Reaching across the table, he touched her hand lightly. "Promise me we won't fight again."

"I hope not." At a loss for words, she gently changed the subject. "Are you going to contact Elena's family?"

At the mention of her name, his bright eyes dimmed. "I've already sent a man with a letter to tell Geoff because I wasn't sure where Rolando is staying. It explained everything. In the letter I told him he would need to buy a coffin and contact a priest to have the funeral tomorrow. Since most of Elena's family is Catholic, I think we should honor that. I just couldn't bear to do any of the necessary things this morning."

"Did you telephone a doctor?"

"Yes, I called the doctor in Tumbaco. I knew Elena was dead, but I kept hoping he would be able to revive her somehow. That was foolish, I guess. He said she died from exposure early this morning and then treated her body. That's why I blame myself for not checking the ridge where Carlos is buried."

"We both know it wasn't the exposure that killed her." Her mouth clamped down on the words. "Marta Brewer killed her."

His sad eyes focused on her. "How can a nurse be so cruel?"

"Tell me everything that happened when you went to see Marta."

"When I returned from the United States, Ramon and Isabel told me they had gone to the clinic to pick up Elena. Well, let me start from the beginning....."

"The nurse told Ramon and me to come back on Wednesday," Isabel said from the doorway.

Their heads swung in her direction as she moved listlessly toward them.

Jillian jumped to her feet. "Here, Isabel, sit down and I'll get you some coffee."

Uncharacteristically, the cook sat at the family table. "Señorita, we took Elena to the clinic in Pachuca because there was a big car race on the highway. We had no choice because her pains were close and I have never delivered a baby, especially in a car." She buried her face in her hands. "I knew when we got to the clinic that something was wrong. That nurse's assistant, what's her name, wouldn't let me stay with her. She said only Elena could go into the patient's room."

Jillian set a steaming cup of coffee in front of Isabel. "You mean Lucia? No, they won't let family members in. It's some silly rule they have about the peasants carrying disease and fleas and it's their fear of thievery."

Eric's face flushed with anger. "Do you mean those poor women go through the pain of delivery without family members present? Anyone who understands the Ecuadorian culture knows that family members are never separated, especially during times of crisis."

"Yes," cried Isabel. "If I could have stayed with her, this wouldn't have happened."

"Isabel, what did you say about Marta telling you to come on Wednesday? I don't understand. This all happened on Tuesday." Jillian pulled a wet stray hair back from the woman's face.

"When we visited Elena after the delivery, she told me to come for her and the baby on Tuesday, but when Ramon and I got into the car to leave, the American ran out of the clinic and told us to come Wednesday not Tuesday. How could we have misunderstood that? She explained that Elena had a difficult delivery and needed to rest an extra day." Here Isabel broke down and sobbed for several seconds. "I feel so terrible. Why didn't we go back to visit her on Tuesday? Why did I think preparing Elena's room for the baby was more important? When we returned on Wednesday Elena wasn't there. The American said she had told us to come back on Tuesday, but she didn't, señor Eric! She didn't!" The woman continued to sob without constraint. "We drove into Pachuca but no one seemed to know where Elena was. It was a terrible day."

"Jill," Eric lamented. "I don't know why I didn't listen to you when you tried to warn me about Marta. Am I so blind that I couldn't see that you knew her better than anyone?"

"Of course you aren't blind. It was hard for you to understand because I found it difficult to speak against Marta and tell you all she was doing in the clinic. I didn't tell you enough. How can you blame

Chapter 36

yourself? It's my fault that all I wanted was my boys back. What did she say to you when you visited her yesterday?"

"When I asked her where Elena was, she acted surprised and said she had left the clinic the previous day. When I asked about the baby, she said it had been born prematurely and didn't survive. I believed her when she showed me the death certificate."

"I tell you and you must believe me, that baby wasn't premature. I saw her in Elena's arms. She was fine looking and pretty as can be." Isabel wiped the tears from her swollen eyes.

"A little girl," mused Jillian.

"A beautiful baby girl."

The three sat in silence. Finally Jillian looked at her watch. "I'll help with the dishes and then I must leave."

"No, no, you go, señorita." Isabel rose.

Eric walked Jillian to her pickup. "I'm wondering if we should go back to the clinic and see if we can find the baby."

"Of course you can go, but I will guarantee the baby is not there and nothing you can do to Marta will make her confess. She will do nothing to jeopardize her clinic and orphanage. She will have made sure no one can find Elena's baby." She changed the subject. "Will you know soon when your mother will return to Ecuador?"

"I'll call my brother tomorrow after Elena's funeral." He leaned against the small vehicle.

"I visited your mother a few weeks ago. She made my friend, Raquel and I feel very much at home."

"Aii!" He hit his forehead with the palm of his hand. "Raquel. You mean Raquel Torres, the doctor?"

"Yes," she replied, bewildered.

"My mother gave me a check for the equivalent of one thousand dollars. It's for the orphanage in Conocoto from our family. She wants me to tell you that the group of government women she has been meeting with is going to raise more money. Jill, her desire was to go out to the orphanage herself and see what conditions the children must live in. Now that she is ill, it is impossible."

"A thousand dollars? How wonderful. Now, maybe those children can get some new clothing and nourishing food. You should see the terrible conditions."

He rubbed his chin. "You know, something has happened to me these past two days. So quickly did I lose everything that I love. I used to love this land more than anything in my life, except my mother. Then one day I met Carlos. Two or three years later I met his dear wife. I was as excited as they were over the upcoming birth of their child. I loved the baby before she was born. She was even in my will, as I told you. And now the three of them are gone and the hacienda can't take their place in my heart." He stood upright. "Would you mind going with me when I deliver the money to the orphanage in Conocoto?"

"Oh yes, I would love to. I'm sure Raquel would love to go there too." She clasped her hands together with delight.

"After the funeral tomorrow we can make plans," he said as he pulled one of her short curls affectionately.

Chapter 37

School was dismissed the day of Elena's funeral. Classes the previous day had also been canceled so that memorial services could be held for those lost in the Papallacta pickup accident. The normal day-to-day activities in Pachuca ceased as the townspeople mourned the loss of their friends and neighbors. Now that the residents realized Elena had indeed been suffering a loss that fateful day, compassion for her united the once divided village and they gathered to pay homage to their lost daughter.

The church bells began to toll, indicating the priest was preparing to leave the church to meet Elena's procession. Jillian walked out of her bedroom and leaned against the balcony railing. Her mind had been in turmoil since her return from Tulcachi the night before, whereupon immediately she had run to see Raquel, bearing news of Elena's death and of her afternoon with Eric and Helen's gift of a thousand dollars. But when Raquel had come to the door, it suddenly struck Jillian that perhaps a chatty visit would be inappropriate. Her friend's haggard face could mean only one thing; the news of Elena had affected her deeply.

"Hi, Raqui. Are you too busy to speak with me?"

Raquel nodded. "Opal, Rolando and I are planning Elena's funeral. Geoff went to Quito for a coffin. Then we must go to Tulcachi to pick up her body. Jill," her voice broke. "How much more can this family take?"

"How is Rolando?"

"He isn't taking it well at all. Actually he's sitting at the table, but all he does is stare into space. When he heard the news, all he said was that it is his fault. What can we say? In a way it is his fault."

"I suppose you'll go to the funeral tomorrow?"

"I'll walk in the procession with the family, but during the ceremony at the church I may slip out. It's important to me that the townspeople see I am with the family, but I can't bear the sad ceremony."

"Why don't you come to my house for a visit during the service? It seems so long since we've been together."

To Jillian's surprise, Raquel hesitated, her face in a frown. "I'll see."

"Please come. I have some important news to tell you."

The gathering of priests passing below her balcony returned her mind to the present. They were on their way to meet Elena's cortege, which waited a few hundred yards to the east. Suddenly it struck her that for several weeks Raquel had been acting peculiar. Something wasn't right. She searched her mind for anything she might have done to drive her friend away. When had we last spent any quality time together? Had we simply been too busy? No, there was more to it. Yes, it was true that Raquel had been spending a great deal of time at her new clinic which was nearing completion. The walls were up and the roof was on. All that remained was the installation of the windows and the interior painting, yet at a time when the young doctor should be her happiest, she seemed despondent. Jillian frowned at the thought. Her mind flipped back to the last time she had seen her, at the accident in Papallacta a few days before. Raquel had shown her no sign of friendliness, but of course, Jillian reasoned, she was preoccupied with the victims. The gnarled and ugly fingers of fear poked at her. Am I losing my dearest friend? I don't know if I can take another loss. What have I done to make her turn against me? Wait a minute. Just because Raquel is acting strangely doesn't mean she is upset with me. Maybe something else has happened. The clinic. Is she having trouble with the clinic? She couldn't shake the feeling that something dreadful had happened to her. Have I been too self-absorbed to have noticed? No, she chided herself. But what is it? When was the last time I saw her happy?

Chapter 37

Between the bell tolls she could hear Elena's procession approaching. The priest, with his curates chanting behind him turned the corner. Several young men followed, bearing the weight of the coffin. Perspiration gleamed on their faces as they adjusted to the heavy load. The Martinez family, in small clusters came trailing after them. Jillian strained to see each face as they came closer. Raquel walked with Geoff and Opal and Mariana and Hector, Elena's aunt and uncle. Rolando walked apart from them, his face set, his eyes seeing nothing. Why, he's in a state of shock, thought Jillian. He looks as if he's ready to collapse. She gazed after him, until she thought of Eric. Her eyes sought him. There was Ramon and then she saw him turning the corner. He was with Isabel, looking very handsome in a black suit. Had he worn a suit to Carlos' funeral? She couldn't remember, probably because she had been so preoccupied that day, wondering if he would look for her. Isabel wept, her head bent into a handkerchief. Eric, guiding her elbow with his hand looked up at Jillian. The cold, glowering look he'd shown her at Carlos' funeral was gone; he smiled tenderly and her heart sang. Jubilant, she saw nothing else. All her thoughts focused on him.

She had forgotten Raquel was coming until she realized the cortege had entered the church and her friend was walking toward her house. She ran down the stairs to open the door. "Go upstairs to the workroom and I'll bring tea for us."

Raquel nodded, turning obediently toward the stairs.

Deep in thought, Jillian put a pot of water on the stove. No longer had she any doubt about Raquel's state of mind. It must be more than Elena's death. There had to be because Raquel hadn't personally known Elena. She moved to Pachuca after the girl had moved away and married. Waiting for the water to boil, she tried to remember when Raquel had changed. She pictured the day they had gone to Helen's house; Raquel had been in a good mood. That's the day she had sent me on to Pachuca and she went to see Rolando. What was it that she said to me the day of Carlos' funeral? She said she had visited Rolando in his hotel room. He was drunk, but he had listened to her plea that he return to Pachuca. He had come, hadn't he? Yes, but she had also said Rolando made it clear to her then that he didn't need her. Might this be it? No, that can't be all. Raquel is too independent, too professional to be affected this way just because Rolando didn't need her, yet I am certain Rolando is the reason. Like a starved dog leaping upon a slab of fresh meat, she seized the thought that Rolando must have done something dreadful to Raquel. But what?

She placed the cups, sugar and plates of buttered buns on a tray and then filled the cups with boiling water and placed a tea bag in each. Upstairs she set the tray down on the long table and turned to face her friend.

Sitting on a bench, Raquel had her chin cupped in uplifted palms. She slowly withdrew her face and turned her gaze on Jillian. "Gracias."

"I was surprised to see Elena's Aunt Mariana and Uncle Hector in the procession. I thought they had denounced Elena."

"Geoff went to their house last night and told them they must forget all their past feelings about Elena and that this is the time to stand together as a family. They listened and came. Earlier this morning, Mariana came to our house, repentant over her actions. There was much weeping. I think with the funerals from the terrible pickup accident yesterday and Elena's today, everyone in Pachuca is re-evaluating his life."

"What about Rolando?"

Raquel's head jerked up; she stopped stirring her tea. "Rolando? Why should I know?"

"Raqui, please tell me what's wrong with you."

"There's nothing wrong with me."

"I know you too well. Something is bothering you."

"I said nothing is wrong."

"Then I must have done something to hurt our friendship." Jillian's voice broke. "You've changed toward me and that makes me very sad. You're the one who started this friendship when you insisted I accompany you to administer those whooping cough shots. I went with you because I felt I could trust you and now I feel like you don't care for me anymore."

Raquel's face crumbled. "Oh, Jill, no. You haven't done anything to make me stop loving you. We're still best friends."

Chapter 37

"Then why don't you tell me what's wrong? If it's not me who has offended you, then it has something to do with Rolando. Are you in love with him?"

"What?" Her voice held genuine surprise. "You asked me that once before. I'll tell you the same thing. In love with Rolando? No!"

"You told me you offered your friendship to him and he said he didn't need you. Is that the problem?"

"I was very upset when he told me that but not because I'm in love with him. I have discovered that people like you and I who want to help those in need are probably the most vulnerable to someone like Rolando. I'm a doctor and you, a missionary of sorts. When we see someone in need we reach out to help. You were right. The problem arises if we mistake compassion for love. You warned me the day I went to see him in Quito. It's true that I have thought a couple times that he might be a little more important to me than he should be, but all I have to do is remind myself of the mess my life would be in if we became involved."

Jillian swallowed the last of her bread. "But he told you he loved you once, didn't he?"

"Rolando is in love with himself, not me. Thank goodness I'm able to see beyond his handsome looks." She brushed bread crumbs into a small pile and crushed them with her finger.

"I met Rolando the other day. We talked for a while. I'm the one who told him Elena was at the clinic."

Raquel's hand stopped playing with the crumbs. "He knew she was here in Pachuca?"

"He didn't tell you? He didn't let you know Elena was at the clinic?"

"No." She shook her head and her eyes took on a faraway look.

"No matter what you tell me, I know that whatever is happening in your life, Raqui, concerns Rolando."

"If I tell you something about Rolando, you must promise me you will never mention it to anyone, Jill."

"Of course you can trust me."

"The day I found Rolando in Quito I told him that Carlos and Elena were no longer in Playas where he thought they were. I told him they had moved to Tulcachi. The next day Carlos died in a tragic accident."

Leaning forward on her elbows, Jillian searched her friend's face. "What are you saying? You think Rolando went to Tulcachi?"

"Yes, I am almost certain."

"You don't think Carlos' death was an accident? You think Rolando may have done something to him?"

"Jill, he hated Carlos for taking his sister from him. Do you know that he followed them to Playas? No telling what happened there."

"This is terrible news."

"I tried to speak with him the night of Carlos' funeral."

"Why? To ask him if he had seen Carlos before his death?"

Tears filled her eyes. "Yes, but he thought it was because I wanted him to be my sweetheart. He flicked me away like he would a bothersome fly. The reason I wanted to speak with him was because I was afraid he had brought harm to Carlos."

"Do you still believe that?"

"I think there is a chance since he is acting so strange. It would be wrong for me to say Rolando killed Carlos when he may not have. I don't know for sure but I have a feeling he went to Tulcachi on that terrible day. If he did, then I'm responsible for Carlos' death and possibly Elena's."

A knocked sounded at the door and Jillian jumped up from her seat.

"Who can that be?" asked Raquel. Do you have a class today?"

"No, all classes were canceled." Jillian bounded out to the balcony railing, peeked over and poked her head back into the workroom, her face a wreath of smiles. "It's Eric."

"Eric!" Raquel bolted up from the bench. "Eric! What's he doing here?"

"That's what I wanted to tell you last night. I'm going down to open the door. Just a minute."

Eric and Jillian returned to the workroom and he reached out to shake Raquel's hand. "Good day, doctor."

"Good day. It is nice to see you this morning despite terrible circumstances."

"Yes," he smiled sadly, as he took a place at the table.

"Would you like a cup of tea?" asked Jillian.

Chapter 37

"No thanks. I must return to the hacienda, but first I wanted to stop by to speak with you, Jill. I'm happy that you are here also, Raquel. Has Jill told you the news about Conocoto?"

"No," said Raquel, her attention riveted on Eric. "What news?"

"Perhaps you have heard that my mother is in the United States. I spoke with my brother today. She had heart surgery early this morning." He answered their questions concerning her positive outcome and went on to explain her desire for improvements in the Conocoto orphanage. "My mother wants to help the children. I have in my pocket the first donation. Her friends will continue to raise money for further help. If it is possible for you and Jill to accompany me one day soon, I would like to go to Conocoto to see for myself how the children are being treated."

"This is good news. Thank you. I see no reason why we can't go on Jill's next day off. Isn't that all right, Jill?"

"Yes, Thursday, perhaps around midmorning?"

That settled Eric changed the subject. "It was good to see Rolando's two brothers, Roberto and Pablo at the funeral. How was Geoff able to contact them so quickly?"

Interested, Jillian hadn't remembered Rolando had two brothers besides Geoff.

"He called Roberto in Quito. He lives there with his family and he contacted Pablo. All of Elena's relatives came, aunts, uncles and cousins, all of them."

"So, for the first time since Elena ran away, the entire family came together," stated Jillian.

"Yes," said Raquel with a weak smile. "I guess it took her death to bring them together. As far as I can tell, this has been the only bright spot in the tragedy."

Rising, Eric walked downstairs to the door, the girls following. "I must go. I will see you here next Thursday. We can go to Conocoto in my pickup."

"Eric," said Raquel hesitantly. "How did Carlos die?"

He stared at her, a scowl frozen on his face and hesitating so long, Jillian wondered if he was going to reply. Then his face relaxed and with a sad gentleness, he spoke. "When I found him, it looked as if he had been thrown from a tractor. It probably rolled over him."

"Did he often drive a tractor?" Jillian frowned, imagining the scene.

"That's what is so puzzling to me. He had never before driven a tractor. I left him alone with it while I rode my horse along the ridge where he waited for me."

"Then you were nearby?" Raquel's head leaned to one side.

"I was, but I must have been gone for several minutes. I didn't realize I had been away so long. When I returned I saw the accident."

She waited several seconds before asking. "Did you see anyone else?"

Eric frowned. "No, why would you ask that?"

"No reason. I thought it was an appropriate question."

He seemed satisfied.

They made further plans for the following Thursday and Eric left. Raquel departed for home a few moments later, leaving Jillian a bit more relieved about their friendship.

Chapter 38

After gathering the dirtied dishes from the workroom, she made another cup of tea and sat in the kitchen reflecting on the day. It was amazing how circumstances had suddenly changed her friendship with Eric. Despite Elena's death and Raquel's suspicions, she was feeling lighthearted. Not until now did she realize how much Eric's absence had affected her. Could it be that he in turn had also missed her? Her fingers traced the outline of the cup. A desire to please God would always guide her decisions. Could it be God's will that she contemplate a relationship with this fine man?

Still in a reflective mood, she rose automatically to answer a knock at the door. There to her astonishment stood Eric. "What a surprise! I didn't expect to see you until Thursday."

"I have something to talk with you about. I made sure that Isabel and Ramon were on their way back to Tulcachi in one of the trucks and I've been driving around Pachuca for the past several minutes hoping that Raquel might leave."

"Come in." She led the way to the kitchen.

In a relaxed manner, he made himself a cup of tea and sat with her at the table. Enjoying the way he felt free to make himself at home, she sat back happier than she had been in many months.

"Jill," he said, spooning sugar in the hot tea. "We must talk about Marta and I want you to be more open about her than you have been in the past."

She was surprised. This was not why she thought he had returned.

"So," he continued. "I have a few questions to ask."

"I'll do what I can."

"Tell me, do you still believe that somewhere Elena's daughter is alive?"

"If Isabel says the baby did not appear to be premature and looked healthy, then yes, she is alive."

"If Isabel hadn't seen the baby, would you still believe she's alive?"

"Yes."

"Oh, God." He leaned back, his face ashen. "It's my fault. Angelita could have been in the clinic when I was there."

"I doubt if she was in the clinic. She was probably in Marta's house or in the old outpatient clinic. Every one of us in a way is at fault. I should have been honest with you years ago when we ate lunch together in the plaza and Rigo questioned me about Marta taking newborn babies from their mothers. If I had been more honest, Elena might be alive today. If any one other than Marta and Lucia are at fault it would have to be Rolando and his family. But you, poor Eric, you were the one bound to the terrible circumstances which called you away from Elena when she needed you the most. How can you blame yourself for that?"

"No, I'm the one who was selfish enough to insist that Elena live in Tulcachi. I promised Carlos I would care for her." He pinched the spot between his eyes as though to rid himself of memories. "Carlos wanted to leave Elena with his aunt and uncle in Quito, but I interfered and insisted I could care for her."

"Is there any person on earth who can say that they have never made a decision they've regretted? Directly or indirectly, we have all made choices about the course of our lives that have affected others. That's why life is never perfect. Have you ever had what you call a perfect day, when everything went just the way you wanted, when you accomplished all your goals, the weather was perfect, your mind was free from worries and lingering thoughts for tomorrow, when you had absolutely nothing on the horizon to disturb your total peace?"

"Not often."

"Those days that seldom occur are long remembered because life is not perfect. It's because we or someone else has made decisions that affect us throughout our lives. Now there are some people who

Chapter 38

have made peace with themselves enough to be content to live with those decisions. Those people did not make peace overnight. They may have had to ask forgiveness from God or make things right with another person, or they may have had to forgive themselves for making some very foolish choices. At one time or another we have all had to forgive ourselves."

"You're probably right, but do you agree that sometimes we must step in and make right a bad decision?"

"Only if it doesn't negatively affect an innocent person."

"Jill, do you want your boys back?"

"I want them safe. Sometimes I fear that if we do something to close Marta's orphanage, the government will take the children and place them in a terrible place like the Conocoto orphanage. I've been informed that I can't adopt them because I'm a woman. The Ecuadorian government won't allow a single woman to adopt male children."

"Are you willing to tell me what you know about Marta Brewer?"

Jillian took a sip of cooled tea. "I think she's from the east coast of America. She's never been married. She is very secretive, reclusive and possessive."

"What about her companion, Lucia?"

"She's insecure, lonely and prone to violence."

"And you chose to live with them?" Eric sounded incredulous.

"No, at the beginning I chose to live with the children who are sweet and loving and who suffer from emotional imbalances because they must live with Marta and Lucia. Eventually I came to need not only the children but the adult companionship. Eric, I was lonely. I seldom left the compound except for shopping days. In time, I became as dependent on Marta and Lucia as the children are."

He was silent for a moment and then his lids closed over a faraway look in his eyes. "So the baby is probably alive."

"Yes, I think so, but you'll never be able to find her."

"Why?" His blazing blue eyes flew open. "I can just go to Marta and ask where she is. That should frighten her into telling me."

"We talked about this the other day. Marta will show you the death certificate again. I know her well. She'll never admit to you the baby is alive."

"What has she done in the past when she took babies from their mothers?"

"She was very secretive, Eric, believe me. Marta did not share her conspiracies with me although I'm sure she had more than one way to send children out of this country. Only once did I hear her talk to a mother about giving up her child. Marta didn't know I was in the clinic and I heard her offer to keep the child, educate her and clothe her. Marta invited the mother to return each year for the child's birthday party, but the mother refused to give up her baby. Yet a few hours later, Marta told me a mother had left her child in the orphanage. Since she was the only patient there at the time, I had to assume she meant the mother I heard only a few hours earlier refuse Marta's offer. The next day the baby disappeared and the same day Marta went to Quito on what she called an 'errand'. I believe she took the baby with her and had it sent to the United States."

"What if the mother came back to see the baby on its birthday?"

"She would tell the mother that the baby died."

"The day we went to lunch in the plaza, Rigo asked you about a baby that was supposedly at Marta's orphanage. The parents were informed they could not remove their child, so they asked for Rigo's help. I can't remember what Marta told Rigo. Do you remember?"

"Yes. Marta was very upset that day. She was determined to keep the baby for herself. I remember how she wept when Rigo came after her. I think Marta told him the baby had been sent to the United States because the parents had agreed, by signing a paper with an 'X' for their signature, to give up the baby. Right after the baby was born she had convinced the mother to leave her baby with her. Of course, neither mother nor father could read, so Marta had conveniently typed a contract that stated the parents must pay her in sucres the equivalent of $40.00 a day for the baby's care, an amount the parents could never afford. Days later, the mother changed her mind about leaving her daughter at the clinic and returned for her. Oh, I remember that day well. What could Rigo do? There was no way to prove that the baby hadn't been sent away. Why didn't Rigo go to the authorities in Quito? Why did he simply let this go? Maybe if he hadn't, we wouldn't be sitting here regretting Elena's death and the baby's disappearance."

Chapter 38

"I don't know," he said slowly. "When I talked to you two years ago, you acted a little frightened of Marta."

"No, not Marta. I'm frightened of Lucia."

"Yes," he said frowning. "You said she was violent."

"Lucia is very insecure and she trusts no one. Although we were good friends at one time, she has hit me, attacked me with a hammer, pulled a gun on me and I'm positive she released the brake fluid on my pickup. The incident with my pickup happened not too long ago. I and those with me could have been seriously hurt. I believe Lucia was the person who did it because that evening after I got home from Quito she went to the home where I park my truck. She waited until dark to pass by but I saw her and followed."

Shocked, Eric struggled with his anger. Finally finding his voice, he spoke harshly. "How I regret not being with you when that happened. You shouldn't be living here alone. You must stay away from those women."

She laughed. "Please don't worry about that. I couldn't get near them if I wanted. Marta has had a brick wall built around her property so now she has a brick wall, a mud wall and a fence encircling the compound. Believe me when I tell you that Marta does not want me near her. She has done everything she can do to make me leave Pachuca. Even when I lived with her, she tried to discourage me from living here. Someday I'll tell you about the tactics she's used this past year to make me leave. But as you can see, I'm still here."

"I'm very happy that you are."

"I've always known there must be someone other than Marta doing all the paperwork for the baby adoptions. For a while Marta was sending the infants to an orphanage in Quito until the government shut it down. When that happened several babies just disappeared into thin air."

"Disappeared? Disappeared where? Could they still be here in Ecuador?"

"I wouldn't be surprised if most of them were sent to the States or Europe for adoptions or much worse to one of the Ecuadorian government orphanages."

"It seems to me that someone must be making a lot of money doing this." Eric pressed his lips together tightly. "I admit I am half

Caucasian and I'm proud of that, but sometimes Americans make me angry."

"Eric," she said tartly. "You can't blame Americans for what a few unscrupulous people will do for money. I believe some Ecuadorians are involved in this also."

"You're right," he said sheepishly. "It doesn't matter where a person is from. I guess I'm angry because the babies are Ecuadorian and I'm most angry that one of them is Angelita."

"I'm angry about what some people will do for money."

"How can we get Elena's baby back?" He asked leaning forward.

"If the baby was taken from the clinic, given another name, given new birth papers and sent out of Ecuador, then I see no way of finding her. Even if you found someone who knew something, they wouldn't tell you anything, not even for a bribe. They would be afraid of you, but unless a miracle occurs, I believe Elena's baby is in the United States right now and we'll never see her again."

"You think she's in the United States already?"

"There's a very good chance since she was born five days ago. That could easily be true."

"Who would take her on the airplane? Maybe we can check the passenger lists."

"It seems only logical to me that with all the missionaries in this country, they, and perhaps embassy employees as well, innocently take babies out of the country in the belief that they are helping out prospective adoptive parents in the United States."

"What about the papers? Don't the missionaries know the papers are false?"

"How would they have any way of finding out? It could be that most of the papers are legal. After all, if the government really believes the babies have been abandoned, then perhaps everything is official."

"I think five days is too fast for her to have been sent away," he sighed, rubbing his chin.

"You could be right, but where do we go from here? I will guarantee she is no longer in Marta's compound. If she is in Ecuador, then where is she?"

Chapter 38

"I don't know, but I may do some checking next week when the government offices open on Monday." He stood and pushed back his chair. "Right now I must go to Quito and call my brother. I want to know how my mother is."

"Please send my love." She followed him to the door.

"My mother will be delighted that we have restored our friendship. I'm ashamed I waited until you came to me."

"Is there a rule that says a woman can't break the silence between two friends?"

His eyes softened with a smile. "I've missed you so much."

"I hope we never separate again because of pride."

He laid his hand on the side of her face and leaned down to kiss her cheek. "I'll see you Thursday."

"You look very handsome in your suit."

He opened up the suit jacket, exposing the vest and satin lining. "Look carefully because I hope I don't have to wear it again for a long long time."

Opening the door for him, she chuckled. "Hasta mañana."

He stepped down and opened the pickup door. Before he got in, he turned to her. "I'm sorry for not taking you more serious about your boys. If I had, maybe we wouldn't be looking for the baby. Instead I'd be taking you to Tulcachi to visit Elena and her child."

She watched after him until he turned the corner.

Chapter 39

The next Thursday Eric sent a message via the telephone office that he would pick up Jillian and Raquel earlier than planned as he had an important stop to make in Quito before they traveled to Conocoto.

"I want to visit a government office," he explained to the girls, taking the main street to Quito's center of town.

Parking his pickup in the same area he had parked the day of Jillian's arrival in Quito, the same boy, older and taller, promised to watch the vehicle, his face wreathed in a smile. Eric led the women to the corner where he flagged down a taxi.

The driver let them off three blocks east of Independencia Plaza, in front of a gray two-story building. Walking quickly through a narrow, windowless lobby they climbed one flight of stairs to the second floor and entered an extended room with high ceilings and dated décor. Long queues of people awaited help from harried workers sitting behind stacks of papers at crowded desks. The air was stale and acrid from body odor and clothes reeking of wood fire smoke. Years of accumulated grime coated the walls.

"Everywhere I go in Quito there are lines," complained Jillian.

"Lines of people and piles of paper," agreed Raquel and turned to her to softly ask, "Did Eric tell you why we're here?"

"Not yet. He said he had an appointment with someone," she replied, shifting her weight to the other foot.

Eric approached a clerk. Nodding his head, the young man pointed over his shoulder to a woman sitting at a desk in a corner.

Chapter 39

Turning, he waved Jillian and Raquel forward until they joined him at the desk. The woman looked up from her work. Stylishly dressed in a sweater and skirt, her hair coifed in a contemporary style, she greeted Eric and then turned her cold dark eyes to the women. They lingered longer on Jillian appraising her with apparent distaste.

On occasion, Jillian had encountered prejudice, the hatred some Ecuadorians had for Americans. She knew from experience Lucia detested Americans because she was jealous and insecure. Jillian wondered vaguely if this woman believed all Americans were typical of the loud, big-mouthed, Bermuda shorts clad, camera-toting type she'd seen herself in some of the fancier hotels. Frankly, she didn't really care what the woman thought about her; feelings of dislike were mutual. The woman made jerky movements as she lit a cigarette and blew the smoke upward in the latest assault against any remaining clean air.

Eric set his hat on a stack of papers and held out his hand to shake hers. After introducing Raquel and Jillian, he spoke. "I called you earlier, señora Flores. We've come to see if you have any records of an infant born recently being readied for adoption. She was born in Pachuca in the Tumbaco Valley a week ago last Sunday night or early Monday morning."

"Adoption, señor?" Señora Flores frowned darkly. "To whom? A family here in Ecuador?"

"I don't know for sure. There is more of a possibility that she is being sent to the United States."

"The United States?" Her gaze swept automatically to Jillian and then back to him. "What is the name of the child?"

"Angelita Tapia or perhaps Tapia-Martinez. We're not sure what was put on her official papers. Her name might have been changed."

Making no attempt to hide her growing irritation, she bristled. "Señor, as you can see I am very busy. How can I possibly help you when you don't have good information?"

Jillian took a deep breath. "Señora, do you have records for orphanages in the Tumbaco Valley?"

"Of course we do." She cast Jillian a haughty look.

"There is an orphanage and maternity clinic in Pachuca run by a nurse named Marta Brewer. The child came from the maternity clinic."

"I still don't understand." The woman squashed her cigarette in a saucer overflowing with lipstick-stained butts.

Eric took over. "We believe Marta Brewer delivered this baby last week, but the baby has not been seen since."

"And you believe she is being put up for adoption?" She continued to grind away at the squashed cigarette, her head lowered.

"We're not sure," said Eric.

"Why don't you ask the child's mother what happened?"

Raquel replied. "The mother is dead."

Señora Flores studied Raquel at such length Jillian wondered if she had heard. Finally she spoke. "Why don't you ask the nurse where the baby is?"

"We did," said Raquel. "She said the baby is dead."

Flattening her palms against the desk top, she stiffened. "Señor Perez, is this a joke? I'm very busy. I have no time for this."

"This is no joke. The nurse said the baby is dead but we don't believe her. We believe she gave the baby away for adoption."

"This is ridiculous," she spat.

"Can you look in your adoption records to see if there is a baby named Martinez or Tapia born in Pachuca in the past two weeks?" Jillian stared down at her.

Again the woman's eyes pierced her with a cold arrogant look. Without another word, she stood and walked toward a door at the end of the room as Jillian pulled her lower lip down in a mock grimace and shook her hand up and down. "Aiii, but she is very unfriendly."

A young clerk working at a desk behind them saw the gesture and chortled until the four of them were giggling covertly.

Several minutes passed before señora Flores returned to sit at her desk, a frozen look on her face. She deliberately lit another cigarette, inhaling deeply. "There is no record at all of a baby by the name of Martinez or Tapia born in the past two weeks and put up for adoption nor did I find any papers signed by Marta Brewer. I believe this office can no longer help you. And again, I am very busy."

Chapter 40

Eric, Raquel and Jillian departed, their spirits chilled by the uncooperative woman. They found a taxi idling by the curb and engaged the driver to return them to Eric's truck. As they neared their destination, Jillian said, "I think we should eat lunch before we go to Conocoto. If not, we might be invited to eat there and, Eric, the food could make us sick."

Depositing them in his truck, he hurried to the end of the block to find a café on the main street and returned with bags of roasted chicken, buttered bread and fried potatoes. "Let's find a more private spot to park before we eat this. We'll have more room."

They found a shady curb and sat in the back of the pickup, stuffing themselves with the flavorful food. Señora Flores' rude behavior was the first topic of conversation and then they lamented over the inefficiency of the government, their frustration in being unable to find any information about Elena's baby. They discussed Helen and her surgery.

"Her operation went well. My brother is pleased, however much to my mother's distress I doubt if she'll ever be able to live again in Quito. The altitude is too extreme for her heart. The same for Tulcachi's high altitude, although I doubt if she could live without all the accommodations she is used to, so she'll probably stay in New York. It makes me sad; her home, her friends and her past are here in Ecuador. New York City is much too crowded for her. Of course, she'll have my brother and his family there, but it's going to be a difficult adjustment."

Raquel frowned, brushing a fly from her chicken. "Did your brother say she will have to live there or is that a decision you two have made for her?"

"It's too soon to say. I speak with my brother whenever I can get a telephone line out. You know what wonderful advances medicine has made. Maybe her heart can hold out here in the sierras if she is careful. I worry very much about my mother."

"I can understand that," said Jillian. "She is such a special person."

"Thank you. Yes, she is." He patted his shirt pocket. "I have the check here for the orphanage from her."

Wrapping her leftovers in a brown bag, Jillian wiped her mouth with a tissue. "We should leave for Conocoto. Cynthia will be arriving soon."

Eric finished off his portion and they tidied the pickup bed and climbed into the cab. Jillian sat in the middle. "It seems you have been away from the hacienda a lot lately, Eric."

Taking his hand from the steering wheel, he pushed back his large rimmed hat. "Yes, I remember not too long ago when the most important thing in my life was the hacienda. I look back on it now and I know I'll never feel that way again. Carlos and Elena changed my life forever. With my mother ill and away, I realize how much I love her. These past few days I have spent a lot of time thinking about my life. I've reflected, repented and resolved to use my life effectively to help other people. That's why I want to go to the orphanage today. My hacienda will function without me. I have many good workers. It's just that for so long I thought it would fail without me." He gave a small chuckle. "There's nothing like a tragedy to open my eyes before I can understand my mortality."

Jillian watched Eric's eyes fill with tears. He was indeed mellowing and becoming even more attractive to her.

When they arrived at the orphanage, Cynthia was waiting for them on the patio. After greetings and introductions, she asked. "We are about to eat our lunch. Would you join us?"

"We've all ready eaten, gracias." Eric sounded relieved.

Chapter 40

"Then I will bring my lunch to my office. Since you arranged this meeting, señor Perez, I have asked someone to help me with the children this afternoon. This way, the four of us can be alone without interruption." She pointed to the end of the passageway. "The door that is standing open leads to my office. Please go in and take seats. I will be with you shortly."

They found their way to the office and sat around Cynthia's desk.

"She must be a strong woman to eat the food here," groaned Jillian. "Raqui, the other day when we came, she was doing her finances behind a screen in the main room. Why wasn't she in here?"

"She's a good caretaker. She wanted to be close to the children, I guess."

Engrossed in their own thoughts, they waited. The room was small with one window facing the bare brown patio. A heavy, wooden file cabinet sat in the corner, leaning slightly as if one side was shorter than the other. A foot high Ecuadorian flag, stuck in a metal base sat atop the file cabinet. On the wall to its left hung a photo of the republic's president; the desk was laden with paperwork and thick dusty tomes.

"Look at those filthy books. Maybe that's why she doesn't work in here. How often do you think she refers to them?" Jillian dramatically poked a finger in the fine film coating the volumes.

Raquel giggled, catching the gist. "Watch out! Don't breathe on them," she said, eliciting a laugh from Eric.

He turned his blue gaze on the girls and then back to the books. In the absurdity of the moment, they began to chuckle, the light-hearted kind of laugh that evokes a feeling of well being, of camaraderie. In another time, another place such a remark would have produced nothing more than a quick retort that would have been quickly forgotten, yet in this moment the laughter was a healing balm.

Silent again, they wiped tears of mirth from their eyes. Eric breathed deeply, his voice shaky. "I needed that. Now I suggest when Cynthia returns we keep our eyes away from those books. It would be very embarrassing to have to explain what we find so funny."

They bantered back and forth until Cynthia entered her office. "Please pardon me for not returning sooner. I decided since you have already eaten that I would take my lunch with the staff and children. They also needed my help as we are short of staff."

"There is no problem, señora," Eric assured her. "We have come at an inopportune time. Now let me explain why we are here. As you know, I telephoned you earlier this week to tell you I have a gift for the orphanage. After Raquel and Jill visited you a few weeks ago, they made an appointment with my mother to tell her about the children's difficulties living in this location. She has decided to give you a gift. This will be a temporary relief until we can organize a group of my mother's friends. They will be raising more money for you. With your guidance, they will buy clothes, toys and bedding. Food, of course will be a top priority. You must have a better menu than you have now." Withdrawing the check from his pocket, he handed it to her.

Her eyes widened as her other hand flew to her breast. She stood, laid the check on her desk and leaned forward to grasp their hands and each of them stood their faces aglow with pleasure. "I will put it to the best use."

"Our government should be doing more. One of the first things my mother's friends will do is come out here, survey everything and then go to the government treasurer. This won't be difficult because many of the women have relatives in the government." Eric smiled broadly.

For Eric's sake, Cynthia invited them to accompany her through the orphanage. Jillian watched his emotions as he looked down on the partially clothed babies, virtual prisoners in their cribs, to the broken glass in the window frames and the overall filth. When they returned to Cynthia's office, Jillian noted the determination in his eyes and she wondered if he would embrace the orphanage to assuage his guilt and pain over Elena.

They made plans and talked of future meetings until it was time to leave. Cynthia again grasped their hands. As she took Raquel's, the doctor asked her. "Do you put any of these children up for adoption?"

"Adoption?" Cynthia looked genuinely surprised.

"Yes," replied Raquel. "You must have requests for adoptions."

"Most Ecuadorians have enough children of their own. To be honest, many of our people feel it is not proper to take another person's child and call it their own."

Chapter 40

Jillian nervously licked her lips. "What about sending the children to America? Many couples there would love to adopt children."

"To America? Oh, we can't do that. At this time we have no adoption policy with countries outside of Ecuador."

"You don't?" asked Eric, perplexed.

"Oh, no," the woman said. "About five years ago a woman from Sweden came to Ecuador. She illegally sent several of our babies to Europe. When the government discovered this, they put a ban on adoptions to other countries."

Eric, Raquel and Jillian looked at each other, too stunned to speak.

"Why do you ask?"

Feeling too weakened to remain standing, Jillian returned to her chair. "Have you heard of an orphanage in Pachuca run by a nurse named Marta Brewer?"

"Marta Brewer?" Cynthia pondered the name. "No, truthfully, I'm not sure where Pachuca is. Why do you ask?"

"Because she is sending children to the United States for adoptions," said Raquel.

Cynthia sat down, her lips parted. "Do you know this for certain?"

"Jill does." Eric pointed in her direction.

"What is this about?" The woman turned to Jillian.

With quickening heartbeat, Jillian knew she was about to reveal incriminating knowledge that might harm her own children. "I worked with Marta Brewer for five years."

"And you know she has sent babies to America? Where did she get them?"

"From a maternity ward connected with the orphanage," said Jillian trying to breathe evenly.

"Why haven't you gone to someone in the government about this?" asked Cynthia, a tinge of anger in her voice.

"Because I thought she was doing it legally," said Jillian lamely.

Eric came to her defense. "Jill always suspected something was wrong, but she had no proof. I know because she tried to warn me and I wouldn't listen. It really is my fault."

"Oh, Eric," moaned Jillian. "Don't take the blame. Cynthia, I didn't come forward because I didn't know who to go to. I had no proof. Only once did Marta make a statement that her records weren't in order."

"What?" exclaimed Eric. "She told you her records weren't in order? What records did she mean?"

"I think her children's records, but they're probably in order by now."

"What children?" asked Cynthia, leaning her elbows on the desk.

Raquel and Eric returned to their chairs and Raquel started hitting the desk with her forefinger. "Children who have been born in the clinic; she's kept some of them, the others she sends from the country."

"And they are terribly mistreated," continued Jillian.

"Mistreated?" Eric sat up straighter.

"Oh, yes. I could tell you terrible stories that would grieve your heart," said Jillian heatedly.

"I still cannot believe you didn't tell anyone about the adoptions, Jill," said Cynthia. "Don't you read the newspapers?"

"The newspapers?" repeated Jillian, bewildered.

"Yes, Sunday's El Comercio three weeks ago."

"I don't think I've ever seen a newspaper in Pachuca." Jillian's voice lowered.

Cynthia stood and walked to the file cabinet. As she struggled to pull out the heavy middle drawer, Eric jumped to her aid and waited expectantly while she looked through several files. Withdrawing a clipped newspaper article from a file, she held it out to him.

In silence, Raquel joined him, leaning toward him while he read. "Oh God, help us."

"What? What?" cried Jillian. "What's wrong?"

Eric leveled his eyes at hers. "Look at these headlines."

She read and then looked up at him. "It's front page news."

"Yes," said Cynthia. "Quito's newspaper picked up a story from the wire services concerning the adoption of Ecuadorian babies to the United States. The president happened to be reading the story while eating breakfast a few days ago and was greatly puzzled because he knows there are no foreign adoptions available in this country at this time due to the past crimes. He started asking questions, but at this point the government has been unable to find the person or persons responsible for illegally sending children out of our country."

Chapter 40

"I'll tell you what it says," continued Cynthia. "A couple from Minnesota heard that babies for adoption were being sent from Ecuador to America. Somehow they found the name and address of a lawyer in Quito who was willing to send them a baby and they wrote to him, asking for a child. Over the period of four months they corresponded. Yes, the lawyer had a beautiful baby in his home that was up for adoption. He was four months old, healthy and ready to be sent to the United States. The couple from Minnesota, thrilled with the chance to adopt a child was more than willing to pay the ten thousand dollars required for adoption. On a particular day, they were to fly to Miami to take possession of the baby and meet the American couple returning to the States from a vacation. The wire service said the new parents took the infant in their arms, opened the blanket to look at him and nearly fainted. The child had downs syndrome and horribly underweight and tests proved he was deaf. Nothing in the letters from the lawyer stated this. The couple from Minnesota was so outraged they contacted the Associated Press with the story. In no time the story reached Quito. The newspaper here picked up the story and put it on the front page. And, as I told you, three weeks ago our president read the paper. You can see what the headlines say: ADOPTIVE ECUADORIAN BABY UNACCEPTABLE TO U.S. COUPLE. As the story goes, our president laid down his paper and asked himself: What is going on? Are we sending babies to the United States?

"What happened? What did he do?" asked Raquel.

"He called a meeting of officials in Children's Services."

"What happened then?" Jillian was on the edge of her chair.

"They have no leads. Everything has been covered up so well they've been unable to find any information regarding illegal adoptions."

Eric picked up the article and pointed to a name. "Here's the lawyer's name, a señor Cristobal."

"Cristobal is a false name. The lawyer's return address is also false. It's actually a small café in El Centro. A boy picked up the lawyer's mail each day. Since the article in the newspaper came out, the boy has not been seen. Originally the letter went through the post office in Lima, Peru before being sent on to Quito. Now you say that this nurse Marta Brewer has been sending babies away?"

Suddenly hesitant and fearful, Jillian shrugged. "I think so. I'm not sure."

Cynthia stood. "Do you know that even today officials of the Children's Services have been in meetings searching for a clue, for a link, the person in the middle of all this? Perhaps we may know who that is."

Jillian fell back in her chair and placed her hand on her forehead. "Oh, I'm so frightened."

Raquel looked at her with concern. Eric leaned on the desk and spoke up. "Cynthia, we went to the Children's Services today to speak with señora Flores. We asked her about a baby girl whom we believe even now is being sent to the United States. She acted as though the idea of babies being sent to the States was unheard of. How can that be if this is such a big story right now?"

"Señora Flores would not help her own mother if she needed it. She is a very cold woman. She knows very well that an investigation is going on." Cynthia went to the door. "I am going to make a telephone call. Please stay here. Perhaps the government officials will want to speak with you."

Chapter 41

After a long delay, Cynthia returned. "If you will remain in Conocoto for a few minutes an official will be coming here to question you. Can you stay?"

Eric looked at the girls and when they nodded he told the woman they would wait. For two hours they visited with the children, took a drive through the countryside and visited the market. When they returned to the orphanage, an official government sedan was parked at the entrance.

Three more chairs were squeezed into Cynthia's small office. Jillian was unpleasantly surprised to see señora Flores sitting on a chair beside the window. To her right was an overweight, well-dressed matronly woman introduced as señora Rosa de Mineo. Cynthia had deserted her spot behind the desk and sat on a chair in a corner. In her place sat a large man dress in a rumpled, pumpkin-colored suit that set off his sallow complexion. He stood to shake hands with the new arrivals. The man was short and heavy and his irregular facial features surrounded one of the biggest noses Jillian had ever seen on an Ecuadorian.

"May I present Ralf Rodrigues, the president of Ecuador's Children's Services," said Cynthia with an air of importance.

Jillian smiled at the man as he shook hands with the three of them, thinking to herself that despite his physical drawbacks he had climbed the chain of command to the top. One had to admire that.

When everyone had found a chair and was seated, Jillian glanced at señora Flores and smiled to herself. The stern woman's hand was nervously twitching and playing with her forearm. Jillian knew she had been pulled from an afternoon siesta and probably was longing for a cigarette. Serves her right.

"Now," said señor Rodrigues, leaning back in his chair. He looked at Jillian, Eric and Raquel in turn, and continued. "I understand you may have some information on illegal adoptions here in Ecuador. Is that right?"

Eric spoke up, his hand fingering the hat lying on his lap. "I don't believe we have any proof."

The heavy man glanced at Eric's two companions. "What do you have?"

Eric motioned toward Jillian. "This young lady worked in a maternity clinic and orphanage in the Tumbaco Valley for several years. During that time she saw a few things which made her think that children were being sent illegally to the United States."

"Is this a government orphanage?" asked Ralf, his eyes narrowing at Jillian.

"No, señor, the orphanage is run by an American nurse."

The man's calculating eyes studied her. "I assume the children were delivered in the maternity clinic, señorita."

"Most of them; however some were brought to us by the parents because they couldn't care for the children."

Sitting forward, the man intertwined his chubby fingers. "I'm aware that an American had an orphanage in Quito not too long ago. We suspected the man was sending children illegally to the United States. Do you know anything about this?"

"Yes, the American's name is Clint Marshall. I don't know how the woman I worked for discovered the orphanage in Quito; perhaps through her lawyer but all I know is that for a short period of time several of our babies were put into that orphanage until papers could be completed and then they were to be sent out of the country. The Ecuadorian government closed the orphanage."

"Yes, I am aware of that," he smiled. "I ordered the closure, however when the government military arrived at the orphanage the children were gone. Fortunately we were able to trace señor Marshall and

Chapter 41

deport him. We've wondered what happened to the other children. Do you know?"

"I'm aware of the situation, but no, I don't know where the babies went. I imagine they are not in Ecuador right now." Jillian looked him straight in the eyes.

He stared back at her. "Cynthia tells me you know the name of someone who is sending babies to America."

"I don't know for sure if she is the one."

His eyes flashed anger and his voice hardened. "You say you don't know for sure. Am I to understand you lived with this woman, yet you aren't sure?"

"I did not live with Marta Brewer as you would live with your family. I lived on a compound with five or six structures. I lived with the children in the orphanage and Marta lived in the outpatient clinic. She had her own bedroom, whereas mine was in another building. Many things could occur without my knowledge." She heard señora Flores utter a gentle snort and the man's mouth settled into a hard line.

Eric interceded. "Señor Rodrigues, I have met Marta Brewer. Believe me, she is the type of woman who could do many things without her companions knowing."

"Babies being born, stripped from their mothers and sent to another country?" His elephantine nose flared. "I find this very difficult to understand."

Jillian felt a great anger welling up within her. "Yes, it is possible. I tried all I could do to find out what was going on in the orphanage, but Marta would give me no answers and it makes me very upset that I find the same problem in your own office."

"What do you mean, señorita?" Ralf asked, his face reddening.

She took a deep breath. "This morning we stopped at your office and asked señora Flores if there were any records on Marta Brewer's orphanage. She claimed there were none. I feel you have allowed an oversight."

While speaking, Jillian refrained from glancing in the direction of señoras de Mineo and Flores, who reacted to her comments with affected, pained exclamations. She continued, "Marta told me at one time that her personal records were not in order, which tells me that she was trying to hide something. If this is true, then perhaps the government should find out what is going on in Pachuca. Could it be possible that your office has no records of an orphanage that has been in operation for almost fifteen years?"

The big man shifted in his seat. "Do you believe that she may be running an illegal orphanage too?"

Her hands shook nervously and she grasped them tightly in her lap. "After thinking this through for many years, I truly believe that she is running an illegal orphanage, sending babies illegally to the United States and though she is a capable nurse who can deliver babies, is probably working without proper papers. What I would like to know is, when was the last time she took nursing studies? She has no way of keeping up with the latest techniques. I've never noticed her reading medical journals or books. Is her nursing license valid? I know the government recently shut down her outpatient clinic because they decided Pachuca didn't need an extra clinic. They inspected her maternity clinic but failed to inspect her license. And what about her companion, Lucia? I believe her only training was a mere six-week first aid course. Does that make her qualified for the amount of time she is left alone with the patients? What if something happened to one of the patients? Is there a doctor available to come at short notice? Marta believes that all Ecuadorian doctors are idiots." She glanced apologetically at Raquel. "Of course we know this isn't true. She should be responsible to someone over her. And what about the children in the orphanage? Did you know there were eleven children living with her when I left, maybe more now?"

Silence descended on the room; each head turned toward Jillian, whose face burned red with the knowledge that she was speaking in heavily accented Spanish before highly educated people. She looked at Eric and Raquel and saw the pride shining in their eyes and could have wept at the support coming from them.

"Well, señorita," Ralf rubbed his great nose. "I guess my office will have to do some investigating; however you must admit, if the American nurse has care of those eleven children, they are probably treated better than the children here in this place."

Hesitating, Jillian spoke softly. "Perhaps, but Marta is not a good mother. I could tell you things about her disciplinary actions that would make you ill. There are some things she does to her children

Chapter 41

that I've never told a soul and probably never will. Someday the children can tell their own stories."

Ralf's face reddened again and he stood to hold out his hand. "Thank you, señorita. I can't tell you now what will happen as a result of your report, but I can guarantee that action will be taken."

Glaring, señoras de Mineo and Flores looked on and then following Ralf's lead, they stood too and shook hands all around. Their limp, unfriendly handshakes did not escape Jillian's notice.

Cynthia beamed her thanks and escorted the three government officials to their car, leaving Eric, Raquel and Jillian alone. Jillian collapsed in a chair, her limbs shaking violently.

"Come, Jill, let's go home." Eric pulled her up and Raquel threw her arms around her. "Good job. I know how frightened you were."

"Did you understand me? I was so afraid I wouldn't be able to explain well in Spanish," cried Jillian.

Eric ran his thumb down her cheek, his blue eyes soft. "I understood every word. I'm very proud of you."

"I can't help but think there are those I may have hurt more than helped."

Raquel took her arm as they walked toward Eric's pickup. "How do you mean?"

"The children may be taken away from Marta and I doubt if señora Flores will ever allow me to have Andy and Ryan now."

"Don't worry about them. I'm more concerned how Marta and Lucia are going to react when they find out what you've told the government, my dear friend."

Chapter 42

Lifting his head from the table, Rolando opened one eye to see if Raphael was near. He needed another drink. Rising he staggered across the room to see if the proprietor had stepped into the back room. In the middle of the filthy floor, among a group of dancers, he collapsed, passing out. When he awoke, he was leaning against the wall beside the saloon steps.

It was Saint Pedro's Day and the festivities had begun early that afternoon with the women of Pachuca setting up their food stands. For days they had prepared for this fiesta, walking to local haciendas to purchase potatoes, meat, havas, ears of corn, animal intestines, frankfurters, lettuce, tomatoes, avocados and onions. They had searched the hillsides for firewood and bought charcoal from local families.

The men had built frames ten feet high from sticks of plywood and tied dozens of firecrackers to each casing. Orchestras had been hired from anyone who owned an instrument and dances in several locations were planned. Elderly women had prepared liquors from chewed corn, which had been spit into buckets and left to ferment for many days.

Farmers slit the necks of squealing pigs and cleaned their bodies on curbs as scrawny dogs watched, ready to pounce on discarded pieces. Shortly after noon villagers arrived in the plaza and began setting up tables and crude stoves filled with wood and charcoal. Wooden chairs, large pieces of plastic and buckets of food filled

Chapter 42

every available space along the curbs. Fires were fanned and great pots of potatoes, ears of corn and meat were placed on grills. On the tables sat bowls of pork, frankfurters, oranges, tangerines, chirimoyas, bananas, chochos and havas.

Later in the afternoon the orchestras appeared to begin their marches around the plaza as the people followed. Hundreds of natives from the surrounding suburbs and mountains converged on the plaza, packing the sidewalks in anticipation of the dances and fireworks.

It was dark when Rolando roused. Men running past him in the street, holding high the frames of bursting, sparkling firecrackers frightened him as he struggled to an upright position. He was groggy but sober. The desire for a drink gripped him and he started to put his hand in his jacket to search for more bills.

Suddenly, as if a curtain had been lifted from his eyes, he saw himself, a young man still in his early thirties, a hopeless alcoholic, alone, miserable and broken. He had despised his father's bond with liquor and had looked on him as a weak, ungodly failure and yet he had become his father. He could not long go on this way. If the liquor didn't kill him, someday someone would. An idea that had been rooting in his mind for the past two weeks blossomed. He knew he no longer wanted to live and he promised himself that tonight would be his last day on earth.

Struggling to his feet, he held his head for a moment and then pushed past the Indians packing the sidewalks. Leaning against them, they irritably made way until he reached Ernestina's corner store. He had never been able to pass this corner without a sense of sadness and now he felt tears on his cheeks. He would never see her again. Since the night she had helped him as a child, no matter how aged she had become, he had loved Ernestina. Standing there, searching for a glimpse of her, he was hassled by the surge of people passing in and out of the doors. In despair, he pushed forward, staggering toward his fateful destiny. One man ran the length of the main street carrying a frame of rockets and blazing firecrackers, illuminating the crowds. Stopping to rest a moment, Rolando looked up and saw Jillian standing at the railing of her balcony as she watched the scene. Elbowing aside a family of Indians parked on her front stoop, he fell against the door and pounded with his fists. At first she could not hear his pounding above the noise of the orchestras and firecrackers. He waited and then began to beat upon the door again until at last the door opened. He fell through onto the cement floor of the entryway.

"Rolando!" She pulled on his arm until he rested on the floor in a sitting position. He knew his face was covered with dirt and his disheveled hair was filthy and he was ashamed. Groaning, he turned and smiled weakly. "You told me I could come when I needed you."

"Yes, of course." She smiled through a frown. "Just a moment and I'll be right back."

He watched her walk into a room off the entryway where she had a makeshift kitchen. Drawing water from a large plastic container, she filled a pan and laid it over a flame on the stove. When it was warm, she poured it into a basin. Taking a washcloth and a bar of soap from the cupboard, she returned to his side. Placing the basin on the floor, she helped him remove his jacket. "Here, sit on this bench."

He pulled himself to his feet and sat obediently as she proceeded to wash his face and hands. As if he were a child, he allowed her to cool his flushed face with the tepid water and he began to feel better.

"You were rather dirty," she grinned.

"I guess I'm in a terrible condition." Embarrassed, he ran his hand through his hair. "Thank you, Jill. I'm beginning to feel ashamed for being here like this."

"Just a minute and I'm going to fix you something to eat."

"Maybe some bread and a little cheese, if you have it. I do feel hungry."

She returned to the kitchen and began to cut bread and cheese. She set the pan of water on the stove again and prepared a tray. As she was pouring coffee, something in him snapped and suddenly tears flowed out of control; tears that had been trapped within his soul for years now gushed forth like a natural spring. Loud sobs racked his body until he fell to the floor in agony, doubled over in pain. She placed a hand on his shoulder.

"I miss her," he sobbed. "I miss her so much. Jill, I love her."

"Who?"

Gasping for breath, he collapsed onto the floor again bathed in tears.

"Who, Rolando?"

Chapter 42

"Elena. I love Elena so much. I miss her." Sobs ripped through him. "I loved her so much. Oh, Elena, my darling beloved Elena, I did this to you." He raised his head, the moans of heartbreak tearing from deep within his belly. "Why did she die before I had a chance to tell her I loved her and ask her forgiveness? Why did I wait?" He tried to stand, stumbling and grabbed at his head trying to control the spasms racking his body. "Jill, I can't stand this pain. I want to die, but I'm so afraid."

He fell back on the bench in agony, weeping with fresh tears. "I am so foolish. I was at the clinic that Tuesday morning, but fear and pride kept me from going in. I could have helped her. Why did I have to be so proud? Oh, God, help me! I can't stand the pain."

"Rolando." Jillian's voice broke as she fought back tears and laid her hand on his arm again. "I'm not sure what I can say or do to take away your pain, but there was no way that you could have known she would die. You can't blame yourself. That would only bring more harm to you."

"I want to blame myself. If anyone should know what Marta Brewer can do to a patient, I should. Why did I leave Elena there? Why didn't I insist on being with her? I need to hurt and suffer. This is what will cleanse my soul. I'm so sick of living for myself. I'm so filthy inside. I've done so many terrible things. I need to suffer."

"That's where you're wrong. By suffering you won't feel any better. Punishing yourself won't gain anything."

"What a miserable life. Why do any of us want to live? I look around at the distress, the sadness, the ugliness and wonder why would anyone want to live in this world?" He looked at her with puffy, red eyes. "I've tried so hard all of my life and in the process I've cut off everyone. Just a few weeks ago I bragged to someone who cares very much for me that I didn't need her, that I could make it on my own. Make it on my own? Look at the mess I'm in. I thought by making restitution to the people I had wronged I could solve my own problems. It helped for a while, but I don't have the ability or strength to change my own life. I just can't do it. Right now, I feel totally helpless with no desire to live beyond this night."

"I don't believe that many people can say they have changed their lives without some outside help."

"There's no help for me. I've tried everything."

"I'm sure I can offer a suggestion you haven't tried."

Raising his eyebrows skeptically, he waited.

"There's no need to live your life with all these emotions bottled up inside you. There is a way to feel clean."

"How?"

"Well, for one thing, all the weeping tonight will make you feel better tomorrow. That certainly can bring a sort of cleansing, but the trouble with that is, in a short time, the results are wiped away by those unresolved problems rising to the surface again. I would like to introduce you to someone who will be willing to have you dump all your sorrows, problems and emotions on him. I can promise you these problems can be resolved. In fact, I can guarantee that with the right attitude you will meet this person, tell him what you want, and your visit will bring changes, some now and some progressively and tomorrow, I believe everything will appear better to you."

"Who would that be?" he asked with interest.

"Come with me. I want to take you somewhere." She stood, pulling on his arm. "I'll take you to see him."

He stood, perplexed and followed her to the door. Pushing their way through the crowds of people, they struggled a few meters from her house to a low stairway leading to a long sidewalk empty of people. Here they were free to walk quickly.

"Where are we going?" he asked.

"We're going to see someone you've known about all your life." She smiled up at him. "Well, I do know him very well and he's someone who will be happy to listen to your problems no matter how many times you need to talk with him. If you'll approach him with the right attitude, as I said before, you'll leave here tonight a different person."

Approaching the wide, low building, she pushed open the big doors and pulled him in with her. Inside, it was quiet, the muffled noises from without strained through the thick walls. They walked up a long aisle until they stood beneath a hanging figure of Christ on the cross.

"Rolando, you have seen Christ on the cross all of your life. The news I have for you is that He isn't on the cross any longer. He was

Chapter 42

there just long enough to die, but now He's alive and He's waiting to listen to even your faintest cry. There is no need too small or no problem too large for Him to handle. You see, that's why He died, so you can live with a soul cleansed from hatred, bitterness and impurities. But the only people who can be totally changed are those who realize they need Him and who come to Him with the faith that He is able to help. You've already admitted you are sorry for all you have done against others and yourself. Rolando, here lies your answer."

He stood for a long time without speaking, and then slowly nodded his head.

"Come, sit with me here." Jillian moved to a front row bench in the quiet church. Rolando followed obediently. "I have been in close contact with Eric Perez. He's visited me a few times since Elena's death in search of answers because I worked at Marta's clinic. We have talked of Elena and Carlos. You may not know this about Elena, but according to Eric, she miscarried twice in Playas. They were very happy together, but there was a period of time after her first miscarriage that she had some type of breakdown. She wasn't a stable person under stress. After losing Carlos, Eric had a terrible time coping with her distress and with the death of her child, she was unable to survive. No one could have helped her with that under the circumstances, so Rolando, you can't carry blame on yourself for something that was beyond your control." She smiled. "Perhaps we can go to Tulcachi and visit with Eric someday. Both Elena and Carlos are buried there together in a lovely spot. I think that might help you too."

Standing, she looked down at him. "I'm going to leave you alone right now. All you have to do is talk to the Lord, just as if He's here, because He is. You can ask forgiveness from Him and He'll rush to help you. Don't forget all we've spoken about. I believe you can walk out of here a different person tonight. Then come back to see me. You still haven't eaten your bread and cheese."

He gave her a small smile and nodded his head as she turned to leave.

Chapter 43

They needn't have worried. Days passed and they heard nothing from the government. Even Cynthia was in the dark concerning the matter and so life resumed in a normal fashion for Jillian; soon other interests replaced her once constant thoughts of Marta and Lucia and the children.

Though now there was one difference. At least one evening a week, Eric and Raquel made a point to spend time with her. During their first few visits, their uppermost concern was of retaliation from Marta or Lucia. Eric cautioned both Jillian and Raquel to remain alert should a hostile confrontation arise. As the weeks passed and the threat of danger diminished, they turned their attention to the fast approaching completion of Raquel's clinic, which had the blessing of the government. It puzzled Jillian that the same government which closed Marta's outpatient clinic using the excuse that one clinic in Pachuca was enough would not have stepped in before the opening of Raquel's new facility. Would this new clinic make Marta all the more angry with her, knowing there was no doubt in Marta's mind that she had been the one responsible for the closure?

The opening ceremony was planned for the day after Saint Pedro's fiesta. The dedication would consist of speakers from Pachuca's town officials and Raquel's own father, a doctor himself and a leader in the Ecuadorian Medical Association. Accompanying them would be a dignitary from the province of Pichincha. Raquel would be presented

Chapter 43

with a letter of congratulations signed by the president of Ecuador. The doors would then open officially the next day.

The day of the dedication dawned bright and warm. From her balcony, Jillian shook her head at the litter that covered the sidewalks, streets and plaza, the outcome of the fiesta. Her eyes were heavy from lack of sleep, but the pandemonium of the night before and the excitement of Rolando's visit had driven her early from her bed. Because of yesterday's fiesta and today's ceremony at the clinic, classes were canceled. The children were still required to go to school for roll call, after which they would be dismissed to attend the dedication if they wished.

As required by village law, Jillian was obligated to keep the curb and street in front of her house clean. She quickly grabbed a broom, dustpan and a plastic pail and made her way through the litter. As she swept, she kept an eye on her watch because she wanted to arrive early at the clinic in order to chat with Raquel before anyone else arrived. She had so much to tell her.

Dressed in her best sweater and skirt outfit, she made toast, spread it with cheese and washed it down with coffee. Grabbing a gift she had wrapped, a leather checkbook, she left to see her friend. Walking past the plaza and to the block beyond, she arrived at the clinic, a four-room cement structure with modern glass-paned windows, good overhead lighting, solid wood cabinets and modern furniture all donated by her parents.

She opened the front door and yelled, "Raqui."

"Jill?" Raquel called in a nervous voice. "Come in."

Raquel met her at the office door. She was lovely with her dark brown hair pulled back in a pink ribbon. Her matching pink linen dress fit her nicely and brought out a crimson flush in her cheeks. Her brown eyes sparkled beneath long, sweeping lashes. Jillian forgot sometimes how pretty her friend was.

"Oh, Jill, if I hadn't so much to do here this morning, I would have pulled you out of bed to find out what happened with you last night."

"You mean when Rolando came to visit me? Why don't you tell me your side of the story first?" Jillian couldn't keep the grin off her face.

"Yes, let me," gushed Raquel. "Opal, Geoff and I had gone to Quito to pick up the desk and chairs for my office. We came here directly to put the furniture in and then we drove the roundabout way to get to our house because all the roads were crammed with people. When we got home, Opal made coffee and a fruit snack. We were talking about the clinic when the door opened and in came Rolando. What a sight! His clothes were filthy and he smelled terrible, but something was different about him. You know we've been quite worried about him since Elena's death. He insisted on taking the blame for it, saying he wasn't there for her when he should have been."

Jillian put Raquel's gift on the desk and then sat in one of the new patient chairs. "Yes, he does. I think he feels he could have prevented her death. The morning she wandered through town asking for money, he'd been on the road outside the maternity clinic. He would have visited her, but he was afraid of rejection and decided to wait until later to visit her with Geoff. He feels he made a terrible decision," explained Jillian.

Raquel frowned. "He's been drinking so heavily lately, I thought the liquor might eventually kill him or he would have an awful accident."

"He had every intention of committing suicide last night. In fact, he was heading somewhere to do just that when he happened to notice me standing on my balcony. One time I told him if he ever needed a friend, I'd be there."

"And he stopped to see you."

"Yes, but he was in such a terrible condition when he arrived, he frightened me a little. I fixed him something to eat and I washed his face. It was quite overwhelming to me, Raqui, because while I was in the kitchen preparing his food, he suddenly broke down and wept like I've never seen a man weep."

"Poor Rolando."

"He just kept sobbing that he missed Elena so much and that he had been so wrong about everything."

"Don't you think that crying is the best thing that could have happened? Rolando is such a complex man."

"Maybe. Anyway, I didn't know how to explain and make him understand how he could be forgiven for his past actions, so I took

Chapter 43

him to the church and showed him a replica of Christ on the cross. I explained how Jesus is no longer on the cross but has risen from the dead and is alive and waiting to have us approach Him with our repentance, our needs, problems and thanksgiving, and no matter how far he would try to run from his problems, or how deeply in trouble he is, the Lord is always just a breath away. And I told him how easy it is to communicate with God and that it's as easy as we're talking together right now."

Raquel clasped her hands to her heart. "Okay! Rolando must have listened because last night, for the first time, he seemed to be at peace. It showed on his face and in his manner."

"I don't know because I left him in the church. I explained to him it wasn't his fault that Elena died. I invited him back to my house for the food he never got around to eating, but he didn't come. I was worried about him. That's why I hurried over here now."

Raquel's face was radiant as she clapped her hands together in glee. "I think he wanted to go home and show us how different he was."

"Then he didn't say anything to you?"

"Actually, no. He said he had visited you. We all saw that in some way he was different though. He said that he wanted to spend the night at our house. I guess he didn't have a chance to say much. He will though, I know."

The front door opened and the first guest speaker walked in. By the time the dedication ceremony had begun, several important people were in attendance. Because the building was small, a decision was made to hold the ceremony outside. Several members of Raquel's family, including her parents, a brother, aunts and uncles stood up front so as not to miss a word. Officials from Pachuca and several outlying villages and towns attended, coming to offer their congratulations. Friends and villagers crowded the street. Many brought gifts of live chickens, fruit, eggs and empanadas. After a few words were spoken by the representatives of Pachuca and Pichincha's district and Raquel's father representing the Ecuadorian Medical Association, Raquel came forward to say a few words. Expressing her emotion, she thanked the people and informed them that she would be on duty the following day.

"I'm not here," she announced, "to take patients from Pachuca's other clinic, but we will be working with each other to bring a better medical atmosphere to this community."

As Raquel spoke, Jillian scanned the crowd for Eric. She spotted him at the back of the group. He waved and winked. Then she saw Rolando, who also waved.

A letter of encouragement from the Ecuadorian president was presented to her and as Raquel backed away with the prize in her hand, the ceremony ended and the crowd dispersed. Raquel returned to her office and for the umpteenth time, checked to see if all was ready. She had hand-picked two graduates from the girls' school in Pachuca and sent for a nurse's aide correspondence course which they had completed in time for the clinic to open.

Chapter 44

After the last guest departed, Raquel's family bade her good-bye and set out for Quito. Her set of close friends then merged in her office, content and proud with what the young doctor had accomplished. They moved from one room to the next admiring the new facilities, even though they had witnessed each new phase in the construction over the past several months. Geoff and Opal, Rolando, Eric and Jillian gazed in satisfaction at the recovery room with two cots, a bathroom with a shower stall, the examination room which could also be used for delivering a baby, the long waiting room and Raquel's office which had addition built on with a modern toilet, shower and cot in case she had to remain the night. In comparison with many of Pachuca's buildings, this was a remarkable achievement.

Returning to her office, they lounged in chairs or leaned against the walls. Jillian realized it was the first time she had seen Rolando in a gathering and she could barely tear her eyes from him. Had he really changed? What was going on in his mind? Had he reached God last night or had God reached him? Had he found peace? No, his eyes looked troubled. She sighed, longing to speak with him alone.

"I want you all to stay here a moment," said Eric loudly, in an attempt to quiet the excited chatter. "I have something in the truck." He departed from the room and they waited in anticipation, laughing at absurd speculations as to what he was planning. They heard noises in the waiting room and then he called for Rolando and Geoff. Jillian followed, too curious to remain behind. She found him with three large baskets and an ice chest at his feet. "Here, help me," he said to Rolando and Geoff.

The three carried the baskets and chest into the office and set them on an examining table in the corner. With an air of mystery, they opened them and peeked inside while Eric pulled out a beautiful white cake with small pink candies sprinkled on top. Jillian's eyes lit up as she looked around the room to watch those who had never laid eyes on a real cake.

"Since you would soon be opening a new clinic here, Raquel I remembered that my cook, Isabel, has sometimes made cakes from a recipe book published by someone who lives in the Rocky Mountains in the United States. Because we live in similar altitudes, she has been able to bake delicious cakes. I remembered my sister-in-law, many years ago had made a frosting called Seven-minute and I telephoned and begged her for the recipe. Yesterday, Isabel baked the cake for you, Raquel. Also, our refrigerator at home makes ice cubes. Here, I have colas and ice."

They look like children, thought Jillian. These young mountain Indians have never seen a cake that looks this beautiful and good. Her heart almost burst with joy. In a flash, her mind jumped back to the days she had lived with Marta. How often she had longed for a moment like this, to be a part of the people, to have wholesome companionships, not the sick fellowship she had experienced with Lucia and Marta, but strengthening, giving, loyal companionships. There was no other place she would rather be than right here. It was hard to hold back the tears as she listened to the excitement and exclamations of her beloved friends.

Plates, glasses and utensils were laid out. Eric handed Raquel a long, sharp knife and she cut into the soft light cake.

"It's called angel food cake," said Eric, as he placed ice cubes in the glasses and poured cola. When they were served, Eric halted them before they began to eat. "Thank you, Raquel, for bringing your talents to our community. I know that you could have earned a great living in Quito, or some other influential section of Ecuador, but the fact that you chose to live and work in one of the poorest areas of Ecuador only proves to us that you are a fine doctor, a good person and a choice friend. Thank you."

Chapter 44

They all voiced their appreciation and sipped their colas. Jillian began to giggle when she took her first bite of cake. It was the best tasting food she had eaten in a long time. Opal and Raquel chattered about the ingredients, delighted with their cake. Geoff, Rolando and Eric wolfed down two pieces before sitting back to pat their stomachs, voicing their compliments for Isabel's genius. Jillian took advantage of the easy conversation to observe Rolando without covertness. He was enjoying himself, but she saw a restlessness there that concerned her. Glancing away, she found Eric's eyes on her. Before he had a chance to blink and turn away, she recognized a look of jealousy. He thinks I'm interest in Rolando romantically, she thought. He really does care for me. His feelings go deeper than friendship! Her heart soared. Eric had averted his eyes, apparently embarrassed. He must not have wanted to expose his emotions just yet. Uncomfortable, he began gathering the dishes.

"Wait a minute," called Rolando, standing, his handsome face anxious. "I have to speak with each one of you."

Eric put down the dirty dishes and sank slowly in his seat. No one moved and all faces turned to the end of the table.

Rolando's face crumbled and his hands shook. "I came to the end of myself last night. I no longer wanted to live and had decided to kill myself. As you all know, I was killing myself slowly with alcohol anyway." He looked at Jillian, a faint smile on his lips. "For the first time in my life, last night, I seriously prayed, really prayed." His eyes swept the faces of his friends. "I told God if He was really alive and if something didn't change in my life right then, I didn't want to live. All of a sudden I saw myself as I really was, full of hatred and bitterness and I looked at Christ on the cross and that He had already paid the price by dying for me and the realization that He is still alive and wanting to help me. Then I saw how helpless I was to change anything in my life. I had bragged how I could change myself, how I could live without help, but as I sat before God last night, I understood how my life lay in ashes at my feet. I remember crying out in the stillness that I didn't want to be alone anymore and that I needed help." He paused, tears glistening in his eyes. "Do you know, in that moment, I felt a peace enter me that I've never felt before? For the first time in my life I feel clean. I was afraid when I woke up this morning that the feeling would have passed, but I'm a different person."

Raquel gasped with pleasure and Geoff, Opal and Jillian wiped tears from their eyes. Eric sat back with a strange look on his face.

Rolando took a deep breath and continued. "I don't know if this is all part of what I must do, but most of the night I struggled with the knowledge that there are a few things I must tell you." He licked his lips nervously. "Geoff, the day of papá's death, I discovered where Elena and Carlos had gone to escape me. I was shocked to find out they had run all the way to Playas, a coastal town in Southern Ecuador. They had been that afraid of me. My intentions were to go there immediately and destroy Carlos. I wanted Elena to come home, for things to be the way they were before Carlos took her away, but first there was papá's funeral and then mamá died. My main concern was money. How would I get to Playas? Then I found several thousand sucres in Geoff's and Opal's bedroom." Tears fell unheeded from his eyes; his lower lip quivered. "Geoff already knows this, but I want everyone to know I stole that money. Over the years, I stole from others too, especially tourists. I stole a knife and took a bus to Playas. It took me a couple days to find Carlos and Elena, but I did. Do you know how long I had convinced myself she hated him and wanted to leave him? Do you know how many years I wasted believing that?" He shook his head slowly. "Imagine my surprise when I first saw them together. Our beautiful Elena, I can see her as plainly as if it had been last night, was standing in the soft rays of the sinking sun; she was so beautiful...." His voice was soft in remembrance. "She was waiting for Carlos to finish his shift in a major hotel restaurant where he had been hired to be the captain of a dining room. Can you imagine? Carlos with an important job like that? I'll never forget how those two acted when I saw them together. I had been so wrong. In that instant I knew how much they loved each other."

He was silent for a moment, regaining his composure. "You would think right then that I would have found a way to come back to Pachuca, wouldn't you? Not me. I followed them with the knife in my hand, ready for an opportune moment to plunge it into Carlos." He stopped momentarily at the loud gasps that met his ear. "But before I could complete the act, someone grabbed me and took me to

Chapter 44

the hotel where I was put under guard until morning. The managers had been watching me all evening loitering. They wanted to have me arrested and thrown in jail. I was so angry. All my planning, all my schemes had failed again. The next morning Carlos came to me and because he considered me part of his family, told his employers to let me leave for home. He forgave me. Now, I look back and realize that God had Carlos' friends there to keep me from killing him. It took me a long time to get over that anger. I had to travel for almost a year, but at the end of the year my anger was gone, but not my despair and guilt. I know now that, though I didn't actually take his life that night, in my heart I had committed the act. That is a burden that would not dissolve. So I convinced myself what I needed to do was find a woman, marry and settle down."

He glanced quickly at Raquel and then his eyes lowered and he ran his fingers through his thick, brown hair. "I was so self-centered I was willing to pull someone else down to my level. Although liquor was almost killing me then, I must say my feelings for Carlos were changing. I have to tell you that when I talked with him in Playas, I almost felt affection for him. To think he refused to press charges and I was released. I had to admire him for that." Rolando's nervousness was increasing, his hands jerking on the table. "Raqui, do you remember the day you came to see me in Quito and told me Carlos and Elena were in Tulcachi?"

She nodded, glancing at Jillian. Sitting up straighter, Eric stared at Rolando, a frown playing on his forehead as the tall man stared back at him. "I went to Tulcachi that day to see Carlos."

Eric cleared his throat. "Carlos or Elena didn't tell me you were in Tulcachi."

"He didn't have a chance. It was the day of his death." Rolando's head hung.

The room was still and then Eric slowly came to his feet. "The day of his death you were in Tulcachi? What does that mean?"

"Yes."

"Why?" A blood vessel was throbbing on Eric's temple. "Why were you there?"

"No, no," cried Rolando. "I wasn't there to harm him. I was there to ask his forgiveness."

Eric's hands were at his sides, clenched then unclenched. "But he did die that day."

"Yes, but I didn't know until the next day that he had died." Rolando wiped his eyes with his hands. "I showed him how to drive the tractor. He wanted to know how but I warned him not to start it moving. I was just trying to be friendly. We had forgiven each other at that point. He had invited me to visit Elena and him at the hacienda one day. He had told me about Elena's pregnancy. I was leaving when he started up the tractor's motor. He must have put it into reverse instead of drive. The next thing I knew he was tumbling down the hill."

"I didn't see you there that day," said Eric suspiciously. "Where were you when I found Carlos?"

"I was running to find help."

"And did you find help? I never saw you."

Rolando gulped. "After I ran several hundred yards, I realized I should have taken Carlos with me. I ran back and then I saw you, Eric. I was afraid if you saw me, you'd think I had hurt him. I was so confused I ran away."

Eric's piercing eyes flashed disgust. "You ran away? You saw me so you ran away? Why? We might have been able to help Carlos."

Geoff rushed to his brother's side as Rolando wept, with his head in his hands. "Eric, I knew about Rolando's trip to Tulcachi. He told me several weeks ago. At that time, he convinced me he had not hurt Carlos the day he died and I believe him. You have to understand what alcohol does to a person. It distorted his feelings for Carlos and Elena and it distorted his decision to run or return that day. Rolando didn't have to confess this today. He just wants to make a fresh start."

"Yes," Rolando said, raising his tear-streaked face to Eric. "There has been so much uncleanness in my life. I want to begin my life again. I swear to you I did not hurt Carlos. The irony is, we became brothers that day. Please believe me." He stretched out his hands imploringly.

Staring at him a long time, Eric's eyes then moved from person to person in the room before finally settling on Jillian. She clasped her hands tightly in her lap, waiting. Eric's continued fellowship with them and his future with her, she knew, hinged upon his decision in

Chapter 44

that moment, for she was aware she would rather remain friends with Geoff, Opal, Raquel and Rolando than choose a bitter, unforgiving man. Holding her breath, she waited as he watched her, knowing he was dissecting Rolando's confession for any untruths. Finally, he turned back to Rolando, the tall, handsome man, now humbled and with a tight smile, Eric extended his hand.

With that, the mood broke and Raquel rushed to Rolando's side, hugging him. Geoff and Opal put their arms around him, tears streaming down their faces. Rolando looked across their heads to Jillian and with one sweep of his arm gathered her to him. He whispered in her ear, "What you told me worked. Jesus is no longer on the cross. He's in my heart."

She looked up to see every trace of pain, disappointment and grief erased from his face.

Chapter 45

Marta Brewer studied the palms of her hands. "See these hands, Lucia? Hundreds of babies have been delivered into these hands." She glanced at the sullen Indian, slouching in an armchair, her chin resting on her chest. "Are you listening to me?"

"I've heard you say the same thing so many times, I could quote you word for word," muttered Lucia without looking up. "Let me finish for you. Hundreds of babies have been delivered into these hands and I've never lost a mother."

Marta's head dropped, the wind knocked out of her sails. "Well, it's true," she claimed, peevishly.

Throwing back her head, Lucia sneered in Marta's direction. "Have you forgotten how many of those babies I delivered? Why is it you always get the credit? Every time we have guests out here, do you ever mention that I have delivered at least half of them? No, of course not. It's always you, Marta. Brag, brag, brag. It's so important that they know how wonderful you are."

The nurse snorted, continuing to study her hands. This conversation was not new to either woman. "You're the one who doesn't want to be mentioned to Americans because, according to you, they are so untrustworthy and hypocritical. I used to brag on you all the time, but any time visitors have mentioned your talents, you claim they are being hypocritical. You are never satisfied." She gazed into the fire on the grate.

Chapter 45

They were relaxing after putting the children in bed. Lucia had been in Quito all day, running errands and visiting distant relatives and had come home, as usual, in her normal, uncommunicative mood.

"How are your aunt and uncle?" Marta attempted a conversation.

"Fine," Lucia muttered into her sweater.

"Did you have a hard time finding a seat on the bus?"

"Nope."

"I did two prenatal exams today. Fortunately no deliveries came in on your day off."

"Ha!" exclaimed Lucia, more animated, her head popping up. "You know why? Because they're all going down to the new doctor's office in the plaza."

"Not all of them," replied Marta defensively. "Things are just slow right now."

Lucia chuckled without mirth. "Well, I might as well pack. Won't my brother and his family be glad to see me when I go rowing down the Tena River in a canoe, heading back to the jungle because I have no job here?"

Marta cast an impatient look in Lucia's direction. "You talk about me repeating the same thing over and over. I'm sick of you telling me you're going to lose your job. You wait and see. The townspeople will soon find out that Ecuadorian doctors are behind the times and don't know the first thing about medicine."

"And they'll all come running back here to you to deliver their babies into your capable hands. They'll remember that you've delivered hundreds of babies and haven't lost a mother."

Marta's thick gray hair bounced as she turned to give Lucia a cold look. "Mark my words, our patients will be back."

"And what if they don't come back? What if we start losing money?" Lucia's small eyes narrowed.

"You've been with me for many years," boasted Marta. "Have you ever gone hungry or have I ever failed to pay you? We've got money, don't worry."

"Yeah, well, if the patients don't deliver babies here, how are we going to be able to send the little brats off to the States?"

"I said I had two prenatal exams today. That means they'll deliver here. No matter what that Raquel, whatever her name is, does she'll make a mistake and the patients will come crawling back here. Just have patience."

"I can't believe you're taking this so calmly, Marta. When things go wrong, usually you are lying on the floor sobbing and carrying on."

"I don't know. I guess things can't get much worse than they are. They've got to start looking up."

"Yeah, who knows?" Lucia's chin dropped into her sweater again.

Marta went back to staring at her hands as her heart began to beat faster and her breath came in short, jerky gasps. Lucia made her so angry. Why couldn't she just tell her what she wanted to know? Why did she always have to ask the same question every time she came home from the plaza? "Did you happen to see Jill?"

"Nope, the house looked deserted."

"Could it be she's gone back to the United States?"

"Marta, we go through this same conversation every Friday. Every time I get off the bus in the plaza, I look toward Jill's house. Every week it looks deserted. That's because she's at some class somewhere. We know she hasn't gone back to the United States because she still has classes going on."

Taping the balls of her fingers on the chair arm, Marta said, "I think the people will turn against her someday soon."

Frustrated, Lucia jerked herself to an upright position and glared at the woman. "You keep saying that. Why would you believe it?"

"Because I told the parents of the children in our school that if they went to a class put on by Jill they couldn't come back to our school again. Don't you think that will scare them?"

"I don't know. I don't think you can trust these people. How do we know the kids in our school don't sneak up to her house for English classes?"

"Because Olivia tells me everything. She's right there next door. She can see everything."

"Then why do you keep asking me if Jill has left Pachuca?" Lucia rolled her eyes upward and then leaned over the side of her chair and made a 't' sound, as though she were spitting. "And as far as Olivia goes, she's watching when she's not hanging around with a man in Quito."

Chapter 45

"We can't be choosy, you know. Anyway, Olivia was willing to file that complaint against Jill."

"She signed it. You filed the report and did you see it work? Did the police take away Jill's visa? It was a mistake to tell the police she has men in her house all the time, especially when they can't find any proof."

"I can't help what Olivia told me. She said there were men at Jill's house all the time," Marta defended herself angrily.

"You know what your big mistake was?" Lucia's eyes flashed. "Using that stupid name, Alicia. I was against that from the beginning. Alicia, Olivia? Bad choice."

"That wasn't my choice. That was Larry Parker's idea."

Lucia clenched her teeth. "Don't even mention their names to me, the idiots. How stupid to rent out a house that belongs to an American and then ask Jill to come over. Can you believe they threatened her? Then two days later, what do you do? You give them a baby you schemed away from an unsuspecting mother here in the clinic. What do you think the Parker's neighbors thought? What about the caretaker? What if someone had been clever enough to check out Larry and Heather Parker? What if Jill had gone back to see them when they had the baby in hand? One day no baby, the next day, a baby. Wouldn't Jill suspect something?"

"No one discovered it," said Marta, peeved. "We were just lucky the Parker's were willing to fly to Ecuador and take the baby to the States themselves, instead of us having to find another couple to transport it. Don't forget, we made a lot of money off the Parkers."

Lucia lowered herself into her favorite pouting position again. "I don't care. I still think we took a big chance."

It was silent for a moment as Marta cocked her ear upward to listen for movement from the children in the rooms above. Satisfied, she settled down to stare in the fire. Their musings were interrupted by the shrill ring of the telephone. Marta glanced at her watch and then met Lucia's startled gaze. "Who could that be at this hour?" She grunted, heaving herself out of the chair.

"Just remember, if it's a delivery, today is my day off," called Lucia.

"Do you think I could forget it?" remarked Marta, trotting for the hallway. She picked up the instrument and in an unfriendly tone,

For This Child

greeted the telephone operator. The verbal battle between the telephone operators in Pachuca and Marta and Lucia went back so far, they couldn't remember what had instigated it.

"Buenos noches. Why are you disturbing us at this hour? My children are in bed and you'll wake them."

"Do I tell your friends what time to call you? I'm just doing my job," snarled a male voice.

"Put my call through, but I won't start speaking until I hear you click off."

Without a reply, the operator told Marta's caller to commence. As promised, the nurse failed to respond until she heard the click.

"Buenos noches, buenos noches, señorita Marta. Are you there?"

"Buenos noches," she finally replied. "Yes, I am here. Who is calling?"

"Can we talk? Is someone listening in?"

"Yes, you can talk. Who is this?"

"Your attorney. I am on my way out to Pachuca right now. You must have the children dressed and ready to go in an hour."

"What?" Marta collapsed onto a chair by the telephone stand. "The children? Ready for what? Go where? I don't understand what you mean."

"You have no choice unless you want to risk losing them. I'm bringing a vehicle."

"What?" screamed Marta. "I don't understand. What's wrong?"

Lucia hurried up behind her. "What's wrong, Marta?"

"The government will be at your house early tomorrow morning. They are going to search your house for the children, their records, your maternity clinic records, everything. I told you someday you would be in trouble if you didn't get those records in order."

The telephone slipped from Marta's grasp and fell to the floor. Lucia grabbed it and watched Marta fall into a heap as she lifted the receiver to her ear. "This is Lucia. Who is calling?"

The caller was silent for a moment. "Where's Marta?"

"She's fainted. What's going on?"

"Listen, I don't have time to explain again. This is Marta's attorney calling. You are in big trouble. You must get the children ready to leave. The government has discovered that your orphanage and the clinic are

Chapter 45

being operated illegally. What is worse, they know about the illegal adoptions. If you and the children aren't gone by morning, everything will be taken by the government. Everything will be discovered."

"But how? How did they find out? I thought you had someone in the government office being paid good money to take care of these things."

"I thought so too," replied the attorney. "Something went wrong. I haven't had time to find out what, but I tell you now, get those kids ready to go."

Lucia hung up, more frightened than she had ever been in her life. Without compassion, she filled a pan with water and threw it on the limp figure lying on the floor. "We've got to get busy or it's all over for us."

An hour later, as the alarmed, shivering children sat in the living room, three sets of headlights appeared in the driveway.

"Why three cars?" Marta blubbered, wringing her handkerchief in her hands. Lucia ran to the door and opened it. In bustled the attorney, a smartly dressed, portly man perspiration glistening on his rigid face.

"Are they ready?"

"Yes," wailed Marta. "Who else is here?"

"I brought the people from the government office that has been helping us out. We figured we would need three vehicles to take the children."

The screen door opened and in walked two women.

"Marta," said the attorney. "Quickly, let me introduce you to señora Flores and señora de Mineo."

But Marta was inconsolable. "Who would have done such a thing to us? Who?"

Señora Flores' cold eyes swept the pathetic woman. "Do you know an American named Jill Townsend? She lives here in Pachuca somewhere."

The nurse's mouth dropped open and Lucia threw her hands up in the air. "So, Jill won after all, Marta," said Lucia softly.

By morning all important papers and essentials had been removed from the compound. The children had been gone several hours before Marta and Lucia took their belongings and fled. It was the first time Marta had ever seen Lucia weep.

Chapter 46

At nine o'clock the next morning, the townspeople in Pachuca were shocked to see a caravan of military vehicles converge on their plaza. After receiving directions, they rolled down to Marta's compound. The military findings astonished them. For the second time in four years, they had secretly raided an American orphanage only to find it deserted. First Clint Marshall, now Marta Brewer had both disappeared from under their noses. Ralf Rodriguez smote his fist in the palm of his hand and cursed. He knew the chances of finding Marta Brewer in a country she knew as well as she did would be next to impossible, especially if she did what Clint Marshall had done and dispersed the children to all parts of Ecuador and the United States. He began to suspect that señorita Brewer was not alone in operating this illegal adoption ring.

Chapter 47

Almost a year had passed since the night of Marta's disappearance, news of which had given Jillian both a mixture of horror and hope, hope of finally being able to contact Andy and Ryan and horror at the consequences for her part in exposing Marta. On that fateful day, Jillian had been driving to her classes in Puembo when the raid occurred. In fact, she had passed the caravan of military vehicles on the highway, but outside of mere curiosity, she had given it no other thought. Upon returning to Pachuca late that morning, she parked her pickup when Gladys approached her in a high state of anxiety. "Señorita, oh señorita, buenos dias."

Her shock at seeing Gladys' apprehension superseded the bounds of propriety failing to greet her properly as she blurted, "Gladys, what's wrong?"

"Jill," called Raquel, running toward her from the end of the block. "It's happened. The military raided Marta's property. Get into your house and lock the doors! No telling what Lucia will do if she can find you."

Gladys and Raquel pulled her with them to her house, relieving her of the school supplies. They told her that military personnel had questioned the townspeople for the location of Marta's property. Curiosity seekers, peeking over the mud walls, reported later that when the government authorities arrived on the scene, only the bewildered maid, Flora was on the premises. After questioned by the authorities, Flora was released to go home. She told the inquiring townspeople that Marta had locked her in her bedroom the previous night while the frightened, whimpering children were gathered in groups and removed from the orphanage. From her bedroom window, she watched as three vehicles departed under cover of darkness. Then in the middle of the night, Marta had come and unlocked her bedroom door and, in tears, hugged the shocked, speechless maid. When Marta turned to leave, Flora tried to follow her out the door, but Marta shoved her back and locked her in again and then she drove off and that was the last she'd seen of her. She did not see Lucia leave, though through the window she'd seen a great deal of movement in the clinic and at the same time she'd heard a lot of noise, the banging of doors and drawers.

Later, when Jillian and Eric had questioned Flora, she could add little to what she had already relayed to the townspeople, except for one good piece of news. At one point Flora had been able to yell for Peter's attention and when the boy had stood outside her door, Flora had quietly instructed him to care for Andy and Ryan in particular and if at all possible, remember to come back to Pachuca when he could and contact her or Jillian. She had only a minute before she heard a reprimand from Marta and then silence.

In the initial weeks, Jillian kept vigil thinking Ryan, Andy and Peter would arrive on her doorstep as Eric had made dozens of trips to the government offices hoping to find news of Elena's baby and the whereabouts of Andy and Ryan, becoming so obsessed with the situation he was parking himself in the offices every day. But as the year progressed with no answers, his hope dwindled and Jillian began to despair.

On one such visit to the Children's Services Division, Eric determined he would not leave until he spoke with someone in charge and had sat and read in the waiting room. Finally señora Flores, still as cold and forbidding as ever, had come forward and told him they simply could not help him. In a flash of anger, he reminded her he had tried to warn her to check into Marta's adoption records shortly after the disappearance of Elena's baby, but instead the government had waited weeks before raiding the property. His outburst had startled the woman to the point that Eric could have sworn he had seen

Chapter 47

fear in her eyes as she retreated to the sanctum of an inner office and did not reappear.

Finally, he was directed to see Rosa de Mineo, upstairs on the third floor. She had invited him into a conference room and seated him at a long table. When Eric questioned her about Ecuadorian children being sent illegally to the United States or elsewhere, the woman seemed to demonstrate some compassion for the situation, but when Eric pressed her to tell him what she knew about babies leaving the country with false papers, she insisted that so far as she knew, legal papers had accompanied them.

"How can that be?" he hammered away at her. Finally just before Eric was ushered out of the conference room, Rosa de Mineo had resignedly admitted that someone in the government had allowed the adoptive children out of the country with a bogus exit paper and that it was true that at least two hundred children had been sent illegally from Ecuador to the United States in the past few years but the government was in the dark as to the perpetrator.

On another occasion, Eric cornered Ralf Rodriguez, the President of Children's Services. The man, in discussing the government search said they had found little to substantiate questionable activities in Marta Brewer's orphanage, except for two pieces of critical evidence left behind by the nurse in her haste to flee. The fat man leaned over to a bottom drawer in his desk and pulled out a leather horsewhip which had been found along with two photo albums stuck back on the top of a portable closet. A week after Eric's first visit, along with Jillian he returned. She identified the children in the photographs and provided the name, age and biological family of each child. Jillian verified that no horses had lived on the property, thereby excluding any need for a horsewhip. The gleam in the president's eyes was hateful. She knew he would love to get his hands on Marta Brewer not only for the torture she had administered to the children but for the havoc she had created in his life.

Through Cynthia, Jillian and Eric knew Marta and Lucia had never been found; they could assume the pair had fled the country and as yet there was no knowledge of the children's whereabouts. It was easy to understand Ralf Rodriguez' frustration for by the end of that year nearly every manager in the Children's Services Division had lost their jobs including Rosa de Mineo and señora Flores. He knew his own job was on the line. Only Cynthia's position had been spared because she had no access to adoption papers or had any scandal tainted the orphanage in Conocoto. In fact, she had been handed a letter of gratitude for her part in exposing the link to the illegal adoptions.

The orphanage in Conocoto had been fortunate in a number of ways. Although Helen Perez had remained in New York with her son, Jorge and his family, she had continued her fund-raising endeavors for the orphanage. It didn't take long, however, for the government wives to realize that no matter how much money they poured into the ancient building in Conocoto, it would never meet their expectations of a modern facility. With permission from the government, a large building several miles north of Quito was purchased. Showers and toilets were being installed; a kitchen, dining room, large playroom, bedrooms and playground would follow. Raquel and Jillian had reflected with satisfaction the part they had played in improving the lives of orphanage children.

Chapter 48

And now, more than a year after the raid they could say that life was good. Not all the loose ends were tied up, but that was normal. She still didn't know where her children were.

It was Friday afternoon and she had just come from her last class of the week which had been held in Tababela. Looking forward to Saturday, she planned to retire early that evening with a good book and with the possibility of sleeping late in the morning. Yawning with the thought, she slipped from the pickup after parking it in the Ortega's driveway. She had been in her house for only two minutes when a knock came at the front door. Groaning in protest, she opened it to find two people from her past, Betsy Wagner and Emily Shoemaker. The two nurses from the American hospital smiled up at her from the sidewalk. So surprised was Jillian to see them, they moved to enter the house before she had voiced proper salutations.

Betsy still appeared the same, unattractive with a light pockmarked complexion, protruding pale eyes and a large square jaw marking her outward appearance. This had never affected her personality or her devotion to nursing. Jillian's remembrance of Betsy dated back to the time she had met her in the hospital when Betsy and Emily cared for one of her babies, Anna. It was never hard to know where Betsy was stationed because of her bubbling laughter and perky conversation. She was an asset to the hospital staff and healing balm to the sick.

Emily was heavyset, dark and very pretty with curly black hair and brown eyes. Both had been roommates longer than Jillian had lived in Ecuador. She had entered their lives at a troubled period in her life. One afternoon, during nap time Marta had spirited the baby in her charge, Anna, away to a place unknown to Jillian. Weeks later, Marta had finally confessed that Betsy and Emily were caring for the infant until they could find a cure for Anna's stubborn rash. For a period of time, after that, Jillian ate her lunch in the nurses' apartment on her errand days in order to visit the baby and then on one visit, upon arrival, she was stunned to hear that Marta had again whisked Anna away and she had been adopted by someone in the United States. Never again would she see Anna nor did she particularly care to visit Betsy and Emily, but now they stood in the entryway of her house.

"Hi, Jill," said Betsy laughing. "Both of us have a day off so we decided to go on a picnic. I remember someone telling me you had moved to the plaza in Pachuca and we thought we would stop to visit you."

"How strange that you should come right now," said Jillian, stepping back as the two walked toward the kitchen. She followed them and began washing her hands in a basin of water. "This is quite a coincidence. I just walked through the door myself."

"Yes, isn't it?" Emily put her purse on the kitchen table.

"Jill, why don't you go with us on the picnic? I'm sure you haven't eaten dinner yet and we have plenty of food."

Jillian lowered her chin apologetically. "Thank you for asking but I've been looking forward to an evening of relaxation all day. This has been a busy week of classes."

"Oh, come on," said Emily. "It's been ages since we've seen you and there's so much to catch up on."

Wondering what they could possibly have to talk about, Jillian continued to shake her head negatively. "No, I just can't. It's late anyway. It will be dark in a little over two hours."

"I promise you that we'll be back before dark," said Betsy. "When was the last time you sat around for two hours speaking English?"

"I can hardly remember," laughed Jillian. "It feels a little strange right now."

Chapter 48

Betsy joined in the laughter. "Come on, Jill. We'll drive up above Pachuca, eat and come back."

"Why don't we eat here?"

"Picnics are for out-of-doors. Come on," said Emily.

Jillian realized she was going to lose and suddenly she wondered if Betsy and Emily wanted to swap information about Marta. "Where are we going?"

"Like I said, up above Pachuca," exclaimed Betsy excitedly. "There's a spot east of here."

"East?" Jillian hesitated. "You mean east, like the road to Papallacta?"

"Yeah, it's close by that road," said Emily.

"I hate the road to Papallacta," said Jillian, a tone of finality resounding in her voice. "I don't think I want to go. I think we should stay here and eat."

The eyes of the two nurses quickly swept the windowless dreary room.

"Listen." Betsy put out her hand. "We'll just go out around the haciendas, eat and come back. Come on."

"Come on," encouraged Emily enticingly.

Unconvinced, Jillian found herself being led out the front door. "I want to tell my neighbors where we're going."

"Oh, come on, Jill," said Betsy, sharpness entering her voice. "We'll be back before you know it."

Nevertheless, Jillian broke away and poked her head in Gladys' doorway. "Buenas tardes, Gladys. My friends have come. They want me to go with them for a picnic up around the road leading to Papallacta. We'll be back in two hours."

Gladys waved her best wishes and Jillian climbed into Emily's little yellow Volkswagen. The trio drove east, exited the main highway and turned onto the narrow road that led to Papallacta. The three conversed about the hospital, the terrible accident now almost two years previously which had claimed two relatives of Pachuca families. They talked about Jillian's classes and their families back in the States when Jillian realized they were traveling beyond the local haciendas.

"Where's the spot for the picnic?" she asked, a frown forming on her brow.

"We're almost there," Betsy called over her shoulder above the Volkswagen's noisy motor.

The conversation lagged and Emily seemed to be driving with more determination. For a brief moment, Jillian wondered whether Betsy and Emily would bring her harm. How silly, she thought, after all they are nurses.

Betsy disrupted Jillian's contemplations. "There's a house nearby that missionaries have built. They use it for a retreat once in a while. Let's go up there for our picnic."

Yes, she had heard about the house, though she was sure it was more than a half hour away. Well, I might as well stop fighting this, she thought. There's no place for me to go but with them."

The scenery changed as the road climbed higher and higher and the canyon beside them deepened. Her anxiety increased and anger with it. She realized things were beyond her control as she wondered again if she might be facing serious trouble. Lapsing into silence, she forced her thoughts away from her anxieties to Eric. He was often on her mind, sending a warm, pleasant glow through her. These past years had been good having him as a friend. Since Rolando's conversion, the six had remained in close fellowship, attending a church in Quito each Sunday. During the course of these several months they had divided into couples, Geoff and Opal, Raquel and Rolando, which left Eric and Jillian together. Often Eric would spend an evening with her, sitting on her balcony, discussing the day's events. This arrangement had suited both of them as Jillian was busy with her classes and Eric with his hacienda and his continue quest for Elena's child. A more serious relationship had not been pursued and truthfully, Jillian was thankful. If marriage were to be considered, it would mean leaving Pachuca for a life in Tulcachi, giving up her classes and her close proximity to Raquel. In fact, she was a little anxious that talk of marriage might ruin the close friendship she and Eric already shared.

Lost in thought, Jillian had almost forgotten the perilous narrow road and deep canyons and that they were traveling further and further from Pachuca, but all of a sudden she was very troubled. Was

Chapter 48

she being kidnapped and facing danger? "Where are we going?" she asked, her voice sharp. "You've been driving more than an hour."

"I guess I didn't realize the house was so far," said Betsy. "We're almost there, I know."

"I don't care," replied Jillian perturbed. "I want to go home."

"We're almost there, just a few more miles," said Emily soothingly.

Chapter 49

Finally they pulled into the long driveway of a white one-story house. Actually there were two houses connected by a double garage. Betsy explained that one house was used by permanent residents who worked at a nearby electrical plant that fed power into parts of the Tumbaco Valley but were away for the weekend. The adjoining house was for guests such as they were for the afternoon. Without hesitation Emily drove the car into the open garage and they got out of the Volkswagen. Stretching her stiff body, Jillian walked to the side of one of the houses, interested despite her concerns. A few feet from where she stood a forty-foot high waterfall spilled into a rushing river which ran behind the house through a lush grove of trees.

"When was the last time you lived in a home with a waterfall outside your bedroom window?" Betsy asked over the roar of the water.

"Not even once," laughed Jillian, feeling a lot better. She looked up at the glowing late afternoon sky, at the towering mountains and trees and relaxed a little. They had topped the Andes Mountain's summit and descended several miles into the verdant fringes of the jungle.

"I'm sorry this took so long," apologized Betsy. "I guess I forgot how far it is, but I knew once you got here, you could relax. On the way home, we can drive very slowly because I know it will be dark, but it just seemed important to me that you get away."

A mild irritation rankled Jillian's momentary peace. "You know, you really didn't have any right to assume I need rest just because

Chapter 49

you're a nurse. You manipulated me by saying the picnic was only a few minutes from my home. This is almost two hours away." She saw Betsy give her a worried frown and then smiled indulgently thinking that soon this would be all over. "I guess you're right. I don't travel very much because it seems my life is taken up in work."

Betsy slapped her friend good-naturedly on the back and withdrew a key from her pocket to open the door leading from the garage into the smaller of the two houses and turned on a light. "Welcome to the guest house, Jill. Now we can eat lunch. Emily, will you make us some coffee?"

Entering the Americanized kitchen, Jillian noted all the modern conveniences, a full range, big refrigerator, a dishwasher and several small appliances. Dropping their lunches on the closest counter, Betsy and Emily went directly into the living room. "I need to go to the bathroom," they said in unison, giggling.

"Jill, you'll be next," yelled Emily.

When they re-entered the kitchen, Betsy told Jillian. "The bathroom is through the living room and down the hallway. Emily will make coffee and I'll set out the lunches."

"Okay." She shrugged her shoulders and obediently followed Betsy's instructions. When she was finished, she returned to the kitchen and sensed something amiss. It was too quiet except for the perking of coffee. To her surprise the room was empty and only one lunch sack remained on the counter. Running to the window, in the gathering darkness, she saw the yellow Volkswagen at the end of the driveway turning toward Pachuca. She was utterly astounded. What was happening? Her first thought was to look for a telephone and hurrying to the living room she staggered from shock and grabbed the door jamb. There stood Marta.

"Hello, Jill."

Momentarily she swayed as floods of thoughts swirled through her mind. Marta! What is she doing here? Am I in danger? Where is Lucia?

"Aren't you going to greet me?" asked Marta, her upper lip quivering, her only apparent show of nervousness. "Here, come and sit down on the sofa."

Her legs weak, Jillian feared she might not make it to the sofa. With determination, she seated herself. "Where are Betsy and Emily?"

"You needn't worry that they have left you."

"But I saw them leave."

"So we can be alone."

Jillian studied the woman as she turned on a lamp and seated herself at the other end of the sofa. Though the lines on her face were more noticeable, she had changed little. For one strange moment it seemed like old times. Memories flickered through Jillian's mind. It was as though time had reversed itself and the two of them were spending a lazy afternoon together discussing orphanage business. To her dismay, she felt a wave of affection for the woman and she pressed back a desire to touch her. *Does this mean I'll never completely stop caring for her despite all she's done to destroy my life?* Just as quickly as it had come upon her, the warm feeling vanished. Her feelings for Marta could never be what they were when they had lived together.

"Where have you been for almost two years?"

Marta folded her hands. "There are a few things I can never tell you. That is one of them."

The woman is too composed, thought Jillian. She recalled the years she had known Marta, the weeping spells, the wadded handkerchiefs, the tantrums. "You've changed. You're too calm. Why are we here?"

"You mean, why do I want to see you?"

"Yes, because I know you hate me."

"Quite the contrary. I never did hate you. I thought I did for a while, but it wasn't hatred. It was fear. I was always afraid that you would take my work, my home and my children away." She laughed humorlessly. "I guess I had a reason for fearing you. After all, as you can see, I did lose all those things."

"Why did you meet me here?" asked Jillian, now almost wishing Marta would fall into a state of hysteria and give her information on the children. This placid mood was beginning to disturb her.

"Because I wanted to see you again."

"Where are the children? Where are Ryan and Andy?"

Chapter 49

"I'm afraid that's another question I won't answer." Marta settled back, her upper lip still quivering. "Please tell me something. I'm very curious about this. If, when you returned to Pachuca after your furlough, if I had given Andy and Ryan to you, would you have taken them back to the United States and left Ecuador for good?"

"You mean, if I could have adopted them? I don't think the government would have allowed me to do that. But, let's say, if you had given them to me, would I have left Pachuca for another part of Ecuador? Yes, probably. I would have been very happy to have moved to Quito, to that little house you picked out for me."

Marta sat back, deep in thought. Then she looked up and asked. "What if I had sent Lucia away and had you stay with me? Would that have worked?"

"I have no doubt," smiled Jillian.

Tears formed in Marta's eyes and immediately Jillian's fear of the woman evaporated. Here was a sad, defeated woman who had traveled back in her mind to the misguided decisions she had made in haste and now she was suffering in leisure.

"Have you married, Jill?"

"No."

"Are you in love?"

"I think so. I care for him very much."

"You know, if you had remained with me in the orphanage, you'd have never met a man. You know how I feel about men courting my helpers."

"It's ironic how devastated I was when you sent me away because I thought I was going to die, but now as I look back on the past many years I've lived in Pachuca and realized all I've gained that you did me a favor. The decisions you made for us may not have been the best ones for you, but they were for me."

The woman wiped her eyes with the palms of her hands and commented unruffled. "Without giving out too much information, I must tell you that Lucia still hates you."

Fear returned and Jillian felt her scalp tingle. "Where is Lucia? Is she here in this house? Is this now your house? Are you two living here?"

Marta merely smiled. "I'm not going to tell you anything concerning Lucia or the children. How do I know you wouldn't tell the authorities that too?"

So Marta and Lucia are still living in Ecuador, probably in the jungle. Jillian turned this over in her mind. Could the children be with them? "Marta, I didn't have much choice in what I told the government. They were already investigating you. The president of Children Services met with me. Actually there wasn't much I could tell them because you had kept so much from me. I knew very little."

"I don't believe that," she said flatly. "You knew everything. You lived in my house."

"Why does everyone think that? I did not know everything. I always suspected the reason you feared me so, keeping me under lock and key when I lived on your property and when you fought so hard to make me leave Ecuador was because you thought I did know too much. Well, I want to tell you right now that I knew very little. I kept trying to tell you that. All your energies to keep me quiet only made me realize all the more there was a lot you were hiding."

Marta sat silent for so long, Jillian wondered if she believed she was telling the truth. Finally the nurse quietly spoke. "Can that be correct? You really didn't know anything?"

"I had absolutely no proof of any wrongdoing. I knew so little about your business, even when people told me they suspected something, I couldn't agree. Remember the luncheon I had with Eric and Rigo, Pachuca's policeman? Remember when you and Lucia were convinced I had told him everything you were doing? You must remember how I swore I had told them nothing. That was the truth. He did ask me questions about the babies, but I knew so little of what was going on, I couldn't answer him. Our outpatient clinic was closed down because of the reasons they told you, that it was unnecessary for you to keep it open with a clinic in the plaza."

"Yeah, even though they let your friend, Raquel Torres, build a clinic," spat Marta, unable to hold back her bitterness. "I suppose her clinic is doing just fine with all my patients she stole."

Jillian refrained from commenting on the remark. "So you see, all of this might not have happened had you believed me."

Chapter 49

"I want you to know that I made many of those bad decisions because Lucia convinced me I had no choice and besides that, I couldn't stand the problems and squabbles you two had all the time."

I really understand the strain you were under, but Marta, I do blame you for bringing Lucia from the jungle into your home and not keeping a better eye on her. You told me when she came to Quito she didn't know how to open a door with a handle or operate a small appliance. She had never seen a water faucet. You had to show her how to turn it and yet you gave her a few days' training as a nurse's aide and then gave her access to the medicine cabinet. She had right of entry to so many drugs I'm sure her mind has been affected. No wonder she's always in a bad mood."

The woman blinked as if it were a new thought. "I've made a lot of mistakes with Lucia, but no matter what, I don't think I could have let her go. She has been such a faithful friend to me."

Jillian looked up in surprise. Night had come so swiftly she hadn't noticed the darkness outside. She reached behind her to turn on another lamp. "I have to go home. It's dark and no one knows where I am."

"You didn't tell anyone?"

She could have kicked herself for revealing this as she still didn't trust Marta. "I want to go home. Where did Betsy and Emily go? I told my neighbor I was going to accompany my friends on a picnic somewhere east, but that I'd be home in a couple hours. That was three hours ago and it's going to take another two hours to get home."

"Don't worry. You'll be leaving for home soon."

"Why am I here, Marta? What is it you want from me?"

She took a deep breath. "I'm not well. I just don't feel well. It could be the altitude or it could just be anxiety. Anyway, you've been on my mind for the past year and I realize I had to see you once more."

Jillian became alarmed. "I don't understand. Why don't you think you'll see me again? Haven't you had a doctor check your health? Shouldn't you go back to the United States for tests?"

"I've had a doctor check me. Can you believe that after all I've said against Ecuadorian doctors, I now have one treating me? Don't worry, Jill." The gray head lowered to study her hands. "I'm no stranger to pain and anxiety, you know."

She's under the influence of drugs right now, thought Jillian. That's why she's so calm.

"Are you hungry?" Marta asked suddenly, her head bobbing up.

"A little."

"Come into the kitchen. Betsy and Emily left food for us and Emily made coffee. It's probably terrible tasting by now. You see, they were telling the truth. They brought something to eat."

"When did you plan this with them?" asked Jillian, following Marta and resting her hand on the sack lunch.

"I got the idea several weeks ago and have been working with Betsy since then. She wanted to wait until she could have a day off with Emily before making the trip as it had to be on a Friday."

"Why?" asked Jillian frowning.

"Because you would be tired and because I know you're usually home on Friday night."

"I know all about Olivia's spying, or should I say Alicia. I know that you used a bogus name on that complaint, Marta."

The woman remained silent and looked sheepish. "I had to do something. I knew you would eventually ruin me."

"You can only blame yourself, but right now all this is in the past. I'm more concerned about getting back home. What about my neighbor? She'll wonder where I am."

"If you mean Gladys Baca, she'll have left for her home and won't realize you're still gone. She'll go to bed without thinking of you. By the time they awaken, you'll be back." She took a lunch sack from the refrigerator. "You might as well sit. The girls won't return for another hour."

"What? Another hour?" exploded Jillian. "This really upsets me."

"Don't be silly. Let's eat." She sat at the kitchen table and unwrapped a sandwich. "Look, roast beef. When was the last time you had a roast beef sandwich?"

Hunger and the thoughts of American food made her open her sack. Inside were a roast beef sandwich, a pickle, potato chips and a piece of apple pie. She ate the tasty food, wondering if she was living in a dream. This entire episode was too hard to believe.

Chapter 50

Marta had thrown out the bitter coffee and was downing a cola she found in the refrigerator when they heard the first patter of raindrops on the windows.

"What's that?" Jillian bolted out of her chair and flung open the door. Through the darkness she could hear the roar of wind, rain and waterfalls. She stomped back into the house. "It's raining torrents."

"It's just a tropical storm. You should be used to them by now."

A bolt of lightning lit up the skies and thunder rumbled nearby. "How do you expect me to get home?"

"I said the girls will be after you in no time," Marta smiled and licked her fingers. She had finished her entire meal before Jillian had eaten her sandwich. Marta always had a voracious appetite. She held Jillian's gaze. "I had to see you because I need to set things right as we may never meet again. I'm afraid to die without making things right and I couldn't see how we could do that with people around. Jill, will you forgive me for all I did against you?"

Thinking quickly back through the past fifteen years. Marta, in one way or another had played a major part in it. But, oh the pain she had inflicted. Forgive her? If I tried to forget the deceitfulness, the cheating and the lies, then perhaps I could but what if Marta isn't exaggerating her poor health and this is the last time I see her? Wouldn't I, in the long run be the winner if I forgive? A passage from the Bible came to mind. All things work together for good to those that love God and are the called according to His purpose. "Yes,

Marta, I will forgive you, but you must forgive me also. I see all the mistakes I made and I don't want to spend the rest of my life regretting I didn't take this opportunity."

Standing, the woman walked to the living room window as Jillian followed. "See, it's already passed. The rain has stopped." She sighed. "Thank you for forgiving me. Now I only hope God can."

"Please tell me where Andy and Ryan are."

"I can't tell you because it will jeopardize me. The night I left Pachuca I lost everything. I really am a broken woman. I have nothing."

"You are saying the children are not with you?"

"All I can say is that I've lost everything."

The compassion Jillian felt was true and she put her hand on Marta's shoulder. Then she moved away, frustration growing. She wanted to go home. It had been dark for several hours now. The two women had been alone for two hours which meant she had been away from Pachuca for over four hours. If she left for home now, she would have been away for six hours. Where were Emily and Betsy? She looked out the back door and almost crumpled with relief when she saw headlights and the Volkswagen pulling into the driveway. "They're here!"

"I knew they would. I told them to be back in two hours. They stayed at a little store in Papallacta. See? I told you nothing would happen."

Relief flooded through her. "Where are you going, Marta?"

"My truck is close by. I'll let you go and then I'll leave."

Jillian stood at the door, ready to leave but turned back to look at the woman who had been her friend. She wouldn't be living in Pachuca or possibly in Ecuador if it hadn't been for Marta. She suddenly remembered the good times, the years they were best friends and with a cry, she ran across the room and hugged the woman, weeping on her shoulder.

Marta broke and wept with her. "Thank you, Jill. Thank you for forgiving me and now I need to ask you one more thing."

"What?" she asked suspiciously, breaking away.

"If someone were to ask about me...just tell them I've left the country."

"Are you going to leave?"

Chapter 50

"As far as you are concerned, yes."

Jillian decided that's all she wanted to know. As she reached the door, she turned once more. Then, trying with all her might, she held back the desire to laugh. Marta had reached into a pocket and pulled out a familiar linen handkerchief; already she was wringing it into a knot. Some things never changed.

Stepping into the garage, she suddenly remembered something and returned to the kitchen. Walking directly across the floor to put her hands on Marta's shoulders, she forced the woman to face her directly. "I have one more question and I must have the answer to this. I know that Elena's baby didn't die. Where is she?"

The question came as a shock. Marta gulped, too surprised to talk.

"I know the baby didn't die," she repeated. "Where is she?"

In those fleeting seconds, Marta in her mind must have bandied the pros and cons of telling Jillian and finally in a small, weak voice, she said, "I can tell you only because you will never find her. I'm not exactly sure where she is, but Elena's baby is somewhere on the east coast of America."

"Thank you, Marta."

"It won't do you any good. You'll never find her."

"Maybe we will someday." With a wave, Jillian ran out the garage and halfway up the driveway where Betsy and Emily were sitting in the idling car. As she reached the door she froze, hearing a clicking sound and then a shot rang out. The bullet whizzed loudly, unmistakably past her ear. In the next instant she heard a second click and the sound of another shot.

Chapter 51

Eric laid a fire and settled back with a book he had bought recently at a new bookstore in Quito's Favorita Mall. He knew he would probably be asleep by the time he reached the fifth page, but he loved new books and relished the feeling of being the first person to touch each page. Lifting it to his nose, he sniffed deeply. Drowsiness settled on him by the time he reached the end of the second page and he laid the book in his lap and put his head back. It had taken several months but just this past week he had closed his family home in Quito keeping only a skeleton staff for cleaning and maintenance. Most of the domestic help had been laid off with letters of recommendation in hand and a list of suggested homes where they might find work. He had retained Isabel and Ramon of course, for they were not merely employees; they had faithfully served the family since his childhood. Isabel had resigned herself to living at the hacienda for the rest of her life and Ramon came with no qualms. Knowing Isabel's disappointment, he promised to remodel the kitchen, adding more modern fixtures and appliances. He had plans to bring water into the house for her convenience so Ramon would no longer have to carry heavy pails from the well. Noticing Marta Brewer's high water tower on her property gave him the idea that soon they could have an abundance of water in the main house hoping this would bring some contentment to his dear friend. Isabel's room would be decorated and a new bed, bureau and cabinets would be bought in Quito and installed. He

Chapter 51

would do the same for his own bedroom. Ramon didn't care whether his room was changed just so long as he had a place to sleep.

His mother might not come back to Quito. For several months he had hoped her health would improve to the point where she could return. He profoundly missed her company more than he could have imagined. The latest prognosis from Helen's doctors stated that her diseased heart could no longer bear the strain of living in high altitudes. Her only hope was for a heart transplant that her body would not reject. For this reason he would not sell the house, in the hope someday she might return.

Thank goodness Jill had re-entered his life about the time he had lost his beloved friends Carlos and Elena and the companionship of his mother. Jill. Smiling, he lifted his head to gaze into the fire. She was always somewhere in his mind. He hadn't realized how much he needed good friends before he met her, Raquel, Rolando, Geoff and Opal. Planning activities with them made him feel energized. Life had taken on a whole new meaning. At least twice a month the six of them socialized, dining in restaurants, picnicking, riding the train to Otavalo, or driving to local towns where the residents displayed special talents in leather tooling, wood crafting and woolen goods hand-woven on ancient looms. Yes, he was loving life as much as he had when Carlos and Elena were alive. Now he wished he had taken more of an active interest in showing the young couple some of these sights. How his focus had changed since then. How he had changed.

Jill. He wondered what she was doing tonight. He knew he would be too tired to drive to Pachuca, so he hadn't made plans to see her. He knew she was also too tired to enjoy company on Friday nights. Without really discussing it, Friday had become an evening of rest for both of them.

His thoughts were becoming jumbled with sleep when the telephone jangled beside him. Starting with surprise, he grabbed it, wondering why someone would call him this late. After the operator in Pachuca had clicked off, he was startled to hear Raquel's voice.

"Eric? Eric? Buenos noches. This is Raquel."

"Yes, Raquel. Buenos noches. Is everything all right with you?"

"I'm not sure. I don't think so. It's Jill."

In that moment, Eric felt his world collapse. "Jill? What's wrong with Jill? Is she sick?"

"No, she's missing. Rolando and I went to her house to tell her something important. Eric, the house is in darkness and the padlock is on the door. That is so unusual. I thought maybe you two had gone to Quito and she had failed to tell me, so I went to her neighbor's store but they had already retired to their home for the evening. I ran to their house and banged on the door until Gladys answered. She was very surprised to learn that Jill hadn't returned home, especially since she was supposed to be back hours ago."

"Back from where?" He felt he was going to be sick. "Where did she go?"

"Gladys said she went east with two Americans in a foreign car but Jill had told her she'd be back shortly."

"Oh Dios mio. Americans?" Now he was more frightened than ever knowing the vendetta some Americans had against her. "How does Gladys know they were Americans?"

"Because they stopped in the store two times today to ask Gladys what time Jill would be returning home from her classes. When she arrived home the two American girls followed her into the house and then a little later Jill told Gladys she was going away for two hours. That was over six hours ago."

"Go back to Jill's house. I'll be there as soon as I can."

Hanging up, he quieted himself to gather his thoughts. With a knock on Isabel's bedroom door, he informed her he had to go to Pachuca. He tried to answer her without revealing the distress in his voice as she worriedly pattered after him, peppering him with questions. Wrapped in her robe, her bare feet peeking from beneath the hem, Isabel followed him as he found his boots, hat and truck keys. "I'll go with you," she pleaded.

"I don't know how long I'll be gone. Go to bed and try not to worry. I'm sure Jill will be home by the time I get there."

He sped through the night, his thoughts creating an anxiety he hadn't felt since Elena's disappearance. Something was wrong. Why would Jill go off with two American women? Who were they? He searched his memory for any mention she might have made of American friends. Certainly one of them could not have been Marta;

Chapter 51

Gladys would have recognized her. To his knowledge, when Jill left Marta's compound and moved to Pachuca, she had unwittingly been forced to cut herself off from fellowship with other local Americans who had chosen to believe Marta's claims that Jill was out to destroy her and her work. He thought some more. He ruled out Larry and Heather Parker, the couple who had used deceit to take Jill into their confidence because Gladys said the two were women. Even if one of them had been Heather, Jill wouldn't have trusted her enough to go with her. Maybe someone had come after her because of an emergency, but what kind of emergency would Jill be able to handle that a doctor couldn't? They hadn't come seeking Raquel and Jill would have mentioned an emergency to Gladys. No, these women were after Jill and he was certain it was with mischief.

His heart sank; the feeling was all too familiar. He remembered Elena and his desperation to find her. Suddenly he felt the urge to cry. There had been too many people in his lifetime that he had loved and lost. What if something dreadful had happened to her? On the other hand maybe the two women weren't up to mischief after all. They could be old friends who had come to take her for a drive, but why east? Unless they had gone to one of the communities where Jill taught school, the only other road leading east led to Papallacta. Why would Jill say she'd be back in two hours? Was she speaking as an Ecuadorian? A couple hours to an Ecuadorian could mean several hours. No she wouldn't do that. East could mean Papallacta, but why would she go there at night? That's a dangerous road in the daytime let alone at night when many terrible things could happen. He wiped perspiration from his brow. The more he thought the more frightened he became. He hated it when things were out of his control. Why hadn't he made more of a commitment to her? Maybe she wouldn't have taken such a chance. No, he knew better. If it was an emergency, she would have gone with or without a commitment to him. For a moment he became rankled with himself. How could he have been so stupid to let her slip through his fingers? If something had indeed happened to her, then he had only himself to blame. How many times had he sat on her balcony, in conflict, wanting to suggest a deeper relationship, perhaps even marriage, but fear closed his mouth. Would it change their friendship? Did she want marriage? Would she shut herself off from him? He knew how important her classes were to her; and Pachuca, how she loved Pachuca and her close friendship with Raquel. Was he being too forward to ask her to give that all up? Would she want to live in Tulcachi? She had lived in Ecuador for fifteen years and a decade of that in the plaza. Was she ready to make a longer commitment to this country and its people? Now, if something fatal had happened to her, he would never know because he had never asked.

He was nearly there. Driving up to Jillian's doorway, he saw Raquel and Rolando sitting on the stoop. The padlock remained securely fastened on the door. Now the fear was so real, he felt like a giant hand was crushing the life from him.

Rolando and Raquel were at the window of his pickup even before he came to a stop. There was no need to ask if Jillian had returned. Behind them, in the dark, Gladys approached in almost a bent, despairing posture. She knew only too well what could happen on one of these mountain roads.

"Buenos noches, Gladys," he said. "Tell me exactly what Jill said to you."

"Buenos noches. She said her two friends had come and they wanted her to go with them to the east. She said she'd be back in two hours." Gladys spoke in jerky sentences. "Soon it will be almost eight hours."

"Gladys said it was a yellow car, one that made a lot of noise. It was little. What kind of car could that be?" Raquel put her hand on Eric's arm.

"I don't know. Let's go to Papallacta. Maybe we can find them. I just hope those two women were telling Jill the truth as to where they were taking her."

"I was thinking the same thing," said Rolando. "What if they told her they were taking her east and took her somewhere else?"

"It's better if we take the road to the jungle and see. We can take my pickup and drive in that direction."

Gladys decided to remain in Pachuca in case Jillian returned. The three started the long arduous trip, traveling slowly, looking for a small yellow car or signs of an accident along the unpaved, pock-marked narrow road. Over an hour later they came to an abrupt halt. Stretching ahead for several yards sat a line of vehicles, silent and dark.

Chapter 52

"What was that noise?" asked Betsy.

"It sounds like someone is shooting a gun. The bullet just whizzed by my ear," croaked Jillian.

"Oh, Jill, that can't be true," said the mild-mannered Emily. "Marta would never shoot a gun."

"Let's get out of here," said Jillian.

"We can't do that. What if Marta accidentally hurt herself?" Emily stopped the motor and Betsy got out of the car.

"No, don't. I was the one being shot at," screamed Jillian after her.

"Shh! Listen!" hushed Betsy.

"What's happening?" said Jillian as she pushed her way into the car.

Emily rolled down her window and the three strained to hear. In the distance they heard voices screaming in violent argument. Jillian relaxed. "Marta is all right. I hear her voice."

"Who's with her?" Betsy started walking toward the house.

In a shaky voice, Jillian called her back. "Don't go, Betsy. I recognize Lucia's voice. I wouldn't go near her if I were you. Not so long as she has that gun."

"I'm afraid for Marta."

"Lucia will never hurt her. I promise you. She was trying to kill me."

"What is Lucia doing here?" asked Emily as Betsy climbed back into the car. "I thought you told Marta not to bring anyone with her?"

"I did. I told her that was the only way I'd bring Jill. She had to be alone."

"Lucia probably hid in the back of Marta's pickup, or stationed herself in the attached house. She's such a wily person. She would do anything to bring harm to me," muttered Jillian.

Betsy turned to pat Jillian's knee. "Are you all right?"

"Yes, I just want to get out of here before Lucia decides to shoot again."

Emily stepped on the gas, revved the motor and started climbing toward the distant summit. Much later they reached the line of stalled vehicles. "Oh, no," she groaned, bringing the Volkswagen to a halt behind a bus.

"What's wrong?" asked Jillian, leaning forward.

"It's either an accident or a landslide. I think it's a landslide because of that heavy rainstorm we had earlier. I thought about the possibility at the time."

Betsy and Jillian got out of the car and Emily found a flashlight in the trunk in order to use the beam. While Emily remained with the car, the girls walked up the muddy road to the front vehicle in line. Already the truck drivers had shoveled through half of the landslide. The two women borrowed more shovels and in the cold mountain air, they joined others digging a pathway through the thick mud.

Jillian was shaking from cold and exhaustion by the time they returned to the car. A narrow passage had been made just wide enough for the cars and trucks. One by one each vehicle took turns from both sides inching through. The three women prayed the rest of the mountainside would hold and not come tumbling down on top of them.

When at last it was their turn, Emily gunned the motor of her little car and safely they reached the other side of the landslide. Amidst loud cries of relief filling the interior was hope that there were no further problems ahead, but at least they were heading for home. Concentrating on the dark muddy road, Emily eased past the stopped vehicles from the opposite direction. Jillian sat on the edge of the backseat keeping sober watch and failed to see Eric's truck until they heard the steady honking of a horn. Her head swung in its direction and then she saw Eric's waving hand.

"Stop!" she yelled.

Emily pressed on the brake.

"Let me out! There are my friends."

Chapter 52

Puzzled, Betsy leaned forward in her car seat to let Jillian out. "Who are they?"

Jillian was laughing with the deepest joy she had felt in years as she ran toward her friends. Descending from the truck to meet her, they wrapped her in their arms and they all laughed. She hugged each one in turn and when she came to Eric she leaned hard into his arms, knowing this was where she belonged. She hoped he would never release her.

Wiping his eyes, he inspected her to see if any harm had come to her. "I was worried. I thought something terrible had happened to you."

"I've got so much to tell you."

Betsy and Emily waited until Eric moved his truck out of line and parked next to the cliff and then Jillian and Eric returned to the Volkswagen for her purse. "I'll say good-bye. I haven't quite decided whether I'm thankful for this experience or not."

"I'm sorry if we did the wrong thing," said Betsy as she scrutinized Eric. "I hope you were able to settle things with Marta. You know we were doing this more for her than you."

"Yes, I know," she said as she squeezed Eric's hand in reassurance that all was well. "But it will take me some time before I decide whether it was beneficial to me."

Chapter 53

They gathered in Jillian's kitchen drinking coffee and eating hard-boiled egg sandwiches. In amazement they listened to her story. The only thing she didn't mention was the gunshots. She felt safe in assuming Lucia wouldn't travel to Pachuca to make another attempt on her life, for too many people would recognize her. As it was, her friends were concerned enough that she had gone with Betsy and Emily to meet Marta. When Jillian finished her story, she took a sip of her cooled coffee and leaned back. It was then she noticed Rolando's arm around Raquel's shoulder. In a split second she knew.

They saw her expression and the two burst into laughter as Eric stared at them puzzled. Jillian stood, her mouth hanging open with surprise, her eyes sparkling with pleasure.

"Yes," said Raquel gleefully. "Rolando asked me to marry him and I said yes."

Rolando beamed as Eric rose and held out his hand in congratulations. "I still can't believe it," he said. "Sometimes I have to shake my head to see if I'm dreaming. I want you to know, Jill, that I love your friend more than anyone in the world. I hope our marriage doesn't interfere with the friendship that the four of us have cultivated."

"Never!" Jillian exclaimed, hugging and kissing Rolando and Raquel. "You have made me so happy."

"I have to get up early tomorrow," said Raquel, her eyes filling with tears. "I think we'd better leave."

Chapter 53

"Thank you for coming after me," said Jillian following them to the door.

Eric stopped them. "I have an idea. I'd like to know how you feel about it. You know Carlos and Elena bought property in Playas. They were in the process of building a beach house. That's when Elena became pregnant the third time and Carlos brought her back to the sierras. Rolando, I know from the look on your face that this may be difficult for you, but I want all of us, including all your brothers to think about it. From what Carlos told me his house plans are at the Grand Hotel in Playas. He had not started the construction; only the foundation is laid. How do you feel about finishing the house and claiming it as a vacation home for our future families? I don't expect an answer now but I want you to know that Carlos told me one evening where the land's deed and the plans are when we were discussing his future." He looked at each one of them. "Let's think about it and talk later."

They all agreed to discuss it later. Rolando and Raquel walked away, melting into the darkness. Eric stood below Jillian on the sidewalk, his blue eyes level with hers. He looked at her for a long time, as if searching for words. Then without a word, he walked back into the house, pulling her with him. With a slam, he shut the door and put his hand under her chin, lifting it to him. He kissed her on the mouth. It was their first kiss and with it he committed himself to her.

"If we can arrange that you'd be able to continue teaching your classes and visiting your friends, could I persuade you to marry me?"

"Marry you and live in Tulcachi?"

"Would you mind living there?"

"I love Tulcachi."

"I would be honored and very happy if you would say yes, Jill."

"I don't even have to think about it. Yes, I'll marry you."

"I have been afraid you'd turn me down when we could have been making plans months ago?" He hugged her to him.

"You probably could have asked me to marry you the first day I saw you in the plaza and not have offended me."

"What a waste of time," he grinned. "You could ask me for anything right now and I'd give it to you."

She thought awhile. "You know that church on the hill in Oyambarillo, the one that looks down across the Tumbaco Valley?"

"Do you mean the church that Geoff is interested in buying and pastoring?"

"Yes, I wonder, maybe the owner would let us use it for our wedding. I'd like to be married there."

"Are you sure you don't want to marry in Quito or in the United States?"

"No, not in Quito or America. This valley stole my heart the first day I saw it. Eric, I want to be married here under the shadow of these mountains, looking down over the most beautiful valley in the world."

Chapter 54

Several years after the raid on Marta Brewer's property, one afternoon Flora closed her school books and made a final note on a stack of notebook papers. After years of study while working at the orphanage and completing four years at the University in Quito, she had been able to secure a teaching position in the Pachuca girl's school. Life had never been more enjoyable. She loved her work, the children and especially the young male teacher who had moved from Quito to begin work in the boy's school. She seldom thought of Marta or Lucia and her past life. Jillian still taught in the girl's school and they retained their friendship, but the subject of their past life had been terminated when no news came of the missing children.

Placing her school work on a shelf in the living room of the small family home, she started toward the back door to help her mother finish the day's main meal before her younger brother and father arrived when she stopped short at a knock on the front door. Opening it, she saw a young man standing quietly on the hardpacked dirt entrance. He was a little taller than most Ecuadorian men which could be attributed to his good nutritional eating habits from birth. Dressed in a clean pull over sweater, slacks and polished shoes, he wore a gold watch. Appearing confident and accomplished, he stood with one hand in his pocket and the other placed casually over his heart region. In his late teens or early twenties, he had fresh skin and clear eyes, but this couldn't hide the Indian origins. He had a low forehead below a thatch of black hair, wide cheek bones, a short nose and full lips.

Taking a deep breath, he approached Flora and then stepped back to peer at her. "Buenas tardes."

"Buenas tardes." Her heart raced.

He seemed to search her face trying to see something familiar. "Are you Flora who used to work at Marta Brewer's orphanage?"

"Yes," she said hesitantly. "You look familiar like my dear friend, Peter."

"I'm Peter," he said with a small croak. "I didn't recognize you, Flora."

"Peter!" She stepped out into the sunshine and looked at him closely.

"Yes, I'm little Peter, but I didn't recognize you."

"Oh, my Dios. Can this be true? You are my Peter from señorita Marta's house. My little Peter?" Her voice broke and she reached over to touch his face.

"Yes, I've come to see you."

"Oh, oh!" She reached for him and hugged him to herself. "Oh how I have thought and prayed for you through the years. I never expected you to come to me. Where have you been?"

Relieved, he laughed. "I didn't know you would still live here in this house. The woman at the corner store said you did." He stepped out of her embrace to inspect her. "You cut your hair and now it's curly. That's why you look different."

Laughing, she plucked at her hair. "Yes and of course I'm older."

"I see who you are now. What is it you do? Do you still work with children?"

"I'm a school teacher in the girl's school. Maybe you remember how I used to study on the dining room table after the cooking and dishes were finished."

"I don't remember a lot. I've blocked some of those things out of my mind."

She took his arm. "Come in. Have lunch with us."

"Flora, would you mind if we took a walk? Do you know I've never walked in the plaza here in Pachuca? I'd like to walk through the town and down to where I used to live."

Chapter 54

"Of course." She turned to shut the door and then she joined him at the road. They walked close, as if recapturing a lost love. A warm glow spread through her knowing he had never stopped loving her as a mother figure.

As if he read her thoughts, he said. "You know, Flora, you were more a mother to me than Marta ever was."

Her eyes misted. "And you were like a son to me. Peter, I have so many questions to ask you. Where did you go after you left here?"

"You mean when we were taken away in the government jeeps in the middle of the night? I can't remember a lot. I think I was only around twelve or thirteen at the time, but my memory is dull. I do remember driving many many miles and it was daylight before we stopped. Sometime in the middle of the night we were divided, the girls were put in one truck and the boys in another. When we arrived the girls weren't there anymore. It was just our truck. I've never seen them again."

"You have no idea where they are?"

He shook his head. "Another thing that is strange is that Marta went with the girls and Lucia stayed with us. I've only seen Marta a few times since then."

"Where did you go?"

"We stayed in Shell Mera for a few days. The government truck left us off and we stayed at a large compound in Shell Mera. After a few days, we took a bus into the jungle close to Tena, took canoes and we've lived in the jungle all these years."

"You've been in the jungle? Oh my." Flora stood still and shook her head.

They had walked passed the plaza and the church and were almost to the end of the road at the marketplace. Turning the corner, they passed the boy's school, the volleyball stadium and started down the road toward the compound where he had lived the first few years of his life.

"Did Lucia treat you well?"

"Yes, she did. At first she was very sad and seemed to be angry all the time, but soon she realized she had a responsibility. She made sure we all continued our education with missionary children and also taught us many trades."

"I'm glad to hear that."

As they drew near to Marta Brewer's property, all talk stopped and Peter walked more rapidly climbing the steep driveway. He stood silently at the heavy gates as Flora followed.

"Who lives here now? What are all those buildings? Look, there's a church."

"I know you don't know anything about Jill's life in the village, but for many years she held classes in all the schools in this district. She had a horse and a little pickup and would travel many miles to teach the children English, music and give them Bible stories. Now that Marta doesn't have the orphanage or clinics, missionaries came after you left and built a school that has enough room for 600 children. Also there is a Christian high school and a church as you mentioned. The exciting thing is that a few months ago they began a university that has classes not only to teach the Bible but many other subjects so that the students can begin productive lives. The pastor of the church oversees all of it so in a way it really belongs to Pachuca and Peter, all of Ecuador."

He placed his head on the gate showing no interest in anything Flora was telling him. "I hate this place. There's the little school building we had to go to. Marta was so afraid we'd become like the town population, she made the teachers come to us. The maternity clinic. Do you know I was never inside? Marta was afraid we'd hurt something or a flea would jump on us. The chosa where we had birthday parties for our real families. No one ever came to see me. Flora, why weren't the families allowed in our house? Fleas again, huh? The outpatient clinic. Sometimes we were taken there for punishment. And those terrible houses where we lived. They were so filled with sadness and fear. We weren't allowed in the guesthouse, but you know about the tiny cement house at the bottom of the property where she would put us when we were bad and then leave us there. It was only as big as a small cell. It was terrible when she locked us in there." He shook his head as if to shake off the morbid thoughts. "Did you know Frankie ran away from our home in the jungle? He left a couple years after we got there. Of course he was older, but he hated everything and everyone connect with Marta. He

Chapter 54

left. Marta showed up a day later, crying and blaming Lucia for letting him go. They had a terrible fight."

"Where did Frankie go?"

Peter shrugged. "He said he was going to join a ship crew going somewhere exciting and jump ship when they got there."

"What about Paul and Tommy?"

"They said they were going to move to Quito, get jobs and make a great deal of money." He laughed. "Of course, even with their education, they probably won't. They'll do okay. Lucia gave them freedom in what they wanted to do and then taught them how to do it. She's a very talented woman, you know."

"Are we talking about the same Lucia?"

He laughed again. "Yes, I remember being frightened at first that she wouldn't know how to take care of all of us, but pretty soon, she did a wonderful job of watching over us. She taught me how to work with wood. I not only can carve, but I can build furniture and cabinets."

"Do you think she just needed to get away from Marta to become a more independent woman?"

Simply smiling, he turned. "Let's go back to the plaza. I don't want to be here anymore."

They found a cement bench in the park and sat before she asked him another question while waving a greeting to one of her students. "Would you mind letting me find Jill and have her come to see you?"

"Jill?" He thought for a moment and then shook his head. "I don't want to see her."

"Why not?"

"Because she is evil."

"Evil?" Flora leaned forward to look at him full faced. "Why would you think she is evil?"

"Because Lucia told me she is the cause of all our problems."

"That's not true, Peter. She loved you children with all her heart."

"Not according to Lucia."

She started to defend Jillian and then changed her mind. "Remember the night you left Pachuca and I asked you to watch over Andy and Ryan?"

"Yes, and I did the best I could. They were still so young."

"Do you know where they are?"

"Yes. They live in Tena when they aren't working at the hospital in Shell Mera. The missionaries have a hospital there and Andy and Ryan work as aides. Lucia taught them many things about medicine so when they went to apply for jobs, the person who hired them said he was very impressed. They go home to Tena on weekends. They love Lucia like I do."

"Do you know that Andy and Ryan were Jill's children?"

"How can that be?"

"She delivered Ryan and Marta gave Andy to her. She was very very upset when she had to leave Marta's house and her children."

"She didn't have to leave. She left because she didn't want to be with us anymore. Then she moved into the plaza and started making trouble for us."

"No, my dear, that's not true." Flora squinted across the street to see if there was a padlock on Jillian's front door. "See that house over there? Jill is married now and lives in Tulcachi, but she still uses that house as a work place. Every morning she comes here to prepare for classes and then attends them. I see that she's not there right now, but I could leave a message for her."

"No, momi Flora, I don't want to see her."

"May I tell her that Andy and Ryan are in Shell Mera?"

He shrugged. "I don't care because they don't know her or anything about her except that she caused a lot of trouble for us. They will never care for her. Well, momi, I see a bus coming. I guess I'd better return to Quito."

"Are you living in Quito now?"

"No, I still live in Tena, but I'm here seeing the sights. I'll return home tomorrow. I'm eighteen now so Marta had to release us. I can do what I want, but I don't want to leave my home in Tena." He reached out to hug her. "I love you for all you mean to me and the way you loved me when I was a little boy."

Tears rolled down her face as she returned the hug. "Please come back to see me. I'll be married in a few months and then I want you to come and stay with us."

"I will." He took a deep breath. "Momi, I don't know this for sure, but I think Marta took the girls to Sangolqui."

Chapter 54

"Sangolqui." Realization hit her. "Why didn't I think of Sangolqui before this? Ah yes, Peter. That's where Marta often took you children for a get away. There's a large house just big enough for several children. I imagine the old man who owned it passed away or moved away. Do you think Marta may have bought it from him?"

"Yes." With another hug, Peter left her and climbed on the bus. She watched until it disappeared and then she went to the telephone office to leave a message for Jillian in Tulcachi.

Chapter 55

Slowly he opened his eyes and squinted against the sun streaming through the window. Automatically he looked at his wife beside him. His beautiful wife. Never did he tire of watching her face, so full of expression and sweetness. In her sleep, she looked like a child, helpless and trusting. They had been married seven years and still he tried to awaken before she did, just to watch her sleep. He thought she had the most perfectly formed eyebrows and lovely, long eyelashes. Her nose was tilted and small in perfect proportion with her face. All of her life she had been spoiled by her father and when Rolando married her, he had happily taken over the privilege. He doted on her.

She moved, coming out of her sleep and opened her lids, revealing brown eyes flecked with yellow and green. Smiling at him, she gave invitation to a kiss.

"We've got to get ready for church and volleyball, Raqui. We have our first tournament this afternoon."

"Did you say you're playing against Tababela?" She yawned and stretched.

"Yes and I believe we can win."

"Of course you can, my love. I wonder if the children are awake."

He grinned. "I've learned to sleep through the marketplace noise on Sundays but there's no way I can sleep when our children are playing in the next room. They're the ones who woke me." Sitting up in bed, he shivered in the cold air and yelled. "Elena, come in here."

Chapter 55

The door opened and a laughing, dark-haired, black-eyed child ran into the room, her bright eyes sparkling.

"Hola, my little love." He hoisted her up and kissed her cheek as Raquel leaned over to do the same.

"What is your brother doing?" she asked.

"He's still in bed playing with his toys," replied the child, pointing toward the door.

"All right," said Raquel. "We've got to get up and fix our breakfast. Popi is going to play in the volleyball tournament after church today and then we're driving out to Tulcachi to eat dinner at Uncle Eric's and Aunt Jill's house. Won't that be fun?"

"Oh yes. Can I ride the pony?" Jumping from the bed, the little girl danced about the room.

"We'll see what happens when we get there. Come and let me comb your hair and then we'll butter some rolls and heat water for coffee."

She rose from the bed and Rolando leaned back, arms folded behind his head, watching the scene. Never would he stop being thankful for what he had. Raquel had opened a clinic a block from the plaza in which she treated patients each afternoon except Sunday. Rolando had bought his own truck and together with Geoff, operated a lucrative business. Geoff, Opal and their daughter, Rosa lived in Oyambarillo in a neat little house on several acres of land while Rolando and Raquel took up permanent residence in the family home. Each Sunday Geoff pastored a small but thriving congregation in the little white church looking down over the quaint community of Pachuca. It was the same church that Eric had purchased from the owners of Hacienda Oyambarillo just before he married Jillian. He had then turned the ownership over to Geoff in order to establish a church. The majority of the members were children from Jillian's school classes and much effort was now to reach the parents. Rolando had long ago repaid his brother the money he owed, refusing any of it in return. Roberto, his brother had remained in the military, choosing it as a career. He had also married and lived in Quito with his wife, working in a downtown office. Pablo had not been as fortunate as Rolando, having died an alcoholic's death the past year.

For This Child

Rolando and Raquel had been married a year when Elena was born. Three years later, Raquel had given birth to a son, affectionately name Pepito.

He waited for a moment to give his wife and daughter a chance to brush their teeth and comb their hair at the water vat behind the house. Listening absently to the marketplace noise, he thought excitedly of the day's activities; the fellowship he would have with the people at church; the volleyball game and dinner with his beloved friends, Eric and Jill.

Raquel beckoned him to hurry and he got up from the bed and took a towel, his pants and shirt with him. The house was chilly, but the sun outside would warm him. He poked his head in the bedroom across the hall and waved to his son, who was being dressed by his mother. The little boy giggled and jumped with delight at the sight of his father.

Outside, Rolando stretched and placed his clothes on a table. He put the towel on the familiar branch protruding out from the mud wall and stopped for a moment, breathing deeply and looking at the green mountains and dark blue sky. He stretched again, absorbing the warmth of the sun. Excitement stirred in him again. He always looked forward to going to church with his family. Now that the congregation was beginning to grow, he was being trained as an assistant pastor to his brother. Maybe someday he would also be a pastor, thinking of so many local areas that needed a good church.

Daydreaming came to an end as he took a quick sponge bath and pulled on his pants and buttoned his shirt. Looking for a razor on the ledge below the mirror he then lathered a shaving bar and placed the foam carefully on his face drawing the razor across his cheek and then rinsing it in a bowl of water placed to one side.

"Popi, hurry and come," Elena called to him. "Breakfast is ready and we have to leave for church soon." She appeared fresh and clean in a dress Raquel's mother had given her, wearing her hair braided down her back.

A memory loomed in his mind and he stared at her for a moment. He had been here before, watching this scene. Shaking his head, he tried to recall if it had been a dream or a distant memory. It was no

Chapter 55

dream. This was real. When? He grabbed at the thought, trying to secure it, but it escaped him.

"I need a hug," he chuckled, holding out his arms.

She laughed delightedly, jumped a little and ran toward him with outstretched arms. He knew she loved the clean smell of his shaving lather. He put down the razor and lifted her above him, drawing her close. Hugging her tightly, careful not to mess her hair, she purposefully stuck the tip of her nose in his lathered cheek and withdrew it with a frosted white nose.

Again he was aware he had been here before, experiencing this. He shook his head, puzzled.

She giggled as he gazed at her intently. "I love you, Popi."

"I love you too, Elena."

She disappeared inside the house, returning in a moment minus the dot of white on her nose. "Popi, Momi says to come right now. Breakfast is ready and we're going to be late."

He stared at her. A thought stirred through his mind, but with a sense of sadness. Elena. Elena, her black hair in braids falling down her back calling him to breakfast. He grabbed at the thought. "Oh, my darling Elena, how I wish I could have loved you the same way I love my daughter. You would probably be alive today."

"Popi, come."

"Elena?" he called softly.

"Did you say something, Popi?"

He shook his head and the mood broke. "No, my carina. Tell your momi I'll be right there." He rinsed off his face, scrubbing it with the towel and looked up at the green mountains and blue sky and thought, what a perfect day it is for a volleyball game.

Chapter 56

The girl had deliberately turned from her guest as she looked out at the great expanse of ocean. With a quick dab, she wiped the tears from her eyes. "I miss her, Martin. She's been my dearest friend all my life."

"Your grandmother was a wonderful woman. I've always admired her strength." He cleared his throat. "Suriana, I need to speak with you about something very important."

"I'm sorry," she said, forcing her gaze from Wizard Island a half mile off shore, and swiveled her chair to face him. "You've come a long way to visit me and I've not been a very good hostess. Are you sure you don't want something to eat or drink?"

"No, thank you. I stopped for lunch on the way." He cleared his throat again and rose.

Suriana Iverson looked at her grandmother's attorney. He was an attractive, trim elderly man with a full head of carefully groomed grey hair. Closely shaven, he wore a high-priced masculine scent. His suit was expensive and tailored perfectly. Martin Rutherford had been a trusted friend and advisor since Sofia Scalfaro had moved to Oregon with her granddaughter Suriana seventeen years previously. She watched as he bent to pick up his briefcase and carry it to the dining table. Seating himself, he opened the case and pulled out a few papers. She was able to remain seated and still be within a comfortable distance. The beach house sat on a high rise above the wild Oregon coast two hours from Portland. The back half of the house

Chapter 56

was one grand room with the living room at one end, the dining area in the middle and the kitchen on the opposite end. The entire wall facing the ocean was a series of panoramic sized windows. She could watch him and also see the towering waves below.

He carefully pronounced her Spanish name and smiled at her. "Suriana, you should have known about this many years ago. I tried to persuade your grandmother when you were old enough to understand but she insisted she would tell you when you were an adult."

Suriana frowned. "Tell me what?"

"What do you know about your life before you were adopted?"

Her frown deepened. "What my grandmother told me, of course. I am Hispanic, born in El Paso, Texas. My mother apparently was too young to care for me and left me in the care of nuns. My grandmother learned later my mother was no longer living and my father doesn't know I exist."

Martin Rutherford cleared his throat and patted his tie. "I have been placed in an extremely uncomfortable position. Several times I warned your grandmother to fill in the areas of your childhood that you don't know. She kept putting it off and when suddenly she was taken by her stroke, I was left holding the information."

Suddenly peeved at the man, she shook her head. "What do you mean? What didn't my grandmother tell me?"

"What do you know about your adoptive parents?"

"Who? My mother and father?" Peevishness was becoming replaced by a seed of fear. "What about my parents?"

"Did your grandmother tell you how you came to be adopted?"

"Yes, she said my parents couldn't have children. I think there was some kind of problem. When they discovered they couldn't have children, they applied for adoption."

He placed his hands on the table and sighed. "Of course you know your parents were very wealthy. Your grandfather came to America from Italy and set up business in New York. He brought his wife, your grandmother and their one daughter, your mother. Your grandfather opened up a small grocery store, specializing in Italian products. You probably know all this, but I must set a foundation for what I've got to tell you. A restaurant was built to the side of the grocery store and word got out that the food was excellent. Within fifteen

For This Child

years your grandparents owned three restaurants and two grocery stores and a bakery. In the following year they opened restaurants in New Jersey, Connecticut, and Pennsylvania and were starting to spread south and west."

Of course she knew most of this. Over the past eighteen years bits and pieces had come up in conversation but this was the first time she had heard about her family in a step by step version and she was mesmerized.

"Your mother was just a youngster when she discovered your father. He was a cook in one of your grandfather's restaurants. After school she would go by to eat a bowl of soup or have a piece of good Italian bread and butter. Of course she chose that particular restaurant because she already had her eye on your father. In time he began noticing her as a young woman instead of the little twig of a thing, as your grandfather called her."

Suriana laughed. "Did my grandmother tell you this?"

"Over the years, we discussed this quite often. She was preparing to tell you, but that didn't happen."

Her humor died and that same twinge of fear nagged at her again. "You are leading up to something very important, aren't you?"

"Very." He nodded and twisted in his chair and then deciding it would probably be more comfortable on the davenport, he rose and seated himself in a corner of the love seat. "Your grandfather didn't like the idea of his daughter starting a relationship with one of his cooks, let alone a young man whose family originated in Norway, of all things, but by the time he realized what was happening the two children were in love. What changed everything was when your grandfather Oscar found out that Ned Iverson was putting himself through college with what he earned as a cook. In their conversations about your mother, Sylvia, Ned was able to offer several suggestions to Oscar on how to improve his restaurant and how to better manage the food and money flow. In time Ned worked his way into the family's heart and Ned and Sylvia married. At first they made excuses as to why they didn't have children and finally to everyone's despair they faced the fact Sylvia was not going to conceive. Years of trying for a child began to take a toll on your parents and grandparents. Oscar would have done anything for his daughter, so in the course

Chapter 56

of an investigation, he discovered he could find a child from Latin American agencies willing to adopt children out. So imagine the women's surprise when one evening Ned and Oscar walked through the door with a baby girl."

Suriana smiled and nodded. This was one of her grandmother's favorite stories.

Continuing, Martin Rutherford took a deep breath. "Well, Suriana, your mother was so surprised. She hadn't planned on your arrival, but your father and grandfather had worked that out too. A large van arrived at the same time with everything a young child would need including a crib, chest of drawers, clothes, toys, a bath, lamps, play pen and high chair." He chuckled with her over the extravagance. "I'm not sure how much of this you know, but according to your grandmother it was love at first sight for the two of you. Your mother had never been around children that much and couldn't adjust to the many changes you brought into their home but taking care of you was exactly what your grandmother needed. In time the bond between you two was cemented for life."

Tears sprang to Suriana's eyes as thoughts of her grandmother surfaced; her black hair pulled back in a bun at the base of her neck, her dark eyes, sharp features and thin body would forever live in Suriana's heart.

"You were one year old when your family decided to celebrate your mother's birthday by sailing on your grandfather's yacht up the Long Island Sound and meet several friends in the Hamptons. However, on that day, you were running a fever and to your grandmother's relief, she decided to stay home with you. She wasn't one for yachting or parties nor was she one to trust the nanny or a servant to your care, but as you know, your family never arrived at the party. Somewhere between the launching and The Hamptons, the yacht exploded and your family perished. Months of investigation followed but nothing and no one was ever found to blame, however your grandmother suspected it was sabotage. She always felt much of her husband's money didn't come from the food industry but had roots in crime. Within a week of the tragedy, she had fled to the Pacific Northwest with you. That's when she followed a recommendation and hired me.

This was the first time Suriana had heard about her grandmother's suspicions. It was beginning to make sense why they had never returned to the east coast.

Martin Rutherford continued. "I'm about to get to the heart of the matter, Suriana. Your family's dealings were only a small part of why you two came to Oregon. The real reason is because you are not Mexican as you think, nor were you adopted from a Catholic orphanage in El Paso, Texas."

Her head fell forward in shock, disbelief enfolding her and her voice faltered. "I'm not Mexican?"

"No, you are Ecuadorian."

She was rendered speechless.

"The reason your grandmother fled with you was because there were many questions about your adoption. She wasn't sure it was a legal transaction."

"You mean I may be in the United States illegally?"

"Your grandfather saw to it that you would never be deported if that's what you mean. I've looked at the papers. It took a huge amount of money, but yes you are here legally." Noting she was in a state of shock, he leaned back for a moment until she could recover.

"You mean my grandfather paid money under the table, as they say?"

"Let's just say that when your mother wanted something, nothing would be denied."

"Do you know anything about my family in Ecuador?"

"I don't know where you were born or if you have a family." He rose to take up his briefcase which was still sitting on the dining table. Balancing it perfectly on his lap, he opened it. With compassion in his deep-set brown eyes, he spoke. "Suriana, I was sworn to secrecy when your grandmother first came to Portland. I was forbidden from ever speaking with you about your past, but now since she has passed away, I am the one who must give you information."

The tone of his voice alarmed her. "Please tell me. Perhaps I am an orphan."

"As far as I know you are not an orphan. Your parents may very well be alive. At least your mother should be. She gave you up when you were only two days old."

Chapter 56

Rocking at the impact of his words, she stared at the vast expanse of the ocean fifty feet below the house. Regaining her composure, she mused. "What a strange feeling. In a moment's time I have gone from having no family to possibly having a biological family. I feel as though I've been robbed of my identity however." She observed a whale-watching boat bobbing offshore. Closer in, two brown pelicans swooped for a meal while surf scoters swam about the swirling breakers, diving before waves broke over them; sometimes she could see their bright multi-colored bills gleaming in the sun. On the rocks in front of the house double-crested cormorants preened while oyster catchers prodded muscle shells open, plucking out the meat with their long bills. Soon the rocks would be covered by the incoming tide and the birds would take out to sea. A black-capped Caspian tern flew past the window, so distinguished by its harsh call. Finally, in a plaintive whisper, she spoke. "Why would my mother give me up? Why would she do that?"

"Think of it this way. You would be living in a third-world country right now instead of in this beautiful home."

For some reason her attorney's logic struck a sour note with her. "Yes, I understand that and I wouldn't have wanted my life to have turned out any differently, but all of a sudden I have a family somewhere. I may have other siblings, aunts, uncles and cousins."

Placing the briefcase carefully on the floor, he stood and walked toward the girl with a folder in his hand. "I have something for you."

She took it, noting her name on the tab. There wasn't much in inside, only a short letter dated eighteen years earlier addressed to her parents informing them a pregnant woman had been found who was willing to give up her child. The letter was signed with a man's name but it was obvious from the stilted, childish grammar that the person was not well-versed in English. The postmark was stamped Peru. "Why Peru? You said you thought I was Ecuadorian."

He had reseated himself across from her. "You are. For some reason this piece of mail was sent from Peru, possibly so it would be harder to trace. You realize that Peru is due south of Ecuador?"

"Let's see," said Suriana, looking through the folder. "Here are my adoption papers. Someone by the name of Romero signed the adoption. The same signature was on that letter. Is he an attorney?"

"He could be. I believe he was the man who did the paper work for your adoption."

"The seal says Republic of Ecuador. I guess that's how you know I'm from Ecuador." She studied the document but there was no mention of her biological parents or her birthplace. "The only names mentioned are my adoptive parent's. There's nothing else? This doesn't tell us a thing about my roots."

"I have something else." He pulled a plain white envelope from his breast pocket. Opening the flap, he withdrew an old, yellowed newspaper clipping. "I had so many questions about the secrecy of your adoption, Suriana, that it was only natural I would be attracted to a newspaper article found among your grandmother's papers. It was published shortly before your arrival in the United States. Supposedly, an American couple had trouble with an Ecuadorian adoption and of course I was very interested. Apparently your grandfather saw it and destroyed all the letters he thought existed from the Ecuadorian attorney. This I'm assuming since none of the letters but that one I showed you is here and we know he must have sent several. I can imagine the moment your grandfather read the newspaper article it was a turning point for them. The only reason that article and letter were saved was because your grandmother pocketed them without your parents notice. At that point she was sure your adoption was illegal and she wanted something with the lawyer's signature on it. Suriana, this is why your grandmother protected you so; no public schools for you. She put you in a private school giving you everything your heart desired. She was so afraid you would someday go in search of your past and discover you were from Ecuador. She didn't want you to find your biological parents."

"That's why she told me I was an orphan from El Paso," she muttered. "Mr. Rutherford, what are my chances of finding my Ecuadorian family?"

"Very very slim, I would say, but possible I suppose," he said, handing her the article and then he opened the envelope flap again.

After scanning the article she took a torn scrap of paper he held out to her. "What is this?"

"That, my dear, is a miracle. Your father and grandfather brought you directly from the Miami airport where they met with an American

Chapter 56

couple who had transported you from Ecuador. They were afraid someone would discover you were brought to the United States illegally so they told no one, not even your mother and grandmother. As the family gathered around you, your grandmother took all the soiled diapers and gowns out of the diaper bag and put them in the bathroom. As she withdrew the articles, this paper drifted to the floor and she picked it up to look at it. I believe it was shoved in the diaper bag by mistake because it had been torn from the original piece. She looked in the bag for the rest of the paper, but there was nothing. As you can see, it was crumpled as if someone had meant to throw it away."

The girl stared at the tattered, yellowed scrap. The print was typewritten and faded, but decipherable. Suriana muttered, "It says bebé Martinez Tapia, then down below that, it says muer....and then below that it says the child was born in...and there's a 'p'. The paper was torn after the 'p'."

"Your last name is Martinez-Tapia," said the attorney, looking at her with a strange look in his eyes.

"What does muer....mean? Is it part of a long word? I'll get that Spanish dictionary." Finding it in the bookcase, a long silence ensued while she flipped to the center of the book and her finger slid down the line of words. "Muer....muerto. Muerto. That means dead, doesn't it? If that's true then perhaps my mother is dead."

"No," said Martin, pulling in a long breath. "I think they were able to get you out of the country by telling your natural family you were dead."

"What? Who?" croaked the girl.

"Whoever instigated your adoption."

"How much did my parents pay to get me?"

"One hundred thousand dollars," he said quietly.

"One hundred thousand dollars," she cried.

"One hundred thousand was mere pocket change for your grandfather. My dear, not a day of your life passed while they lived that your family regretted giving that much money for you. I'm sure they would have given much more."

She gave him a bittersweet smile. "Thank you. What does this 'p' mean?"

"I think that is where you are from," he said, adjusting the knot in his tie.

"P? What if it's a B or an R? However I don't see a line coming down from the loop even though it's been torn there. I still think it's a P."

"Well," Martin Rutherford stood. "That's why I wanted to see you. I realize I took a long time to bring this to your attention, but actually I had intended to talk to you after the funeral. I've debated with myself whether I should or should not tell, but, Suri, you have had a month to grieve and now you must know. Many times I tried to talk your grandmother into telling you your birthplace."

"Did she ever tell my parents about his scrap of paper?"

"No, they never saw that." A frown gathered on his brow. "But you must realize that you may not be Baby Martinez-Tapia. Maybe that paper didn't belong to you."

"No," she protested a little too loudly. "I am Baby Martinez-Tapia. I'm sure of it."

Chapter 57

Following Martin Rutherford's departure, Suriana sat quietly assimilating the news she had just received. At long last she understood the veil of secrecy surrounding her adoption and now realized from an early age she had been told little of her youthful years. She hadn't thought about questioning it and most inquiries had been waylaid. All this time she thought she had been born in Texas and that her biological parents were dead or hadn't made efforts to find her.

Her first thought was to make plans for traveling to Ecuador but as she stared out over the Pacific Ocean, the high tide now washing over a series of tall rocks directly in front of her house, reality set in. She knew no Spanish and with her dark coloring all the Ecuadorian nationals would expect it. She'd need a visa and a little more preparation, a tutor to teach her Spanish, a trip to the library to search through all the atlases looking for Ecuadorian towns that start with P, B, and R.

Within the week she contacted Martin Rutherford and asked him to close up her grandmother's townhouse in Portland. She would no longer live there. The local public library provided information on the type of visa she would need and all the particulars of living and traveling in Ecuador. The atlas offered additional information, but the librarian cautioned her that there could be hundreds of villages unknown to cartographers. The adventure lying before her seemed to be growing, for now she had to consider the possibility of living in Ecuador for a year or more. The librarian was also able to direct her to a capable Spanish speaking high school teacher. One year later, six months past her nineteenth birthday, Suriana Iverson left her beach house in the hands of caretakers and flew southward to find her roots.

Chapter 58

She decided to use Guayaquil, Ecuador's largest city as her base and found a hotel close to the airport and from there she planned her next move. Possessing the rudiments of Spanish, she located through trial and error, a taxi driver whose fares were consistent with the advice she received from the hotel management. The two took several day trips to hamlets and villages many of which were not shown on her maps. The librarian at home at been correct; maps are not inclusive as few foreigners had traveled to the remote areas. The taxi driver was more than happy to help her ask the townspeople questions about her parents, but no one remembered a couple named Martinez-Tapia. At the end of three months they drove to the Peruvian border to renew her visa, a stipulation on her visitor's permit.

Now, except for townships along the coast, there was no other village to search that lay within a three hour's journey from Guayaquil and she was beginning to broaden her plans to travel north and locate in another large city. She was feeling more secure in her Spanish and knowledge of Ecuadorian customs and released her driver to travel on her own.

After another month of searching by bus travel along the coast, wearied she began to wonder if she should forget the quest and return home to Oregon for a long rest and return later for a search from Quito when one day she descended the bus steps and looked about at the little town of Playas. Standing a block from the plaza, she embraced the familiar tang of the sea. She found a room in the Grand

Hotel and lay down to rest. By now her search had settled down to a pattern. She would rest an hour, eat a good meal and then set out, going to each store, each restaurant and each public place. She would speak with public officials and stop any person on the street who looked older than thirty-five. She figured her mother could have been eighteen or perhaps a little younger when she was born. Of course, she could have been a lot older, but Suriana had settled on eighteen. Eighteen years plus her nineteen would put her mother close to age forty.

Taking lunch in the dining room, she found herself increasingly homesick for her beach home on the west coast. The restaurant's ocean side wall was nothing more than several long boards which dropped on hinges during meal hours, revealing the blue Pacific Ocean. Somehow during these past months, she had been able to assuage her loneliness, but now, lounging beside the ocean, she suddenly wanted to go home. The calm tropical waves, the clear turquoise sea and white sand were so different from the wild Pacific Northwest where steep cliffs, rocky surf and leaning wind-worn pines adorned the shore. Neither the waiters nor the clerks had heard of her parents. The managers were away for the day, but they would return that evening. She planned to see them later.

With that, she wandered toward the plaza to begin her trek through the business section. It was a few minutes before the siesta hour when she entered a little grocery store. Behind the counter stood a girl about her age, slender, a red ribbon woven through the long black braid that fell down her back. She too had not heard of Suriana's parents but, catching the look of despair on her face, the young woman called to her mother in the back room. A middle-aged woman, with a shy smile greeted her and as she stared at Suriana, her smile faded and a puzzled frown gathered on her brow. Hesitating, she held out her hand.

"Buenos tardes, señora," said Suriana, clasping the extended hand. "Perhaps you can help me."

"I will be happy to do what I can," replied the woman. A flicker of recognition crossed her face as she studied Suriana. "I'm sorry, but you remind me of someone."

Chapter 58

Suriana's eyes widened. "I do? Actually that's why I'm here. I'm looking for a married couple named Martinez-Tapia."

The woman caught her breath. "Martinez-Tapia? Why do you want to know?"

"Because I believe they are my parents. You see, I was sent to the United States for adoption and just recently I found out that I was born in Ecuador. I have never seen my parents, but I'm most anxious to."

"Well, many years ago I had a dear friend by the name of Elena Martinez-Tapia. She and her husband, Carlos, lived here in Playas for almost two years. Elena and I were very good friends because we had gotten married about the same time and had many similar experiences."

Suriana tried to settle her breathing as her heart was pumping madly. This could be the town where she was born.

"Are you all right, señorita? Here, my name is Anita. May I ask your name?"

"Yes, please call me Suriana," she said, recovering from the shock. "Do you know where I could find Elena and Carlos Martinez-Tapia?"

"Do you know, that's why you look so familiar?" Anita searched Suriana's face. "You look like Elena, here, right across your eyes." She swept her hand in front of Suriana's face. "Your smile belongs to Carlos. I didn't know him as well as I did Elena, but he would come in here with her sometimes. Elena said when he smiled his face looked like the sun." Her voice softened. "She gave me a hair clip. I still have it, but I treat it like a treasure. If you will come back later I will show it to you."

Suriana felt tears welling in her eyes. "Yes, I want to see it. Do you know where my parents are? You said they lived here only two years."

"They moved to the Quito area." Anita tilted her head to one side, studying her. "I see so much resemblance."

"I think they may be my parents. When I was an infant, somehow I was separated from them and sent to the United States."

"How can this be?" Anita recoiled in disbelief. "I can recall the joy Carlos and Elena expressed when she discovered she was pregnant.

I cannot believe Elena would be separated from you. You weren't born here. You were born in Quito."

"Quito? In the sierras?"

"Yes, your parents came from there. I remember they had a sierra accent." She paused, memories crowding back. "Your father worked in the Grand Hotel. Perhaps you should ask them if they remember him."

"I did ask but the workers must be too young. This evening I plan to speak with the managers."

"Please forgive me. I was so absorbed in talking with you." She turned behind her and drew the young woman forward. "This is my daughter, Elena. I was pregnant with her when your mother lived here. I named my daughter after her."

Now Suriana was crying with relief and waves of deep emotion. "Thank you. Thank you for telling me this."

"Your parents lived in a little house near the hotel. I don't know if their house is still standing but you might walk by. Walk south of the hotel along the ocean. It was the middle stick house."

Suriana kissed Anita and Elena good-bye, promising to see them again and hurried back to the hotel. She walked along the ocean front, keeping her eyes open for three stick houses, and when she spotted them, she approached noting they had fallen into ruin. Boards had been stripped from the sides for firewood most likely, but the floor, atop stilts remained. It had once been a two-room house. She leaned on the floor and looked across the ocean. My mother and father stood on this floor, she thought, looking out over the blue expanse. She closed her eyes and tried to imagine what they looked like. My popi had a smile that glowed like the sun.

Waiting restlessly for the evening hour when the managers would arrive, she tried to read a book. At Suriana's request the desk clerk rang her room upon their arrival. Replacing the telephone receiver, with a pounding heart, she approached the office.

"Come in," a male voice called out.

She opened the door and walked into an office twice the size of her hotel room. Two polished wooden desks stood in the middle of the room on thick beige carpeting. Twin side tables rested beside a long, rich brown sofa and two matching recliners. Soft lights glowing

Chapter 58

from the lamps enhanced several pieces of contemporary art adorning the walls. A man sat behind one desk working from piles of paperwork. He looked up when she entered and then stood.

"Buenas tardes, señor."

The Grand Hotel's manager greeted her with a handshake and pointed to one of the brown chairs.

"Thank you." She lowered herself to the cushion's edge and looked at the man as he returned to his seat. He appeared to be middle-aged, older than forty, dressed in a slightly rumpled lightweight blue suit. His dark hair was thick and untidy, his dark eyes looked tired. She hoped he would remember her father.

He introduced himself as Pedro Fuentes. My brother, Marco who is co-owner of the hotel is overseeing the kitchen right now. How may I help you?"

"My name is Suriana Iverson. I'm visiting here from the United States and I'm looking for information about my parents. I believe they worked here at one time."

Leaning forward on his elbows, he frowned. "Why don't you know where your parents are? And who would you mean?"

"I was adopted by American parents soon after my birth. Just recently I learned that Carlos and Elena Martinez-Tapia may be my birth parents." Her voice shook.

"I don't remember Carlos and Elena Martinez-Tapia. When was this?"

"It had to have been about twenty years ago."

"Oh, perhaps that's why. You can imagine how many people come and go from our hotel. We've had many workers here in the past twenty years."

"Do you have employment records?"

"Yes," he said, leaning back in his chair. "Records from twenty years ago would be in storage."

"I would appreciate it if you would bring them out of storage. I've come a long way to find my parents."

He pushed his hand through his untidy hair and stood. "Eduardo, one of our janitors has been here longer than twenty years. He's almost eighty years old now so he might remember. I'll see if I can find him."

"Oh, thank you."

She waited several minutes. During this time a waiter appeared to offer her a cold fruit drink. She was sipping from the frosty glass when Pedro returned with an old man.

Eduardo shuffled into the room and saw Suriana. Removing his dirty, stained hat, he bowed his head in her direction. "Señorita, buenas tardes."

Suriana rose to shake his hand and waited to be properly introduced. The ancient man chose to remain standing.

"Eduardo," Pedro took his place at the desk. "How long have you worked here?"

Stoking his chin, his mouth opened in a toothless grin and his eyes ageless. "I started working here before you were born. I used to work for your Popi."

"Do you remember someone by the name of Carlos Tapia?"

The hesitation was lengthy and Suriana clenched her fists in anticipation.

"Tapia?" Eduardo looked upward seeming to study the ceiling. "Carlos. I think Carlos was our dining room captain for a few months. He wasn't here long. Before that he was the landscaper."

With a small yelp, Pedro's fist hit the table. "The landscaper, of course. The boy who came here with his wife. Remember? He was the one who made these grounds so beautiful and then he trained several men to carry on when he was promoted to the dining room."

Suriana almost collapsed with relief and scooted her body toward the chair's edge. "Do you know where he is now?"

Weaving a little, the old man planted his feet further apart to gain better balance. "Now? No, I haven't seen Carlos since he took his wife to Quito. She was with child, you know. He wanted her close to a good hospital because she had lost two other babies."

With difficulty Suriana absorbed this new information, trying to hold back her tears. *My mother had lost two babies and when she moved to Quito she must have been carrying me. If my parents left their home and job to make sure my mother delivered in a good hospital, then why did they give me up for adoption?* Her joy dimmed.

Eduardo continued speaking. "You know, they owned that piece of property down the road a few kilometers."

Chapter 58

"That's right," exclaimed Pedro.

"Where?" cried Suriana.

"Yes, somebody has built a house on the property. Sometimes the people who stay there come here for meals," said Eduardo.

"People who stay there?" Suriana swallowed nervously.

"It's only a vacation home but it must be owned by several couples. Sometimes they all come together, sometimes a smaller group." The old man shrugged a slumped shoulder and shifted his feet again and added with a touch of pride. "I know they are from the sierras because of their accents. I recognize different accents, you know because I've worked here so long. I guess they must be Carlos' family."

Suriana was on her feet. "How do you know that?"

"Because the property hasn't been up for sale. Whoever built the house must be related to Carlos."

"Who are the people who come in? Does anyone here know their names?" Pedro asked Eduardo.

"Not me. Maybe the dining room captain knows who they are."

"I'll go find him." Pedro pointed his chin in the direction of the door and Eduardo followed him after bowing to the girl.

Returning to her chair, she sat and again tried to assimilate all the additional information until Pedro returned with a middle-aged man dressed smartly in a black suit and tie with gold clip, gleaming white dress shirt and white handkerchief neatly stuffed in his top pocket. He was introduced to Suriana as Alberto.

Pedro explained to Alberto their need for any clue that might identify the visitors that live in the beautiful vacation home that had become a focal point for many nationals and visitors. Rafael nodded his head. "I don't know everybody's name, but once in awhile we have several couples come in who say they're staying in the house. There's a tall gray-haired man with an American wife. I think I heard someone call him Eric. Sometimes there are two men with their wives and children that come with them. I guess they are the older couple's children because I've heard them call the American woman, momi and she called one of them Ryan. That's a name I've never heard before. That's why I remember it. Other times, another rather tall, man with his pretty wife come in. One time he called her doctor and their children laughed. One holiday they all came together and brought another couple. They occupied almost half of the dining room and had a very festive time."

"We wouldn't have records on them at the desk because they don't spend the night here," said Pedro. "Can you think of anything else? Did they mention where their permanent resident is?"

He shook his head slowly, thinking. "Well, you can tell they are from the sierra because they use that dialect, but nothing else was mentioned."

Pedro dismissed the captain and leaned back in his chair. "I wonder if Carlos gave us a forwarding address when he left."

"Would that be in his records?" asked Suriana.

"I don't know," he said as he lifted himself out of his chair and headed for the door. He suddenly stopped and whirled around. "I just remembered something. I remember one night when we caught a man trying to harm Carlos. Wasn't that Carlos? I believe I'm right," he bellowed, his eyes brightening.

"What? What man? What did he do?"

The man's face darkened, trying to remember. "If I recall correctly, we thought we saw a loiterer on the grounds. We were afraid he was going to steal from the guests, so my brother and I followed him. Then we noticed he was going toward those old stick houses we had on the property years ago. That's where Carlos and his wife lived. Yes, I remember it clearly now. We watched him as he spied on Carlos' house and then when Carlos and your mother left the house, he followed them. The next thing we saw was a flashing, like light flashing off an object. We grabbed at his hand and found a knife."

Suriana stifled a yelp of fear. "What was he doing with a knife?"

"We thought he intended to harm your father."

"What did you do?"

"We captured him and brought him here," he said flatly. "We kept him here all night. The next morning we called Carlos in to see him."

"Who was he and why did he want to harm my father?"

"I'm sure he was a relative. I think he was your mother's brother, if I remember right."

"My uncle? Why?"

Chapter 58

"I can't remember any more than that, except Carlos came in to talk with him and after that the man left Playas and didn't return. Soon your parents left us and we didn't hear from them again."

She rubbed her forehead. For so many years there had been such a dearth of information regarding her past and she was having a hard time believing this was happening. "Did you say there was a chance we could see the records?"

"Oh, yes." Pedro rushed to the door. Fifteen minutes later he returned with a notebook. Suriana followed him to the desk where he opened it. In neat handwriting someone had copied information concerning each employee. He flipped the pages to the middle of the book and handed it to Suriana. "Here, I found your father's pages."

Almost reverently, she picked up the notebook. "Perhaps you should help me with this Spanish."

"It says here that your father began work at the Grand Hotel as a gardener. In less than a year he was working as the dining room captain. We rented them a little house nearby which they fixed up and lived in rent free for a year and then they offered to help fix the other two houses. We gave them another year rent free." He paused, taking the book from her and turning the page. "Carlos was an excellent worker and was given three raises. They departed for Quito after living here a little more than two years."

Craning her neck to see over his bent shoulder, she said, "Is there an address in Quito where I might find my parents?"

He flipped another page and stared. Paper clipped to the next page was a letter. "Look, a letter to your father is attached. It hadn't arrived before they left." He scanned a note written on the back and read it aloud. "Letter arrived after Carlos left employment. Will give it to him when he returns from Quito."

"That means they were planning on coming back to Playas. Why didn't they?"

"Let me read further in the records." He lifted the book to waist level and continued reading searching the page and flipped it over. "There's nothing of importance here. Oh, wait, yes, it says here that we should hold his job open for a year because he was planning to return with his wife and child. It also says that should we run into any problems with his property or finances, we should contact his attorney in Guayaquil. He planned on keeping a few hundred sucres here to have when they returned. He said permission was given to my father, who was manager then, to gain access to a box we kept here for Carlos. Apparently all the papers for the house were also in the box for safekeeping. The box has since been moved to a safe location in storage but now I wonder if the new owners are part of Carlos' family, they may have been able to retrieve it."

"Who are the people staying on the property? Could they be my parents? No, that's not right. He would have come back here. Why didn't my father return to his job?"

Pedro slowly shook his head.

"May I see the letter?" She studied the yellowed envelope. "It's from a....what does this say?"

He took it and turned it toward the lamp light. "It says it's from Jose Sandoval."

"Is there a return address?" she asked breathlessly.

"Yes. Here, let me open the letter. Don't you think that's all right?"

"Please."

He slowly opened the envelope and slipped out the letter, unfolding it and then silently read the first few lines. Looking up, his gaze locked with Suriana's. "Apparently Jose Sandoval is your father's uncle. He mentions his sister, Laura, who is Carlos' mother."

Suriana stepped back and held her breath for a moment. "My grandmother's name is Laura."

"Yes, and you have an aunt and two uncles because he mentions your father's siblings by name, Jerman, Joel and Yolanda. At the time he wrote this letter, your grandmother Laura had just visited him in his Quito home. He speaks of your mother, Elena and her brother, but doesn't mention his name. Oh, your mother's father, your grandfather passed away and soon after Elena's mother, your grandmother."

Tears sprang into the girl's eyes. "My grandparents are dead."

"Yes," he said softly. "Here, you take the letter. It seems he didn't know a lot of the details. Most of the letter is nothing more than consolations."

She took it and quickly scanned the contents and then she stuffed it into her sweater pocket. She would peruse it carefully later. "How can I find my parent's property?"

Chapter 58

"I'll find a taxi driver who will take you." He lightly took her arm and led her toward the door. Turning, she thanked him profusely and he acknowledged the thanks with a nod of his head and a small bow.

They walked through the lobby and stood under the long portico. With a snap of his finger, Pedro drew the attention of a dozing taxi driver. He sprang to life, replacing his hat and starting the car's motor in one sweeping motion. Pedro opened the taxi door and placed her inside. "You know, that property should belong to you. I assume you are their firstborn."

"Firstborn. Yes, I'd be the firstborn."

"Come back to see me when you return. We'll find the box containing information about the house and perhaps one of us can accompany you to the attorney in Guayaquil. We'll find out who has the deed and who built the house on your parent's property. My aged father may be able to help us. We'll work to see that you have ownership of the property. Whoever has claimed it probably doesn't know that you exist."

"Thank you. I'm very anxious to find out who it is that is living in my parent's home during their frequent trips to Playas."

They parted and she settled back against the seat, her heart thumping against her ribs. *What if someone is staying in the house right now? They could be my biological family.*

The taxi driver stopped in front of a fenced-in yard. He turned to look at her inquisitively. "Is it your family that visits here during the year?"

"I believe so. Do you know anything about them?"

"No, because they usually drive their own vehicle." His head leaned to one side. "You have the accent of a foreigner. Are you not from South America?"

"No, sir. I am an American." She had the car door open and was stepping out.

He recovered his manners and jumped out of the cab to help her. She pressed several sucres into his hand and bid him good-bye.

"Would you want me to wait? I will take you back to the hotel."

She solemnly shook her head. "No, gracias."

As the taxi cab disappeared down the dusty road, she leaned her head against the tall iron-rod fence. It was beautiful, the land sloping down to the sea. Several years ago someone had planted shrubs, trees and a lawn, a splendid landscape in a terrain of hard, unyielding earth. Someone is maintaining the yard. Her father was a landscaper. Did he create this beautiful garden? A house sat at the edge of the trees, close to the sea. If her parents had bought the property, that could only mean they love the sea as I do. Something about this place had claimed their hearts even as the coastline of the Pacific Northwest had claimed hers, but why had they chosen to remain in the sierras? Why hadn't they come back here to live permanently? Or are they here somewhere? Is it my family who has kept this property as lovely as any garden in the United States?

She would leave for Quito after her visit with the attorney in Guayaquil. Now she had her best lead of all, the address of her father's uncle. She would find out from him where her parents live. He could tell her why they had come to Playas in the first place. Maybe he would know why her mother's brother had tried to harm her father so many years before.

Suriana followed the fence until she came to the edge of the property and then turned with it to skirt the sea. A seawall had been built along the ocean front to discourage trespassers and hold back high waves. A set of stone steps was barred at the top by another iron gate. The house was visible beneath the umbrella protection of the trees. It was a two-story white stucco, with closed red shutters, large enough to lodge more than one family. The house looked contentedly asleep. She walked onto the beach and found a log. Sitting with her back to the sea, she stared at the house for a long while. Tomorrow, she thought, I must continue my journey, my quest to find my family. Who comes here to visit? Who had invested so much money in this property? It must have been very expensive to create this lovely spot. Surely someone must be paying for its maintenance.

The sun was quickly setting, painting the house a bright golden hue. Suddenly she was afraid, more afraid than she had ever been in her life. Even the death of her grandmother had not caused the apprehension she now felt. Abruptly she turned toward the sea. Why hadn't my parents returned? Who were the gray-haired man and his American wife? Was she really an American? How could the restaurant captain know her origin simply by her accent? He said that they

Chapter 58

have children. Who is Ryan? Are they related to me? Who are the pretty doctor and her husband? Why hadn't someone seen my father and mother since the day they left Playas? Am I really sure they are my parents at all? So far, all the proof I have is a piece of paper from my diaper bag and Anita, the store clerk. She had simply said that I resemble a couple named Martinez-Tapia whom she knew many years ago.

A thought loomed as large and dark as a thundercloud. Could my parents be dead? That would explain why they hadn't returned. Have I come all this way for nothing? No, there has to be an explanation. Maybe my parents sold the property to the gray-haired man and his wife.

She stood and brushed off her skirt. Looking once more at the house, she shook her head. No, I know that my parents have lived here. Somehow I know I will find them.

Taking off her shoes, she walked along the beach, kicking the golden sand and wading in the sun-soaked sea.

Tomorrow.

The End

CPSIA information can be obtained
at www.ICGtesting.com
Printed in the USA
JSHW022052110721
16743JS00001B/3